The Gin Drinkers

The Gin Drinkers

A NOVEL

Sagarika Ghose

HarperCollins *Publishers* India

HarperCollins *Publishers* India Pvt Ltd
7/16 Ansari Road, Daryaganj, New Delhi 110 002

First published in 2000 by
HarperCollins *Publishers* India

Copyright © Sagarika Ghose 2000

All rights reserved. No part of this publication may be reproduced, stored in a retrieval system, or transmitted in any form, or by any means, electronic, mechanical, photocopying, recording or otherwise, without the prior permission of the publisher.

ISBN 81-7223-413-9

Typeset in ElegaGarmnd by
Nikita Overseas Pvt. Ltd.
19A Ansari Road, Daryaganj
New Delhi 110 002

Printed in India by
Gopsons Papers Ltd
A-14 Sector 60
Noida 201 301

For Rajdeep, who's always at the receiving end

Acknowledgements

Bhaskar Ghose read all the drafts and showed me the way on many occasions. As did Ranjana Sengupta. Chitralekha Ghose brought me up to be exactly like her. And Ishan and Tarini Sardesai made my world miraculous. Ravi Dayal read conflicting drafts and gave me the benefit of his wisdom. Amitabh Mattoo, Brinda Datta, Gauri Gill, Giti Chandra, Janaki Bahadur Kremmer, Leela Gandhi, Mary Mount, Manjula Padmanabhan, Mahesh Rangarajan, Namita Gokhale, Pranay Gupte, Rathin Roy, Ruchir Joshi, Sanjeev Saith and William Bissell helped in valuable ways.

Chandrabhan Prasad and Raja Sekhar changed how I perceived many things. Vinod Mehta exasperatedly gave me leave from work. Tarun Tejpal threatened me with dire consequences if I wrote bad sex. Without Pankaj Mishra's encouragement I would never have had the confidence to complete this book.

Renuka Chatterjee was a source of good cheer and vodka.

1

Uma heard about the disappearing books for the first time at Jaspreet's party.

In Delhi, where sultans looked for treachery in court and viceroys outlawed quit-India rebels, bazaar and citadel have always existed nervous cheek by uneasy jowl. And nowadays, it's war. Lurking shadows break into flowering villas at night. By way of revenge, imported cars cut down pavement dozers at dawn.

So when Uma heard about the strange theft of rare and antique books from the well-appointed houses of the well-read, she couldn't believe it. It sounded peculiarly intelligent, most unlike Delhi.

Book burglars, for God's sake. Thieves of books. With a taste in Samuel Butler's *Erewhon* and recent translations of the two ancient Tamil classics, *Silappadikaram* and *Manimekalai*.

Uma was stupefied.

But Jaspreet said it had been going on for months. At first people thought the books were simply lost. Or maybe the servants were being cheeky and had hidden them. Then more books went missing. Then the first complaint to the police was filed. Then there were more complaints.

They never took ordinary books. Only books that were old or very rare. Heirlooms. The local police inspector had picked his teeth indifferently. Arre sahib, we don't believe in wasting time on these kitab chors, he had chewed. Theek hai, theek hai, koi padha-likha aadmi hoga.

When robbers play by the book, cops don't care, the dailies had laughed in single column.

Earlier that evening Uma and Sam sped through the neon-lit smog of a Delhi evening.

"*Aami chini go chini tomaare, oh go bideshini,*" sang Uma.

"Didn't get that," apologised Sam.

"I recognise my foreign friend who lives beyond the Indus," translated Uma shyly. She skimmed into a fountain roundabout, grazed up against an Opel Astra and accelerated away leaving the Astra brooding against the dribbling fountain.

"Beyond the Indus, in er...let's see, in South Kensington," smiled Sam.

She squinted at him through her spectacles. Gorgeous. His body, faintly lit at the edges, the body of a Grecian athlete. No, not an athlete. He was too tall and thin to be an athlete. He was David Copperfield, brooding eyelashes under a nineteenth century hat. She had read about him for many years, lying alone under a dusty ceiling fan in her room.

"It's crazy, you know. You. Here."

"Hey, I'm ecstatic."

"I never thought it would happen."

"Why not?" Sam looked at the black and yellow painted traffic islands and thought Delhi looked a bit like Cairo. "What's the fucking nation-state, anyway? Humbug. Friendship's been around since B.C. The nation-state," Sam stepped down hard on an imaginary brake as Uma did something nasty around an autorickshaw, "is only, what? A few hundred years old."

Uma felt a quick kick of panic. She longed to tell him that thoughts of their future made her nauseous before meals and leapt into her throat like pre-exam fright.

But their relationship was still cruelly polite.

"Geography is just…" Sam waved, "…nothing."

Uma took her hands off the wheel and made my-country-versus-your-country, between-me-and-you gestures but couldn't think of a reply.

"So how would you say my name in Hindi?" Sam asked distractedly pointing at the steering wheel, as they bucketed down Akbar Road, a wide boulevard with government commandos picking their noses under the giant tamarind trees.

Your name, she thought, swerving hideously. Not Shyam. Not Samudra, either.

"Samuelo," she shrugged at last. "'Samuelo'."

Uma had thick eyebrows in a thin-boned face. Slanting eyes shone behind small round glasses which rested on a long sharp nose. Her hair was a black mop of unruly curls and she was tall — only a few inches shorter than Sam — and slim-hipped. At first glance, she could pass for a curly-haired mahogany-brown schoolboy.

"Uma," Sam narrowed his eyes, made his hand into a revolver and issued a threat from The Mob, "don't fuck with me."

I wish I could fuck with you she thought swiftly. Just once.

He reminded her of Daniel Day Lewis in *The Last Of The Mohicans* (except for his glasses). He tied his shoulder-length dark hair in a ponytail. Behind his spectacles, his heavily-lashed eyes flitted about with the restless intelligence of men who have travelled almost the entire world by the age of twenty-two.

His eyes made him compelling to look at. They were the colour of deep green waters in high mountains, the only evidence, he said, of his Irish ancestry.

They revved into Jaspreet's father's bungalow. A pillared colonial verandah led to the party inside. A small water tank gleamed under a paved tree: diyas and rose petals floated on the water.

Bare limbs and shining hair crowded into a white-walled living room. Cadres of bottles marched on a long white table along a peeling wall with a lizard poised in the centre. Cups arched for air in a thicket of whisky, rum and wine bottles, mugs and tumblers and bowls of salted cashews and pistas. Beyond the garden doors stretched the lawn, manicured and flatly fluorescent, lit by lozenges of sodium vapour.

A murmuring crowd squirmed fleshily. The air coiled around it like perfumed marsh mist. A dusty chandelier waved in the glasses and in Uma's spectacles.

"Hi Uma! Uma! HIIIII!"

Uma's friend, Jaspreet laughed in a circle of people. They were all clad in regulation black and held drinks against their cleavages. A small blonde wearing a nose ring stood among them.

"Hi, Jassi," Uma smiled shyly, scanning her friend's face for the coldness of a two-year absence. But Jaspreet looked as bemused and as kind as ever as she shouldered through the throng to plant a wet kiss on Uma's cheek and welcome Sam to India. She was about to announce their arrival when the crowd suddenly surged. Jaspreet lurched up against Sam, jackknifed backwards on a stained glass topped table and scraped her elbow against the wall.

"Oh my God," called the blonde in a trembling American sob. "I have some cream in my bag, if you want."

Jaspreet was an industrial photographer. Her impressions of life were as pale and as vague as beautiful watercolours but she had the warmest of hearts. She was long and tall with beads around her ankles and a henna tattoo on her upper arm. She waved and went to find drinks for them. Uma turned to Sam but he had already materialised next to another bottle crowded table at the opposite side of the room and was talking intently to a slightly built man with floppy hair and spectacles whom Uma didn't recognise. That's funny, she thought. I didn't know he knew anyone here.

More people arrived and passed glasses around. Bottoms bumped and eyes glanced down each others' necklines. Rivulets of sweat ran between Uma's breasts. She charged towards Jaspreet.

She had e-mailed Jaspreet about her English boyfriend. Her boyfriend who wasn't her boyfriend, her lover who wasn't her lover.

"How's," Jaspreet whispered, "*he* liking it?"

"He's," she whispered back, "liking it."

She had dealt with Jaspreet better on e-mail than in person. Technologically liberated from truth. Now, face to face with her, she knew she wouldn't be able to lie for too long.

"Guys," Jaspreet smiled and extended an arm towards the group, "meet Uma. She's damn clever. She's just come back from Oxford and all."

No, no, thought Uma feverishly. Please don't say that. I went there, that's all. Purely by accident and it's left me with a life full of lies.

"How are aunty and uncle?" she asked, changing the subject quickly.

Jaspreet rolled her eyes. "Gone out. Thank God. But they're dying to meet you, yaar. They keep saying look at Uma, look at Uma. Why can't you be like Uma. You," Jaspreet beamed and hugged her, "are such a pain. Better tell them all about it. They're just dying."

Yes, thought Uma. I'll tell them. I'll tell them there are all kinds of things wrong with everything you hear about The Third World Student In a Western University. My grandfather, the late S.N. Bhattacharyya, may have had a pince-nez and silk cravat and thought of England as his soul's resting place, but my sojourn was an act of will. An act of will rather than a crowning achievement and I had to work very hard at the anecdotes.

"By the way, did you hear," said a lawyer. "The Rashtrapati Bhavan library was robbed."

A hush fell on the group.

"Really?" whispered Jaspreet. "The *President's* library?"

"Yes," said a PR professional, "imagine that. Actually they don't know when it happened. It might have happened weeks ago. These kitab chors are amazing."

"But how did they get in there," asked Jaspreet loudly. "With all that security. And what did they take?"

"Surf, no," shouted Mathew Kutty V.C., the software genius, "Why don't they surf, no, if they want books?"

Roberta Flack, honey and gold and generous, flowed from the player. Glasses clinked on the table.

"A tiny percentage in India," said the blonde sagely, "have access to the Net? Besides, the Net gives you information? Not wisdom?" Every statement trailed upwards into an indignant questioning cloud.

Uma dredged her brain for the most suitable reaction to a book heist at the presidential palace. Unlike Sam, she was unsure about moral choices. Steal now or be forced to steal later, kill instantly or kill slowly over the years, she didn't know which was better. She decided she would work on a short exposition later as to why stealing was okay if everyone remained unhurt.

"They took the Census Records of India. Old ones. Compiled by the British. You know, castes, tribes. Several volumes," said the lawyer.

The others began to talk excitedly about the gang. Who could they be? An emerging breed of criminal academics? Poor students who couldn't afford books? But how could they have entered Rashtrapati Bhavan if they were just petty robbers. They must be big time. The same marauders from the slushy metallic outskirts who scream into the city with arsenals in their Maruti Gypsies.

"By the way, who's she?" Uma whispered to Jaspreet, pointing at the blonde.

"Christine," said Jaspreet. "Haven't you met her before? She's also spent some time in Oxford."

She shut her eyes. She had come back to Delhi only a week ago. Come back with Sam. Not so that he could meet her parents, simply to visit for a few weeks because she had invited him and because he had a month to spare before he started on his job with McKinsey's Consultants in London.

She had taken Sam to the new discos.

Nightclubs in Delhi still thrashed in an area of insecure pleasure. The first one that Uma and Sam visited was deafeningly decadent where women wore shiny saris that were tucked only a hair away from the pubis. Girls in bikini tops with glitter in their cleavages shouted emotionally. A gargantuan Sikh gambolled at the mike, belting out Punjabi rap. Security guards stood outside with walkie-talkies to keep off 'anti-social elements'.

The second one had been surreal and fun. It had posters of a Texan bar and a Manhattan club on the walls. Waiters clad only in leather waistcoats and shorts threaded past couples with New Bodies wearing DKNY and Versace, hopping anxiously to Venga Boys.

Uma, Sam and her ad copywriter friend Aditya had sat at a dark table, drinking glasses of warm Kingfisher beer. Revolving coloured lights dripped from a tin lamp stand.

Small executives with rosebud mouths and barrel stomachs lolled in dark recesses nipping at brimming glasses and leading dual lives: one life at the site of their physical presence, the other on the mobile phone. Bleached blondes curved at the bar, grim with sex appeal.

"Why the hell did you come back, yaar," Aditya had said. "This place is going only one way." He had turned his thumb downwards at the floor. Aditya's eyes were bloodshot because he drank most of the time. He said he buried himself in drama to escape. He was an amateur theatre director and had once raved for days in a locked bedroom and refused to eat until he was allowed to perform all Shakespeare's soliloquies in full length and detail without an interval, without any form of glamorous packaging, without lights, music or concession to audience fatigue. Pure drama, without dreadful demeaning accessories.

"But you do need," he turned a dour gaze on Sam, "a shit load of money. To shut out," he jerked his head towards the redheads, "all this shit."

That evening Aditya offered Uma the part of the ghost in his new production of *Hamlet*. Experimental, he said sternly. Nothing to do with cheap entertainment. Or with the need to please anybody.

Uma opened her eyes quickly but couldn't see Sam.

"Have you seen him?" she asked Jaspreet.

"There he is," she pointed, "with Jai Prakash."

"Who's Jai Pra..." began Uma but Jaspreet was no longer standing where Uma remembered her. Instead she found herself addressing an evil-looking journalist who said that Jaspreet had gone.

She stared across the room at Sam as he stood with his head bent, listening to what the floppy-haired man was saying.

The man was, well, *different*. His hair was oily and he wore a faintly synthetic sweater. His skin was the colour of blue-black ink and his gestures were splay fingered.

He was small and sharp-featured and he looked, Uma thought, like a desi bhaiya. Someone who couldn't possibly recognise a Delhi Gymkhana sandwich if he saw it or cry "Good Lord!" if he was jostled in a crowd.

Two competitive groups inherited India from the British in 1947, Uma had read somewhere. The brown sahibs and the desis. The sahibs sipped consomme and promenaded in metropolitan gymkhanas in tailored suits. The desis traded mithais in the old quarters of smaller towns and wore the dhoti — or regional equivalents — as their badge of Indian self-respect.

For one group, the state and high industry were once simply a gathering of close relatives. The other became provincial postmasters and local legislators. Nehru was a sahib. But Sardar Patel was a desi.

Of course, this simple distinction, as Uma knew, is often complexly blurred and desi grandfathers have sahib grandchildren and desi wives live happily with sahib husbands. But nonetheless the unspoken separation remains indelibly sharp in most memories and Uma was able to recognise Jai Prakash instantly. What could Sam be talking to *him* about so intently, she wondered drifting moodily through the glass doors and into the lawn.

She sat down, lit a cigarette and stared out across the shining yellow grass. Five years ago, taking the eight a.m. bus to St Stephen's College everyday, past the Red Fort and through the Delhi Ridge where crumbling Mughal caravanserais now operated as Five-minute Photostat and Fax centres, she had sung a popular advertisement ditty about an ointment many times for the captain of the college chess team (and son of Secretary, Petroleum) who lived next door and always sat next to her in the bus: *Zandu Balm, Zandu Balm, pira hari Balm!*

He had smiled a lips-drooping-downwards mama's boy smile and shyly confessed that the single virtue he looked for in women was a sense of humour.

They had tried to get rid of with their virginities once in his living room under a giant portrait of Indira Gandhi hung with dried marigolds. But failed.

After they left for Oxford and Brandeis as sons and daughters of India's civil servants often do, he sent her an e-mail from Brandeis saying that they hadn't been able to do it because their zodiac signs weren't compatible. But by then Uma had met the lively Sam who was teaching her how to make Colombian coffee, speak Spanish, how to read maps and question whether Doubt was a greater virtue than Conviction and was very far away from zodiac signs.

Uma met Sam a few months after she arrived in England, in a Political Theory class. He had been sitting a few rows away from her and talking about the months he had spent in Brazil. He had listed his complaints against a consumer society. New generations of TV and Net cruisers were growing up illiterate and amoral and far too rich, Sam had raged.

Michaelmas Term had been bitterly cold. Black clouds had dashed against the tall windows and an icy wind had beaten against the ornate pillars and curlicues.

Uma had been amazed by Sam's emerald water eyes. Vulnerable eyes. Hurt eyes. Hurt by the rotten money-oriented world. As they wandered out after class, she tried to entertain him with little skits of the Politics tutor, thrown her arms about in a parody of another don, whom she heard say "Oh fuck a duck," when the papers he had been carrying had been blown away by a strong breeze shooting past the Radcliffe Camera.

She had essayed a little play on her impressions of Oxford. "If only I had my elephant here to bear me on a howdah to the river," she babbled. Sam had laughed curiously.

"Eccentricity," Uma had cried suddenly, gratified that she had made him laugh, "Eccentricity is the only weapon against the trap."

Not all her ideas were an attempt to impress him. She had become agitated after going abroad. Pored over books and magazines beneath the stained glass window Magdalen Library and bitten off her nails during lectures by a range of gesturing gurus.

She had discovered that she wasn't just Indian, but that she was also Black with many new responsibilities.

For the first time in her life, she had been confronted by how brown the colour of her skin was. Her hair and eyes were jet black. So was the fuzz which appeared on her upper lip every few days. So was the spiky hair on her legs.

The smooth whiteness of her tutorial group slanted onto her eyes like shafts of piercing laser in a dark room. She had begun to feel ugly and ethnic and by consequence intellectually adventurous. Her perceived ugliness spurred her creative juices. The way she talked had begun to change. Theory had become a refuge, hyperbole a shelter from the horrid truth.

Her clothes had changed too and become antiquated. She had altered her grandfather's tweed jackets and his old pleated pants with suspenders when she had come back on a holiday once. Had even uncovered a velvet coat from her mother's trunk and cut it to fit her slim contours. She had bought herself a frock coat.

She had interpreted India in so many different ways to so many people that she had begun to feel like its gatekeeper. She had become a one-woman travelling circus for an entire country, desperately seeking parallels to prove that she needn't be baffling. She was embarrassed at her power to surprise, embarrassed by her conflicts and potency and the fact that she'd been witness to bloodily questionable human nature while her new friends had slept with teddies on heart-shaped pillows. This may not have always been the case. But she was painfully conscious of their barely audible intake of breath when she spoke and was flustered for them and herself.

"Is it not difficult, Uma," Sam once asked her, "to put on your rouge every morning?"

Sam was the first man in Oxford to invite her to his room. He was the first man who didn't treat her as one. And he was tall and laughing and at the centre of many gatherings. And he had eyes that made you feel you were scuba diving.

He had dropped in to see her everyday, cooked with her on some nights and played the guitar so well that she would never have guessed that after school Sam had considered becoming a Catholic priest.

It was only last year when they had been allotted the same college house and she had helped him move his books — Maritain and Merton, St Augustine and Ignatius Loyola — that she had begun to understand that Sam was an anti-Enlightenment kind of guy.

Tolstoy had it right, he once told Uma, when he said that life dictated by human Reason alone was meaningless. *Conjectures Of A Guilty Bystander* by the American Trappist monk Thomas Merton as well as his autobiography *The Seven Storey Mountain* occupied a prominent place on his book shelf.

Sam had grown protective towards her over the last two years. He got firsts in all his essays and let her read them if she wanted to. He never let her spend a weekend alone, always invited her to spend brief argumentative Christmases with his mother in London and had taken her on a weekend to Amsterdam to shrug his shoulders at drugs and pornography, and drink himself into oblivion about the modern world.

On the way back on the freezing ferry, he had spread his long coat over her shoulders, pulled her towards him and let her shiver in his lanky chest. He spoke fluent Spanish and said the next time they decided to go on a holiday they should go to Granada and see the Alhambra palace where she wouldn't be so cold.

He had also confessed that he wasn't equal to the task of Real Love.

"You have to be strong and unselfish to love. Love has to set the other person free. It must be generous and not make demands. I just don't think I'm capable of it."

She had been to church with him one Sunday at Blackfriars and sung all the hymns with gusto. She had told him that she too had grown up singing *Make Me A Channel Of Your Peace* in a convent run by Irish nuns.

She had turned to look at him and found that he was kneeling on the pew, his eyes tightly closed and streaming with tears, his fingers white and clenched. As she watched him get in line to take communion, she saw that his head was bowed and tears still rolled down his cheeks.

On the way back from church, he had held her hand so tightly that she felt she was supporting a tall wounded soldier in a War and Peace sort of way.

"Please stay with me, Uma," he had said as she had turned to go back to her room. "Let's...let's make some coffee."

His sentences had become silences, she had heard the dot dot dot in his pauses, but hadn't known what to think.

And then there was the sex. Or rather, there wasn't the sex. And there probably wasn't, at the way things were going, ever going to be any sex. Sam was the sexiest man in the Western world. But he didn't believe in sleeping with anyone whom he wasn't ready to marry.

She had been aghast for days when he told her this. Hurriedly tried to explain that her family had always been 'progressive' and rejected old fashioned values like virginity and arranged marriages. That things were changing in India, that there had always been a thin modern crust. That he needn't worry about *her*.

But Sam had frowned and asked what on earth was wrong with old fashioned values? Old fashioned values were good.

Uma had sighed, panic-stricken about her wretchedly intact hymen, shocked that the reckless Sam was so fuddy-duddily moral and more convinced than ever that she was ugly.

She heard a faint sound. Christine, the American blonde from the party was standing a few yards away from Uma. They smiled at each other through the brilliantly-lit smog. Uma had missed the perfumed pollution of Delhi. Pollution was grittily urban, a Big City lethality.

"Everytime I go to a party...I think...they're so...sort of... empty?"said Christine.

Uma frowned. She liked parties. All racial and cultural awkwardness with Sam might be sorted out if they constantly drank in a white-walled bungalow with a thousand-watt lawn outside.

"Are you okay?" said Christine hunching her shoulders.

Uma inhaled and coughed. "I just...got a bit tired."

Christine sat down next to her. Uma noticed that there was a mark in the centre of her forehead, a dot, like a bindi. She was very small with a heart-shaped face and in her grey clothes she looked like a lost kitten.

"Would you like some Shankhapushpi? It's really good? It'll help you?"

Uma had seen the advertisements. "Shankhapushpi: Tonic for good mental health."

"Shankhapushpi?"

"Try it," said Christine, pulling out a hip flask from her pocket. "It's completely harmless? I promise. It'll make you feel better."

Uma tried to push her hand away but Christine reached around and forced the open flask into Uma's unsuspecting mouth. A trickle of sticky brown liquid snaked in between her teeth.

"Excuse me," cried Uma, wiping her mouth and swallowing the sticky minty taste on the tip of her tongue. "D'you mind?"

She pushed Christine's hand away and stared determinedly at the garden. Christine held out her hip flask again, like a child offering toffee.

"It's not a drug or anything like that? It's sort of natural, like, herbal?"

"No, thanks."

Christine smiled and spread her hands.

"I'm inviting you to try it. Don't worry. Nothing will happen to you? You can sue if anything happens?"

Uma threw her cigarette away, drank a little and handed the flask back.

"Thanks," she said.

She glanced at Christine to find her staring at her expressionlessly. An oddly helpful person, this Christine. Offering cream to Jaspreet. Offering Uma her Alternative syrup.

"What brings you to India?" Uma asked.

"The Third World elite," Christine ripped out a clump of grass as a Paris *citoyen* might have ripped the hair out of an aristocrat during the French revolution, "is one of my areas of study? That's why I'm here? To do...um...like...field work?"

"Here?" Uma asked.

"Yeah, you're one, right?" Christine grinned suddenly. "Upper caste agent? Instrument of social oppression?"

Uma's head snapped back towards the garden. Nothing to worry about. Christine was only making a joke.

"What's in a name, that by any other...as Shakespeare said," Uma shrugged.

At close quarters she could see that Christine's face was almost sweet and young. Her complexion glowed. It was well hydrated and wiped.

"Oh my God. Shakespeare," muttered Christine reproachfully. "Serious Dead White Male stuff. That's crazy that you should quote from Shakespeare, you know that?" She shrugged. "But maybe it's not surprising considering the Indian upper castes have monopolised everything for so long? They've not given others a chance? That's why society here has decayed?"

Uma stared at Christine in silence. Christine ran a hand over her face and her nose ring became a little dislodged.

Uma's brain became crowded with possibilities about Christine. She was a Stalinist vegetarian fighting for the oppressed in the Third World. An Indologist who now loathed Indians because she'd never recovered from tropical diarrhoea.

"I have to go," she said at last, rising and dusting the grass from her pants. "My parents will get worried."

But as Uma began to walk away, Christine struggled to her feet and ran up behind her. "No, hang on. Wait. I apologise if I upset you? It's just that…um…I sometimes try and sort of…shock people into thinking about themselves. It's a you know, like, a device?"

Uma stared dumbly at her. Christine sighed, picked up a stone and threw it into the lawn with impressive force. Uma flinched.

"Jai Prakash wants to meet you," said Christine.

"Who?"

"Jai Prakash. You'll like him. Trust me."

Uma laughed cheerlessly.

"I'm sorry. I was just trying," Christine shrugged, "to get to know you? But I guess it didn't come off?" She laughed. "No, it didn't."

Uma shook her head, pushed on her shoe which had come off her foot and walked back into the party. She signalled to Sam that they should leave. He detached himself from the wispy man who Jaspreet had said was Jai Prakash who seemed to be well known to the mysterious Christine.

On the way home, Uma asked who he was and how he had met him.

"Oh, that was Jai Prakash," said Sam airily. "He was in Oxford for a year working on a book. That's how I met him."

"He was in Oxford?" asked Uma disbelievingly. "How did he get there?"

She became urgently hopeful of solidarity with Sam on this quick point. The educated of the world versus the uneducated. Perhaps that could be the unifying idea for the rest of the evening. But Sam only laughed formally and his expression became disapproving.

A black and yellow taxi rattled upto the Habitat Centre—a cavernously thoughtful red building crammed with offices, bars and restaurants, with a giant open space in its centre where rows of plants stood under a monumental iron trellis overhead.

A tall slim-hipped woman with curly hair sat in the taxi.

Dr Madhavi Iyer of Columbia University, New York was carrying her briefcase, a set of files and her one-and-a-half-year-old daughter, Mira, tightly bound in pampers and a travelling suit.

Two suitcases — a massive red one with a fold-up pram stretched under the clothes and the other, a large black one, crammed with feeding bowls, toys, pampers, socks and blankets — bumped in the boot. Mira shoved her hands down Madhavi's kurta and squeezed her breast.

"See, tomato*kutty*, this is Delhi," murmured Madhavi, easing the chubby hand out, "Where mama used to study years and years ago. Awful place, no? Really awful. Now I'll attend my *seminar*, so you sit *quietly* and then when I finish we'll go for a *walk* and then we'll play and then we'll have *ice cream*, and *then*, after *that,* we'll go...where shall we go? There's nowhere to go."

Mira nestled closer, inserted her finger into Madhavi's mouth, stroked her teeth, then tried to push her finger up her nose.

"Mama-lita nee mama," said Mira coquettishly, pulling her mother's cheeks.

"*Kutty*papa, tomato," replied Madhavi happily. "We'll unpack the new potty just now."

They climbed out. Madhavi bumped her head hard on the door as she slid out holding Mira flat against her stomach, her files clutched between her thighs. Her briefcase fell open and a few papers fluttered down.

Clutching Mira with one hand she snatched at them as they lay on the road. She twirled the crumpled papers with her feet, holding Mira on her lap and struggled to close her briefcase with her heel.

She gave up after a few tries and jammed it, still open, under the files. She stood for a few seconds in a pond of bags, papers and baby, immobile in chaos while Mira pulled out strands of her mother's hair and dressed them around her thin-boned face. Madhavi screwed her finger into the soft cheeks. Mira flung herself against her mother in a teeth-mashing, tongue-biting snuggle. Madhavi looked sideways at the little squashed profile. Cheek like the moon and eyelashes like a boat.

"Arre chaliye, madam, bag nikaliye," shouted the driver irritatedly.

"Ek minute. Ek minute," she replied breathlessly.

Of course it wouldn't occur to him to give her a hand. No. No help. No consideration for a mother and child. Simply class war. The Machismo Of Poverty. Inner Darkness. Barbaric North Indian modernity or get-rich-quick mentality. Or something.

She was wrong. He heaved an exasperated sigh, flung out of the car, dragged out her suitcases and struggled with them into the reception.

He gave her a sideways look: I know what you're thinking, rich bitch.

She looked back straight: Alcoholic wife beater, judging from those hooded eyes.

She looked down at the debris. Perhaps if I strap her and the papers to the black one and hold the red in the other hand, no but my files and briefcase will fall. I could wheel the suitcases in with both hands and put Mira on top of them. Perhaps if I just sweep everything — including her — up and hold everything ahead of me like a giant potted plant. No. Too heavy. Could I tie the kid to my back? I should have pushed the files into the suitcase. I should have had another bag for the files. Why, oh why don't I have more limbs? I could be, I should be, a self-sufficient many-limbed universe for her.

The receptionist had no idea who she was, why she was here, why they were supposed to have a reservation for somebody with her name, indeed why she had bothered to come to India at all.

She explained patiently as Mira bounced on the counter. A room, she panted. I'm going to be here for almost a month, there's a reservation. Please check. Please check.

Her hair, which she usually wore severely clasped in a pin at the top of her head, came a little undone and fell about her thin sharp features. Her fine slanting eyes were untouched by make-up. Her only embellishments were a long black line drawn in the centre of her forehead and a silk dupatta to match her churidar and kurta.

They found the information at last and she was sent away to her room accompanied by a baggage handler who stood very close to her in the lift and informed her slyly that since she had arrived during the festival season, he knew he could expect a bit of tea and water from her.

They arrived at her room. It was large and comfortable, and, the handler assured her, would be sunlit during the day. A big double bed squatted in the centre of the room and a fleshy sofa oozed in front of the television. Little glazed pottery lamps lit up corners. She paid the boy his Diwali dues and lowered Mira relievedly on the bed.

"Don't roll, Miraamma," she called, checking the bathroom for grime, "if your grandfather was here, he wouldn't allow you to roll on the bed. The child will fall! The child will fall! Be careful, be careful, he would say."

She spoke to her father every week for news about cousins' divorces and aunt's deaths. Whenever she came to India on seminars she would briskly shower him with gifts and spend a few days discussing politics and family weddings.

Home looked as it always had in the days before cable television when India was still Black and White. Her father's bamboo table mats. Glucose biscuits and upma on Sundays. Wet haired Vividh Bharti afternoons. After breakfast, lying in bed, waiting for lunch.

The slow luxurious ease of time, the shout of the distant fielder in the cricket match outside, the sun between the toes, in perfect straight lines on the bed. The world consigned happily to the periphery because in the centre there was only her father and herself and their special aeons contained in every random ritual.

After the seminar here in Delhi, she would visit her father in Bangalore.

She pushed her suitcases to one side and dived in after Mira.

Little blonde baby of a new glossy time, you may never understand your mother's secrets. When I was small I didn't look like you. I had anklets on my feet, kajal in my eyes and my frocks were made of old saris. I used to eat with my hands off a steel thali not bash my spoon against Pocahontas painted on an unbreakable, non-toxic plate like you do. I used to place my books at Saraswati's feet and ask her to bless me before my exams.

Mira's birth when Madhavi was thirty-nine had brought all sorts of changes. Her body had become broader. Not fatter but broader. She had acquired a maternal width. And her breasts had become a dead weight, lumbering against her rib cage where once they had skipped and whispered.

She pressed Mira closer to her chest. Mira ran her tongue near her mother's neck and tried to lick off her sweat. Madhavi pressed the little body into her skin. Sometimes she would lie on her back in bed, lift her clothes and spread Mira out on her bare stomach.

The baby would squirm seductively and spread her little arms like a tadpole trying to swim.

"It's me you want," her eyes would say to her lustful mama.

'Mira' was a compromise name. Madhavi always felt she understood Mirabai, the sixteenth century princess who neglected her home and sang and danced ecstatically all her life, mad about Krishna. Being married to a Rajput chieftain must have been a deadly chore. Mirabai became a musical saint because she was bored stiff.

Peter hadn't liked the Mirabai story but said it was a great name.

The telephone rang. Who could have this number? Who could have possibly got through?

"Surprise!"

Peter had the number. He had calculated the exact time it would have taken her to get here from Indira Gandhi International Airport. He might even have e-mailed the Habitat Centre.

"Pete."

"Everything okay with you guys? How did she travel?"

"Oh fine. We're fine. She's happy." She looked down at Mira. She's a celebratory pig. And I'm going to gobble her up.

"Are you feeling good?"

"Oh yeah. It's good to be here. How're you doing?"

"Fine. We have a leaky floor, though. There goes the weekend."

"Oh. Sorry."

"E-mail me a list of addresses of the IR faculty at JNU? I may send out some letters. Also could you see if the book's available in stores out there?"

"Sure. Will do."

"Kiss her for me."

"Kiss you from us."

She hung up. Then took out her photograph of the Meenakshipuram temple that she always carried with her and set it up on the bedside table. She switched off all the lights except for one little lamp, drew the curtains, washed and changed Mira and gave her a bottle of milk. Then she opened her suitcases, showered, changed into a T-shirt and track pants and jumped in next to the sucking child.

She smiled down at her. The infant's face was jowly and jolly, a retired rear admiral's face. Daddy called. He said to kiss you. Not me, you. I know you two have secrets. I've seen the addictive eye contact, been excluded from the bands of blondeness.

Professor Pamela Sen had invited her to Delhi for the first Mahatma Gandhi Foundation seminar. Pamela was her former teacher and now director of the prestigious new Foundation. She had seen the pictures. A grey stone and plate glass building, low slung and breathing easily under layers of soft leaves with phlox and poinsettia growing through the year in a greenhouse at the back.

Pamela was about to retire and was to nominate her successor. Madhavi had seen the smart advertisements in a couple of journals and sent in her application almost immediately.

In reply the Foundation had invited her for its first international seminar. After the seminar, the letter said, Pamela, in consultation with the Board of Trustees would announce the name of the new director.

The Foundation didn't know she would be bringing her baby. But then this was an unconventional seminar and she was sure they would be kind enough not to mind if her baby farted at the other end of the room while they discussed *Challenges before Indian Politics in the Millennium*.

She pulled Mira's cheeks.

"Doodoo little moondoo."

"Mama-lita," the baby slurped.

Pamela stepped into the gathering darkness in her garden to check on her hibiscus plant.

She was a tall thin woman who still held herself upright, although the parting in the middle of her curly mop of grey hair was becoming a slowly widening forest path. Deep lines crisscrossed next to her eyes and at the corners of her lips. Her large slanting eyes had become heavy. Her face, in repose, looked serene, but sometimes when she spoke, her features twitched violently and she had to wage a quiet war to govern her insurgent lips and chin.

She had given up gardening after her stroke last year. But she still went for her morning walk among the trees of Nizamuddin where she lived. Occasionally, her sari rode up her calves as she strode along past Hurhayun's tomb with her cane, oblivious of the sniggering security guards and the flirtatious ayahs who hung around them.

She walked around the semicircular garden in front of her house as she waited for Benedicta to finish cooking her soup and vegetables for dinner. Benedicta had come to her after her stroke and they had become friends. Pamela felt soothed by Benedicta's 'missy baba' English and the big wooden cross she wore around her neck. Felt comforted to know that she, Pamela, was keeping Benedicta away from the poverty of a convent in Ranchi or from the slavery of a housemaid's life in the house of a Dubai sheikh.

The worst fate of all, Pamela always felt, was not to be of any use to people. Why else, after all was one alive, if not to be of clear and direct use?

Benedicta's blind mother had three younger daughters and had told her that since she had the heftiest body among all her sisters she better go off and work. And Benedicta and Pamela had been relieved to find each other.

She parted the weeds with her cane, peered at the dying plants, then looked at the sky.

Would the atmosphere be kind to the hibiscus seeds she had recently planted? Would cloud and sun conspire in her plan? She poked around with her stick, wondering what to say if Benedicta inquired why she had planted the hibiscus when she was about to leave Delhi and this flat.

"How you will do packing, madam?" called Benedicta as she stirred and chopped in Pamela's kitchen. "Call some labour, na."

Shelves of books leaned out from the walls of her living room. Her Jamini Roy painting had been taken down from the opposite wall and was propped up on the floor. In the kitchen, a heap of cutlery lay on the small wooden table, ready to be cleaned. In the long bedroom with the bay windows looking into the garden stood an iron frame bed. On it, a Bengali novel, *Devi Choudhurani* by Bankim Chandra Chatterji and Pamela's round reading glasses.

"Myself," stated Pamela, looking up from the seeds. "I shall do all my own packing. I always have and I always will. No packers. Koi nahin chahiye humko."

Pamela, the nay sayer. A letter inviting her to be lecturer at University of Wisconsin? No, thank you, too many responsibilities at the moment here in Delhi. Senior fellow at Sussex for four years? No thank you, for six months only, if possible, have taken on far too many projects in India. Visiting Professor at Texas? No, but how utterly kind of you to think of me. Visiting Professor at Yale? No, very kind of you, I'm honoured that a university such as yours has complimented me. For your great university to even consider someone like me is a reward, but no. No. No. No. Visiting Fellow at Oxford? Only for a year, please, and only because I was a student there once.

Pamela Sen, teacher of History for forty years at the University of Delhi. The permanent fixture among the jet set, scouring Nai Sarak and Chauri Bazaar for old books. More books. Let's build together with all our heart and soul, a library, *here*. The lone figure in the History department library, painstakingly looking through the catalogue when evening shadows slanted mournfully on depleted corridors. The occasional article in a newspaper: *Creating the Historical Mind*.

A letter to the Birla Group of Companies, and to the CEO of Infosys Technologies: Sir, if I may introduce myself, would you care to finance an extension of the History library building at Delhi University? No, it's not for a computer centre. No, it's not for religious studies either. It'll just help young people, that's all. That's all.

She had been invited to become director of the Mahatma Gandhi Foundation by the Vice-President of India. Although the Foundation was privately funded, the Vice-President was its honorary chairman. He had written to her praising her for, 'Your rare and extraordinary commitment to the spirit of enquiry.' She had been at the Foundation for the last two years. Not her Foundation. No, *not* hers.

"So much samaan, madam," said Benedicta chopping beans and carrots. "You need lot of boxes. Big big boxes."

Pamela didn't hear. She went back into the room and smelt along the book shelves. Prophets rearmed and armed, discoveries of India and of Europe, revolutions and putsches, questions eastern and trading, leviathans and social contracts, The prince and the city state, drain of wealth and wealth of nations, economies planned and affluent, people subaltern and courtly, gardens in nineteenth century Europe and women in American public life.

History. History in its pulsating futilities and its retrospective failures. History, that great rearing hydra head of blood and aspirations and love and government. History was the catch in Pamela's breath and the goose pimples on her cheeks.

These books, these scores and hundreds and even thousands of books resting in their functional iron book shelves, she would have to seek help for them. How would they fit into any human container? What wood or steel was big enough to bulge with their contents, forewords and prefaces?

On a small table near her faded armchair stood a glass hurricane lamp which she had brought to Delhi from her family house on Lansdowne Road, Calcutta. A house encircled by supari trees and a riotous basti at the back. Long red cement verandahs, ornate railings and rooms with four-poster beds with mosquito nets floating above them. Downstairs, a black and white photograph of her father, Karun Chandra Sen, a lifelong devotee of the great Brahmo leader Debendranath Tagore.

Her father had sat her down one evening to say that the most important thing was to make sure that one's life was as rational and sensible as possible. Not bound by ridiculous rituals and the degraded worship of idols.

He had given her an anglicised name and packed her off to Gokhale Memorial School and after she completed her D.Phil. from Oxford, he had died almost immediately, in sheer relief that his life's mission had come to fruition.

Pamela stroked the hurricane lamp, carefully trying to remove the dust from its inner wall but it was fragile and teetered under her unsteady hands. Benedicta heard the sound of moving glass and leaped to rescue it, bumping into Pamela on the way. Pamela stepped back at the impact and pushed against the Jamini Roy painting which slid onto its side and fell flat on its face. Luckily, the glass didn't break.

"Aiii, madam. Take care, take care," cried Benedicta, wiping her hands on her apron and settling the hurricane lamp and the painting.

But Pamela was already striding away towards the kitchen. Now, she would have to take all the delft down one by one, clean them and arrange them back again. She danced momentarily against the cabinet, her shoulder hitting the wooden surface. This damned unsteadiness.

"Want soup now?" Benedicta asked.

"Not just yet, Benedicta," Pamela replied. "Just leave it all in the kitchen, please. You go to your quarter now."

The chords in her voice rattled. She had smoked cheroots for forty years and her voice sounded like a dragging axle of an old car. Benedicta bustled into the bedroom, pulled the sheets and straightened the blankets. She smelt of raw vegetables and detergent.

"No, no memsahib. First you eat. Come sit."

She shepherded Pamela to her armchair and settled a bowl of hot chicken soup on her lap. She always drank her soup in her blue porcelain bowl.

"Okay, madam?"

Okay? *Mono mor megher shangi, ure chole dig diganter paane.* My mind flies across the universe. No, I'm not okay.

To please Benedicta, Pamela spooned up some soup although she wasn't hungry. Some of it dribbled down her chin and sank into her grey jumper like ghosts shrinking into gravestones, but she didn't care. She suddenly felt painfully tired.

"More?" Benedicta's voice pierced the darkening tunnel of Pamela's vision.

"No thank you, Benedicta. You go to your quarter."

"*Intoxication filled the cup. Youth's frenzy took me by the hand, a city populated by love and adoration.*" Which of her Independence heroes had said that? She couldn't remember. Was it Nehru? Or Maulana Abul Kalam Azad?

But in those early days of independent India, Reason infused the world. Reason not faith. Socialist reason. To be socialist was, they believed, the only way towards sense. Pamela's husband Sailen believed that socialism was not simply an idea: it was the only road to justice in a country of the poor.

Sailen had died within the first ten years of their marriage, leaving her his collection of cigars and cheroots. She still loved him, of course. And missed him so much that she had tried to become him. To smoke his cigars and uphold what he would have upheld.

She thumped the bed. "Benedicta!"

"Want smoking now, madam?"

Pamela smiled. Her arm snapped up as if she was writing on a blackboard. "Please."

Benedicta lit a cheroot for her and frowned as Pamela puffed and coughed. The soup bowl shook, buffetted by Pamela's coughing. Benedicta lifted it swiftly and placed it on the little table with the hurricane lamp.

"Coughing and coughing. Tomorrow putting tulsi-honey in hot water. Then having it."

Benedicta looked worriedly at Pamela for a few minutes then went back into the kitchen.

"Achcha, ja raha hai, memsahib," she called.

"Theek hai, Benedicta."

Pamela waved frantically as she watched Benedicta let herself out of the kitchen door and climb up the spiral staircase to her room on the terrace.

She sat smoking in her bed for a few minutes. Then broke up her cheroot on the little table and walked out to the garden again. Must look at the hibiscus.

Humayun's tomb, opposite her house — the official residence of every Foundation director — loomed out at her through the darkness. Humayun, opium-addict father of Akbar.

Akbar was the hero. Akbar saw things others were too inhibited to see. Akbar, the illiterate, who grew up with an empire and became the greatest Mughal of them all. In him the nomad Genghiz merged and soared with the urbane Timur.

If Sailen and I had had a son, thought Pamela, turning back to the house, we would've named him Akbar.

She sat down on her armchair and looked through three applications for the post of director of the Foundation. Whom should she choose? Whom, for example, would Akbar have chosen? Whom would Sailen have chosen? She read through the applications and gazed at the photographs attached to them. She had read the personal statements many times but she read through them again. One of them she looked at particularly carefully and held up against the lamp. She read painstakingly, marking out portions with her pen.

Outside her house a group of people assembled quietly. They wore dark clothes and their movements were light and quick. They spoke to each other in low voices, moving swiftly under the amaltas and neem.

One of them was plump and galumphed noisily. He was pushed by the others with a loud *shshsh*. The moon sailed out behind Humayun's tomb. Crazy drug-addict of an emperor who fell down the fucking stairs of his own fucking library, one of them laughed to the others.

At the Nizamuddin roundabout they jumped into a couple of cars and raced off in different directions. One of the cars was a Zen, the other was a Maruti 800: young cars, cars in a hurry.

Coincidentally, as they disappeared, the lights in Pamela's house were switched off.

2

On the way home, as she told him about what she had heard about the kitab chors, Uma was conscious of something happening to her body. Her arms and legs felt intriguingly rested. Her neck had become long and slow like ET's neck. As she turned to look at Sam through gentle eyes, she found that he was shaking his head disbelievingly.

She drove aimlessly into the depths of South Delhi when she should have turned off, before the Seva Nagar flyover, towards her parents' Lodi Estate bungalow. The white Ambassador car with a sheathed flagstaff on its bonnet bumbled along. The Ambassador, still the chariot of the obstinate nomenklatura.

It was late now. Through the trees the colonies of bungalows in the Graeco-Hindu, Disney and Sci-Fi styles, gleamed with brazen wellbeing. But the tattered roses in their gardens were growing black with soot. On the streets gap-toothed urchins created combinations of intoxicants as they squatted on municipality sewer lines. Perhaps they too find a certain rough drugged happiness, thought Uma. They must. Their lives can't just consist of unremitting difficulties. There must be things that work it out for them in the end: festivals, street fights.

Glittering women chattered outside a wedding shamiana and paan-chewing vigilantes lounged outside half-open shops. A new shopping mall snaked along a road, like a python with light bulbs along its body.

The roundabouts surrounding Raj Path, encircling statues of India's founding fathers still looked the same. But just a few minutes' walk away, in Connaught Place, the rubble of new construction loomed through a permanent haze of dust. Chrome and glass strained out of mud. In the government colonies, white or yellow-washed bungalows with their bougainvillea garlands teetered on the edges of clamorous flyovers dotted with new hoardings. Delhi was changing muddily.

In her parents' bungalow, her room looked bare and thinly occupied. Her music collection reduced to a Tracy Chapman cassette, another of Celine Dion and one of Mozart's *Greatest Hits*. And her book collection, P.G. Wodehouse and John Le Carre arranged in a single neat row. The books and music she had acquired in England under Sam's tutelage, the catalysts that had made her life more refined and complex were still unpacked, resting in cardboard boxes in her mother's dirty storeroom.

Her parents were unchanged. Her intoxicated and elfin mother, Anusuya chiffon-clad and short-haired, with her shelves of Tibetan incense, portrait of Zarathustra, photograph of the Bom Jesus church, carved ivory Ganesh and photographs of dead family members. And hidden strips of Calmpose, Valium and bottles of Blue Riband and High Ball gin.

She was a tiny Madonna of the Rocks, or a Madonna on the rocks, given her proclivities. The stunning Anusuya, cigarette in a black enamel holder poised against frosted pink lips, a party flower who once had a face of such bursting warmth and rose-tinged sadness, such delicate shoulders, huge eyes and short bouncingly straight hair that Uma had sighed hopelessly at her own angular silhouette and decided that eccentric clothes would be her only salvation.

And her father, Shantanu, a civil servant in the ministry of education who wore printed bush shirts and had a grey beard, piercing eyes and a secret ambition to command a battleship.

The evenings with them in their cool crumbling government bungalow with the high colonial ceilings, long corridors, dark cement floors and interconnecting rooms. Glow worms hid in the hedges that lined the flat square lawn in front. In the damp untiled bathrooms, fat glistening cockroaches would stick their heads out from the drain and fly at your mouth if you tried to kill them. Sam had been installed in the guest bedroom with the silverfish-riddled book shelf and dusty orange curtains. The bougainvillea still rioted over the open front verandah. Pansies, carnations and roses burst on the rims of the long lawn and beyond it frail Ashoka trees leant against the red brick walls.

Inside, Anusuya's crazy and half-hearted watercolours of horses and village scenes decorated the walls. Round white lampshades were dressed with cobwebs and threadbare Bhutanese carpets lay between the dusty flowery sofas.

Her mother would sit in front of a video of *My Fair Lady*, a glass of gin at her elbow and her father would read Churchill's letters and speeches, dashing at the circling mosquitoes with a fly swatter. The evenings didn't vary much except for the occasional catastrophe.

Uma's family were 1947-junkies. Her Congress grandfather (when he was alive) and Communist uncle (before he became a raving capitalist) had experienced severe cold turkey if they hadn't stood to attention at the Republic Day parade or frowned critically through the prime minister's speech from the Red Fort, their skins prickling with patriotic goose pimples.

Or spent Sunday afternoons listening to records of Donald Swann and Michael Flanders live, on an LP, at the Royal Albert Hall. Or received 'special passes' for concerts by visiting ballet troupes from Beijing where the best seats were always taken by dozing octogenarian ministers and their AK47 bearing commandos.

At the airport, Uma had leapt back a few paces at the sight of her parents. Anusuya wore a pale silk sari with a fading zardozi border. Shantanu in a full-sleeved white shirt, with his grey beard neatly trimmed wore scuffed black shoes. They had looked gallantly poor. Worn. Civil. Besieged by the new raucously prosperous laughter all around them. For a few affronted seconds Uma tried to treat them like distant relatives whom she had coincidentally happened to meet in the arrival lounge.

She wished, for Sam's sake, that her parents couldn't speak English, that they were clearly and distinctly foreign. That they had acres of politics and literature of their own instead of being so embarrassingly tied up with Stratford-upon-Avon and Lady Diana lore.

The welcome had been dull to say the least. Anusuya had made a weak attempt at pleasure. Shantanu had seemed irritated rather than pleased at his daughter's failure to emigrate to the West. Uma had tried to ignore the sweaty taxi rank outside Indira Gandhi International Airport and the crumpled kith and kin from Gurdaspur with their steel boxes and bedding rolls effecting the hourly resettlement to Leeds.

The smell of starch on the sheets on the first day as she lay in bed watching the sun beat against the handloom curtains and listening to the calls of the vegetable seller.

Call of the vegetable seller, Uma had thought. Perhaps she could write a long essay about it. A dusky woman, with a bright veil and a vegetable cart trundling between the heavy machinery of imported cars. The Unbearable Lightness of Being an Indian Vegetable Seller.

She had instructed Anusuya not to betray too much awareness of the British royal family, but Anusuya had not been able to stop herself from revealing to Sam that she had followed the investigation of Lady Diana's death in critical detail and had a pretty good theory about it herself.

Sam hadn't been able to take his eyes off Anusuya when he first saw her. As he shook hands politely with Shantanu, he continued to look at her and on the way back from the airport had insisted on stopping at a roadside stall to buy her a bunch of flowers. Anusuya had snatched the bouquet away, fenced with it a few times to shake off the water and jammed it, head first into one of her plastic bags.

All through the last week Anusuya had strained away from him, veins standing on her neck and shoulder bag digging into her flesh. If he asked her a question, she directed her answer to the sky. When Sam tried to pay for a meal, she glared at him and asked if he thought they were so poor that they couldn't pay for their guests.

Sam had been introduced to Misri, the cook and Vishweshwar, the chauffeur.

And he had been introduced to Hari Ram, the telephone 'line man', who was almost a part of the family now. He had restored their phone line so often that they had taken him into their bosom, had begun to share family confidences with him, irrespective of the fact that he was an employee of the government and was always hostilely preoccupied with his own clan.

Anusuya had forced Sam, through a combination of helplessness and blackmail, to accompany her to the INA market and blamed him if things were too expensive, saying it was the British who were responsible for everything that was wrong with India. She whispered about him to Uma in his presence and rolled her eyes heavenwards if he asked how she had liked England when they had visited a few years ago.

She would arrange her Ganesh and Durga statuettes aggressively on the table every time Sam sat down to eat. If Sam suggested that he would like to visit a church, she clapped her hands on her ears and shut her eyes as if she had heard a loud noise.

The day they went to the sale at the new Liz Clairborne in South Extension market, Anusuya demanded to know why British stores employed Indian slave labour. She told them a shocking story about the mother-in-law of a cousin who had been so upset by a trip to England that when she came back to India, she had lost control of her bowels and until today defecated horribly all over the verandah.

As they sat in the coffee shop of the Imperial hotel one night, Anusuya asked the waiter if he thought Uma and Sam would make a proper couple, considering his hair was longer than hers. The waiter shrugged contemptuously, Sam looked away, Shantanu concentrated on spearing pineapple chicken with his fork and Uma prayed to the entire pantheon of global deities ranging from Zarathustra to Ra — even directing an appeal or two to St Peter's — that Sam would be blessed with the fortitude to place Anusuya in historical context.

The gods heard Uma's prayers. During one of their meals, Sam whispered to Uma that Anusuya was the most beautiful creature he had ever seen.

At the sight of Sam, a light contemplation had settled on Shantanu like a sheet. He barely registered Uma's presence, asked vaguely about her future plans and what sort of job she now planned to do, didn't wait to hear her reply and heartily congratulated Sam on the successes of the Labour government. He then delivered a long commentary on what a shame it was that ancient Nalanda in Bihar had been allowed to fall into ruin when Western universities were so well preserved.

As they wandered amidst Jamaali Kamaali, the Red Fort, Tughlakabad and the Lotus Temple; Shantanu repeatedly examined the first-past-the-post principle of the electoral system in Britain and wondered aloud if proportional representation was far better suited to India's needs.

When Sam had asked when the Lodi Garden was created and who designed the houses of parliament, Shantanu ignored his questions, warning him instead that it suited the BBC and CNN to relay biased reports on India and Sam shouldn't believe everything he heard about the child sacrifices, burning of widows and trade in human organs. Sam had looked startled, stuttered that there should be laws against such unfair journalism and had hurriedly gone back to asking about the seven cities of Delhi. But Shantanu still remained suspended in a quiet frenzy and every time Sam asked him a question, responded with detailed comparative examples between India and England.

As they drove into the house after Jaspreet's party, Uma noted thankfully that the light in her parents' bedroom was off and they were safely asleep.

Mira rolled herself into a lazy snail. Her eyes were huge and didn't miss a thing. She always spotted insects on the wall well before her mother did. She was pleased with the new blue potty decorated with Antz cartoons which mother had bought for her before they came to Delhi. Good for mother. She seemed to be getting the point at last. Give goods, receive love. No goods, no love. Mira yawned and slid into contented sleep.

Madhavi looked out of the window into the darkness at the faint tree-bumped skyline of Delhi, with whitewashed low buildings stuck among the trees. A groaning, stink-bedecked, stimulating, spiteful and exciting city, she thought.

A city of creeps, politicians, intellectuals, grey stubborn bureaucrats, bearded artists and bejewelled thugs with the complaining cripples in their wheelchairs, the naked beggars, one of them, she remembered, with a bit of livid prolapsed rectum peeking out innovatively from his bum, the flower-decorated

BMWs on their way to drop off a honeymooning couple to the airport, the art exhibitions in tiny alleyways and the poetry in theatre basements. The booming enterprise of cake manufacture in a housewifely kitchen. The villages of artisans and carpenters supporting an empire in garment export from a tin shed on a wire-crowded roof. The stockpiles of weapons behind temples on the city outskirts. In this city death and orchids, creamy sauces and diarrhoea existed to help each other.

Life was lived here over speedy generations from jhuggi to housing colony to marzipan villa in astounding succession. Intricate monuments were buried by high-rises and ancient stones breathed humbly under auto-repair shops and electricity substations.

Small dust devils rose and whirled in mossy tenements and crowded chawls, in Presidency outhouses and suburban colonies in Lucknow and Kanpur, Ludhiana and Barmer. They churned and spun as they rushed, burning, to burst upon Delhi's boulevards.

The city screeched into them. The rich conmen, the beautiful fixers and the powerful rogues danced on the glowing coals of the dust devil's heart. Another unknown boy and girl from somewhere takes Delhi by storm! Where did they come from? Where would they go? The city was a wicked whore. She'd only fuck those who had the fire and urinate on the sad ruins that had lain nearby for centuries.

Yet Madhavi was hopeful for Delhi. It would one day rise and claim its place in the world. It had done it before. It would do it again.

She liked the way history ran, casually and neglectedly in all the stones and shrubs from the crumbling walls of the fort of Siri to the Hauz Khas tank and the imitation Acropolis on Raisina Hill. Looking up one night at the stony cliffs of Purana Qila gloomy with dim illumination, skeletal black trees dancing along its walls, she had seen a dark figure sitting cross-legged on the ruined turrets.

A breeze had blown away his cowl, and underneath she had seen a long aristocratic face. Perhaps a phantom sultan, stopping off in the city of his tomb before being driven away again by the carbon monoxide and liquefying tarmac.

The Mahatma Gandhi Foundation in Delhi was a trendy new idea. It was intended as a place where scholars, journalists, writers, film-makers, artists, dancers and playwrights could 'interface' and 'synergise'. Roughly translated, Madhavi grimaced to herself, as fornicate and stab in the back. It was, the blurb said, 'aimed at placing subcontinental popular culture on the Millennial map'. It had received a huge endowment from Non-Resident Indians and corporate houses and unlike most other such institutions in India didn't lack for money. To Madhavi, it was a prize worth leaving a husband behind in America for.

She ran a finger along Mira's spherical sleeping cheek. But the competition, tomato*kutty*, was stiff indeed: Dhruv Mathur, former editor of the popular newspaper *The Republic*. He was already additional director at the Foundation, for which he had even given up his job at *The Republic*. After Pamela's stroke, Dhruv reportedly did most of the managing and she had heard that Pamela was considering him very seriously for the job.

Like her, Dhruv too had been one of Pamela's students. Like her, Dhruv too had completed his D.Phil. from Oxford.

She knew him. Suspended in a night sky between seminars from Prague to Buenos Aires, she had sifted her memories carefully. She couldn't imagine what it would be like to see Dhruv again. Again. Dhruv again.

In the Magdalen College Fellows Garden, swept by a pub-laughter breeze, he had pushed his foot against her crotch, pushed it against her fading damp jeans. She had pointed out (breathlessly) that the moon was tossed like a ghostly galleon. He had groaned and told her to stop quoting school poetry. God, didn't she read anything but juvenilia? She wasn't serious enough. She was a wet blanket. He was smelly in those days. He smelt of hash and booze because he hardly ever bathed. The Love-Like-Hate-Adore test for their names showed 'hate' for them both. Yes, they hated each other. She would black out the test savagely, exasperated by her own frivolity, let down by her true nature that seemed to burst and bubble at any foolishness, not progress clearly and calmly as her grave ancestors would have expected.

If it all works out, no, tomato, she told the sleeping child, then we'll come and stay here and then we'll go for holidays to Bangalore. Nice, no? Very nice. And maybe Daddy will come too. But even if he doesn't, it'll be okay with you and me. Of course it'll be okay. We don't need Dad.

Her five-year-old marriage to the scholarly Peter was a civilised exchange of professional achievements. They took well-organised holidays sometimes in San Francisco and sometimes in Bangalore. His work was bringing him closer to the administration and there were rumours that he might even be offered a position at the Asia Centre at Harvard University. His open pride at his well-read and ethnic wife among their small circle of friends at Columbia was obvious.

They looked in on her as she sat in her glass showcase, and approved.

But recently her careful self had seemed to come apart. After Mira's birth, dry books and papers gave way to wet hormonally changeable emotions. Peter was surprised to see his soft-spoken Asian Flower who looked so beautiful when she sat quietly at dinner parties suddenly begin to crawl around on the carpet, subsiding into loud giggles or sobbing over the crib.

She felt absent from long periods of her own life. Most of her twenties and thirties had been lived among people who were now brushing past strangers in different time zones. In New York, on hectic evenings, when Happening people in Greenwich Village hailed taxis and music trumpeted in bars, she sat alone in her apartment whispering to her baby in Tamil and feeding her *payesam*.

Peter hadn't understood why she was so eager to get this Delhi job. He was happy for her but she had to understand that he couldn't possibly come with her. Things were going so well for her in Columbia, she had just been given tenure, why on earth did she suddenly want to relocate? And he couldn't just give everything up and go to India, not when his Mandarin was improving so rapidly and his articles on Hong Kong had even been circulated in the White House. She was expecting far too much from him.

He would just have to remain in New York. They could visit each other over the holidays. Madhavi seemed to do whatever she wanted to, she always left him out of her decisions. The American view of a partnership was based on joint decisions. Did she realise that? Did she agree with it?

She had insisted that Mira come with her. Why, he had demanded. Because Delhi was nice in winter, that's why. But why did she want to spend an *entire* month there? Whom did she want to meet?

Pamela, she had replied. She wanted to meet Pamela, the teacher she had once idolised. And Zahra Reza, her friend.

But Mira's too tiny to register her mother's old friends, Peter had said impatiently. Did she honestly expect a baby to get excited about people she had never seen and wouldn't recognise? For Christ's sake, Peter had said, hurtling into belligerent silence.

Madhavi found Zahra's number and dialled. Several years earlier, Zahra and Madhavi had arrived in Oxford together, Madhavi from Delhi, Zahra from Hyderabad.

"Zahroo? It's Madhavi."

Madhavi's voice was clear. A voice hung with two long plaits and a ribbon tied at each end.

"Muds!" Zahra's was throaty and deep. She would be considered beautiful anywhere in the world. She had ivory skin, masses of brown hair waving below her shoulders and sparkling Miss Universe eyes. Madhavi had lost touch with Zahra over the last few years, distracted with her books and her baby.

How *are* you, how *are* you. Darling. How have you *been*. How have *you* been. I arrived only a few hours ago. With your baby? With my baby. Oh my god, your baby. I've been wondering if she'll be okay with the potties here. Come on, stop being an NRI! Mira? Yah, Mira. We named her Mira. How's Peter. Shit, we're past forty. Imagine, yaar, did you ever think we'd be middle aged? I'm really sorry about your divorce, Zahroo. But it's all for the better. Better to be happy, na, whatever it means. Listen, is there some…do you have someone?

There was a sudden sharp silence. A silence that opened up unexpectedly like a gorge between two mountains, a steep sheer drop into a dark crevasse below. Have you met someone, Zahroo? Madhavi asked again. Silence still, still that dark fall. Madhavi sat up and brushed off her fear. But, there had never been any silences between Zahra and her, for God's sake. Chatter was their security blanket. They had always burrowed deliciously into confessional razai and wriggled their toes.

"Zahroo, another thing. Dhruv."

The silence shifted and became less sudden. It was awkward now, but social, a silence of manners as when waving at someone and they look away.

"He's fine," said Zahra at last. "He's not worried about you, darling."

"Oh," faltered Madhavi. "That's good then."

Another silence. Madhavi hurried into the void.

"I'm just desperate to see you, Zahroo and…"

"You've just had yet another successful book, I hear," interrupted Zahra.

Zahra had written her first book on the Indian National Movement. Critics had called it 'adequate' and Zahra hadn't written anything else since.

"Oh that. It's all over now, anyway. I'm ready to move on."

"I'm sure you are."

"Must catch up on your life, Zahra. And tell you about my life and thoughts!"

"Your life and thoughts. You sound like Bertrand Russell. You're very big, darling. A celebrity. " She rang off.

Madhavi stared at the telephone. No, she was imagining the silences. It would all be all right when they met. Everything would be sorted out in their special words in inverted commas. Words that they made bizarre by their meaning and the way they used them. 'Concatenation' and 'germane'.

Zahra used to laugh at the ghastly clothes she had worn in Oxford in those days. Frock coats and antiquated frilly shirts. Dhruv used to curse when he was trying to pull them off. He was always clumsy anyway, no finesse. He was crude and cruel. She had called him a dumb fuck. He had looked as if he was about to burst into tears and said she was a bitch. They always called each other such terrible names. The hatred never abated.

She had bundled those old clothes into a bag on her last trip to Bangalore and given them away to an orphanage.

She turned on her side and tried to sleep.

The champa tree outside Anusuya's window was fuzzy with dew. Shantanu and Anusuya were tossing in their blackened bedroom beyond the dining room, television room and study. Across the living room, down a short corridor, Uma's room looked out into the front lawns and opposite, the guest room, where Sam stayed. Nicely separate but close enough.

She turned the front key and let them in. Sam's bed had been neatly made by Misri. The bedside table had been freshly wiped. On it a flask of water and a glass and in a corner of the room the smell of sweet poison from a tablet of mosquito repellant.

"Not sleepy are you?" he asked as she turned towards her own room.

She heard the loneliness in his voice but didn't know whether she was imagining it. She always imagined him buried in his own world, wreathed in layers of interconnectedness with others. He would look askance at her if she tried to claw at the wall of courteous understanding that they had erected. Or, if she tried to get her feet wet in a whirlpool they monitored together from a clever and polite distance, he might be embarrassed.

She shivered. Her tongue began to tingle with life. Her memories became perceptive, she felt insightful. The effect of Christine's Shankhapushpi, perhaps.

"Sam…" she began.

In his attic room in Oxford they had sat talking for hours. Whenever it got too late and she tried to touch his arms or hair, he would push her away firmly and say that she must be tired and should sleep. Then he would close the door with a soft but determined click.

One late night after he had banished her with a friendly pat on her shoulders, she had gone back to her room painfully intimidated, with an aching longing. She couldn't help feeling that his resolve had as much to do with her bony legs as it had to do with the Vatican.

But shopping in Sainsbury's together she caught him gazing at her while she read the labels on a pickle bottle.

"Uma," he had said, "I wish that sometimes you would look at me straight, do you know what I mean? Don't dance around all the time. Just steady on…let me…" he had sighed and trailed off. She had been confused. She had always assumed that her impromptu performances were amusing to him.

On their last Sunday, Sam had asked Uma to accompany him to church, but she had refused thinking his invitation to be only a formality. She hadn't wanted him to feel that he was obliged to take her everywhere he went. Besides, she didn't want another argument about Absolute Values just as they were about to leave for India.

Sam was keen on Absolute Values. Moral relativism had led directly to the rise of Hitler. There were certain things that were Right and certain things that were Wrong, irrespective of culture. Culture shouldn't matter, only values.

But, she had sighed inwardly, unless he understood her culture, how would he understand her? Unless he understood the hapless class of Indians who grumbled in the space between Enid Blyton and the Taj Mahal, how would he ever know why she reacted to things the way she did?

But Sam was suspicious of the culture argument. The way you speak or dress didn't ultimately mean anything. If you believe, everything falls into place.

She wondered if one day he would be found near the Amazon, cultivating a farm or leading a life from a Graham Greene novel in Central America.

She composed letters to him from Delhi. She would write him into missing her, convince him by her winning fluency that she, schooled in Irish convents, was as much a Christian as he was. She knew all the hymns, all the saints, all the miracles. She knew much more certainly than he did of Hinduism. In any case, she wasn't really a Hindu. She only liked the clothes.

She had once swept into a puja pandal in an antique lace sari and been much admired by the Sarbajanin Puja Samiti of Lodi Colony.

She had even written a Political Theory paper on how religious differences should be openly demonstrated in public fancy dress parades in order to further civic peace. There should be religious fairs where every denomination would have a separate stall. There should be a carnival atmosphere.

This wasn't the end for them. Hadn't he said that nation-states didn't matter? He must have meant it. He would go back to England, join McKinsey's and laugh in wine bars while she yearned and ached on fantasy-ridden nights, a million miles away. But she would keep writing to him. She would send him e-mail. She would see him again. He would be her lifelong English friend.

And Sam, looking down at her felt certain that he would never meet anyone like Uma in his life. No other woman would inspire him to come to a country which he knew nothing about and where he felt he stuck out like a sore thumb. But was it her or did he simply wish to pedal off into the tropics, a crazy white man on his bicycle, (as he had read in a poem he couldn't fully remember) carrying a medicine for which there was no disease?

He had had a kitbag for Uma in Oxford, brushing off her fears of racism and laughing at her intimations of exclusion. Was it wrong to want to 'cure' her from such terrified and rather passé innocence, to protect her somehow from wounds he could only dimly realise. His mind was being whipped like thick cream by the clashes and juxtapositions for which he could find no divine purpose, no links to the edifice of knowledge he had already accepted as true and good. Was that the selfish reason which was keeping him here? The challenge which was like a sexual charge that goes on and on but demands that you never succumb?

As he stood at the door of his room, his eyes were as impenetrable as rockpools. She reached up to kiss him. He hugged her and slapped her on the back as he always did when she made him laugh.

"Cheers, baby," he said.

"Goodnight, Sam."

3

Most invaders who galloped into India through the Khyber stopped in Delhi and there were ghosts everywhere. And the day after the party and the effects of Christine's Shankhapushpi, Uma saw a queue of them. But they weren't medieval.

Or she may have imagined them. Or perhaps she saw them because although she tried to tell herself that she was happy to have Sam here, she was becoming insecure about him, and his presence glared into her life and lit up its furtive corners. The ghosts made her feel more inferior to him than ever.

The day began as it always did. Shantanu had gone to the office. Anusuya sat up in bed smoking, rubbing Oil of Ulay on her bare arms and painting her eyes black and green. She made a few loud uncharitable remarks about Uma and Sam, saying now that Uma was Oxford-returned, at least she should get a job instead of fooling around with her worthless friends and Sam should travel around the rest of India, not just sit in Delhi and eat Misri's food.

After breakfast, Sam said he needed to change some money. Uma drove him to the 24-Hour Open Central Bank Money Changer counter at the Ashoka Hotel, to the faint smell of old leather and to the lobby decorated with an astonishing fusion of dusty destroyer class chandeliers hanging in front of concrete

Mughal screens. This state-owned hotel in decline ruined by new private competition turned out to be the appropriate venue of an Oxford reunion.

Uma followed Sam into the lobby, feeling cold with unexplained foreboding. Across the lobby stood P. Venugopal, former alumnus of Merton College. Venu had been in Oxford for the last four years but still looked as if he had never set foot anywhere outside Kilpauk, Chennai.

Skinny, squeaky clean and wearing a heavy blue anorak, he was coughing and kicking opposite the 24-Hour Open Money Changer which was now firmly shut.

Six copies of his bound D.Phil., sepulchrally examining the effects of the WTO regime on Indian development rested in his suitcase. Venu was passing through Delhi for a day before taking the connecting flight to Chennai.

Uma's heart sank at the sight of him. The dank anorak reminded her of the bleak stairs behind her parents' home. Or the musty interiors of a neon dark office where she would one day hunch over a creaking table and find herself staring up the nose of a depressed typist.

"Hi Venu," Uma called.

Venu jerked his head and his spectacles flashed. "Yah, er...Oh it's you," he pointed out.

He slid hurriedly into an alcove, gave Sam a weak smile and sank into a sofa in a squelch of plastic bags. She sat down next to him. Around them the hotel straggled governmently. Conferences for Waste Recycling, Modi Xerox luncheon, reception in honour of the Latvian premier. Receptionists in dull suits and crumpled saris rudely told everybody off. A thin garland of rajnigandhas hung on a carved sandalwood Saraswati.

"So we're both back, Venu," Uma announced, "Back to the beauty of the doomed…"

"Yah, doomed? I don't think so," arrested Venu stiffly. "There's progress in every sphere. Every sphere, er...that's it."

This Bengali woman has always been depraved, he thought. Her entire effort has centred on foreign men and generally leading a useless life. He still remembered that summer ball where he had been dragged against his will and forced into parting with an obnoxious amount of money for the ticket. (Thankfully he had subsequently recouped the money by winning a cash prize for a venomously comprehensive forty-page essay on how Third World governments can cut fiscal debt.)

At the ball the idiotic Bengali female had been behaving like a goat. Literally. She and some feathered foreign friends had been impersonating animals in a zoo, and Uma, Venu remembered cringing, had been braying in a Bengali accent.

He shuddered at what she must have been up to last night, judging from her bloodshot eyes.

Venu was clear about his own priorities. He had his impeccable qualifications. Now he would begin the unstoppable rise up the World Bank where he had a job waiting for him as soon as he had completed his family visit to Chennai and bent his head in dutiful assent when his mother inquired about finding him the right girl.

Venu wasn't worried. He knew that wherever he was in the world he could always visit the Venkateswara temple nearby.

"Economic policy has been the biggest break from the past," he began formally to Sam. "The main thing about today's India is the...you... economic change. Today, in India it, that is, liberalisation of the economy in 1991, more than any other single event, divides the generations, er...that's it."

Uma looked pityingly at Venu. He had led a permanently offended life in Oxford, never venturing into the uncharted territory of the cultural ambassador. All Venu's friends had been

Indians and he had eaten only Indian food. Perhaps there were unseen international conspiracies working to keep people caged in suspicion of each other. Invisible organisations that profit from mutual distrust.

She tried to picture Venu in his World Bank office, cursing his bosses under his breath.

Venu glanced at Uma scornfully. He knew all about her vile lifestyle, her quicksilver changes of clothes and this long-haired boyfriend. He had heard her speak to him in a fake accent. She spoke differently with different people. She was, basically, a woman in search of an accent, concluded Venu, turning to peer down the corridor to see if the bank had opened. As he turned back, he almost choked.

Shravani-Rani Prasad and her Norwegian boyfriend were upon them.

Shravani-Rani Prasad had been named Smita at birth. But at Oxford, had decided that she would much rather be known as Queen of the Indian Spring. In England, Shravani-Rani had undergone a metamorphosis that would put the lead character in *The Fly* to shame. Where there was once a stringy plait, salwar kameez and white sneakers, there now stood a wind-blown neohippie.

Masses of curls, dangling earrings and anklet, flaming red ghagra with black leotard top, arms jingling with silver bracelets, high-heeled boots pinching on long gym-tuned legs.

After three years in Oxford, Shravani-Rani had become an Orientalists' wet dream. A made-to-order East, confirming every Western hope of pyramids of spice and odd gods. Her voice had changed too. From high pitched and inquisitive, she had acquired a Marlborough huskiness.

"Hiiiii!" she shouted, sweeping regally towards them as Svenn shambled admiringly behind. "Imagine seeing you all here, of ALL places!"

She dug a green fingernail into Venu. "Still cowering, haa, still scared. Going away had no effect. No effect at all."

"And what about the Bangaali bhadramahila," she said whirling in front of Uma. "Are you making it happen or not? Haa? Kya hai? Kuch hai? Batao, batao!" she laughed shrilly. "Oh you both know Svenn, na? I've dragged him down to the little desh, just like that, giving him the Heat and Dust. Just as Uma's dragged you. You see, Svenn's ready, at last. He's," she lit a cigarette, "ready to just *be*. You know, just *be*."

Sam lit a cigarette too: "That must help."

"Hi Shravani, hi Svenn," smiled Uma. "Good to see you both."

"Arre, lovely yaar. Lovely."

Shravani-Rani's engagement to Svenn had been a well-publicised event, as was her future life in Oslo, where she had a job with the Lutheran World Service programme for Third World women. While her parents ran their private medical practice in Delhi and thought wistfully of the high life in New York, Shravani-Rani had already become a global player. Her degree in psychology had prepared her for every human impulse. The self, gender, experience and emotion were codified and docketed as efficiently as she had prepared for her examinations.

The names of her boyfriends unfailingly typified national types. She had conquered a Greek by the name of Niko, an American called Bud and now, the Scandinavian Svenn. If Shravani-Rani ever slept with a Native American there was a good chance he might be called Wounded Knee.

"Sam. Uma," smiled Svenn, an International Relations scholar from St Antony's, blazer and cream trousers soon to be badly rumpled.

"Ah, yah, er...International Relations! The subject of the future," declared Venu in loud relief, "most of the...er... yah...Wall Street millionaires, NASA scientists, all...Indian only...Indian only...er..." Venu made money-changing gestures with his hands.

"*Mashaallah!*" cried Shravani-Rani. "Did you hear what he said? He's so gritty. So nitty. Too sweet. You know, Sam, the first time I met Svenn," she began, "I was trying to reject the Asian Woman image. Understand? Rejection of the Asian Woman image. I was standing on a diving board in Ralph's house. I was feeling positive because I was *down* to forty-eight kgs, think of it, forty-eight kgs, man. Too good! I just decided to shock everybody. All evening I had been answering polite questions on widows in India and sati in India and bride burning in India. So I just broke free. Free. D'you know what I did? I just took my top off. Just took it off.

"Svenn, don't you remember how fantastic it was? The night stars, the swimming pool, that diving board, everybody daring the Eastern Temptress to emerge out of the chrysalis. Everybody looking, thinking, how could an Indian woman do this. My god, look at that Indian woman go. Well the Indian woman ain't what she used to be, my dears. She ain't what she used to be. Don't you think so, Uma?"

Shravani-Rani blew smoke into Venu's purple nodding face and delved into her bag.

"Now, where did I put those traveller's cheques, Svenn, darling?"

Uma felt panicky and restless. She hated hotel lobbies. They always reminded her of everything that was wrong in her life. She felt her hands become clammy and nervous.

The India Institute Library in Oxford, was the way she liked India best, air-conditioned and in books, raw material to be harshly exposed and used, with a carpet underfoot and spires dreaming outside.

She felt detached from the others and looked away, beyond the uselessly expensive hotel shops, the long marble corridors that smelt of nothing, at the greens and reds and yellows of clothes. Then she saw the queue of spirits.

A long line of people stood at the counter, changing money.

They had just come in from somewhere and their skins were dry and brown, the apologetic brown that lurks in bright supermarkets and tiptoes down the road at night anxious to attract as little attention as possible. A resigned and mournful brown, drooping with far too many labelled suitcases.

Around them the hotel bustled but these people were curiously quiet, huddling before the hard-faced clerk, hands shaking over different coloured currency notes, scraps of documents, multi-hued passports, diaries, legal papers of different kinds. They whispered in small groups. Their eyes were blank, their movements slow and heavy.

"Uma, where have you disappeared, you're not listening to anything at all that I'm saying," Shravani-Rani sounded hurt.

"I was just looking," muttered Uma.

"Er, yah...looking at what?" asked Venu.

"Have you seen someone you know?" asked Svenn solicitously.

"What's up, Uma?" Sam asked.

"Those people, I was just looking at those people in that queue," said Uma half-heartedly.

Shravani-Rani, Venu and Svenn peered in the direction Uma was pointing.

"Oh my God, what on earth is this deluded individual talking about?" demanded Shravani-Rani. "What people? Where?"

"There doesn't seem to be anything there Uma," said Svenn, "what are you looking at?"

"No, there, there. Can't you see those people there, there are those people, come on, those people with their passports, changing money there, can't you see them?"

"Yah...er...there's nothing at all sad about changing money, that's it..." said Venu incredulously.

Sam put an arm around Uma and she sat down heavily. She looked at Shravani-Rani and Venu. No they couldn't see the queue. Only she could see them. Only she could see that procession that wends its way around the world, pockets bulging with currencies of different countries, visas, passports and documentation that makes it possible for them to exist. It filled her with nauseating sorrow.

She would one day be part of that procession. She would one day join the ranks of itinerants, greedily seeking opportunities and wealth in the face of scorn and pity while the sun set on her ordinariness in different cities around the globe.

All my friends are becoming ghosts, she shouted urgently to herself. I belong to a generation of immigrants and exiles. Ceaseless travellers with their multicoloured documents, their camouflaged skin colours, changing their accents faster than they change money. Where were the builders, the role-models, the childhood sweethearts, the beauty queens, the jokesters? Where was the captain of the college chess team? Where was the amateur boxer? They had ceased to be themselves. They were only numbers, standing in a queue for their green cards.

She looked at Shravani-Rani. In Oslo, imprisoned in her new persona, her armour against domination, a feeble attempt to resist conquest by Svenn. She was an unutterably sad courtesan.

She turned her gaze on Venu, with his D.Phil., unknowing about who he would ultimately serve and for what purpose he would finally bend his scholarship. He would contribute to the growth of enterprises that couldn't spell his name. Vote for political parties who wouldn't understand who he was. Derive a shabby pleasure from a laundromat every Sunday morning and a Mercedes parked in his garage.

The crowd moved away from her. She could see that they did not need her sympathy. She looked at their efficient folders, their neatly arranged papers and felt like crying. They reminded her of home. Of family occasions. Of the little worlds of large families. Of the smell of her father's worn briefcase. His old fashioned aftershave, Old Spice, floating behind him as he left every day for work.

Her mother. The brave rings and necklaces. In her heart, photographs of the dead. Flowered sofas from which the dust never rose. The more you dusted, the dirtier they became. The blue and green of various forms fluttering under paperweights in studies without electricity. The documents of voluntary exile and cowardly goodbyes. Her parents' crumbling house where skinny mechanics streamed in and out all day wearing *Sesame Street* T-shirts.

"You're a foolish girl," said Venu, unable to restrain himself any longer.

The counter opened and they all began to hurry towards it.

"You know, this might just be a complicated expression of something," said Shravani-Rani, enviously. "A sort of psychological Black Hole."

As they hurried off, Shravani-Rani turned and called over her shoulder.

"Bye, Uma. I'll write to you. From Oslo."

Uma sat on the Ashoka Hotel sofa and felt Sam's arm on her shoulders. The ghost queue shuffled past. Each of them had a recognisable face. Venu, Shravani-Rani, the captain of the St Stephen's College chess team. And herself. She waved them away desperately and edged closer to Sam. He, more than anyone, could protect her from them.

She waited numbly for him to finish changing his money. Sam and his bristly cheeks and hidden chest. Of whom she was so afraid that she simply couldn't bring herself to use the word 'love'. How could she, when he could barely see her as she stood at the end of a never-ending queue? She decided to tell him, today, that she was madly in love with him and ask him, flat out, if they could have a future.

He was a *Where Have All The Flowers Gone* soldier wandering between the borders of new countries. He was literary and separate from her tattered world. His voice sounded like a standard for her grandfather to emulate. She would have to tell him. She would have to grasp at his trueness and use it, pragmatically, cruelly, for herself.

But after Sam finished changing his pounds, he said he would like to go to Chandni Chowk because he had to meet someone there, in front of the Bata shoe shop.

"Chandni Chowk?" she asked in surprise.

His eyes were opaque, "I just need to meet someone."

"Meet someone in *Chandni Chowk*?"

"Actually," he laughed, "I just want to see what it's like."

"See what it's like? You'll get killed."

"Uma," he protested.

She got the hint.

"Don't be late because we've got Kamini's party tonight. And I want to tell you something."

"Can't wait."

Chandni Chowk was the heart of the Old City of Delhi where once the grand Jama Masjid may have opened onto a street of merchants and hawkers selling fruit and silk. Crowds burst at Sam as he got off Shantanu's Ambassador. Trucks, cyclists, cows and vendors fell on his back. Birds circled screaming overhead. The nerve-rattling honking of edging cars and milling crowds and street-side stalls dispensing everything from clips to clothes to jewellery and parrots crowded him into his own chest and pressed his arms against his sides. The purplish sores of a beggar-cum-salesman of tissues waved in his face. The heat of frying samosas and aloo-tikki ran around his head. Parrots screeched. A massive Mitsubishi Lancer nudged a pathway through the crush. A frightened monkey leapt away from its minder. Children fluttered onto the road and dashed away in the face of swerving Marutis and Sam bellowed: "Uma! I can't move!"

She sat distractedly behind the wheel still thinking about her ghosts, still thinking how she could tell him about herself, how to finally make everything clear. She heard Sam's shouts but couldn't reply. By the time she stuck her head out of the car to see if he was all right, it was too late.

He was carried away in a mighty surge while scooters and cycle rickshaws scampered madly after him. A vast truck carrying vegetables scraped past a road-side sugar cane juice vending machine, but miraculously — for such things are not short of the miraculous — missed it.

Giant hoardings of Sumeet Kitchen Machine and the latest Bollywood blockbuster glared down. Rival gangs of eunuchs and unemployed youth taunted and chased each other between the roadside shrines to Hanuman, Santoshi Mata and technicolour photos of Jesus.

Uma reversed, blind to Chandni Chowk's jagged frenzy which could (if you allowed it to) squeeze the quiet areas of loneliness and contemplation into fruit juice. But Uma was in another world. She was planning her big confession.

That evening, on Kamini's breezy barsaati terrace strewn with rum bottles and cushions her friends waited to meet Sam.

The young at heart lived in barsaatis. Their landlords and landladies lived downstairs and sometimes provide food with surrogate parenting or bills with malicious hostility.

Kamini's landlady was the beautiful Mrs Visvam, once a Bharatanatyam dancer. She always wore fresh jasmine in her hair and painted long black lines around her eyes.

Her friends cheered as Uma and Sam walked up the stairs.

There was a power cut. But it didn't matter because the weather was mild and the terrace was huge and still, enclosed by potted rubber plants, cactii and fanning palms. Candles glowed inside clay lamp shades. Chips were set out in wooden bowls and plates of shammi and seekh kababs rested on the low central table. Rum and coke, whisky and water, glasses and teacups sat on the ground. Inside, on the walls of the lamp-lit bedroom, a Raja Ravi Verma print and a poster of Picasso's Guernica that Kamini had bought in London.

Kamini worked in a glossy fashion magazine and liked to keep in touch with the world. She was frail and slender with flyaway cheekbones, long lank hair and laughed — so her friends said — like a giraffe on heat.

Why do all Bongs get excited about goras, she had written to Uma in England. *Forget him. Forget the white world. Why should he give a shit about you?* But Sam won Kamini over almost instantly. Not just because he was charming and lively but because she was expecting a blonde god and instead she got a bespectacled Mohican.

There were other friends there. Gitanjali, the lawyer with thick black hair and thick black clothes.

Ashish, the economist wearing his army boots and Sachin Tendulkar T-shirt. Geetanjali's boyfriend Vir who owned a travel agency and Kamal and Manish the gay fashion-designer couple who wore loose salwar kurtas and took holidays in contrasting cities.

And the strapping dark-skinned and Castro-bearded Dinesh Krishna, alias Deekay, who ran an NGO for blue-collar workers laid off by newly liberalising industries and whose westernised Gujarati parents ran a chic architecture firm in Mumbai.

Deekay was older than they were and much busier. His days were spent organising demonstrations in support of the world community of oppressed people. He sometimes took part in councils of war on sexual harassment on the university campus where he would be the only man in a room full of khadi-clad women. He once became so disturbed at the report of a caste riot in Bihar that he resolved to set up an internet army that would log on to all computers in the tribal belt and tap out messages to rural caste militias reminding them that all men were equal.

In an awareness campaign about the vanishing rain forest, he had created a small shrine to the Amazon in his one-roomed flat in Hauz Khas consisting of a clutch of moneyplants arranged in a Help Me pattern. He was an active member of schemes to rehabilitate the children of the Orissa cyclone and regularly sent as much money as he could to people he insisted were freedom fighters killed in Kashmir.

He had staged demonstrations against the shahtoosh shawl, the nuclear tests, the Narmada Dam and against plastic bags. In a battle with the management at the Kamani auditorium, he had questioned why they had not provided for wheelchairs in the theatre. He had objected to an aquarium in a sea-food restaurant saying the proprietors shouldn't display their cruelty to marine life.

In protracted negotiations with a local legislator, he had pointed out that on Delhi's streets, the racism against African students was so bad that unless laws were introduced he would write, no, not simply to the chief minister of Delhi but to the United Nations. He regularly wrote articles on the need to stop Kentucky Fried Chicken and McDonald's from expanding in Delhi as children were not just contracting disease but their worldview was being damaged by lewd advertising. He had demanded that the public wake up to the fact that whole villages were being ruined by the incursions of the market economy and unless something was done to protect the apple farmers and the silk weavers he, Deekay would be forced to withdraw support from the ruling cabal in parliament.

His tiny flat was hung with notices against dictators in every country and he was frequently bare-bodied and clad only in track pants to indicate his solidarity with the fate of the Sri Lankan Tamils, Aung San Suu Kyi and the Dalai Lama at the same time. He never ate chocolate on the grounds that the cocoa growers of Africa were being steadily impoverished while Nestle's and Cadbury's were netting super profits. He was vegetarian, which suited his Gujarati parents and never drank milk, which didn't. His parents sent him to the Delhi School of Planning and Architecture so that he might take over their business, but he dropped out, spent all his money on a trip to the US and came back determined to fight. Deekay fought on many fronts and always had surplus energy for more armageddons.

He told his parents that he would never return to the money-centred world of Mumbai and would only agree to take a small stipend from them if they didn't pressure him into getting married.

Deekay was universally adored (and loved by Kamini) because he was an indefatigable campaigner for everybody's rights with scant regard for political niceties. No questions asked, no explanations required, just point him in the direction of the injustice and let him roll.

His friends knew him well enough to realise that Deekay had little time for the complicated twists and turns in the Revolution. He just wanted to be useful and feed people. If Deekay hadn't been a world-hater he could easily have been the head of a large household, builder of efficient cities or a chef.

In fact, he was an excellent cook. He would prepare a huge pot of vegetable stew and a moist pineapple halva served with vanilla ice cream which he would pass around to his friends in his Hauz Khas flat with the gravitas of an aid worker among the famine victims of Ethiopia, or an *intifadah* warrior saving his colleague from death. Khao, yaar, khao, he would say, gazing at them conscienciously while they chomped in drooling solidarity.

Tonight, he had made a delicious *undhiu* for Uma and Sam and after the introductory flurry, spooned out a large portion and pushed it into her mouth. The *undhiu* was delicious, tender and spicy-sweet.

"So...Uma, now what? Kya karegi?" Deekay poured himself a cup of rum.

Gitanjali clapped: "Arre, let's make Uma prime minister."

"Are you mad or what?" Ashish was incredulous. "Did Laloo Prasad Yadav go to Oxford?"

They guffawed and drank. And clustered around Sam and Uma, throwing their arms open and snuggling their circle closer. They had been children together and they wanted nothing to matter but the old jokes.

Uma glanced at Sam. His eyelashes had dropped low over his emerald lakes and a stubble was beginning to sprout on his cheeks. Sam had a thick growth and sometimes had to shave twice a day, unexpected virility in someone so negligent about his maleness.

"Mujahideen lagta hai, Uma," giggled Kamal, following her gaze, "kahan se pakar ke layee hai?"

She felt proud of him. Proud of his long black hair, dark stubble and pale skin. Like a sexy Mohican-Mujahideen. Man in all his violence and angst. Man stretched to his limits. Man betrayed by life. Passionate. Wrung out.

"So," smiled Manish, striking up his guitar and looking slyly at Sam, "you like India? Or," he looked around at the others, "you only like Indian women?"

Sam sat back against the wall and grinned. "So far, only the women."

"My problem with Catholics like you," said Deekay turning to Sam, "is the present pope, yaar. The guy's too backward looking. He's just, I don't know. Eh, I got a problem with the pope, man."

His tirade broke over their heads. Sam smiled quietly and poured himself another glass of rum. His hair was slicked down, his cheeks were flushed and his eyes were hooded with lashes.

Uma's brain paused for a split second. How had Deekay known that Sam was a practising Catholic? Nobody knew. She hadn't told anyone. How did Deekay know?

The others hooted and fell about with noisy disagreements. Gitanjali craned her neck towards Vir.

"Vir, let's tell everyone."

"What?"

"That we're getting married, na," Gitanjali sang.

"Never."

Laughter rose up and floated out into the surrounding trees. They settled down to the food and rum. Kamal put on some music. Sam got up and came to sit next to Uma. Vir and Gitanjali were going river rafting, Kamini's mother was sick and could Deekay please help her, Ashish hadn't filed his income tax returns and might go to jail but Kamal and Manish said the police would never jail a Sachin Tendulkar fan.

"You *don't*?" Kamini asked Uma in the bathroom, as they pissed together as they had always done.

"No."

"Why?"

"I don't know." If she had said God, Kamini would have thought she was being perverse.

"Shit! Is he into virginity and stuff?"

"It might be because...you know...the way I look."

"Then he should tell you!"

"Oh come on how can he tell me? How can he say, Uma, I don't want to sleep with you because you're ugly?"

"You're not, ugly anyway," said Kamini loyally. "Nobody could say you were ugly."

UB40 mourned in the player. Sam drained his glass, filled another and lit a cigarette.

Uma turned over different sentences in her mind, all of them beginning with Sam. Vir drew Gitanjali towards him and stroked her hair. Ashish lay on the bed, playing a wrestling match with his own feet. Kamal and Manish dug into the food. Kamini stared up at Deekay and wondered if they would ever get it together.

They drank while the night grew darker and wan beams from streetlights shone down on sneaking cats and Deekay delivered a familiar oration on global problems.

After Sam goes back to England, thought Uma, I should vow never to speak in English, master Bengali and live in Santiniketan in a sari with a hibiscus in my hair for the rest of my days. It's just as well he's rejecting my body. It'll teach me to go back to where I belong.

"Vir, let's go for a real Arya Samaj thing? Vedic rituals and all that. Theek hain, na?" Gitanjali pleaded.

Kamal yawned. "Somebody marry the girl from Ludhiana before I kill her."

Deekay stood up, suddenly angry.

"Eh, I'll tell you one thing, man. I may not know about Byron and shit, but I got my commitment to the whole shit, okay. I got my commitment, man. You guys just kill me, yaar. Shit, I'm not playing any games or anything like that, you know. Not playing any games. You people are all assholes, man."

"Excuse me, did I miss something?" inquired Manish, sitting up. "What games? Who's playing games?"

Deekay looked around the room and threw up his hands. Then he grabbed a can of beer and ranged over to the terrace railings.

"Eh, tum saale chootiya ho, yaar. You people just don't know about anything. You chootiyas, yaar. You got no commitment. You can't live in a fucking country like India and just...just...fuck around."

"But nobody's fucking around!" wailed Kamini. Too true, echoed Uma silently.

Deekay poured himself another cup of rum. "Don't laugh," he growled.

So they laughed again. Uma rolled her head from side to side. Sam was stretched out on the floor on his back, with one arm raised, a cigarette burning between his fingers.

But what about the circumstances to which I've returned, she shouted silently. Christine who accused me of class prejudice has never seen my mother. My mother who may be privileged or cocooned or whatever but you can't get a more miserable victim of Pax Brittanica. Day in and day out, only sorrow, deep sorrow from everything ranging from dirty tea sets in the Calcutta Club to the dust on her window sill.

"You can't just keep doing all this, you guys," harangued Deekay. "You've got to wake up. You've got to have some commitment at least. Otherwise, fuck off abroad, yaar."

Aditya, the ad copywriter and devoted dramatist, Uma's friend, lived with his parents in a house crowded with flowering creepers, pomegranates, jasmine, bigonias, hibiscus, plants in pots, teapots, old bath-tubs and matkas. His mother was a manic gardner and their double-storeyed khus-scented Golf Links villa with chiks rolled neatly upto the ceiling commanded a superb view of the golf course. His parents played bridge every Saturday while Aditya retched in his room, Shylock one day, Uncle Vanya the next, Mac The Knife, the day after. His collection of plays crawled under the bottom shelf of his CD cabinet.

That night the gang came when Aditya was asleep. His insomniac mother was digging up a pot in the dark balcony when she heard a faint thud thud. She thought it was probably Aditya playing the role of Puck and continued to dig. Meanwhile the gang took away the magnificent Wells and Taylor edition of the *Complete Works of Shakespeare*, *Don Quixote* by Miguel de Saavedra Cervantes and *The Collected Plays Of Anton Chekhov*.

The electricity came back and the party ended.

Vir stopped playing, stood up and raised a toast. They hugged and slapped Uma.

"Full marks for coming back to India," said Deekay. "Although coming back is not enough."

They went back to the rum and sang *Seasons In The Sun.* Two arms came around Uma from the back in an unexpected hug from Deekay.

"See you, man, I'll see you. Achcha, Sam. Salaam."

He swayed out of the terrace with Kamini following close behind.

As they drove back in silence, Sam said:

"Poor Shah. No one takes him seriously."

For the second time that evening, Uma's brain paused. How did Sam know that Deekay's surname was Shah? Nobody had mentioned it. Deekay had introduced himself as Dinesh Krishna, being opposed, in principle, to surnames and caste names. How had Sam remembered the surname of her old friend that even she may not have remembered if she had been asked?

"Have you met Deekay before?"

"Never had the honour."

She must have misheard him. She was going a little crazy. Seeing ghosts. Hearing things. She better tell him what she had decided to tell him. Tell him of her true feelings, how desperately she needed to know if he felt anything for her at all.

As she sat on his bed and waited for him to come out of the bathroom, her eyes fell on his books. *A Confession* by Leo Tolstoy. *City Of God* by St Augustine of Hippo.

"Sam, you're my *priya bideshi*," she smiled.

He wagged a slightly sozzled finger at her.

"Now wait. That was...was that Bengali?"

"Yes. It means my dearest foreigner."

He leaned over and touched her cheek. "Got it right this time."

"Yes."

She sorted out several strands of thought and wet her lips. What would be the most tasteful way of saying it? What if he laughed and said he thought of her as a sister all this time? He pre-empted her.

"You said you wanted to tell me something, Uma." His voice was quiet.

"I hope," she said hesitantly, "I haven't sort of...put you under pressure...."

"No pressure, memsahib."

"Just going and plonking my friends on you...."

He flipped over in bed.

"Coming and going and plonking! Oh madam I am being very very sorry, oh blimey I am being coming and going and plonking!" He began to laugh.

Uma froze. She reached for the mountains on her lip.

"Gosh, you're totally tiddly."

Sam nodded his head from side to side and thumped the pillows.

"Oh madam I am totolly toddly. Oh totolly totolly toddly!" Sam giggled.

"Sam," Uma felt a stain on her cheeks. But he wasn't listening. He jigged his head and wagged his hands.

"Sam!" said Uma loudly and wildly, seeking an escape from this terrifying mimicry.

"Sam, what I wanted to tell you was this. You know. I believe. I believe love's just a product. All emotions have been coopted by industrial houses. Nostalgia, integral to the use of cellular phones. Sentiment, bound by images of coffee. The spirit of adventure, linked inexorably to fizzy drinks."

He sat up and jerked his head from side to side.

"Oh blimey! Buying and feeling! That is notta notta very very good notta very very good."

Uma's trembling voice rose in a frantic arc over his skit. Oh help. Oh god. This was awful. This was the return of the East India Company. This was the Battle of Plassey. The agitation against the Rowlatt Act. He hated her. He hated her friends. Poor Kamini and her sweet barsaati party. Poor old Deekay and his commitment. He had hated them all.

"To feel is to buy," she cried. "That's why I don't believe in love. There's no such thing. No such thing. It's just a con." She shouted the last few lines, drowning him out. He nodded and giggled.

She felt breathless. She felt tears gather in her nose. Had he parodied her accent like this in England? He had never done this before. Suddenly, he had her in his power. He hated her for inviting him to India. He hated India. He had nothing but contempt for her. He was tiring of her.

He hid his face in his hands and shook with laughter. Totolly toddly, he mimicked. Tears welled up in Uma's eyes and clouded her vision. She ran about in a jagged maze but couldn't find a way out.

"Don't make fun of me," she choked.

He stopped laughing immediately. His expression changed and he sat up.

"Hey," he pushed the hair out of his eyes, "you're upset!"

The sudden remorse in his voice tipped her over the edge into full-blown sorrow. Tears tipped over her eyes and snaked out from under her spectacles.

"Oh my God," Sam ran a hand through his hair, "I'm terribly sorry. My God."

"I never make fun of *your* accent," she wept.

Sam stroked her hand. "Hey, come on. Please stop. I'm sorry. I had no idea you would react like this. I was just kidding around, Uma."

Tears ran down her cheeks.

"D'you know how happy I am to be here with you? To meet everybody? I thought Deekay and Kamini and the others were terrific." Sam's voice was quiet. "Do you know that I would be destroyed if we had just said goodbye in England? Do you know that Uma?" His palms were warm.

"Love's been made into a product and it's being bought and sold," she whimpered.

He stroked her hand and pressed her palms. "I was just fooling around Uma, believe me."

"You weren't even listening to what I was saying," sniffed Uma, wiping her eyes.

"Of course I was. But I thought you were just...being facetious."

"No, I wasn't," said Uma thrusting her chin upwards. "I mean it. Love is a load of crap. It's shit. I don't believe it."

There was a pause. He got up, drank some water and went to the bathroom to brush his teeth. He came out and said that love was central to his beliefs. He could never accept, as she had said, that it was nothing more than a commodity. Without love, life made no sense to him whatsover.

She sat tremblingly on his bed. You believe in love but you don't love me she thought. That's clearly why you don't want to sleep with me. You're only being nice to me because you see me as a representative of the Indigenous Peoples. What is this love anyway which is so ideal and so unattainable.

She felt suddenly sure that he could never love her. How could he when she was so far away from his ideal of love. And in any case someone like him should streak his convertible around a sun-rippled bay with a golden Juno by his side, not gaze at her brown hairiness and listen to her bleak tales of oppression. And her funny accent.

After she went back to her room, Sam wrote agitatedly in his diary:

She distrusts love and thinks it to be some sort of Judeo-Christian plot. And I have followed her here like a puppy, hopeful of her acceptance. Hopeful of the very thing she seems to despise. The greater truth that seems to me to be life's main objective, she seems to regard as a Western conspiracy. If I'm to be made a representative of 'White' people all over the world and if 'home' and 'culture' are so much more important than achieving love, then I simply don't see the way forward. What the hell was I thinking? Why did I come here?

Lajpat Nagar and Defence Colony face each other across a busy crossing. Poms walk in Defence Colony's parks and ladies bake broccoli with boursin for their kitty parties. In Lajpat Nagar stray dogs chase their tails on patches of grey grass and small publishing houses bring out books on social theory in flats above families of seven.

Narrow crowded houses with artillery divisions of washing strung on their front verandahs whistle with the sounds of pressure cookers. Wobbling vegetable vendors on cycles push past new Cielos that swell in the alleyways and nudge their way over stones, tracks and precipitous ridges that pass for pavements. Lajpat Nagar is not beautifully low, it's simply neglected and weary.

Jai Prakash lived in a flat in one of the narrow Lajpat Nagar houses, with bright yellow windows and a patch of brownish, grass-ish vegetation in front. Next door to him lived Mr Aggarwal with brilliantly henna-ed hair who happened to be, coincidentally, Shantanu's Lower Division Clerk in the Ministry of Education. Mr Aggarwal had once taken Jai Prakash to his office and introduced him to the bemused Shantanu, who was the 'burra sahib' of the office. Jai Prakash, Mr Aggarwal had said to Shantanu, was also a Great Man.

That night, Jai Prakash, neatly dressed in grey trousers, white shirt and pale blue jumper, sat upright at a dining table crowded with papers, books, biscuit packets and cups. Stacks of paper stood in almost every corner of the room and the floor was piled with books. A thin board outside announced Shiksha Andolan.

Carefully and slowly, he folded sections of paper, some computer print-outs, some hand written, checked to see if they were accurately numbered and placed them in neat brown envelopes which he sealed with small strips of cellotape. He finished sealing about a dozen envelopes and selected a couple of books. Together with the sealed envelopes, he pushed them into a canvas bag for dispatch somewhere.

Two threadbare sofas stood on either side of the study table. A clump of agarbattis burned in the corner. A couple of framed photographs stood on the computer: one of the Buddha and another of a bald man in a suit.

Under the window which looked out into the Madras Canteen restaurant, lay bunches of papers bound by thick twine. He extracted a few and ordered them into neat sections. The kettle whistled. He walked rapidly back to the kitchen and made himself a cup of tea with lots of milk and sugar. He carried the sticky brew out into the room and sat down to look at the papers again.

He was light and quick on his feet and as he walked his floppy hair bounced. Directly opposite him was a book shelf. Most of the books were in English, but some were in Hindi. Uma would probably not recognise their names. The books didn't bear names like Manto, Premchand or Harivansh Rai Bachchan. There were other unknown names: Ekalavya, Majhi, Parashuram and Bechain. He put his cup down and wrote out a list of things to do in neat Devanagari.

The doorbell rang. His head jerked up and he hurried over to open the door.

Christine came into the room and threw her arms around him. He held her face in his hands and kissed her forehead, so that his hair dropped over her head. They sat down on the durrie on the floor. She turned her back towards him and giggled as he massaged. She shook him off and bent towards the papers.

He pulled her back onto his lap and whispered something in her ear. She threw back her head and laughed. He offered her his cup of tea. She opened her mouth wide and bit down hard on his hand. He laughed and tickled her waist. She laughed again.

The doorbell rang for a second time. They got up quickly and smoothed down their clothes. Christine answered the door and more people came in. An Indian woman in a sari wearing yin and yang earrings, a tall brown-haired white couple and two dark Indian men, one of them with a long untrimmed beard. They clustered around Jai Prakash and Christine.

Jai Prakash put his hand on Christine's back and pushed her gently towards the kitchen. Tea, he mouthed. The others sat down on the durrie and pulled out papers and books from their bags. Outside, a thin dinner time crowd straggled into the Madras Canteen.

Jai Prakash showed around some papers to the others. They nodded and passed them around. The yin and yang woman began to talk. The brown-haired couple seemed to disagree with what she was saying and pointed to the papers as if to say that it was simply not worth it. But the woman continued to argue and got up on her knees aggressively.

Christine brought in a tray of tea. Jai Prakash waved his hands as if trying to pacify the others. He pointed at himself and said something which made them all laugh. Then he pointed at Christine and they laughed again. The yin and yang woman sat down and they resumed their discussions.

Christine lay back on one of the sofas, drew a small hip flask from the pocket of her jacket and drank. Instantly, Jai Prakash was by her side. He snatched the hip flask away, walked to the kitchen and emptied the contents into the sink. A brown sticky liquid flowed out. He walked back to Christine who was still lying on the chair and shook his head in mock reprimand.

She looked down at her feet like a guilty child. He ruffled her hair and looked towards the others who were still talking.

"We better be careful of our books," said Jai Prakash looking up suddenly, his face deathly white. "These kitab chors must not attack us also. These bloody kitab chors!"

"No," said Christine her eyes filling with tears. "We should keep our books safe."

"The rich people and big people can buy new books, but if they take ours, what'll we do?" said Jai Prakash with a gleam in his eye. "What'll we do?"

The others shook their heads and made angry and agitated sounds.

Jai Prakash began to talk. He spoke quietly and rarely blinked so that his gaze was steady and a little disorienting. When he spoke he sat very still as if his body was a battery being charged by his own speech. His gestures were minimal and unfussy, there were no flourishes in his manner. But when he laughed he threw back his head and bellowed so loudly and infectiously that everyone found themselves joining in but avoiding his eye lest they see uncomfortable truths swimming quietly under the mirth. Jai Prakash may have seemed nondescript to Uma but he was an effortless and charismatic leader of men and women.

4

Madhavi and Mira exploded in Lodi Garden.

Mira screamed. Madhavi danced. Please stop, please stop. Okay one minute, see there's a bird. Big bird. No, wait, see big bird is going to come and pick you up and fly away. Look there he is! There, *there*. See see. See tomb. See sky. *Vaanam. Vaanam.* Please *Kannakutty aa. Chinnakutty aa.*

She felt fleshy and abandoned. They had spent all of yesterday sleeping and eating in the room. She had wiped gook from Mira's eyes with her finger, giggled at her farts, stuck M&Ms up her own nose to amuse her. She had smeared chocolate on her hands and had Mira lick it off. Early this morning when a thick green slime had burned in Mira's nose, she had wiped it off with her hands, then rubbed her hands on her kurta. She had crawled under a table and teased out a cobweb from its damp underside and played with it on her fingers. The child had rolled after her, howling murderously for cola.

Being a mother is to overcome squeamishness in all its forms. Wiping off snot spirals from a plate, dashing talcum powder on a wound to make the blood less conspicuous, black depression one moment, a conquering spirit the next, living in the rain shadow of vomit. Losing out almost completely on finer feelings because of the continuous flow of viscous liquids.

And because a laughing back flip on a bed could lead to permanent brain damage or a playfully trundling pram to sudden death.

All mothers are secret and dangerous subversives. When your intestines have been spilt onto a table, when you've crushed your breast into a bottle and pumped it for milk, when a crowd of hands have groped themselves half way up your vagina searching for the baby's head, somewhere deep down you lose the reason for crooking the little finger when drinking tea.

You try of course. You maintain a tenuous attachment to graciousness as well as you can, but deep down, a maniac prowls. In a crowd of women, Madhavi could recognise a mother at once. An abandonment around the mouth, flexible hands that could become saucers, sponges, even knives, calf muscles that could defeat Michael Jordan in the race to get a farting bottom on the pot. Wrists that trembled when the telephone rang, was the child dead and lost or had she simply wet her pants?

Before Mira was born, she had not known about the rickety barricades that parents put up every day against different kinds of loss.

Mira arched backwards and yelled louder. Madhavi put her down on the grass and peered into her pampers. No potty, no susu. Come on, come *on*.

Sikandar Lodi's tomb squatted benevolently in the sun. The sun lit up the huge acres of surrounding woodland and glade, once Lady Willingdon Park, later redesigned in the Fifties by a Japanese landscaper.

October, the golden. October of the silken sun and the blossoming trees and hardly any power cuts (even if there are it's pleasant so it doesn't matter). What better October can there be but the one in Lodi Garden?

Just then Deekay came jogging up. He bowled along the track, black hair bouncing up and down, sweat running down his bare body. He looked like a long hairy black deer, leaping morosely through the bushes.

Mira screamed even louder at the sight of him. She clung to Madhavi like a koala in a gum tree. Madhavi danced. Darling one, beloved one, please please.

Deekay stopped. Madhavi smiled and continued to pace, bouncing Mira up and down, gasping and singing.

"Having some trouble?" Deekay had a huge grin, a chef's satisfied smile at the taste of a rare herb.

Madhavi skipped and nodded.

"You want me to try? I'm good with babies," said Deekay, holding out bare sweaty arms.

"Oh, no thanks," panted Madhavi, "she's just a little disturbed. I think she's missing her father."

"She's cute, man," he said, rubbing his fingers on Mira's hanging cheeks and round nose.

A cloth bag hung open from Madhavi's shoulders, a milk bottle and a fold-up pram lay on the grass.

Mira uttered a high-pitched shriek and cannoned into Madhavi's shoulder. She yelled rhythmically into her mother's ears, cupping her mouth for better acoustics, screamed and clawed at her mother's face. She located a few loose tendrils and pulled with all her might.

"Hey, stop that!" cried Madhavi. "Stop that, *kutty*papa, don't!"

She pulled Mira's hands away, in the process pulling out some of her own hair. She moaned and brushed the torn hair away from her face.

"Arre, why don't you let me try. I'm really good, believe me," said Deekay, peering around Madhavi's shoulder towards Mira.

She held the baby out hopelessly. Deekay lifted Mira out of Madhavi's lap in a high circle. He swung her through the air, so that she became a little Superbaby wheeling above a mountain. He swept her towards him, cradled her up and down on his lap, then made blowing sounds into her face. He bent his head down towards her, so that his beard became a cushion on her stomach, then ran around under the tree. Some of his sweat dripped onto her chin.

He held her stationary in the air for a few seconds, then whooshed her down to the ground. Then up in the air again and whoosh to the ground. Then again. After a few half-hearted harangues, she fell silent and licked her finger.

"Mama!" she called over his shoulders.

"A miracle," smiled Madhavi. "Where did you hone your skills?"

"Eh, political work, man. Demonstrations. Protests. Hiding from cops. I had to learn to keep everybody quiet."

"Childcare in political exile, and why the heck not," she widened her eyes. She swung Mira down onto the grass and watched her waddle to a flower bed.

They smiled victoriously at each other. His eyes, reassured by success, became interested.

"You live in India?" he asked.

She shook her head. "No."

Deekay pulled Mira back from the thorns and crossed his eyes at her. She frowned back, craving lebensraum. Madhavi reached over and scratched Mira's neck. Mira rolled over and became an overturned turtle.

They exchanged names and professions. They both loved Delhi in October and both liked Amitav Ghosh's novels. Deekay had begun work on a doctorate, Madhavi was wondering what book to write next. She noticed a scar on the back of his hand. He said, no, it was not police torture, simply an accident with a knife. His NGO work took him out of Delhi a lot. To Arambagh in West Bengal where the communist land laws weren't working at all well. To Bhilai in Bihar where workers had been laid off ever since they could remember. Not enough time for his academic work.

"There's still a whole lot of shit happening here, you know what I mean? A whole lot of shit."

"Quite," agreed Madhavi. "Inevitable, I suppose."

Nationalism and pampers, society and piss, governments and goo. I'm going mad.

He said she looked very young for someone so accomplished.

"You must have children?" she found herself asking.

"Kids? Eh, man, no way. I'm just a tapori. Long way away from that. Not even married. *My name is Antony Gonsalves. Main duniya mein akela hoon.*"

She relaxed a little. My God, she hadn't heard that song in years and yet when Deekay sang, it seemed as if the song had been in her mind all the time.

"And your husband?"

"Peter also teaches. At Columbia."

Was he missing her? She pictured him fixing the floor, then going to his gym in the evening, eating yogurt with muesli, confused by her reactions to things. She stared across at the Lodi tombs.

On weekends she trundled Mira along the Brooklyn Heights waterfront and looked across the East River to Wall Street, or sat in Central Park, watching sharp buildings sprout from red trees, and thought obsessively about Bangalore. She had grown up in a house with moss on the walls and ikat curtains blowing in the evening breeze.

Her twilight father, becoming drolly obsessed with death, regularly sent her lime pickles and *muraka*. And a rudraksha when Mira was born, as a blessing that a child born so late in life was normal and healthy. Her mother would have been so happy, her father had written and would have wanted the baby to have a rudraksha. He had even sent a packet of 5 Star chocolates. Peter had taken a bite of 5 Star and thrown it away in disgust. He didn't know that 5 Star was the best chocolate in the world.

On a recent trip home, Madhavi had gazed at the new shops bursting with Mars bars, Twix packets and Coke cans. The banners of concerts and patriotic fundraisers sponsored by Diet Coke and Pepsi. Years ago she had straggled home from school with just enough money for pani-puri.

Her doctorate on three women politicians in the Indian national movement had been published as an important book. Since then, she had written two more on the role of women in political movements for Independence, resurrected unknown heroines of the Indian freedom struggle, dashed between Manhattan and the National Archives in New Delhi, between morning sickness and excitement at new records. She had always enjoyed her work.

"Do you like Delhi?"

Mira began to eat fistfuls of mud. She blew a spitball, it hung on the grass like a circling soap sud.

"Oh God, I hate it, man," began Deekay warmly. "It's all so fucking fake. All the 'fixing' shit, influence shit. The privilege of people here. The opportunities they get, eh, it just kills me, man. Just kills me. I'd like to do something more, you know. I'm trying. In my own way, I try. Eh, outside, man, that's where you got to see India. This city's all crap and..."

He looked up at the trees. They rustled down at him, massively indulgent.

"Well, I suppose it's in transition," she cut him short in a voice that Deekay couldn't understand.

She sounded as if she was choking and suddenly said she must go. Mira had begun to fidget again and would soon want to eat. She must feed her, then tidy up and show her face at the Mahatma Gandhi Foundation before Pamela decided that she had lapsed into wet and slimy motherhood and was unfit for the job. Yes, Pamela Sen was her old teacher. The new Foundation, gasped Deekay admiringly. But that's major. Yes, but Pamela's pretty major, too, she said.

She extended her hand and said it had been nice to talk to him. She told him where she was staying. He promised to drop in. He watched her place the baby in the pram and wheel her quickly down the path. She looked back to find that he was standing under the trees, looking after her.

Smoky room, holding hands in anguished nights and walking in leaf-falling meadows. She had been there. She knew the routine with these sexy world-changers. But she had no time for all that anymore. She had mouths to feed and pampers to change.

Peter held Mira upright on his chest, as men normally do. But Deekay had held Mira the way she had seen her own father hold babies, horizontally using his arms like a cradle.

Dhruv Mathur walked through the India International Centre, towards the Mahatma Gandhi Foundation. The Foundation had suited him well this past year. He had liked being part of an international fraternity of creative people who straddled the dining rooms between culture and government.

He delighted at strolling in its lawns, rejoiced in its hip glass and slate surfaces and felt active and engaged when sorting out the Foundation's new programme at working lunches.

As institutions went, he far preferred a place like this to Magdalen College in Oxford from where he had completed his D.Phil. almost two decades ago. In Magdalen he had struggled through English pudding in a dim wood-panelled hall, felt awkward during grace before meals and had known that the portrait of Henry VIII was suspicious of him.

Dhruv, Madhavi's rival for the post of director was also a successful journalist. But Dhruv had already completed a year as additional director here. He was a few inches over six feet tall with brown eyes in a thin clean-shaven jawbone centred face. His thick black hair was heavily streaked with grey and he had the loose leggy walk of men who were gangly as boys. A few years after discovering the treadmill, his body was far more impressive now, in middle age, than it had been when he had really needed it.

His looks and size were the source of at least the first five minutes of conversation between people who had seldom seen an Indian man above six feet or one to whom the term 'goodlooking' could be truthfully attached. While Madhavi glowed with the colour of polished mahogany, Dhruv's wheat-skinned sheen was sometimes compared to Omar Sharif, without the moustache.

A secretary and a receptionist sat in the hushed neatly carpeted entrance. They looked up and smiled deferentially as he walked in.

On the right was a long ballroom-like room, with polished white cement floors empty except for a life-size portrait of Rabindranath Tagore on the central wall. Leading left off the reception area was a square carpeted reading room. Along the sides of the room stood freshly painted empty book shelves. A kidney-shaped reading table sat in the centre. Untouched journals and newspapers were neatly arranged on racks along the walls. Roses burst against the glass windows. Next to the window, overlooking the rose garden was a large bulletin board. Concealed lighting gave the wall a halo.

The rooms were deserted and the smell of new furniture rushed out at him. He walked into the computer room, sat down and began to type.

The sun streamed in through the window. It was so bright that he had trouble focusing on the screen. He wrote a few sentences, then deleted them. He wrote a title but changed his mind. Damn it, he couldn't concentrate. Impossible to think straight this afternoon.

Certainties lasted for a lightning short while for Dhruv. Every time he thought he had cracked a foolproof formula, something happened that made him change his mind immediately. His deepest truths were maddeningly unreliable.

He felt as if he was scrabbling for a hold at something all the time, conviction was nothing but a firefly. At night when he ran after a lantern that would show the way across dark water, he woke up and found he had been dreaming. During the day he opened windows to let in the light of clear perspective but only leering phantoms crowded in. Contradictory hatreds and unrequited lusts boiled in his secret self, where there should have been, he felt, growing wisdom about the world.

Twenty years ago, he had gone to Oxford from Delhi, a westernised pot-smoking Marxist. But in England, he had discovered how wrong he had been about himself and his country. And so, he had come back to India, a kurta-clad England-returned Hindu.

Like so many Indians — even perhaps like India's first prime minister — Dhruv's discovery of 'India' or what he thought was India, began while he was a student in England. His patriotism had grown through his Oxford tutorials and his youthful immaturities still ran for cover under grey British pavements.

In those hectic pioneering days in Oxford he had told Madhavi that henceforth he would regard Swami Vivekananda as his role model. Swami Vivekananda who in the nineteenth century preached Hindu doctrine and social service had the answers for Indians like himself. Why on earth, he had asked her incredulously, had he turned his back on the passionate Vivekananda for so long and embraced the European Marx? Why had he ignored his own heritage?

She had only laughed derisively and said colonial self-hate was as old as Gandhi. He felt suddenly self-conscious, as if she was watching him. Had she changed? She would still be scornful, he was sure about that.

He wondered what she thought of him now. She knew everything about him. Knew about his ideological dodges and feints which began in college and were such a dominant feature in his life that she had jeered that for Dhruv, Belief was simply an unattainable beauty queen on the catwalk.

She knew about his college days. In the mid-Seventies, St Stephen's College in Delhi was still heady with the vestiges of violent Marxism and student protests. Almost as soon as he joined college, he had become fascinated with the adventures of his young lecturer who had been a Naxalite. He had stayed up all night listening breathlessly to tales of a movement that began when he was still in school.

His lecturer told him many stories. How, when anti-Vietnam protests filled American streets, affluent young men from Calcutta and Delhi crouched in small-town backstreets and hid in village alleyways, passing along guns and cartridges to their comrades. Or lived among ununionised workers to teach them about proletarian destiny.

Or hid in tribal huts in Bihar. Teenagers who loved the Beatles but crawled through slush on smooth bellies trying to overthrow the state and sacrifice their lives.

Dhruv had been agog. He had begun to detest his parents' gin and tonic life. When his teacher became part of an underground movement during Indira Gandhi's Emergency, Dhruv had written the occasional article for magazines circulated under cover of darkness.

He graduated with an unexpected first class and applied for a scholarship to Magdalen College, Oxford from where he completed a D.Phil. in *Peasant Insurgencies in the Indian Princely States*.

He had abhorred India's maharajas ever since his schooldays at Mayo, the public school where he had suffered at the hands of well-built sons of nawabs because of his skinny thoughtfulness. At Oxford, at first, he had been an unruly dissident. He had railed against India's land laws and first nuclear test. Against Margaret Thatcher, the Falklands war and Indira Gandhi. Then slowly, he had begun to change.

He had wandered, still in his kurta, down the High Street struck by the efficiency of fun, travel, sex and food. He had rejoiced at the absence of inhibition and the fact that irreverence was a primary virtue. Yet somehow, the more time he spent in England, the more the conviction began to grow that he was counterfeit, a brown copy of the white ideal, that the Third World outpost where he was born was a Disneyland of caricatures, that he had lost everything and gained a photocopier instead of a soul. Help me, he appealed to her, I want to burn myself. Everything I've believed in so far is revealed now as monstrous. I want to cauterize myself, but how?

Sitting in his room in Oxford's cold cloisters with his posters of Jimi Hendrix and Lenin, he had discovered his own nationalism. He became convinced that the genius of India was being stifled by an ideology that was invented in nineteenth century Europe. He began to feel secretly ashamed that India's anglicised Left exercised such a dominant influence over the country's intellectual life and that he had believed in it for so long. He was no longer proud that his own role models so far had been Che and Dylan Thomas.

Sitting in the King's Arms pub, he had set off on what was to become his lifelong search for his own country.

He had begun to speak only in Hindi to his Indian friends. He had gone to the India Institute Library almost every day to read *The Times of India* and *The Hindu*. When asked to contribute food at house cook-ins he had always made subzi with lots of chili. He rang his mother to ask for the dates for Ram Navmi and Navratri and even asked her to send him some Hindi novels.

The vernacular languages, he had proclaimed on late evenings, India lives and bursts and laughs in the vernaculars. Tamil, Bengali, Telugu, Gujarati. In dreaming villages and under banyan trees. Beside rivers and waving paddy. English? English is just the language of the rootless and the deluded. Why do we all speak and read English? Why. Why. Why. He had bought himself a copy of Tagore's *Gitanjali*, in English with Yeats' famous introduction.

By the end of his time in Oxford, the *Bhagavad Gita* (again in an English translation) appeared on his shelf.

The Indian populace had floated in his dreams like a ghostly throng over Tom Tower in Christ Church College. He felt as if he had understood them at last.

But she hadn't understood his tranformation. Hadn't understood why, here in England, he had begun to only say 'namaskar' and 'phir milenge' instead of 'hello' and 'bye'. She had made fun of him as just another dumb man drifting from one idea to another as if they were brothels. She hadn't understood his need for India.

There was a knock at the door. Madhavi walked in.

"Dhruv," she smiled, clutching Mira close to her.

He looked terrific in blue jeans and and white shirt stretching across his map of Africa chest.

"Hi Madhavi! My God, my God, my God!" His smile cut deep welts in his thin cheeks.

He opened his arms. She walked into them. After they separated she thought how different he smelt. His chest had once been long and boyish. Now it was broad open plateau. There was an uncomfortable pause.

"Back to the homeland after millions of years," he said, smiling down at her.

"I've come many times but never seen you," she smiled back.

Look at you, she thought, just look at you. No beard, no shabby kurta, no spectacles. Those muscles and that hair cut. Jesus.

"You look...very glamorous," she said.

He laughed and rocked back on his heels.

"But you," his eyes stared into hers, "look the same."

There was another pause as he suddenly turned away and settled his papers. The pause stretched into silence. Outside a DTC bus shouted by. Mira drooled. Dhruv turned and squeezed the baby's cheeks awkwardly.

"Sweet baby. So," he ran a hand over his face, "you brought your little one as well, haan? Starting her early."

She, of all people, was the thorn in the side of his easy ascent. She of all people was the one obstacle in his takeover of Mahatma Gandhi Foundation. Strolling in, cosying up to Pamela, expecting to be anointed director instantly just because she had the stylish uterus and the trendy tubes. Earth mother as director.

She squared her shoulders. "Yup, I'm starting her early."

A tired trick, my dear, he thought, in a leap of stabbing hatred. Don't think I can't figure out the Madonna trick. Don't think I don't know about the mother-and-child image. Woman with baby, woman with biological fluids, sustaining womb and nurturing limbs. Make me director because I can reproduce.

He leaned against his chair and shoved his hands into his pockets. "Fabulous to see you."

"Yah. You too."

He peered at Mira and tickled her chin. She bit his finger. Madhavi wrenched her away. "Ooops! Sorry about that."

A social butterfly, she decided. The sort who'll justify anything as long as there's a drink available. Obsessed with money? Trying to stop the ageing process?

"No worries." Dhruv sucked his finger.

"So how've you been?" she asked. "I keep hearing about you. You're famous."

"Forget it," he waved. "Not as famous as you. Listen, let me tell you about the programme. Have you met Sen yet? No? Achcha, let me tell you then. See, first there's a talk by Ikram Gilchrist, then..."

"Isn't it funny," she interrupted quietly, "all of us being here together in Delhi. Me, Zahra, you and Pamela."

"What...?" he looked distracted, "Oh yes. It's funny."

But he had managed to persuade the famous writer Ikram Gilchrist to deliver a lecture at the Foundation. Think about it. The great Gilchrist. Could she imagine that?

Ikram Gilchrist. Ikram Gilchrist, mused Madhavi. Ikram with his moth-eaten importance, his increasingly bitter anonymity, his hot-protesting decline. How surprising that Dhruv should invite Ikram of all people for an inaugural lecture and treat him like a sought-after treasure. She looked at him with sudden sympathy. He seemed redeemed by his devotion to a magnificent has-been like Ikram. Less on the ball. Fatally linked to gramophones and dank bungalows and short-sighted tottering drivers in dirty caps. Still dreaming about Ikram Gilchrist when the rest of the world thought of him as a boring joke. Dhruv was curiously old-fashioned sometimes, for all his smart talk.

She had him taped. She had him on the drawing board with nails in his skin. She made searing notes while he squirmed.

But he didn't notice her gaze and chattered on.

After the lecture, there was the seminar. Zai Cheever, the film-maker, Kumudini Rai the dancer, Lady Lichfield of course. Did Madhavi know Lichfield, relative of Mountbatten? A friend of

India. Or perhaps aunt of India. If she agrees to endow a chair here, we're made. Well and truly made.

"After the seminar, Pamela will make the formal announcement which," he looked at her sideways, "I hear has already been decided."

She let his excited words rush around her and looked around the computer room. Half a dozen terminals, faxes, e-mail, laser printers, Xerox machines, even a huge black and white photograph of S. Radhakrishnan, India's philosopher-president.

She put Mira down on the floor and walked to the window and looked out at the waving shadows on the pavement.

"You know, I've been telling Pamela that the Foundation's got to talk to people," said Dhruv, addressing the window, "it's got to be, you know, accessible. Sociable. Multimedia. Audio visual. The days of the purists are over. A good television documentary does far more for the subject than a footnoted book. Everything's changed out there."

Madhavi guided Mira away from the computer cables with her foot.

I don't think so, she thought fiercely. I'm going to hold out to the bitter end on that one. What about the integrity of research, hours of work, encouraging the young to break new ground. None of that matters anymore, I suppose. Grammar and rules don't matter anymore. The old learning has gone. Education, forget it. Dump it in a dustbin. Who needs education anymore?

"Not necessarily for the better," she said.

Mira crawled to the plant and began to eat lumps of clay. Dhruv looked down at his papers.

"How's your husband?"

"Fine."

There was a third pause.

"Chal," he said finally, "let's meet soon and talk. We must see you."

She stared at him openly. 'We'? He read her thoughts. "Zahra and I must see you," he revealed. Oh I see, she thought. His eyes monitored the ceiling for jealousy.

"Seeing you again...is..." he spread his hands and his eyes smiled then became embarrassed, "very nice."

He reached across and squeezed her shoulder. She turned, fitted Mira securely onto her hip and said she must go. It was good to see him but the child was getting hungry. She touched his hand but he withdrew it quickly.

She hurried into the hall and dumped Mira in her pram. For some reason her heart was imitating the first steam engine. She leaned against a wall and looked across into the reading room. On the blank blue bulletin board was pinned a single sheet of printed material. Obviously an important article of some kind judging from the prominent place in which it was pinned, bang in the centre of the board.

Opposite the reading room, across the corridor, a closed white door announced in small letters, *Pamela Sen, Director*. The single sheet on the bulletin board stared out at her. Curious, that there should be only a single notice on such a large board. She walked in and read it. The paper was a review of her latest book, *Women Leaders in Militant Hindu Movements*, from a journal of Third World writing. After a few paragraphs, the reviewer had written: *'Iyer's own upper-class background limits her enquiry and her book remains confined to an urban westernised mind-set, biased against rural communities. A shallow and silly work.'*

Madhavi flushed and felt her feet grow cold. What a gross criticism. Her work had never been described as shallow or upper class. No other reviewer had ever made such a misguided attack on her. And as for 'silly', how could anyone use the word 'silly' in a review?

My God, this reviewer has completely missed the point. Obviously someone who knew nothing about her. Someone who hadn't even bothered to read her book properly, someone motivated by an unknowing dislike.

She read the name, blinked and looked again. No, it couldn't be. There must be some mistake. She reached instinctively for Mira and wound her fingers around the child's hair, frowned and stared again.

At the bottom of the page in bold type was the name of the reviewer: *'Zahra Reza, Delhi University.'*

Dhruv's flat in Panchshil Park was large and airy but cleaned out of most of his furniture by his ex-wife, who had pulled up at his door one morning in a monster tempo, yelling that for all the time Dhruv spent at home all he needed was a bed anyway. His bedroom was spare and his cane bed piled with sheets, pillows and newspapers.

When the gang came, Dhruv's Ranjit who had belonged to his father and now belonged to him, who cooked and cleaned and drank Dhruv's whisky was sleeping off a hangover on the October sun terrace. He had left the doors open. In any case, the Mahadev courier company in the flat downstairs was always busy so there was plenty of to-ing and fro-ing all day.

The beat reporter, hanging around despondently in the thana that evening, got some interesting news for his sleepy editor.

And *The Indian Express* giggled the next morning:
The Kitab Chor gang last night took away a priceless edition of Tableux Pittoresques De L'Inde *containing rare steel engravings by the famous De. W. Daniell. The book was published in Paris in 1836 and belonged to Dhruv Mathur, Additional Director of Mahatma Gandhi Foundation.*

Shantanu and Anusuya were to take them out that evening but Anusuya had taken vivacious leave of her senses.

She had spent the day rushing and swaying from room to room, spraying the wrong spices in the wrong curries much to Misri's fury, snatching down photographs of family members and forgetting to put them up again or cradling them for several minutes on her lap and singing with half-closed eyes. Her pallu trailed behind her and her breasts bulged out from her blouse. Uma was horrified at the way drugs always re-sexualised her mother and hurried Sam out of her way in a mad rush to not look at her.

She dragged Sam into her bedroom and distractedly tried to show him her books. Sam perched on her study table trying not to notice Anusuya for Uma's sake.

"So," Anusuya staggered in, lipstick smeared all over her lips and black eyelashes painted on her cheeks, "you've seen everything in Delhi, na?" she slurred to Sam about half a dozen times.

"Yes, Ma," Uma had said looking sheepishly at Sam. "He's seen."

Silence. Anusuya's head lolled forward and she goggled at them with awful seductiveness. Anusuya's silences were a result not only of her daily drug and gin intake but also designed to provoke Uma into self-damning disclosures. In conversations, Anusuya would remain silent until Uma, desperate to elicit a response would make some sort of frantic confession which Anusuya would then seize upon and use as a lever for the next few days.

"Ma, please go and sleep."

Anusuya wandered out at sixty degrees, shaking her head but turned and charged back into the room, like a suddenly rampaging bull and knocked over Uma's bedside lamp.

"Why should ah-I go? You go. Ah-I run this house on my own. Entirely on mah own with no help from that goat in man's clothing. You get out if you don't like it. Only mah dead body will leave this house, head first." She raised her thin arms so that her pallu hung away from her wan body and her stomach and bosom blared out at them, heaving in sozzled excitement.

"Feet first," corrected Uma automatically, averting her eyes.

"Go naow. Go naow," her mother yelled, clenching her teeth and pushing at her table weakly. The other thing that happens to her when she's wasted, Uma noted, is that her accent becomes a Lodi Garden version of the American deep south.

Sam shrugged soundlessly and spread his arms comfortingly, trying to ease Uma's horror. Anusuya turned on him, her head wobbling.

"Would you like to have some pastries? Ah-ve made some. Ah-ll just get it," she said, weaving out of the room.

"She's feeling sad," Uma explained quickly. "She goes nuts when she's sad."

During the day, Anusuya had taken at least three Valiums and perhaps a Calmpose or two washed down with Blue Riband gin. In her darkened room, bottles and strips of medicines lurked in secret corners behind statuettes of deities. From the walls giant photographs of her dead family glared down on Anusuya's divine drug store.

As a child Uma would dust and tidy up her mother's dressing table, carefully wiping the wooden surface, washing out the lace mats, vigorously cleaning sticky, crusty bottles of dry nail polish and jars of rouge, throwing away empty gin bottles and wiping the photographs of the Bom Jesus church and Zarathustra.

Then she would arrange them in perfect order and even place a photograph of herself against the mirror, just to remind her mother that all was not lost. Anusuya used to be dimly appreciative, but in a few short hours the dressing table would be shattered into lipstick-smeared, powder-dusted neurosis.

After a few minutes Anusuya cruised in at sixty degrees again, bearing ageing pastries and pale coffee.

"Please have, please have," she said sweetly. "And teach your friend how to talk to her mother. Just because she's gone to some foreign university, she thinks she's great."

She sat down heavily on his bed and stared accusingly at Uma with huge darkened eyes. Uma used to leave magazine cuttings on *How to Conquer Addiction* and *How to Deal with Denial* from *Femina* and *Woman's Own* strewn around for Anusuya. But she never read them and always angrily asked the jamadarni why she let scraps of paper remain and didn't sweep properly.

"Really nice, Anusuya," Sam lied, nibbling at a crumb.

"Why should they not be nice?" Anusuya cried. "Ah made them you know. Ah made them, that's why they are nice. Because ah made them."

She looked at Uma again with a mixture of pride and detest.

"Everybody says we pulled strings to get her the scholarship to go abroad," she said loudly. "But Uma's father would never pull strings. She got it all on her own. We never had to talk to anybody. She works hard. I don't know when she has the time because she's always with people like you. You're jealous of her."

"Ma, please!" Uma cried, red-faced and shaking.

Another silence. Anusuya stared at her daughter as if she was a complete stranger.

"Now she's thinks she's a big intellectual," she sneered. "She's always been pretentious. She can't kill cockroaches in the bathroom even. Just because she thinks she knows good English. Hah! Mah father was the one. He knew good English."

"It's okay, Ma, I'll just finish everything. You just take it easy," Uma said desperately.

"Ah've never had any opportunities, you know," Anusuya screamed at Sam, weaving in front of him like a small white moth, "Ah've never had anything. Except mah looks. Otherwise...nothing!" She giggled ferociously. "Everyone says I'm so sweet. I'm so small. I'm so small. But I'm not! I'm not sweet. And I'm not small. Do you think I'm sweet?"

"Never," smiled Sam.

Anusuya buried her chin in her chest and stared malevolently at Uma like a vampire about to begin the night's work. Then suddenly stumbled against the door and flew like a newly risen phoenix away to her room. When Uma, Shantanu and Sam crept out for dinner later that night, Uma knocked tentatively on Anusuya's door.

"Ma, we're going for dinner. Want to come?"

Silence.

"Okay. Ta ta."

Only the sound of a few ragged snores.

Shantanu placed a hand on her head.

"Come, Uma-ma," Shantanu said. "Leave her to her own devices."

They walked downstairs to the white Ambassador under the champa tree. As her father and Sam were getting into the car, Uma glanced towards her mother's window. And looked again.

Anusuya was standing by her window, clinging to the bars, peering through them like an inmate catching a last glimpse of visiting relatives. The champa tree was rioting outside. Uma couldn't see her mother's face in the darkness, but her white nightie made her look like the Lady of Shalott hiding in her tower.

After a few seconds, Uma waved tentatively. But Anusuya didn't respond. Her head rolled forwards and her lit cigarette dashed against her forehead.

As they drove away from the bungalow Uma stole a glance at her father's impassive profile as he drove. She tried to picture what he would do later tonight, after they came home from the dinner. He would come back to the house, shabbily hot after the air-conditioned restaurant, change into his vest and pajamas and go to his study to look through his father's diaries. And not say a word to anyone about anything. Never buy himself any clothes, wear the same shoes for at least a decade.

In the morning, he would try not to look at Anusuya as she sat in her bed tearing through the newspapers and dusting family portraits. He would put on his safari suit and flee to the hopes of 1947.

Uma had visited him in his office in Shastri Bhavan many times. The stretch of corridor outside his room was so broken down that it looked like a kutcha village road pitted with ditches and potholes every few steps. One evening, the electricity had gone off and the babus had to pick their way over the cement ravines and brick gorges with torches, journeying fearfully through the gloom to small green rooms where columns of files towered.

"Baba," Uma had said, "your office is awful."

"Only outside," Shantanu had smiled. "Inside, it's very comfortable."

His room — as befits every secretary to the government — was perfumed with a sickly sweet smell and hung with giant portraits of national leaders. The table was bare and the leather sofas were tight and hard. Above a sink in the corner, on a ledge rested Shantanu's chosen cosmetics: a small sliver of Lifebouy soap and a clean comb. Uma was struck by the fact that her father actually thought it comfortable. But perhaps it was better than his home.

Homes, they say, are sanctuaries. But even in sanctuaries, the outward peace of the birds and deer belies the brutal struggle to stay alive.

They arrived at Have More restaurant at Pandara Road market, recently redone from its mess of higgledy-piggledy cars and running urchins to a paved kitsch with blue and green lights slamming onto a line of energetic fountains.

"Uma?" said Sam as they waited for Shantanu to park the car in the long lines stretching outside Pandara Road.

"Yah?"

"I'm sorry if I upset you, sweetheart. After Kamini's party. I'm really sorry."

She felt like crying every time he called her sweetheart.

"No, no, Sam, I overreacted. I'd seen... I'd seen something."

"You know, I'm glad I've never been to India before."

She stuffed her handkerchief into her mouth and chewed.

"People in England have always used India," he said again. "First, the empire and all it implied. Nowadays, for themselves. To make a statement. To prove they're adventurous. To lose weight. I've always felt that's terrible."

Gosh, how kind of him to say that. How kind. How kind. How sheltering. Why did she always misjudge him? She never gave him a chance. She had stupidly taken up arms against him last night. He was on her side.

"There's far too much baggage for comfort."

"Achcha," she said after a pause.

Well, maybe he wasn't completely on her side.

"I was thinking of taking a trip, for a few days outside Delhi. Do you mind?" he said.

"A trip?" She pushed her spectacles up her nose. "Where?"

"You know, travel around a bit. Let you get on with your own thing. Don't want to burden you with my presence. I know some of the trains."

No, no you're not a burden, she wanted to scream. You're the only thing I have. You're my only achievement. My old associates have educated themselves away from their homes and are vulgarly happy about it. They've become members of a ghost queue. My mother's as frail as a blade of grass. But you, you're distinct from my parents and their wordless hell.

She felt she was ranging around on some desolate landscape with a single tin shed for shelter. When she looked up at its roof, it was full of holes and a chilly wind blew down on her. She was

Neanderthal man, hewing a cave through howling stormy Ages. How could he leave her now?

But over dinner Sam said he had made up his mind to go to Badayun in western UP with a friend. Which friend, Uma asked jealously. Oh, Jai Prakash. Remember we met him at Jaspreet's party. He's invited me to visit him.

Uma felt her mind break up like a shattered jigsaw and the seekh kabab turn to tissue paper in her mouth.

Since Jaspreet's father was a minister of the state in the government, the bungalow with the classical pillars and the tamarind trees was guarded by a posse of security guards who used their AK-47s as sticks, pillows and armrests. Tonight, dew hung like a spider web between the trees and pie dogs howled on the horizon. A truck hurtled past.

The tradesman from out of town turned on his side under his blankets, cursed the hard pavement and snored. He had a small business in combs, clips and brooches and found it more economical to sleep on the pavement since he was from Moradabad and it would be foolish to spend money on a boarding house near the station when he could simply snatch a few hours on the road before taking the early bus home to his wife and cool pucca house with a courtyard running with chickens and cats and his in-laws' business in brass tumblers.

Once a serious young woman with kajal under her eyes had approached him and said she would be marching for his cause to parliament. He didn't know what cause she had been talking about. She had shown him her banner 'MARCH FOR PAVEMENT DWELLERS' written in Hindi. Oh, he had said, reading it slowly. Can you read, she had asked in surprise. Of course, he had said, puzzled. And I don't sleep on the pavement every day. Only when I come to Delhi with my business.

As he slept and the commandos polished their guns, two black-clad figures crept their way along the walls of the white bungalow. They kept close to the wall as they sidled along the sides and over the bright lawn into the kitchen. They pushed the door. It opened easily. Almost immediately the dog started barking and Jaspreet's father came running down the long corridors in his velvet dressing gown.

They jumped on him and one held a hand on his throat. The other ran through the house with a bag, down the corridors hung with black and white photographs of the Himalayas, past the Buddhist tankhas and Chinese porcelain, sprinted over the Kashmiri rugs of the living room with its bulbous white sofas and through the glass doors into Jaspreet's father's library.

Jaspreet's father struggled and kicked but the grip on his mouth and shoulders was surprisingly strong. One arm was locked behind him in a professional arm lock. His mouth was covered by a warm soft hand. He strained to get a look at the attacker but he was wearing a mask. Jaspreet's father struggled hard, but his attacker held him down harder. The minister of state didn't exercise much and wasn't very strong. His assailant, by contrast, seemed to be a gym-trained athlete.

At last the other came back with a bulging canvas bag. They shoved Jaspreet's father to the ground and melted away across the lawn as Jaspreet's father began to scream and the commandos came running in and Jaspreet's mother wandered out in her nightie and curlers.

The commandos bowed their heads. No, sir, kuch nahin dekha.

Jaspreet's father ran to his CD player, the television, the locker, the saris and the china. All intact. He hurtled to the bedroom, the cupboards, everything untouched.

"I don't understand," he panted to Jaspreet's mother, "they don't seem to have taken anything."

"Your books, daddy," said Jaspreet who had just come in.

Commandos, dog and parents rushed into the library. The priceless copy of *Ayeen Akbery, or The Institutes of the Emperor Akbar*, by Abul Fazl translated by Francis Gladwin published in Calcutta in 1783, still spelt in the old British way and Sir John Malcolm's *A Memoir of Central India including Malwa*, published in London in 1823, were gone.

"Kitab chor, sir," grinned one of the commandos. "I've heard of them."

"Shut up!" bellowed Jaspreet's father. "I'll suspend you if you say one more word. What do you mean kitab chor?"

"Book stealers, sir," the commandos mumbled. "They only steal books."

Jaspreet's mother's eyes fell on something shining on the floor. She picked it up.

"What is this, Jaspreeta?" Her mother called her Jaspreeta.

Jaspreet snatched it out of her hand and put it in her pocket. "It's an earring. Mine. I'd been looking for it."

Jaspreet stood quietly at the door. Long and tall in her pajamas with a henna tattoo on her upper arm.

"Did you like the butter chicken?" Uma asked, after they'd come home.

"Very nice," Sam said half-heartedly.

Oh help. He didn't really like her food. He was too Christian to appreciate Indian flavours. She was the only Indian woman in the world who was trying to have a relationship with an Englishman who was resisting becoming an Indophile. Show me the way forward God. Cleave the question, raise up the answers.

He lit his Camel. Rugged, anti-system men, he said, always smoke Camel. That's why I can't give it up, because it's an ethos. And that's why I already hate McKinsey's and everything it stands for.

He rocked back in bed, holding the cigarette close to his mouth. Sam's hands were big and workmanlike. Sailing hands which had helped his father sail his boat and grow his dope.

Masterful hands that might hold and not let go. Hands that might....But no. No. Stop it.

A year ago, Sam had driven her to Wales to tell her about his life's greatest crisis. When he was fifteen and on holiday from school, his girlfriend had become pregnant. He had run through his mother's flat, weeping, vowing to get a job to support the child. But the abortion was agreed to calmly by both sets of parents who had coldly asked why he wanted to ruin a young girl's life by saddling her with a child. The only cure for his desperation and remorse had been the priest at school.

"D'you know what I found most shocking? I couldn't understand why everyone was so normal about it. She's still so normal about it. Her parents. My parents. Really nice and understanding. I hated that. I hated the fact that I wanted to be punished and nobody was strong enough to punish me. All that weak Sixties oh-let's-understand-the-child stuff. What I did was wrong. Morally wrong. That's why I think it's so bloody important to have a moral authority, an unapologetic moral source."

"My parents have no moral source," Uma had been forced to admit.

He hadn't slept with anyone since his fifteen-year-old vigil at the hospital. At University, his tall attractiveness and easy laugh had won him a circle of admirers. But he had ignored the barefoot nymphs who ran ahead of him on flower-strewn paths and chosen, instead to take Uma to dinner to a Lebanese restaurant in London and ask her to give him some books about India. She'd recommended a few titles which he bought and read in less than a week.

He said he promised to spare her the stereotypical Western reaction and until now he was being true to that promise.

One day, as an experiment, she had decided to tell him the truth about her birthday parties. The lie might have been easier for them both. She could easily have sketched a believable scene of riotous Indian ritual. Kinfolk coming bursting in, the demonstration of ancient social documents such as the tika and the tying of the red thread around the wrist. A small puja being mounted and bells chiming in the temple indicating the number of years that had passed.

But instead, she told him the truth. Shantanu tripping resentfully on a cheese straw, oppressed by loose streamers and the failure of Pin The Tail On The Donkey. Anusuya, tipsy from the morning, starting loud arguments with parents of other children, by turns fiercely protective of Uma then seemingly revolted by her existence. Her frightened friends cowering in a corner, eating potato chips and stale jam sandwiches with damp hands.

Surprisingly for Uma, Sam hadn't been in the least confused by her birthdays. Instead, he had said that her parties sounded similar to his own and convinced him that as usual she was making far too much of the cultural differences thing.

One evening in Oxford on the way back from a film when she had been trying to impress him by sharp arguments about the film's mawkish romanticism, he had suddenly come up behind her and wrenched her towards him. She had drawn back, astonished.

He brought his face so close to hers that she could see that he was controlling himself from something. What? Anger? Or could it be, could it possibly be, lust? Could it? She had put her hands tentatively on his arms. He had drawn her waist into his stomach.

"Is love so difficult for you, Uma? Must man's most noble state be nothing to you but an opportunity for fucking jokes?"

Then he had abruptly pushed her away, said sorry, he didn't know what came over him and they had resumed their discussion on the film.

"Sam," she stubbed out her cigarette, "do you really want to go to Badayun of all places? It's really yucky."

"It might be fun," his eyes were narrow through the smoke. "Come?"

"I can't. It wouldn't," she sighed, "look right."

"He's probably very, you know, very," Uma made dismissive gestures, "probably licks dal off his fingers and says 'gnat' instead of not and 'vort' instead of 'what'."

"Now, now, memsahib," yawned Sam, lying back in bed, with his eyes closed, "don't deny me."

He stretched and was already half asleep. Not surprising considering that they hadn't had much sleep since the two parties and the amount of beer he had drunk at Have More. His long dark hair waved on the pillow and a tanned arm stretched across the sheet.

Now why is it that when I am asleep I look like an aged turtle with scaly skin and tufts of oily frizz on my head, but when Sam sleeps he could be in an opening sequence of a Hollywood film. Damn my colonised imagination!

She tried to imagine what his body looked like under the sheets and whether he slept on his side or on his back. Did he sleep naked?

That night she dreamt that Anusuya had died. Uma was looking around her room on one of those watery mornings that always mean there's been a death the night before. The room had been cleaned by alien hands, no spilt sindoor on the dressing table, the bed untouched, tightly made. Sunlight in corners which used to be dirty with hair. She saw the triangular shadow of Anusuya's bewildered presence. The hair in its characteristic short bob (a hair cut which was an effort to please Shantanu, Uma knew), hiding behind the dressing table as if she was afraid of Uma.

Then as she turned to say a final goodbye to Anusuya's bedroom, there in the unknown sunlight stood Sam.

"Hey, Uma," he said.

Anusuya had always been in her dreams. But now, thank God, thank God, there was also Sam.

5

The next day, Madhavi shook Dhruv out of her mind, pushed Peter into it, packed Mira into her pampers, got a taxi and set off towards Nizamuddin, where, opposite the red sandstone of Humayun's tomb, lived Pamela Sen, benevolent mother of a hundred doctorates.

It had been a little over a decade since she had seen Pamela last, in that one year when Pamela had been the reluctant visiting professor at Oxford, marking time to be back in the paan-stained university which her colleagues couldn't wait to leave.

She had been Madhavi's supervisor. Sceptical of innocence but worried by too much cynicism, holding out against fashion in clothes as well as in thought. Pamela never used words like 'crypto' and 'quasi' and wore tightly knotted saris with heavy walking boots. Pamela had no time for sandals and slippers.

The unremarkable aspects of life, she would say, were just as important as its exciting pronouncements. The battle against boredom was not in the least bit important. The truth, Pamela often said raising her eyebrows in genuine surprise, can never be boring.

Madhavi walked up to the house. Pamela's garden looked unexpectedly barren. Gardens were Pamela's treasures, she had always been fussy about her plants. Things sprouted between her fingers faster than in the rainforest. But the optimistic Amazon that Madhavi remembered from England had given way to a huge lawn that was just an expanse of brown twigs. The arched doorway was dusty and the doorbell didn't ring.

Madhavi knocked. There was no answer. She knocked again. Still no answer. An old Premier Padmini, presumably Pamela's stood rustily in a corner.

She pushed Mira around to the rear of the house, littered with milk packets and scraps of paper and looked in through the huge glass doors into a dim hexagonal room. Fading pink curtains hung in the windows. A cloth duster lay over a Jamini Roy painting propped up against a wall. A hurricane lamp and a bowl of porridge stood on a small table next to an armchair, opposite a grand sweeping cream-coloured sofa. Walls of books closed in on all sides.

The living room didn't look like Pamela's either. Pamela's rooms were always decorated with polished artefacts. They were full of sunlight, smells of malpua and tea sitting in the kitchen. It was most unlike Pamela to let a beautiful flat like this go to seed. Most unlike her. She pushed open the doors and crept in.

She peered through the gloom and noticed a head of curly grey hair resting on a faded maroon armchair. Pamela was asleep.

"Pamela*di*?"

The old woman's skin hung from her cheeks and lapped at her shirt, like a tired tide on a fading beach. Her once straight jaw had disintegrated into a line of bumps and troughs. But her body still looked long and robust.

Her eyes opened at Madhavi's question. Her mouth and chin dashed away to one side and then back. She bit down hard on them in an admonition. Then her brow furrowed and her eyes crossed. She shook her head impatiently. Spit collected at the corners of her mouth, the chin slowly slackened then snapped up towards her teeth. Her lower jaw began to slide towards her ear then shuddered and became like stone.

Madhavi held Mira in front of her.

"Hello ma'am. I'm Madhavi. Madhavi Iyer and this is my daughter. I live in New York now. I teach there. In Columbia."

"Please excuse me," said Pamela preparing to go back to sleep. "But I'm very tired."

Madhavi dropped Mira onto the carpet and let her crawl towards the bay windows.

"You invited me to come to the Gandhi Foundation seminar, ma'am. You wrote to me."

There was a spreading wet patch on Pamela's stomach, spilled water or a new tea stain. She shook her head from side to side and coughed a phlegmy smoker's cough.

"Let's see, Mountbatten's administration, is that you?"

Madhavi shook her head and sat down on a little stool opposite her.

"No. Women leaders in Congress. Madhavi Iyer from Columbia University. Come on, ma'am, you must remember me."

Pamela had written to her off and on after she left, always with some advice. Self-scrutiny, after a certain age, was pointless. The way forward was to move beyond the limits of the self.

But after the first few letters, Pamela had stopped writing.

Her latest book analysing the Congress party — *The Caste of the Cadres* — was full of facts, exact details, tables, minute classifications and lists. The spirit of a time, Pamela had insisted in her introduction, is not known by its greatness but by its daily toil.

At a seminar in the University of Chicago, glamorous postmodernists had giggled that in times of triumphant theory, old bat Sen was still banging on with facts and figures in the Fifties style.

Pamela shut her eyes and her lips and mouth chattered a little. Madhavi grasped her elbow almost as if to stop her from being swept away by a strong breeze. Gusts of forgetfulness.

They had known each other for only a year but Pamela had been a little bit of home in those early foggy cold-feet years in Oxford. Her old-fashioned Nehruvian accent had always reminded Madhavi of her father. Her muffler, scented by cheroots, had kept Madhavi warm when the oaks had rustled with winter. How could she not remember her?

"Who's that child?" Pamela asked after a pause.

"Ma'am, this is my daughter," cried Madhavi, her voice becoming higher pitched. "My daughter, Mira. I'm Madhavi. I've sent in an application to be director of the Gandhi Foundation. I used to be your student. Don't you remember? Dhruv, Zahra, me, we were all your students in Oxford!"

"Ah, Dhruv," Pamela held up her finger, "Dhruv is doing a fine job. He's good-looking."

"Pamela*di*," she shouted, "I'm Madhavi Iyer, I've also applied to become director here, don't you remember me? Ma'am, please, come on, look at me."

Mira began to grumble. The steam engine inside Madhavi's heart took off down a tunnel, whistling continuously. Pamela closed her eyes as if hurt by the sound of Madhavi's voice.

"Switch on the television, will you?" she sighed. "And see if the cushions on the sofa need a thump. Benedicta's gone to the market."

Madhavi stared around the room hopelessly. She rushed over to the ancient television and banged it on. It flashed and went dead. She hurried towards the huge sofas and thumped the cushions viciously. A cloud of dust rose.

Pamela straightened up in her chair and reached for her porridge. Madhavi pummeled the cushions. She hit them so hard that one of them burst open and some stuffing oozed out. She beat them hard with her fists. More dust clouds flew.

"Mama!" objected Mira sternly. "Nee, Mama. Nomanee. Nomanee."

Pamela looked up, her mouth an open cave crowded with stalactites and stalagmites of porridge.

"The child is right," she said calmly, "there's no money."

"But there is money," Madhavi threw the pillows away, her cheeks flushed. "I visited the Foundation. Impressive isn't the word. It's staggering. I met Dhruv there. He told me about the summer programme. Congratulations are due to you."

Pamela continued to eat her porridge in noisy slurps. She wiped some off from the bowl and licked her finger.

"That Foundation. All *that*...it's too dazzling for me. Me with my," she pointed to her migratory chin, "disastrous handicap. It's not meant for someone like me. I'm not good-looking enough. Dhruv is. He's good-looking."

Madhavi sat down heavily on a stool again, pulled Mira onto her lap and punched her rhythmically between the shoulder blades. Mira coughed.

She was already in Columbia by the time Pamela retired from Delhi University and took up the directorship of the Foundation. News of it had spread fast. Sen's Taj Mahal. Her last hurrah.

Pamela jerked her shoulders and reached for a packet of biscuits. Using the biscuit as a spoon, she lifted lumps of porridge into her mouth. A flash of blue light shone in her eyes for a brief second. The porridge bowl clattered and swayed dangerously on her lap.

"Why can't you recognise me?" asked Madhavi tearfully.

"You," said Pamela looking at her through distant eyes, "don't have to insist that you're my student. You needn't. You needn't keep reminding me. Please free me. Free yourself."

Pamela extended a shaky hand in no particular direction. An ageing Noor Jehan, once a powerful queen but staring at the royal court she helped create from a broken window of retirement.

The dust from the cushions drifted towards the kitchen. Madhavi rose, settled Mira into her chest and looked around the room. Pamela had started to eat again. A photograph of a smiling woman stood framed next to Pamela's armchair.

"Your daughter. She's married now, na?"

"Yes," said Pamela still eating.

"To whom?"

"My son-in-law is in the business of relations. Relations between the public, I'm told. Public relations."

Pamela looked up at Madhavi and suddenly, she smiled. Immediately her face became the one Madhavi had carried in her heart all these years: clever, serene and kind. And in spite of her confusion, Madhavi couldn't help grinning back. Pamela would never be at peace with post-modernism or PR.

She settled her teacher's bowl of porridge securely on her lap, covered her knees with a blanket and walked out. Mira complained loudly. Her mother had absentmindedly forgotten to straighten the straps of the pampers so that they had become thin twisted plaits digging into the little football stomach. Mira cried out but Madhavi didn't hear.

She strode blindly out onto the road, staring out for a taxi with swimming eyes.

Sam drove off to see Jai Prakash to talk about his trip. He had travelled in China, Brazil and Argentina and was always remarkably well-prepared with train tables, guide books and background literature.

Uma confronted Anusuya across the breakfast table, across a brass bird swinging on a stand and a lamp floating in a bowl of water: the uncomfortable decorations that Anusuya had installed this morning to impress Sam.

Today, Anusuya would do what she did everyday. Sit in the living room, alone, looking through her endless albums, or painting her face in lurid colours, maroon on the lips, red on the cheeks, black and purple on the eyes, while the champa tree poked knobbly arms through her window, like a wicked spirit, trying to enter her.

"If you become an immigrant," said Anusuya sucking an orange, "I'll never talk to you. I'll cut you out. OUT! I won't put up your photographs on the wall."

"All your family are immigrants, Ma," said Uma dully.

"That's different," shouted Anusuya. "They had no choice. Look at you with all your opportunities. You should stay where you were born! Live with dignity. Running after foreigners all the time! Be proud! Be proud! You can't do anything about your birthplace, remember that!"

For Anusuya, countries were like marriages: unchangeable givens. If you were unfortunate enough to be born where you were or married where you were you just had to lump it and alleviate your misery by taking drugs or looking through albums. She would be a staunch ally of the Men in Black.

"You can't *ever* live in India if you marry a foreigner. Nobody will accept you! You won't be invited anywhere," warned Anusuya.

"Marry a foreigner?"

Silence again.

"Your fiance," yelled Anusuya without warning.

"Oh," said Uma nervously. "Ma, it's nothing like that."

"Is he your fiance or not? Haan? What is he? Then why has he come with you if he isn't your fiance?"

This time it was Uma's turn to remain silent.

She scratched the back of her neck, leaving apprehensive welts under her pitch curls. Misri came in with a plate of idlis, noticed that Sam wasn't there and took them back in a rage.

"*All* white people hate us," declared Anusuya. "They don't donate their organs to Blacks. I've read about it."

Uma couldn't think of an appropriately reassuring answer.

"Has he agreed to marry you or not? Has he set a date?" asked Anusuya again.

Uma swallowed.

"He'll never get over the language barrier," predicted Anusuya.

"What language barrier? We speak the same language."

"I can't speak or understand English," shuddered Anusuya. "How will I talk to him for the rest of my life?"

Uma made her hand into a fist and pummelled the breakfast table.

"And what are you speaking now, esperanto?"

Another long silence.

"Don't talk to your mother like that," snapped Anusuya. "Learn to show some respect. Show some respect. D'you know how the placenta separated weeks before you were born? *Weeks. Still,* I gave birth. I carried the baby without a placenta. Is there any other woman in the world who has carried a baby without a placenta? Tell me, tell me! It's a miracle that you were born normal. Only *I* could have done such a thing."

Uma looked at the antique clock swinging on the wall.

"I'm going."

"Where?"

"Khan Market," said Uma, pushing back her chair, unable to look at Anusuya any longer for fear of recapturing those horrible drunkenly erotic images.

"There's a wide gap between the English people and us," Anusuya called after her. "Don't try to be too big for your boots! Licking the shoes of the English all the time! Drinking mineral water! What sort of Indian are you if you can't even drink our own water? Mineral water! Bisleri or something."

Anusuya's voice echoed after Uma as she wandered out of the dining room and Misri brought in Anusuya's nimbu paani, and whispered, would memsahib like it sweetened with her medicines?

"I never drink mineral water, Ma," Uma called back. "I always drink our own water."

Anusuya whistled through her teeth in disgust.

In the two years that Uma had been away, Anusuya had sent her a variety of gifts. She sent the gifts with anyone who was visiting the Western hemisphere, from Alabama to Czechoslovakia at any time of the year irrespective of whether or not they would be anywhere near England. Anusuya never provided the correct address. Whoever was unlucky enough to be chosen to bear gifts for Uma had to toil through local telephone books in different countries, ring embassies and friends and then spend a fortune on postage.

She sent bags of choora. A pair of puppets. A wall hanging. A picture frame and a moth-eaten sweater belonging to her father. She sent soggy packets of *sandesh*, kolhapuri chappals and papiermache vases. Anusuya would be outraged if Uma said she didn't need puppets or chappals. But the Rays next door liked it, she would retort. She had even sent her a Bankura horse once, with a scrawled warning saying, *'Remember who you are'*, delivered by a sullen diplomat who had complained that the horse's legs had smashed in his suitcase and bits of Bankura clay had got into his Harrod's clothes.

As Uma walked along past the hedgerows, expertly dodging gangly little men wearing neatly ironed clothes whose arms veered towards her breasts or crotch, she wondered where Anusuya bought those gifts. She certainly could not have bought them in Khan Market or else Uma would have easily recognised them and placed them accurately in the shop of their origin.

Khan Market was Uma's shrine. It was where she had bought her first pair of jeans and seen her first flasher with his penis encased in what had looked to her at that time like cellophane. As paper went, she knew cellophane very well in those days. She used cellophane to cover her scrap books on dried flowers. It had seemed to her the strangest thing in the world that the man should cover his penis with the same cellophane.

Now kanjeevarams and tweed jackets promenaded the market's front walkway. Lovers exchanged glances and linked fingers as they disappeared into Anokhi. Housewife-entrepreneurs shopped for supplies at Saluja Dairy and avid Europhiles snapped up kiwi fruit and Brussels sprout from spilling stalls. Khan Market was an island of smoked ham and cheddar in a sea of sizzling samosas and diesel fumes from the surrounding car repair shops.

But walking into Khan Market this time, Uma stopped short. There was a new department store that she hadn't seen before. Behind the main market, where there had once been a littered park — where clerks and telephone operators from Lok Nayak Bhavan opposite ate their tiffin, and exuberant youths who had no reason to be happy because they were all unemployed, whipped into quick gymnastic exercises— there was now a brand new department store. Uma stared at it in surprise and wonder.

The Aladdin stretched towards the sky in three floors. A coconut tree stood at the corner of the shop. Clumps of coconuts hung between the leaves. A ferocious chowkidar stood at the entrance. In the centre of the shop, a giant brass Shiva maintained the tandav pose in cosmic discomfort. On the ground floor, Persian carpets, brass lamps and glazed pottery winked like a customs official's haul for the year. Bales of brocade and silk glittered evilly, as if the material had been freshly snatched from skilled suffering weavers. On the mezzanine floor, a furniture show room displayed wrought iron staircases and antique colonial chairs which East India Company nabobs might have killed for. And on the top floor, reached from an external staircase, in the beauty shop, beauticians waited to grind customers' faces into bowls of rose flavoured mud. The Aladdin was a behemoth of exotica, established here in Khan Market obviously to cater to the market's large diplomatic clientele.

As Uma stared, a plump woman came running out of the Aladdin and threw herself at her. It was Mrs Khurana. Mrs Khurana whom Uma knew.

One winter evening in Oxford, Uma had cycled down to a small Kashmiri stall on Cowley Road to buy a packet of agarbattis for a party. Incense was de rigeur, after all, in an Indian woman's room.

She generally tried to avoid Cowley Road, believing it to be not a fashionable manifestation of Low Culture but an example of the humiliations of South Asian immigration, inhabited as it was mostly by Indians and Pakistanis.

She had ventured there only a few secret times taking care not to wear the trademark raincoat or a cap that may in any way place her in the same queue as citizenship papers and residency permits. Her time in Oxford must not be reduced by the quest for permanency. Dignified transience had been her creed. She would soon return to where she had come from, breezily dismissive of the West's seductions.

The owner of the stall, Mrs Roshan Khurana from Punjabi Bagh, wearing a salwar kameez and bright red lipstick, had been sitting behind the glass counter studded with jade rings, fake silver cups and imitation ivory chess sets. The stall was small, dirty and cheap. "Why don't zyou come for dinner to our place, beti?" Mrs Khurana had invited eagerly. "Zyou'll have full home food. Yes, typical sarson da saag and makki ki roti. Zyou will really miss India," she whinnied, chafing for an evening of melancholia. "Please come, beta. Come, na."

Her face was runny with fat and marked with tear aqueducts from her eyes to the middle of her cheeks. Her breasts were water-filled gunny bags sloshing over her stomach towards her navel. She was butter-coloured and her curving lips drooped at the corners. She looked like a melting caramel custard wearing a salwar kameez of cheap nylon. And her loud guttural accent would have sent Anusuya running to her gin.

"Beti, zhou must wisit us," Mrs Khurana had urged. "I vill ring zyou up in zyour car-ledge and inwite zyou!"

"No!" Uma had shouted, "There's no phone in my college, no phone. There's only pigeon post, but the Lodge also is closed."

Mrs Khurana had smiled sadly.

"Don't vurry, beta. Zyou remind me so murch of my darter. She studied lah, zyou know. But then she gave hurr degree to me as gift. But now," she wiped her forhead, "she vonts to be singer."

"Singer?" said Uma.

"She is vith band," said Mrs Khurana, as conspiratorially as she might say, she-is-with-child. "Sometimes zyour uncle and I we go for hurr caan-serts. Haw much can zyou just sit alone every evening, just the two of us? Beta, zyou'll come and see me, na? Please say zyou'll come. I'll show zyou pictures of Gurleen."

Uma had a swift vision of a sulky Gurleen with pierced nipples, swinging to fusion, while her pathetically poverty-stricken parents applauded dutifully in the audience. She clutched Mrs Khurana's hand. Something about this fat loud woman had seemed heart-breakingly pure. Her breasts and stomach seemed to collapse by the sheer weight of the affection she carried in them. Uma had felt suddenly enraged with the absent Gurleen. How could this jurist rocker have turned her back on such a fat vulnerable mother?

Mrs Khurana had sobbed big-heartedly and lashed at her wet face with her dupatta.

"But zyou will come and see me, no beta? When I look at zyou, I can't help but crying! A poor motherless girl here in Oxford. One look at zyour face and I just want to spend the whole night crying."

She had left messages for Uma at her college for a few weeks but Uma had been too embarrassed to respond. What would Sam say if he ever had to meet Mrs Khurana with her scraping 'y's' and her 'w's' that sounded like 'v's' and her rubbery face and crude manners? He may never want to be seen with Uma again.

Her home in Cowley Road would probably be cluttered and damp, a cheap glitter sitting on plastic doilies and linoleum tablecloths. She would wind her way around Marks and Spencer, smelling of achar and wearing a dressing gown instead of an overcoat. Sam would knit his eyebrows and be patient and kind. What else could he be? He would have to be kind. Kindness would be his only option. Not engagement, not admiration, but kindness. She hadn't been able to bear the thought of Sam being kind to Mrs Khurana.

Now Mrs Khurana wept ecstatically.

"Arre, meri gudiya, meri choti si rani, tu yahan hai, *puttar?*"

"Aunty!" Uma stepped back in surprise and leaping pleasure. "What are you doing here? When did you come back?"

Mrs Khurana's face streamed with tears and she waved vaguely in the direction of the Aladdin.

"I verk hair now, rani. I verk in this shop. England chor diya. Batterr to be in own country, no beta? Batterr. Some loved ones are hair, bachoo."

Oh good, thought Uma, feeling relieved and comforted. She's escaped from Cowley Road. She's found a job in this store and at least has spared herself that terrible life in England. She's probably earning a little more too and missing her daughter less. In time she might become senior shop assistant or deputy accountant. She'll be able to move to a nice flat with neighbours and family and riotous noise all day without a moment's loneliness.

"So how are you, aunty? It's so nice to see you," said Uma, blinking back tears. "Really lovely."

"Oh my beti. My little girl. Patli si hai bechari."

Mrs Khurana dragged her into the Aladdin. It blinded Uma momentarily by its shining plenty from Ladies to Home Decor to Kidswear.

"Dekho," she whispered to a woman who looked like another shop assistant, displaying Uma in front of her as a fishmonger displays fresh fish, "I have found my Gurleen. Mujhe meri Gurleen mil gayee."

They talked for a while. Gazing down at Mrs Khurana, Uma felt her own eyes beginning to moisten. Why was this heaving swollen woman driving her to tears? And why had her heart leapt with such joy at seeing her? The thought of Mrs Khurana's life in England and India depressed her. Being the adopted daughter of this sad returned immigrant who was now employed in a triumphantly kitsch store made her clammy with helpless unclear emotions. Mrs Khurana's spittle-rimmed mouth reminded her of a womb, of mothers as they should be, not as they were.

Uma freed herself from Mrs Khurana's grip and ran home as fast as she could.

Something furry brushed past Madhavi's breasts as she stood in Lodi Garden and watched Mira play in the grass.

"Hey!" she brushed it away absently. The furry thing was a hand. The men closed in, skinny and shorter than Madhavi, Rambo hair cuts and jutting bums. She could see the yellow wedges of food sticking between their bared teeth.

"Get out, saale! Niklo yahan se," she hissed.

One of them put his hand on her buttocks. The other stroked her cheeks. He pushed the back of his hand against her breast.

"Choot degi?"

She pushed out with her arms.

"Chale jaao, saale, chootiya sala haraami. Dekhta nahin bachi hai?" she yelled in the remembered voice of her student days.

"Oye, maadarchod, saale," boomed another voice. A ringing, male and tall voice. Deekay, sweaty and huge, loomed through the trees.

"Randi," they tossed at her and fled. Madhavi staggered back against a tree.

She felt the familiar loathing rip through her body and an evil bloody hatred churn in her mouth. She could have murdered, skewered, run lead through their tongues.

"I'd forgotten about eve-teasing."

"Bastards."

He gave her shoulder a reassuring squeeze. She felt cold relief flood into her calves and palms, making them tremble. He jogged here every day, he told her. These gardens gave him hope. The acreage, the huge trees and the beautiful tombs. Poor Sikandar Lodi. He might have felt diminished from Afghan valour at the thought of his tomb being considered restful.

Not so restful, Madhavi added. But you've rescued me twice now.

Mira flapped her arms like a chick trying to fly. Deekay knelt and kissed her. He smiled up at Madhavi and rubbed his beard against Mira's cheeks. He rubbed the baby's sides and she blew a spit bubble.

Deekay threw her in the air and caught her deftly. She chuckled and he did it again. Tears collected behind Madhavi's eyes. She blinked them back hurriedly.

She was not used to being so unprotected, buffetted by jealous friends, mad mentors and streetside molesters. Peter had spoilt her. He had mollycoddled her. She was surprised to find herself inviting Deekay to her room later that evening.

He came punctually. They fed Mira and listened to her babble into sleep. Then they opened the bottle of wine she had bought from Khan Market and sat across each other in mutually approving silence.

"So," asked Deekay at last, "you were going to meet your old professor today, na? Sab theek thak?"

Should she tell him about her meeting with Pamela? About the flood of self-pity that was straining at the banks of her mind. No, he wouldn't understand Pamela. To him, she would probably be an old comprador, living off the fat of a rich foundation.

He turned his head towards her. His face was big and bony and notwithstanding his proud man-of-the-soil stance, his wrists were aristocratically slender.

He's wondering about me she thought. A little woman with a baby who has her breasts squeezed in a park and hopes to become the director of a grand foundation that occupies half a stretch of road.

"Let me tell you one thing," she said. "Delhi's really changed."

Deekay burst into a crack of laughter.

"Let me tell you *one thing*. We all say that, man. Let me tell you *one thing*. One *thing*."

Madhavi smiled. "Yah, I guess it's a common phrase."

Deekay scratched his head. "It's still not politicised, here, yaar. People just don't have any public feelings. Detached. Totally on their own trip. It's weird, man. I can't be like that. I can't sort of...just...cut myself off. Pretend as if we're not living *here*."

Madhavi shifted away from him and looked towards the door as if she expected Mira to come in.

"Yes," she said, switching to classroom-speak, "society remains far too hierarchical. Probably why there isn't any public-spiritedness. But there's a change, no? Something's happening. I think."

Outside the darkness was settling in shaky waves. Headlights danced up against the wall of the Habitat Centre and fell away again, leaving an inky stain.

"Yah," said Deekay, "You're right. Definitely, it's changing. You don't have to be like a fucking intellectual to sort of figure it out."

He asked why she hadn't stayed on in India. I made a choice, she replied and once one had made choices one must stop grumbling and take their consequences on the chin. In any case Gender Studies are designed for exiled academics. The conferences never stop and I get to see my father often, she laughed.

"Peter doesn't understand why I make such a fuss. That's because an American stays an American wherever he goes. But what's an Indian accent? A Peter Sellers routine. India's an immigrant society. Immigration's become a part of most families."

"Sahi hai, yaar," Deekay whispered. "You know sometimes when I was in America, I felt really sick about the whole thing. Indian means, some sort of a dog or something. Indian is like shit."

Now there's a serious confession, she thought. A confession of closeness, a confession she had heard before from someone else at some other time. Deekay looked at Madhavi's mouth. Her mouth was wide in a small face. It made her look warm and open, like the faces of women who stand behind their men but tend to your every need if you visit their house. He knew them. On his field trips, he had stayed many times at the homes of those unwanted caregivers. He drained his glass and stood up abruptly. So did she.

He saw her breasts bounce under her kurta, small slightly drooping breasts, the breasts of a woman who's nursed children. Not like Kamini's wonder bosom which flashed around him at night inviting him to stroke and admire. What did Kamini know about caring for a child?

She watched from her door as he walked towards the lifts. She should ring Peter tonight and tell him about her drink with a young NGO worker. She would dismiss him in a witty phrase, a hairy activist. She would laugh at his pain. She would scoff at his immature radicalism. It was skin deep, anyway. It always was. She knew. She had seen it before.

She wandered into the bedroom where the baby was sleeping. Airborne Mira, when Deekay had swung her into the air. She could have swung like that on the rusty swing in her parents' back garden in Bangalore. The swing next to the washing line which had been central to her life when she was twelve.

Did I leave New York under a nasty constellation? My friend is a hostile stranger and my teacher is senile and in Lodi Garden, demons are abroad. Pamela's pedestal must have crumbled years ago, I just hadn't been aware. I probably never meant very much to her anyway.

She felt her vision becoming cloudy again. Crying, Pamela used to say, didn't necessarily mean you were unhappy. It simply meant that you had an excellent grasp of the situation. In fact sustained weeping might even imply heightened intelligence and sensitivity. The old Pamela with her sudden grin and her Parker ink pens. Nobody uses ink pens anymore. Or writes long smudged letters on carefully chosen letter paper.

Like the old Bangalore of cycling streets in a cool drizzle. Of typed manuscripts in an embroidered jhola.

She lay down next to Mira and tried to snuggle into the little arc of the child's body. Her own mother had died years ago, reaching out from her hospital bed, whispering, white-eyed to her daughter: "Bye bye *kanna*, bye bye *kanna*." Madhavi had just turned thirteen. After the funeral, as she peeked through the curtains into the drawing room where the grown-ups stood murmuring, a crowd had bloomed strongly around her. Her aunts, with iron in their grip and tears bursting in their hearts, two grandmothers and one favourite uncle. She had been so quickly and effectively enclosed that she later realised that her mother must have felt left out. On the edges of the crowd that held her close, her mother's shadow had pushed and run, trying to get in, squirming for a place. Remember me. Miss me. Cry. Cry for me.

She hadn't been able to understand why her mother's shadow had been so frantic until the day Mira was born.

Uma sat on Sam's bed, watching him pack. He was very neat and folded his T-shirts and trousers carefully into his bag. He was to leave for Badayun tomorrow. Jai Prakash had a house in Badayun and his family lived close by. It would only be for a few days. Uma needn't worry.

I promise not to be a Westerner who discovers truth in a rural landscape, he grinned at her. Instead, I shall demand Pepsi and air-conditioning at all times.

He said Jai Prakash and Christine were running an education programme called Shiksha Andolan and wanted him to help them. Christine would be coming along with them too.

Uma had a fast forward of Sam falling in love with Christine. Would Sam come back from Badayun and tell her that he was about to marry Christine? Would Uma become the eager pagan scratching at the glass of a tasteful Christian union?

When nationalities are intertwined with infidelities in relationships, how much greater must be their damaging effects. If an Englishman found his Chinese wife having an affair with a Chinese man. Or if a Chinese man found his English wife having an affair with an Englishman. Othello's conflict. Not simply a betrayal of the heart but a burn on the skin.

As it turned out, it wasn't Christine whom Sam fell in love with.

Just then the doorbell rang.

"Uma!" Misri called. "Hari Ram *esche.*"

Hari Ram was tall and stooped with very few teeth and sunken eyes. The parting in his thick hair was insanely straight, not a hair this way or that. Sometimes Hari Ram was moody and irritable. At other times he was unctuous and deferential. Hari Ram could cut off lines, add phones, add disturbances on lines, 'fix' a bill and install caller-identity machines in twenty-four hours. Or he could vanish for months without a trace.

Telephones and electricity were the twin muses for the city's citizens. If you had them together for a clear month, you might become recklessly creative. If you didn't you could plunge into self-questioning despair.

And the telephone 'line man' was the monarch of a rough madness. It was the madness that those who hadn't experienced a dead telephone line could not understand. At his wish, swathes of houses could be cast into the lonely middle ages. At his whim, they could be accepted back into a brave new world with their phone lines quiveringly, joyously restored.

Uma had even been to Hari Ram's house in Trilokpuri. Not lovely sewers and beautifully filthy tenements spilling children dotted with boils. Not film festival shock art which would keep Deekay in permanent outrage for the rest of his life. No, none of that.

Instead, Hari Ram's house manifested the day-to-day holiness and cleanliness of life next to the shit-and-marigolds garbage. Video films in a green room with a twenty-member family, all equipped with Akai TVs and imitation Nike shoes. Bright nylon curtains strung up by delicate string between the toilets that divided the families. Tinsel garlands on busy portraits of gods performing perfumed, reptilian miracles. Gold ornaments packed in trunks next to sinks that ran with phlegm.

Hari Ram stood at the door looking at Uma with the fierce excitement of a scientist who has just discovered a rogue gene.

"What about a scholarship for my older son," Hari Ram, said in precise Hindi, snapping out a pen and paper and waiting with poised pen as a journalist waits for a scoop.

Uma struggled to maintain a smile of tolerant amusement. "Scholarship?"

"Yes!" shouted Hari Ram. "Come on, come on, tell me where I can get information about your scholarships. Tell me just now. I don't want to waste any time."

"Your son can't get scholarships," she reasoned. "You see, you need a working knowledge of English. Maybe you can ask my father for a government grant..."

He stepped towards her threateningly. She shrugged off the trepidation and faced him squarely. She better be careful. Hari Ram's good humour was a wavering souffle. Any sharp words or sudden noise would make it collapse. He would then sink to the bottom of the earth and cut off the telephone line.

"Your father!" Hari Ram waved impatiently. "He's useless. What kind of officer is he? He doesn't even get angry. He never shouts or gives gaalis like other powerful officers."

Uma tried to frame a suitable reply but Hari Ram moulted into a different personality and became a benign father figure. "Uma sir," he said smiling paternally, "just give me some advice. Now you are getting married. Show me also some generosity. Do something for me, sir."

When Hari Ram wanted to be ingratiating he called everyone 'sir'.

"What?"

"Scholarships!" he bellowed, transmuting his personality again, this time into a fire-breathing demagogue. "For UK, USA, Germany! All countries. As many countries as possible..."

"You're mad!" she cried. "I told you, your son can't get a scholarship to England when he can't even speak English. Come on, be reasonable."

"There must be others," Hari Ram grumbled, "where you don't need to know English. Come on, you can do it. You can do anything." He became a sly leprechaun. "Ask your firangi.

How much does he drink, by the way, do you know?" He leant towards her conspiratorially. "People say in the bazaar that he polishes off a bottle every morning? Is it true? And I've heard," Hari Ram introduced casually, "that in the bathroom he only uses *paper*. No water. Only paper."

Bum-cleaning, that important dividing line between Orient and Occident. Water versus paper. She had, as in all other aspects of her life, grown up with an uncertain fusion. Water to wash and paper to wipe.

"Look," she said, trying to keep calm, "I can't help you. My scholarship is meant for people who know English, you see. That's the trouble. It's unfair. You should try a different tack."

Hari Ram took a deep breath.

"So what will you do now? Will you," he stared at her with clinical detachment, "become an officer?"

She stared back at him, puzzled.

"My son," Hari Ram beamed, "will definitely become an officer. I'll see to it. I have contacts."

For dinner that night Misri brought in freshly made chapattis and mutton curry, and Anusuya produced a salad from the garden vegetables. Sam said that Jai Prakash had told him that there was a social revolution going on in India at the moment and that the Shakespearewallahs were being shoved aside by the dehatis.

Utter rubbish, Shantanu exploded. Don't believe those blighters. When Shantanu most disliked people he called them blighters. Most of them are mentally underdeveloped and those that are educated are stubbornly militant. That's why they don't get anywhere. They should be grateful that there were people like him, Shantanu, still around to make sure that things worked the way they should.

6

Sam left the next morning. To first meet Jai Prakash and Christine and then hire a car to Badayun.

The sudden painful emptiness was too much for Uma to bear and she rang Aditya to tell him that she would be available for the part of the King's ghost after all.

She would uncover a new ease with Sam through Shakespeare. She would rise to the common humanity thing.

"Shakespeare as a *means*," exclaimed Uma enthusiastically, "of realising how differently the same language may be spoken."

Shut up and come for a rehearsal at the Shri Ram basement tomorrow, grumbled Aditya, depressed after the theft of his plays.

Your Englishbabu drank only a cup of coffee in the morning before he left and didn't eat a single thing, Misri yelled furiously, clattering out of the dining room with the dishes. He's not a man with a big stomach who can eat like a tiger and burp like a king. Not like my husband, Chaitanya, poor man, left behind in the village while I throw myself like a dog in other peoples' houses.

It was Anusuya's mother's death anniversary that day. Five years ago, Kamala, the cordon bleu bonsai creator, poisoned by renal failure and weakened by years of widowhood had suddenly died. Anusuya had gone to Calcutta where her mother lived and come back madder and more addicted than before.

The day passed with Anusuya locked in her room. In the evening Shantanu returned from the office and knocked on Anusuya's door. Uma wandered from room to room trying not to think about Sam. They ate dinner in silence and went to their rooms to sleep. Uma tossed and turned in bed, trying to sleep, read and think at the same time. Late at night, in the middle of a patchy dream, while a mad jagran jangled in the temple beyond the outhouses, she was awakened by a familiar whistling sound.

Uma jumped out of bed and looked out of her window into the Very Important Garden tended by government malis and always freshly verdant.

Her mother was sitting in the middle of the administrative bower, swaying as if to a silent tune. Around her were scattered several pieces of jewellery. Heirlooms, earrings, lockets, bangles, a heavy kundan set, a sparkling navratana and pearl strings which had once belonged to Kamala and been bequeathed to Anusuya on her wedding day.

As Uma peered through the window bars she noticed that Anusuya had pierced a flower through her nose, in place of her usual gold nose ring. Anusuya had worn a nose ring for twenty years and the hole was wide and painless. The flower that she had smashed into her nose was a carnation, that badge of refinement, now roughly impaled in her nostril. She was a white smudge in the darkness, a small iceberg in a glittering delta of jewellery, with a plant flapping in her nose.

Uma examined the possible outcomes of the night. Anusuya could remain there all night, to be discovered by the gardeners next morning and carted off to the municipality office blinking, in a wheelbarrow. Several forms would have to be filled, in triplicate, photocopies organised, money paid to the municipality office to get her back.

Or Anusuya could gather up her jewellery, wander into the streets and disappear forever with the neighbourhood thief. Or

Anusuya could stay where she was and wait for the press to arrive in the morning, and subsequently declare her a newly Ultimate guru. Anusuya might refuse to give interviews, smash a few television cameras, then pass out and step over to the Other World in a huff.

The effects on Shantanu's career may not be all bad. The civil service, sympathetic with their brother officer, would appoint him defence secretary. Shantanu would stride about on INS Delhi pointing to technical defects in the new Sea Harriers.

After a few minutes she saw her father walk across the garden towards her mother. He was in his pajamas and his hair was dishevelled. He was carrying a Bengal Sweet Home plastic bag. He looked at Anusuya for a few seconds, picked up all the pieces of jewellery and stowed them carefully inside the bag. Anusuya watched him impassively. Then suddenly keeled forward and fell, face down on the lawn like a rag doll.

Shantanu checked the garden to see if there was any more gold lying around, then went back to the house, padded up to his study and locked the door. Anusuya lay on the lawn, a carnation in her nose, her nightie billowing around her, the wind kissing her varicose veins.

Uma was seized by sudden determination. She rushed through the living room, through the verandah and out into the lawn. She lifted up her small mother and staggered back with her into the living room. As she laid her down on the sofa, Anusuya's head lolled back and her mouth fell open and Uma saw that her tongue was crusted with tablets. She placed a cushion under her head and turned her on her side, so when Misri came in the morning, it would look as if memsahib was sleeping.

Then she hurried back to her room, lay down on her bed with her pulses racing about:
a) the free availability of sedatives
b) the dangers of traditional people trapped in a modern marriage

c) her mother's lack of inner resources and
d) the human being's failure to deal with death.

She had barely been asleep for an hour when she heard a faint scratching. She scissored out of bed and opened the door to find Anusuya weaving outside, making hieroglyphic marks on Uma's bedroom door with a black eyebrow pencil.

"What are you doing now, Ma?" cried Uma.

"Signs," Anusuya stated matter-of-factly.

"What signs?"

"To keep the spirits out. I have to protect you in case they take you away also."

"Just stop this! It's very late. Go to sleep."

She pushed her mother across the dining room, past Shantanu's study which was bolted from the inside and into her own bedroom. Anusuya smelt like a chemical factory. As Uma helped her lie down, she impulsively pulled Anusuya's tiny body close to hers. She was shocked at how good it felt and how clearly she remembered Anusuya's chest. No matter how weird mothers were, their remembered laps were thin havens.

The champa tree outside stuck wobbly arms alongside the window of her cold bedroom as Anusuya drifted off to sleep. Uma rushed back to her room and tried to comfort herself with the notion that mothers who didn't fit the stereotype were good for character building.

Anusuya remained in her kaftan the next day, chain-smoking shakily, smearing honey and wheatgerm on her face, ordering the servants to hose down the dust that settles on Delhi's windows every morning, instructing Misri to prepare dishes that Shantanu most disliked and foggily questioning passing salesmen on why they had failed to clean her house. They smilingly reminded her that they weren't in her employ and shook pamphlets of fungus repellants and washing machines in her face.

She wandered back onto the lawn and sat down on the grass with a thump. The wet earth soaked into her nightgown and leaves clung to her feet. She left the house that night.

Earlier in the evening, Uma sat on the sofa, silently thanking God that Sam wasn't there to hear glasses crashing and the grubby sofa being thumped repeatedly. Anusuya lurched around the long corridors at speed, inarticulately enraged. She commanded Shantanu to talk to his travel agent and buy her an air ticket to Calcutta so she could spend a few days with her dead mother's sister. Just take a train, Shantanu suggested. Train? screamed Anusuya. No trains for me, my friend.

Shantanu turned up his nose at the sight of her and refused. She screamed that she had always been far too upper class for him. Flakes of mud drizzled off her hands and feet. She looked like Rochester's mad wife in *Jane Eyre*, decided Uma.

At the appointed time in the evening Uma switched on the television set to watch *Yes Minister*.

"Ma, please sleep," she said, turning up the volume.

Silence from Anusuya. She sat upright on the floor, staring at Shantanu, who was reading a book with studied attention.

"My mother only drank champagne," she whispered. "She used to be the best dancer at the Calcutta Club. The jitterbug. The twist."

"Not very well though, it must be said," Uma clarified.

"Tell him," Anusuya bellowed.

"What?" Uma was rivetted by Sir Humphrey Appleby.

Shantanu looked up from his book at Anusuya as if she were a cockroach.

"Go to sleep, for God's sake. Stop making a spectacle of yourself. What if the Englishman was here to see you?"

Anusuya tightened her jaw in a terrifying leer, struggled to her feet, pulled out her family album from the book shelf and threw it at Shantanu.

Anusuya's family had once been determinedly eminent but now were either dead or overseas. Her grandfather had been an immensely powerful patriarch from a small village outside Dhaka who had pulled his many brothers and sisters out of lower middle class gentility and by the time Anusuya was born had installed them firmly in the upper echelons of the English speaking professions.

There was an uncle with a grand piano in his bedroom and an aunt who collected porcelain dogs.

There were civil servants and doctors, corporate executives and lawyers. Anusuya's doctor father Ranjan and her pearly mother Kamala were dead. Her brothers had drifted off to America and Australia, leaving Anusuya in New Delhi with nobody except her husband and daughter which may have been enough for some but was simply not for Anusuya who yearned to tumble in a noisy menage.

Shantanu got up from his chair in a rush and flung the album at her feet.

"Throw all this garbage in the wastepaper basket," he said.

He preferred his own father's diaries and photographs. His father, S.N. Bhattacharyya, of the Indian Civil Service, the bureaucracy created by the British. S.N. Bhattacharyya who would probably get severe *ombol* — that form of indigestion only visited upon Bengalis — up in heaven if he knew that nowadays you could even take the civil service exam in an Indian language.

Anusuya picked up the album and threw it at Shantanu again. Shantanu opened its thick worn pages, deliberately tore up a few of the photographs and distributed them over her nodding head. Anusuya filled her glass with gin and tossed it at Shantanu. He spluttered and pushed at her, she toppled backwards and her head banged against the cement floor. She crawled to the stairs that led up to her bedroom but was too intoxicated to climb. She sat at the bottom of the steps, swaying from side to side.

He wiped off the gin, smiled at Uma and went back to reading Churchill's letters.

An hour passed. Anusuya sat at the foot of the stairs, Shantanu read and Uma watched *Yes Minister*. Then Shantanu went to the kitchen and helped himself to some dry sabzi and chapattis which Misri had left for him in the hot case. He placed a hand over Anusuya's shoulder and with some concern asked her if she would like to eat something. She brushed his hand away, and resumed her nodding and swaying, staring fixedly at him with glazed eyes.

Uma climbed over her carefully and went to her room, hoping that by some miracle, her mother would be back in her bed tomorrow, screaming at the servants and wiping layers of dust from the windows with her hands. But when they awoke the next morning, Anusuya had gone.

In normal circumstances, since this was a fairly common occurrence, Shantanu would become worried, ring up all their friends and relatives, then all the hotels and fetch a drowsy Anusuya back from the neighbourhood Ray family or from the dirty Kohinoor hotel nearby, behind Khan Market, where she would invariably go.

The staff at the Kohinoor were quite used to Madam Anusuya with her delicate wrists and kohl-blackened eyes sidling through their lobby at two a.m., and plodding up the steps to a garish single room at the far end of the corridor, in the long line of rooms in which lecherous politicians with money in their crotches sweated and heaved.

But this time Shantanu seemed unmoved. He bathed, shaved and ate his half-boiled egg and toast in silence.

"Baba, aren't you going to find Ma?" urged Uma.

"No," Shantanu replied.

"Perhaps she's lying under a bus," Uma suggested.

"I don't think so. There would have been a commotion."

"Perhaps she's gone to your office and is showing your minister her album." Shantanu's minister was still under fifty with a superb head of hair and a cellphone growing from his ear. He was an authority on the quotations of John F. Kennedy and even maintained two wives.

"I hope not."

"Aren't you going to find out?"

"No."

He deftly separated the napkin from its holder, wiped his face, picked up his briefcase and walked out to his white Ambassador car, waiting to speed him to the bowing and scraping refuge of the government.

Uma spent the morning in busy detective work. Visions of her bedraggled mother wandering the streets, clad in her nightie, brought shivers of mortification.

If only she would listen to Uma. If only she would abandon all pretence at being a mother and simply become Uma's student. Several things would then become clear. Uma would explain it all to her. Explain what she had worked out while reading her books in her room. She would explain that Anusuya couldn't understand relationships that weren't defined by tradition. She had no idea how to *create* a relationship. When people died she indulged in ritual grieving which others saw as hysteria. When daughters went abroad on a scholarship, she took it as rejection. She expected her husband to be a stern patriarch like her grandfather and despised him for weakness if he tried to be nice to her.

She had no idea how to be 'modern' and a mother at the same time and mistook gin and Calmpose as the salient feature of such an entity. She was all the rage at Delhi's cocktail parties that took place under freshly-watered palms accompanied by freshly-polished silverware but her pallu-slipping helplessness became confusing for the vigorous nuns at Uma's convent when they met during parent-teacher meetings.

She rang her parents' friends. They were used to these calls from Uma and tried to sound comforting. She would be back, she had probably gone for a morning walk, don't worry. Uma rang the Kohinoor. No, Madam had not come this time. Uma paced in the garden, hoping that her mother might burst through the earth. She examined the trees in case they were whispering to her about death. She scrutinised cloud formations in case they were sending her messages of mortality.

Whenever her mother went missing, Uma scanned the elements for answers. Anusuya seemed united somehow to the landscape. Poor Ma. Poor thing.

At noon when Anusuya walked through the door, upright in a sari with a small overnight bag, Uma felt like falling at her feet and thanking her for standing on two legs and speaking through her mouth. Yes, she had packed her things and gone to spend the night out, Anusuya said briskly.

She had simply walked to a taxi stand and hired a taxi. But why had she not called. Because there was nothing to worry about, she had simply spent the night out, that's all. Anusuya could be chillingly impatient about the apocalyptic.

And where had she gone? To the Kalibari, of course. She knew the priest well and he had opened up a guest room for her. She had spent the night praying for Kamala and had even seen her mother's spirit saunter in the temple compound. The spirit had looked quite healthy and had conveyed to Anusuya that she would be receiving a letter from her soon.

She went in for a bath, leaving Uma to rush to her bedroom and fall on her bed, thanking Kali for restoring her mother to the household.

But when Shantanu came back in the evening, she was nodding drunkenly again.

"Ma," Uma asked exasperatedly, "why are you like this?"

Silence from Anusuya.

"You're a drug addict, Ma. One day you'll be lying in a subway in London with a syringe up your forearm. Indian mothers aren't supposed to be like this."

"Silence! Have some manners!" scolded Anusuya, "Don't talk to your mother like that. You don't know how to talk," she said jaggedly painting her long finger nails a wan pink.

"Pop stars are drug addicts, young poets, male writers, daily labourers, the unemployed, not Indian housewives," Uma pointed out.

Silence from Anusuya. She charged into the kitchen and returned with a plate of cold banana fritters.

"Have," she said, "have some. I had made them for your friend."

Uma munched on a fritter, trying to imagine the strange state in which Anusuya must have knocked up these sour savouries.

"He'll be back soon."

"You're very stupid," Anusuya said. "I'm not any of those bad things."

"As they say in the West, you're in denial. You see, you don't *know* anything. You haven't discovered psychoanalysis. Mental illness. Freud. Ma, you've heard of Freud, no?"

"Who?"

"Freud."

Another silence from Anusuya.

"You need to see someone, a doctor, a counsellor. You're sick," persisted Uma.

"What do you mean by that?" shouted Anusuya becoming red with fury. "Do you think I'm mad? How dare you insult your own mother just because you have an English boyfriend! Just because you think you're a big intellectual. You're nothing compared to my uncle and father, understand? Nothing. They didn't have the advantages that you have. You only do phyach phyach in English all the time like a *tyash goru*! Besides," she blew on her finger nails, "I'm going to start Feng Shui classes soon."

Uma reached for another fritter.

"Baba tries to be nice to you but you keep putting him off. You're a manic depressive. You're not normal, Ma, believe me."

Another long silence from Anusuya. She continued to dab paint on the tops of her fingers instead of on her nails.

"I don't need your father," she said haughtily tossing her head and lifting a small shoulder. "The Bhattacharyyas have always been *murkhos* compared to my family."

"*Nobody* would call you normal," insisted Uma.

"I'm *not* abnormal," said Anusuya argumentatively. "I'm normal. Don't be rude to me just because my mother's dead and I don't have anyone in the world."

Uma grasped her mother's tiny polish smeared hand in her own and pressed it against her own cheek.

"You don't even have my looks," said Anusuya, snatching her hand away. "That's why the Englishman doesn't want to marry you. Because you don't have looks. Or figure."

She confronted her father the same evening as he sat in his bare study with the Bajaj Automobiles calendar showing Krishna gorging on butter flapping on the wall. Shantanu's study was bare of carpets or ornaments. His half sleeved cotton vests were spread out on the lone wire chair and a picture of INS Vikrant hung on the wall. He dusted his books every weekend and arranged them carefully against the green limestone walls of the bungalow.

"Baba, Ma's quite sweet," she ventured.

Shantanu looked up from a back issue of the *Times Literary Supplement*.

"She has a number of creditable qualities." Silence.

"But you don't like her," Uma accused. She wanted to ask what he had done with her jewellery. Had he put it back in her safe? Or given it to a mistress? Either way, Anusuya would never know.

"She thinks she can do what she wants because her family's rich," Shantanu said coldly.

He patted his grey beard carefully and dusted some crumbs off his brown cotton trousers.

Of course, had this not been the age of 'Love', thought Uma, naive beautiful women and ascetic professional men might easily have made a tolerable marriage. Shantanu could have become a pillar amongst a community of enlightened men and Anusuya would have been cosseted under the family umbrella.

But according to modern fashion, they felt the need to be exclusively In Love with each other, with all its attendant fantasies and 'important moments' and sadly couldn't manage it at all. No wonder Uma was convinced that Love was a terrible problem and no wonder she couldn't bring herself to use the word easily with Sam.

Shantanu continued. "She's embarrassing sometimes, Umama. It's difficult for me, you see, because I was brought up by a very admirable mother. My own mother was a tremendous personality. Tremendous," said Shantanu, looking appealingly at his daughter.

Shantanu's mother, Umadevi was a freedom fighter. She used to swim strongly in a frothing river when she was the Collector's wife posted in a district town. Before she was married off against her will, Umadevi had been imprisoned during the freedom movement, become a member of the Congress, and always loudly argued about politics with her husband S.N. Bhattacharyya, ICS. She had given a lecture series in Norway, written articles on women's education, poured scorn on Anusuya's mother, the fluttery Kamala and ended her days as principal of a women's college. Shantanu had insisted that Uma be named after his mother to ensure that she had the correct role models.

"I suppose marriage can never be a delicate exchange over a dinner table," said Uma helpfully.

Shantanu inclined his head and went back to the TLS.

If only my parents spoke to each other in Bengali, and not English, Uma told the absent Sam, looking into her mirror. They would have got on much better. Life in an English speaking universe robs them of honesty. They try too hard to be imagined characters. They don't have the words to be themselves. All sorts of Bengali proverbs get them through the day and advise them about human nature. But the proverbs are furtive, hidden deep away.

In a class on land laws in British India at Oxford, she had wondered why there were no emotions in History. What about a history of parents? Parents who crumbled under the probing fingers of time, and of their own children, crumbled like the old walls of Delhi.

She imagined what Mrs Khurana would say if she told her about her home. Mrs Khurana would weep with breast-shaking sympathy. She would stroke Uma's cheeks and hair and burble: "Bahut dukh dekha hai, guddi." She would bring her aloo parathas and achar the next day.

The kitab chors pulled off a kidnap that afternoon.

Mathew Kutty V.C. , the software genius, was festering in his flat, unshaven and dirty, surrounded by the history of the universe, chaos theory and the super nova.

Mathew Kutty V.C. was umbilically wired by invisible cables to the world of the computer. He would often fall silent in the middle of a conversation or halt in his tracks in the middle of the road or suddenly stop eating and look suspiciously at his food or run out of the auditorium in the middle of a film if his brain magically began to receive a feed from somewhere about a recent breakthrough on the Net.

Mathew Kutty V.C. had set up a website called H20.com that told you everything you wanted to know about the chemical composition of the drinking water available in different countries. The website had become indispensable for the tourist trade and Mathew Kutty V.C. had become rich. But even though he was a millionaire, he lived in a smelly one-room flat in Mayur Vihar in a housing society that was Stalinist in design and the Tower of Babel in decibel level.

If Mathew Kutty V.C. had wanted he could have bought himself a superb mansion but so obsessed was he at this time in investigating the nutrients available in certain insects and so incredulous was he at the fact that the human race had neglected to develop a taste in eating insects when in fact some of them could be almost as nutritious as some plants, that he had forgotten about his money.

The gang walked into Mathew Kutty V.C.'s crowded room. It was a snake pit of writhing cables, terminals, modems, running electronic mice, voltage stabilisers, uninterrupted power suppliers, CD-Roms, discs, printers and print-outs.

"Yaaah!" cried out Mathew Kutty V.C. for whom receiving a visitor was roughly the same experience as being stabbed in the abdomen. He looked up through thick mottled glasses and a wild hedge of hair.

"Come," said the gang.

"No," said Mathew Kutty V.C. definitely. "I can't turn anything off."

"But our library needs to be computerised," they pleaded.

They led him into a car and took him where they wanted to go. They fed him biryani and cake which they appeared to be carrying with them, (the gang was nothing if not classy), methi roti and sabzi, choora and Pepsi and dropped him home after four days.

Mathew Kutty V.C. never noticed people or the newspapers and thus had no idea that there was anything strange about the rows of antique books that they showed him.

He had heard about the kitab chor gang at that party but they couldn't possibly have anything to do with these people, one of whom Mathew Kutty V.C. knew quite well.

When the gang logged on, they found that their information and library had been classified and filed in a manner they didn't think was humanly possible

As Madhavi was getting Mira ready for an expedition to Connaught Place, the baggage handler knocked and delivered an invitation card.

> Dr Pamela Sen, Director, The Mahatma Gandhi Foundation invites you to an evening with Ikram Gilchrist.

Underneath Dhruv had scrawled, '*Come. D.*' And under the note his mobile telephone number. Under it: '*Call me*'.

Madhavi looked at the card for a long time. Should she tell Dhruv that Pamela hadn't been able to recognise her? No, she couldn't trust him with her sorrows. He would only use the opportunity to be nasty about misty-eyed expatriates like herself.

He always tried to be imperious with her. Wearying attempts to gain the upper hand. He just didn't realise how far ahead of him she was now. She hadn't always been, but now she was. What had he become? A journalist. A mere journalist who would probably be incapable of writing more than a few sensational paragraphs even if Britain reconquered India.

His handwriting hadn't changed. It was still unformed, as if he was writing with his left hand. Boyish handwriting in a note under a book at the India Institute Library in Oxford, inviting her to go to London with him. Quotes from the latest Hollywood film, jokes about Sardarjis. What an idiot he used to be. She had teased him so hard once that he had dashed his hands against his eyes so she wouldn't see his tears. She used to hate him if he was happy, skipping around with his irresponsible visions.

Nothing but a public school jock. That's what she had called him and watched his face fall.

As he began to change before her eyes, suddenly acquire an exaggerated Indian appearance and refuse to listen to any music except Indian classical, telling everyone who cared to listen that he was above all, a Hindu and a kayastha she had shouted at him, for becoming a dishonest poseur.

She had even made fun of his thesis. She said he was interested in the princely states only because he was secretly ashamed that he wasn't a maharaja or a Rajput aristocrat. She mocked him for discovering the *Gitanjali* in Oxford. She had grown up with the *Mahabharat* and the Gayatri mantra. She didn't have to come to Oxford to find them. She didn't need to find the soul of India in England. Kapow! Take that!

She had watched him grope for repartee. She had watched from a roof beam like an evil owl. She had felt better to see him crushed. He couldn't know, of course, that she spent almost every evening thinking of him.

Years later he used to send her his articles at *The Leader*, where he worked at that time. She would send them back with disparaging comments. The last mail she had received from him was an invitation to his wedding.

She had read his didactic editorials in *The Republic*. She had been so outraged at his ideas about '*this* is Indian, and *this* is *not* Indian, Dylan Thomas' poetry was *not* Indian, bhangra pop was Indian' that she had e-mailed a friend to meet him and find out whether he was serious about his jingoism.

Suguna had e-mailed her back saying Dhruv still missed her. Madhavi had missed him too. Missed him with the shocked realisation that at night, under clouds of darkness, devoted mothers still dreamed about men they really couldn't be bothered about during the day.

She was still thinking about his wedding card when she bumped into Zahra in Connaught Place. Connaught Place was now officially called Rajiv Chowk but no one used the term and she remembered it as CP. Before they went abroad, Dhruv and Madhavi had completed their Bachelor's degrees from Delhi University. They had wandered in CP sometimes where hippies dodged eve-teasers, brushing past office goers hurrying to the bus stops opposite the state emporiums, or on Parliament Street. A desultory penis had rubbed itself dry against her college-girl thighs. I wonder if he's still there, she thought, lurking near the pavement bookstores, where jokesters turn neat tricks with match boxes and where they used to sell pirated videos and perfumes between the paan stands.

But Connaught Place was not only about girlhood penises. It had once been a swinging circle where young people had courted formally. In the Fifties, CP was a cup of coffee and a bus ride away from St Stephen's. Clubby ghosts riding in family Cadillacs still hid in the coffee shop above the Regal cinema. In the Seventies, when Madhavi and Dhruv came here, Dhruv used to buy cheap hash at The Cellar.

"Zahra, hey Zahroo!" she called, as Zahra walked past New Book Depot.

Zahra's face turned paler under the alabaster. Madhavi threw herself into Zahra's arms. Zahra took a few steps back, steadied herself and hugged her thinner friend and her baby.

Zahra looked ethereal in white trousers and blouse and a black pashmina shawl swinging off her shoulders. Her hair fell down below her shoulders in brown waves. Zahra's mother had been the loveliest student at Indraprastha College. And Zahra had been the fairest of them all in Oxford. An old-fashioned beauty of besan, mehndi and haldi. Of cup-sleeved blouses and flowers in the hair.

"Madhavi," she breathed, "hi, darling."

"Still as beautiful as ever, Zahra. Look," she pointed towards Mira, "this is the little one."

They stood across from each other, the two old friends who hadn't seen each other in many years. They were about the same height and their eyes were on a level. Yet they couldn't bear to look at each other for more than a split second.

How foolish I was in those days in England. Constantly in odd clothes, my unmanageable hair. But you in chiffon salwar kameezes and jootis cut so that the ends of the toes showed, you always had the men drooling. I was the bitch. You were the distant mystery.

"Muds," said Zahra huskily. "You look the same as ever."

Still the young-looking face, the tall figure and springy hair, thought Zahra. Always on top of everything. Intelligence that was so startling that it was almost comic. Intelligence that fizzed through a lecture room, leaving Pamela smiling in pride and the rest of us shifting in envy. I didn't feel equal to her then and I don't feel equal to her now.

"See *kanna*. This is Zahra. Zahra *khala*. Isn't she purty purty?" said Madhavi to Mira.

Zahra pushed her long hair away from her face.

"Let's meet after the seminar, darling. You know how Dhruv is. He's really making me work. I have no time."

Of course I know how Dhruv is, thought Madhavi. Didn't I once hold his hand as we discussed threadbare where everybody had gone wrong? But then I became dispensable. Perhaps because I wasn't beautiful.

"Zahroo," said Madhavi, "you didn't call me."

Zahra tossed her head, so that her nose tilted against the street and her hair swung back from her ivory face. You always demand surrender, she thought. Unilateral admiration, a series of compliments about your latest achievement, while you sweetly acknowledge how nice I look. *I* sound strange. Y*ou're* always normal, there can never be anything wrong with y*ou*.

"Things have been so rushed," replied Zahra.

Madhavi picked up Mira from her pram and dandled her on her shoulder.

"The seminar can't be taking *that* much time."

If you're worried about the absence of devotion, Madhavi, you should be. For years I was led by you. Led through the nose. Told about your thoughts, forced to agree with things which I later discovered that I didn't. You're not comfortable with anything but a straight acknowledgement of your dominance. You have to be top dog. You have to be the main act.

"It's just that both Dhruv and I have been working damn hard, darling. Bloody hard. You know. Invitations are there. Seminar lists are there. Many things."

"I saw your review."

Zahra looked away. Do I *have* to admire you, does everyone have to always applaud? Is criticism of you necessarily the other person's problem? You're always perfect, everyone else is always wrong.

Madhavi swung Mira from shoulder to shoulder.

You don't fool me, she thought. None of this is about my book. I know that. You're just Dhruv's creature. You go from one guardian to another. For years you treated me as one. Now you've switched your dependence to him.

Zahra sniffed and knitted her brows. She puts me on the defensive, even when she's trying to be nice. She always compliments me on my looks, never on what I'm doing.

She used to lecture me on my identity. How could she possibly have known what it was like for me? She just took it for granted that I was the same as her. How condescending she was.

Madhavi danced up and down with Mira. Zahra chucked Mira under the chin, shrugged and changed the subject.

"How's Peter?"

Madhavi threw Mira up in the air. Peter, yes Peter. Peter who dutifully accompanies me to Bharatanatyam performances at the Julliard school. I've learnt to cook a Thanksgiving dinner. We have apologetic sex after getting a little tipsy at book launches. And afterwards, we clean the house.

"Oh, he's fine. I'm fine. We're all fine. Really."

See, there. There's my confession falling on the blank face of your hostility. I'm brave that way. I confess even when I know confessions are not welcome. I'm a closeness junkie.

She made the signs of inverted commas when she said really. Really spelled ' g-h-r-e-e-a-l-l-e-y', sick spelled s-c-i-q-u-e or yes spelled y-a-y-h-a-y-a-s. For some reason we found the misspelt words hilarious, they were our efforts to sidestep language.

The photo of your parents in their baroque house in Hyderabad, with velvet curtains and painted portraits. An old-style bearer offering them soup and kababs on a tray. Your father, the nawab, a friend of the prime minister. My father, the civil servant, for whom Westminster-on-the-Ganges held out hopes of upward mobility. Your Ramadan, my pujas. But our word-world was so enclosing and so warm.

"Little bacchi kachchi," said Zahra, smiling at Mira.

"It was nice chatting to Dhruv the other day."

Zahra stepped back.

"Which day?"

"Oh, didn't he tell you? At the Foundation." Zahra's eyes seemed to become smaller. "Oh."

She fidgeted, tugged at her shawl, kissed Madhavi hurriedly and said she had to go. Madhavi watched her float down the street, hair streaming behind.

"Bye Zahra," she said to herself.

She took Mira to the crowded patch of grass in the centre of Connaught Place and whooshed her in the air as Deekay had done. The baby giggled. She bought some chocolate for her, an ice cream for herself and sat down on the grass. If this hadn't been Delhi she would have lifted her kurta and let Mira lie spreadeagled upside down on her stomach.

Bone for bone, flesh for flesh. Zahra and Dhruv. Dhruv and Zahra. Why the hell not. She just didn't belong anywhere anymore. Didn't belong to any of the concentric circles of closeness that had formed without her. In Peter's self-contained world, she was a well-behaved guest.

She lifted Mira onto her legs and swung her this way and that in a maternal merry-go-round. For God's sake, for God's sake, Zahra. Please don't reject me. Please don't let a mere man come between us. Remember how it used to be between us? Don't you remember me? Don't you miss me? Of course you miss me. Don't tell me you don't miss me because I won't believe you. I won't.

Outside her father's house in Bangalore stood the black Ambassador with windows that had to be pulled up by hand by the cantankerous Anjaiah, the cook-cum-chauffeur. Generations of their families were bound no longer by ties of master and slave but simply by bad habit.

She remembered Anjaiah and her own five-year-old hand stuck in the railing. How he had rubbed soap and oil to slide it out. She had remembered him as spare and tall but on one holiday, when Anjaiah had come to meet them at the airport, she had been shocked at how small he had become.

Go away, Pamela had said. Go away.

I'm free, she thought. Free to do exactly what I want. When nobody remembers you, you become free. She felt insane. She felt as if there was a lunatic sleeping in her intestines who was suddenly stirring and yawning.

7

Sam's mother, Felicity, telephoned that weekend and was relieved to hear that Sam wasn't there.

"But darling," she told Uma, "he's terrifying."

Felicity was a striking blonde with Sam's eyes who ran a successful kilim exporting business from Istanbul. After years of driving around in the Turkish countryside in search of rare threads, Felicity had acquired an almost permanent tan and soft Mediterranean consonants, so Uma was able to place her, quite easily as a Delhi Gymkhana bridge player and slid into a confiding relationship with her.

Felicity had once been a rollicking hippie. She and Sam's father, Michael had rattled around India in tie and dye clothes when they were nineteen and enrolled in an ashram in Nepal.

Krishna's a child, Felicity often enthused, loving and playful. Not, she had said crossing her arms across her chest and knitting her brows, as forbidding and far away as Our Father.

Sam returned to Catholicism, his parents' rejected religion, as soon as he was old enough to rebel against his mother. Not only against her but also against his parents' bitter divorce which included a long battle over him when he was only six.

After excellent A levels, while his friends were 'year offing' in India and China, Sam shunned India — far too painfully tied up with his parents' dharma and karma youth — to do a gruelling pilgrimage to Santiago de Compostela in Spain. That was when he had learnt Spanish and begun to read *The Spectator* regularly.

"I wish my mother wouldn't insist on being my friend," he had told Uma once. "Mothers should be mothers and fathers should be fathers. All this stuff about we-are-all-individuals and we-are-all-friends — is simply a cop out from responsibility. Just a fucking cop out."

Felicity swept into Oxford whenever she had time to take Sam and Uma out for long boozy lunches. Uma was always awestruck at the money Felicity spent on the food. Sam smiled quietly through the meal, refused to order anything except the cheapest salad and didn't say very much.

After lunch, he would thank his mother for a lovely time, wave her off as she sped away in her Jaguar and spend the rest of the evening reading in his room.

She had once arrived looking as breasty and rich as ever and had announced that she was about to give them a very special treat. Sam had shrugged and said he wished she hadn't insisted on coming this weekend because he had to prepare for his McKinsey's interviews.

"I used to roar up to his school," Felicity smiled, ignoring Sam and blowing a kiss in Uma's direction, as they drank coffee in the kitchen, "Roar up with the dogs and picnic baskets and my guitar. Sam was always thrilled to see me. Much happier than when his father turned up in that ghastly Mini with his Cup-a-Soup. Sammy darling, don't you remember what fun we had? I've always looked years younger than I am, you see and nobody could tell that I was Sam's mother."

"But you're not my mother," Sam had looked straight at her, "You're my best friend."

"Sam, of course, I am," Felicity clasped Uma's hand in soft puzzled palms. "Right darlings, ready for lunch?"

"No thanks, mother," Sam had stubbed his cigarette out resolutely. "I've got some reading to do. And I have to meet someone at Blackfriars in an hour. I did tell you this weekend wasn't good for me."

Tears had dug trenches in Felicity's rouge.

"But I drove all the way down, Sammy," she had said in a breaking voice. "Come on now, don't disappoint your old mum."

"Sorry, mother."

Uma had rushed to Felicity, arms flailing, with a first aid kit. Could Sam not see how much his poor mother adored him?

"Would you like to eat here? I'll cook something."

"But I'd made a reservation for us at that new Italian place," said Felicity in a small voice. "Sammy? Sure? No lunch?"

Sam had kissed her and gone up to his room.

"If you really want my honest answer, darling," said Felicity on the phone, "I think it *must* be the sex."

"Oh?" Uma asked fearfully.

"*Quite* unnatural. I mean. I don't care *what* the reason is. All that stuff was years ago. Why on earth doesn't he want to make love with you now? It's *horrible*. There's something very wrong with him. He's a bigot."

Felicity hadn't been to church in over two decades. She had married and divorced twice, drank lots of champagne whenever she was under pressure and went through phases of oxygen therapy, high protein diets, milk baths and cucumber face massages. Uma could see Felicity and Anusuya communicating quite satisfactorily. And they did, the few times they had spoken on the phone.

"Have you noticed how he avoids looking at me?" she cried. "I sometimes wonder if it's something *dreadful*. Some sort of Oedipal *thing*, you know. Perhaps he saw me in the shower one day when he was little. You know how it all comes down to us poor mammas in the end…"

"Sometimes I think he just doesn't find me attractive enough, Felicity."

"Doesn't find you attractive?" Felicity screamed loudly. "Doesn't find you attractive indeed! You're beautiful, darling. Your lovely skin, your figure. Never say that to me again. No, it's not *you*. It's those extraordinary ideas. Truth and things."

Felicity showered Sam with love. Jeans, CDs, chocolates, a set of aromatherapy massage oils, Chinese silk paintings.

Sam never even bothered to look at them. He would just dump them in his bicycle and cycle off to donate them to Save The Children.

She sent him e-mail with funny cards, telling him how much she loved him and missed him. His bedroom in her flat was always ready for him, whenever he wanted to come, she had said, decorated with books, fresh flowers and pictures of dogs.

Sam would delete her message almost as soon as he received it.

Uma had been sitting in Sam's room one cold rainy night when Felicity's housekeeper had rung to say that she had been taken to hospital. Sam had hurtled down at midnight to find Felicity in Emergency, bruised and sleepy. Her slashed wrists were taped and her eyes gummy.

Sam had stroked her bloodless arms and sat by her bed all night.

Felicity had been delirious and rambled on about her Turkish lover, his sexual techniques, the way he liked to stroke her breasts, liked her to shave her pubic hair, the money that she had spent on his underwear, his fetish for watching her bathe. And now the news that he was married, had been for fifteen years and could never leave his wife.

Sam had held her hand and assured her that everything would sort itself out. It was only in the morning when she was properly awake that Felicity had realised that her nocturnal confidant hadn't been the night nurse.

Ignoring the trembling appeal and apology in her reaching arms, Sam had bought her fresh croissants from the nearby bakery, waited to see her get up and walk around, then driven straight back to Oxford.

Felicity spoke to Anusuya to invite her to spend a few weeks with her in London.

"Come, Anusuya," Felicity breathed. "Please come."

Anusuya put the phone down with a secret smile on her lips.

"Very nice lady," pronounced Anusuya. "Much better than the son."

Michael had come to see Sam sometimes too, skidding along in his Mini with his German Shepherd. He was a computer programmer who once surprised Uma by quoting from the *Rig Veda* in Sanskrit. But he said he was an atheist. Atheist, Sam had laughed afterwards, more like a dope fiend than an atheist.

Lunches with Michael were very different from the ones with Felicity. He would take Sam and Uma to a country pub, absent-mindedly buy them whatever he imagined they might require, insist on sitting outside so that he could sit as far away from them as politeness would permit and smoke a joint.

Unlike Felicity's continuous chatter, Michael hardly spoke, except a few quick queries about Sam's grades. Sam was very cordial with Michael. Uma never saw them have any physical contact except a lip-pursed handshake.

After one of Michael's visits, Sam said: "God existed for minds like Tolstoy and Merton, but He doesn't seem good enough for my father."

At another time, he had exclaimed to Uma, "My mother's a Flower Power fascist."

"She's not!" Uma had protested strongly, not fully clear what he meant. "She's incredibly human."

"I mean," Sam had said seriously, "that she takes Flower Power to ridiculous lengths. She would stand in a Nazi concentration camp and say, oh live and let live, darling. Musn't apply our own standards, darling. Musn't impose anything on anyone. Must never use the word Good and never use the word Bad, darling. Live and let live darling. She's so scared of taking a strong stand."

Uma had been confused by that analogy. But surely it was good not to take a strong stand?

Madhavi spent the weekend gazing at Mira, thinking that the best love songs were those that could be sung to children. For the first time since Mira was born, she saw her daughter not at the centre of a whirlpool of her own confusion but as an individual with traits and tics.

Deekay had invited her to to see *Sakharam Binder* but she had refused as diplomatically as she could. Instead, she made a little picnic lunch for Mira and herself and took her to Nehru Park. She even took her to Jahanara's grave, inside the Nizamuddin shrine. Poor accomplished princess Jahanara who followed her father into captivity and nursed him until he died.

She hadn't been to the Foundation or to see Pamela again. Dhruv had sent her a copy of the paper he would present at the seminar about two weeks from now. She had been appointed 'discussant' and would have to lead the debate after he had finished reading out his presentation.

She sat back on the sofa in her room, her kurta pushed back over her chest. Mira lay upside down on her bare stomach like a white rabbit, her arms hanging down on either side of her mother's waist. Her small breaths ruffled the down on Madhavi's midriff. A Sunday night quiet surrounded her windows.

She read Dhruv's paper, held high above Mira's body. *"Challenges Before Indian Politics In the Millenium."*

Dhruv had written her an accompanying letter.

M—

Here's my revulsion for my own life's purpose in the last decade of political journalism. The tawdry realisation that India's founding fathers were nothing more than a huddle of awed Indian students in England.

The bags of money that change hands in every dawn that breaks over a putrefying skyline that you perhaps only dimly remember. You haven't been in India for long. That is, you haven't lived here for any considerable period of time.

But I have. I've seen those who pick their teeth in the guise of popular power, the heavily prosperous thugs that rule my life, the class of clowns that carry the flame of the Constitution, it's awful and I've seen it all. Consequently, would you believe, my mind has become a sewer rat and crawled away under a pipeline!

I find that I despise most the pathetic vanity of journalists. They are like maggots, eating pieces of other people's lives. Every time an earnest newcomer comes to me with a 'story' I find myself despising the juvenile ego that forces them to launch into what they misguidedly believe is 'the action'.

Of course I can't say any of this. No seminar can accommodate my bile. Seminars assume mental ease. Seminars are for my mask. The 'successful journalist' that I'm supposed to be. My request from you is just sympathetic treatment from you. (The second 'from you' was crossed out.) Don't tear up this letter. Just sympathise a little. Call if you have any queries. D.

'Queries' she thought. An unlikely word to use in a personal letter. But his written language had always been officious.

They had cycled out to Port Meadow when the trees were bare and the grass was wet and uncomfortable. He had told her how he had grown up in a tree-lined colonial bungalow in Delhi's Civil Lines, built after 1857 to segregate colonial officials from the rebellious sepoys and later extended to house visitors to the Delhi durbar of 1911 when George V processed into the empire.

How his mother played the piano every evening and his father surrounded himself with the divine rightness of the Congress party, while the chiks rustled in a hot breeze and the servants' children yelled in the outhouse. In the evenings, their giant uniformly long-nosed clan sipped Beefeater and insisted on a tyrannical taste in Vilayat Khan and Beethoven.

The afternoons were exclusively his own. All India Radio afternoons dominated by the voice of Anant Setalvad and the actions of Sunil Gavaskar. Always Sunil Gavaskar. Scoring centuries in Port of Spain, the brilliant double century at the Oval.

She had wondered why men converted their childhoods into shrines, why they mythified their own boyhoods. Perhaps it was a grudging admission of the fact that it was the only time in their lives when they weren't corrupt. She worked much harder than him. He had been flashier with many more friends. Aquiline and angry. Different from those round-faced, yellow-eyed Bengali men who loomed up at her behind Oxford street corners in those days.

She and Zahra had giggled about him over coffee. He was a joke, an enraging, exasperating joke. Her irritation with him was boundless. God, would he ever get serious?

A feminist schoolboy. His anguish at the commodification of women, quoting from Germaine Greer. Notices of different kinds above his bed. Middle Common Room march against apartheid, a Noam Chomsky lecture which she must attend. After he went back from Oxford he would join a worker's union. He hated Oxford, of course. It reduced him to a khidmatgar at a royal durbar.

He would cook a vat of dal and store it in a saucepan under his bed, in his room. Whenever he was hungry he would spoon out a portion, spread it on some bread and chew. He cared a hang for High Table.

After he began to discover his 'Indian-ness', he refused to cut his hair saying short hair was a Western convention and in ancient India men always wore their hair long. He only wore chappals with socks even in the biting cold of Michaelmas Term.

At Pimms parties, Dhruv used to wear crumpled pajamas and baggy sweaters with his hair so thick and long that he needed a headband to keep it off his face. He would speak in an exaggerated Indian accent and use Hindi phrases even with the Master of the college.

She had secretly admired him for being brave enough. Of course she couldn't tell him that she admired him. Never.

Her telephone rang.

"Madhavi? Hi, it's Deekay."

"Hey Deeks. What's happening?" sparkled Madhavi, sitting up straighter, throwing her papers to the ground. Mira shifted. Madhavi balanced her on the little curving hill of her belly.

"Listen, do you like Shakespeare plays? You know. Shakespeare plays."

"Sure, Deekay. I love Shakespeare. Which play?"

Mira squirmed. She patted her rhythmically. Go to sleep. Go to sleep.

"*Hamlet*. This friend of mine, you know, she's acting in it. It's kind of different. Next week. In case you want to come. We could...sort of...go together...if you...er..."

Madhavi smiled into the phone.

"I would love to go. Thanks, Deekay."

Deekay chuckled.

"Achcha. So you won't see *Sakharam Binder* but you'll see Shakespeare, haa? Just the kind of thing for you bourgeois gentry folk! No Hindi, only English!"

"Deekay," she protested, "stop abusing me!"

Mira grumbled. Madhavi slapped her on the back, hard. Keep quiet, child. Quiet. Quiet.

Bourgeois. That used to be Dhruv's word too. Bourgeois. Square. What had he called her once when she wouldn't agree to swim topless in that cheap pool in France? Madhavi of the Squares. Miss Boring Iyer. What a card he used to be.

"It's very nice of you to ask me, Deekay, but what shall we do with Mira?"

"Arre, bring her along, yaar. I'll take her out if she bawls."

She had met a clone of Dhruv's earlier self in Deekay. Dhruv had changed so dramatically. All his wranglings about himself and who he was seemed quite forgotten in his new success and his looks. Deekay might go the same way too. At forty he might shave off his beard, acquire a Body, a new set of clothes and style and gel his hair and insist on the need to sell everything. His younger rebellious incarnation would hide most of the time but ocasionally surface in a late night study and prod him into embarrassed memories which would subside once he gazed at his good looks reflected in the mirror.

He would forget about right and wrong, forget about being foolish, forget about vulnerablity, forget about his country and his relationship with it and why he should care more and which language he should speak. Instead, he would care only about dominance and fads. He would forget about ageing teachers with unassuming libraries inside their heads. And he would forget about critical little girls who had high hopes for him and turn instead towards high-rises and helipads.

"Not just the mother but also the child. You're a generous guy, Deekay."

"Anything for you, man. You know that."

She put the telephone down and straightened Mira roughly on her stomach. But she was uncomfortable and began to wake up. Peter would be shocked to hear that she was thinking of taking Mira to a play. But you won't enjoy it and neither will she, he would argue logically. Not that Peter wasn't devoted to the baby. He had paced all night with Mira asleep on his shoulder, singing and pointing to the stars. After she was born, he had insisted on learning to bathe her. Mira squirmed again and sneezed.

Madhavi groaned, took her to the bed, laid her on her side and pushed a bottle roughly into her mouth. Spoilt little daddy's girl. *Sleep*!

Kamini's landlady, Mrs Visvam the Bharatanatyam dancer, kept her beautiful home spotless, which was no mean achievement in a dusty city like Delhi. Long cool Italian marble floors were spread with chatais and pastel coloured rugs. Brass lamps and bronze figurines were encircled with agarbattis and fresh flowers by their side. Pure white cushions sat on delicate cane furniture. On the open verandah a hanging Gujarati swing was nicely set off with tiny mirror-work pillows. Huge flower arrangements bloomed under lamps and the glass on the carved tables shone so well that it was invisible.

Kamini had lived in her barsaati above this lovely house for the last two years. Her rent was paid for by her busy newspaper-publisher father. Her mother, soft-voiced and aristocratic and sister to a famous actress presided over framed pieces of Spanish tapestry and antique chests in their double storeyed farmhouse several kilometres outside Delhi.

Mrs Visvam had secretly telephoned Kamini's parents one night when Deekay had stayed on in Kamini's room. When she had told them that she wanted to marry Deekay, her mother had said that if she did, she wouldn't come for the wedding. That NGO worker with the beard and that awful way of speaking?

Please keep in mind what our family always stood for! Kamini had vowed to take revenge on Mrs Visvam.

As she walked up the stairs to her terrace, she heard a commotion inside her bedroom. She peered in.

Mrs Visvam, tiny in a white sari and huge red bindi with jasmine and marigolds in her hair, was in a fearsome state. She paced the floor of Kamini's room wringing her hands and blowing on her fingers while her servants stood in single file watching her worriedly.

She launched herself at Kamini as she entered.

"Kamini, my child, my books!"

Mrs Visvam performed a mudra of despair and touched her forehead with her wrist. All her dance books. The history of Bharatanatyam, those big picture books, her *Questionings On Criticism And Beauty* by Arthur James Balfour written in 1909, and her *Nritta Manjari* by Leela Row, published as far back as 1948. All gone.

"Ooops," whispered Kamini.

Mrs Visvam turned to her, her mouth quivering downwards and her thin sandalwood scented fingers shaking.

"Could Deekay have taken them, Kamini? Perhaps he's taken them. Ring him up at once!"

"Deekay?" Kamini smiled. "Books on dance? I don't think so."

Mrs Visvam rushed downstairs and shouted across the balcony and the bougainvillea to Mrs Talwar in the equally beautiful home next door.

"Where are my books, have you seen them?"

"I don't know about any books-shooks," shouted back Mrs Talwar.

"Then where are they, maybe your son..."

"My son," Mrs Talwar was chopping spring onions for her prawn and cheese bake and waved her knife at Mrs Visvam, "doesn't need books from you. He has his own books."

"Then where are my books?" screamed Mrs Visvam. "Where are they, you stupid woman?"

"Just a minute, please," Mrs Talwar sniffed to her feet, "Please don't raise your voice. We know as many people as you do, remember that. I know very well where people like you come from. I told you I don't know about any books. Aankh ladaati hai mere saath!"

She steamed away towards her new three-in-one oven.

Mrs Visvam dialled Deekay. Arre, kya aunty, calling me so late at night. Nahi, re, I don't know about any dance books. You must have lent them to someone, God, how do I know, aunty.

Kamini stared down from the terrace. The lights from the techno-mandir opposite beamed into her eyes. A strobe light had recently been fitted on the temple shikhara and flashed as smartly as in a disco. Anamika boutique had closed but the flower stall next to the temple was still open.

"Oye!" Mrs Visvam called down from her terrace "kisi ko dekha hai yahan aate huye?"

The flower seller looked up and bared his gaps and gums. "Nahin dekha."

Dirty lower-class creep, sighed Mrs Visvam. Thug. He's probably burnt my books as raddi. Used my *Nritta Manjari* for paper bags.

Kamini stood quietly on the terrace. Frail and small with long lank hair and flyaway cheekbones.

8

Sam had promised Uma that he would remain unaffected by his trip to Badayun because anything like an upset stomach or transformed worldview might just be far too much of a cliche.

But as it turned out, the few days that Sam spent with Jai Prakash in Badayun, a small town in western Uttar Pradesh, did change his life.

He glanced at Jai Prakash as they rattled along in a taxi down the crowded highway towards Badayun, past Khurja and Aligarh. Untidy hair fell over his spectacles like a child's overgrown fringe. His face was thin but still looked young.

There was a directness to his manner. Behind his square scholarly glasses, his eyes were intense and steady. Under his cautious clothes, his body was edgy and restless. To Sam, he looked like a trade union leader or a student leader in a provincial university.

His open-palmed gestures suggested a robust easy sexuality. Virginity? Lost it with the village prostitute at the age of ten, he might guffaw.

Christine sat in the front seat, her fair hair blowing out of the window.

Chai stalls and dhabas, ramshackle towns and sudden statues of Dr Ambedkar standing upright in meadows, Hanuman mandirs and clusters of mud huts and maize fields ran by. Don't be fooled into thinking it's beautiful, Sambhai, Jai Prakash said. It is savage.

"*A Brahmin,*" he recited, "*sees the beauty of water, flowers, lakes. But an Untouchable's eyes sees only the fish under the lake so that he might catch and eat.*"

At the time of the sultanate, Badayun had been a great city with 'ladies in palanquins and noblemen riding on elephants'. Now it was a crowded and narrow small town, crisscrossed with cyclists, cows, battered Marutis and the ubiquitous white Ambassadors. Roadside nalas ran with filthy water. The trees next to the houses were burnt and brown. The market was festooned with banners, ragged election flags stuck out from tin roofs and peeling posters of the local MP were pasted on shuttered grimy facades and rained on by the urine of men and dogs.

They pulled up at a small house in a tiny alley, enclosed by exposed brick walls. The house had a dish antenna on its roof.

At first glance Sam thought it was a despatch room of a private courier service. There were sheafs of paper tied with string stacked in every corner. A large flat table was piled with papers and large brown stamped envelopes. Swaying badly-made book shelves were crammed with books, in Hindi and English. Loose handwritten sheets of paper had been dumped in a cardboard box sitting open on the floor. A laser printer whirred on the floor.

A tall bearded man sat at a computer, typing fast from a handwritten script. Another man in kurta pajama ticked off items on a checklist. The woman in yin and yang earrings was buried in a book.

"Sambhai," smiled Jai Prakash, extending his hand. "Welcome. Welcome to my home."

A speckled mirror hung on the wall. On a narrow ledge running the length of one wall, agarbattis had been freshly lit and thin spirals of sweet smoke curled against the mirror. Sam noticed two photographs on the wall. One of the Buddha. And who's that, Sam asked. Ambedkar, Jai Prakash answered, the Untouchable draftsman of the Indian constitution.

"Friends," said Jai Prakash pointing to the group at the dining table, "meet Sambhai. This is our group. Our name is the Shiksha Andolan. We compile and distribute written material, from books and from the Net, to people who want to learn. We call them," he looked around at the others and laughed, "our Study Packs."

At the back of the house, across a small courtyard was a tiny dark kitchen with exposed brick walls and a single tap. Sam could see a few steel utensils arranged on rough stone ledges. Next to the kitchen was a room, its door firmly bolted with a heavy padlock. Between the kitchen and this room was a flight of stairs leading to the roof where a couple of boys were flying kites. Christine went into the kitchen and came back with two steel glasses of water. She set them down on a wooden table, drew up a couple of rickety wooden chairs and sat down at Jai Prakash's feet. She seemed, noted Sam, quite at home here. A thin little boy ran in with a plate of samosas and small cups of sticky tea. Jai Prakash ruffled his hair.

"Come, Sambhai. You must be tired after the journey. Come, eat Shankar's mother's samosas. And drink some of our sweet tea."

Jai Prakash drank his tea quickly, set his cup down and gestured towards the plate. Sam chewed. "Hmm, achcha laga."

"Bahut khoob!" Jai Prakash raised his hands to an unseen protector of native tongues and proferred thanks. "You have tried to learn Hindi. That is good."

The Andolan seemed hard at work. The yin and yang woman licked the envelopes with a long pink tongue, then banged them with her fists to make sure they stuck. The bearded man continued to type and the other man looked over his shoulder at the screen.

"I wanted you to come here, Sambhai," said Jai Prakash "because I wanted you to help me with my work."
"Work?"
"Yes."
"What work?"
"We," Jai Prakash looked down at his hands, "run a kind of study circle here. We try and read as much as we can on certain important subjects and we condense them into articles which we circulate to our subscribers. Our focus," he looked steadily into Sam's eyes, "is to teach people how to think. Not simply give them information, which is what the Net does."
"But how can I help?" Sam asked.
Jai Prakash laughed. He took a gulp from his tea. "Tell me, do you think about poor people?"
"Only sometimes," grinned Sam, helping himself to another samosa, "I'm ashamed to say."
Jai Prakash laughed too. "I know you do, Sambhai. I have seen it in your face. I know you can help me."
Sam coughed. The tea was scalding and sweet.
"It was my good fortune," said Jai Prakash, "to meet you at Jaspreet's party. Because it was a party meant for people like you, not people like me. And I thought that perhaps you vould not like to be friends with someone as non-civilised as me. I'm not an Ox-phord intellectual like you. I did not want to...how you say...impose...and..."
He opened his mouth wide and burped loudly. Sam reined in an involuntary shudder as expertly as a jockey reins in a prancing horse. Jai Prakash grinned at Sam's presence of mind.
"There's no imposing," said Sam.
"Christine has spoken rudely to Umadevi, Sambhai. She has really done bad thing. Really bad. But don't be angry."
"I'm not angry. I'm sure Uma isn't either. She just pretends to be."

"You see," Jai Prakash smiled, "I have not learnt manners like you. I am dehati, a total...how you say it... barbarian... a nobody."

"So am I," said Sam.

"Tell me Sambhai, do you know about India's negroes?"

"India's negroes?"

"I will tell you about them. They are people whose skin is as black as the negroes of America. As black as mine."

He began his story. He said he didn't know how old he was but according to rough stars and even rougher moons he was past forty. He was born in a village near Sahaswan, close to Badayun, here in western Uttar Pradesh.

He belonged to the caste of scavengers who ate the meat of dead animals and used the hides for leather and tanning.

Untouchable caste, Sambhai, you understand? Dalits, as they are called. The lowest of the low. Dirt poor. Never owned land. Never went to school. Never been anything other than the eaters of dead animals. India's negroes. Except the only thing is, that unlike the American negroes, they are still invisible. Still unseen.

But things changed for his family in the early part of the century. Jai Prakash's grandfather heard rumours that far away in the Americas, they were building a new canal and there was work and dollars available. He and his friend gathered all the money they had and boarded a ship to Panama. For months, he toiled on the canal site by the Caribbean, his flesh eaten up by wild mosquitoes and flies, his ankles sunk in a swamp for weeks at a time. But by the time he came back, after four years, fluent in Spanish with even a small business in Panama City, he was rich.

Rich enough to buy twenty acres and become a landlord. The first scavenger in the village who became a landlord, imagine that, Sambhai. He even opened a small grocery shop much to the fear and hatred of the upper castes in the village. Many years after he came back from Panama, Jai Prakash's grandfather would sit on his charpoy in the middle of his courtyard and declare proudly that he was the recipient of a pension from none other than the US government.

The family became prosperous. Prosperous enough for Jai Prakash's father, Sheoraj to build himself two pucca houses and indulge in his hobby, wrestling.

Wrestling was a popular profession in those parts and Sheoraj enlisted with a local akhara and hired out his muscles for kushti competitions and displays. Jai Prakash's mother Kitabo was the district beauty with waist-length hair and olive skin, whose love Sheoraj won by a particularly skillful display of wrestling once when she had come to the Badayun fair in the days when there was no television connection even in any of the pucca houses.

One day when Jai Prakash was seven years old and Kitabo was pregnant with her sixth child, she summoned him to massage her aching legs. As he was rubbing oil on her calves, he sang her one of his poems.

"The birds fly with their wings, leaving me to fly only with my eyes."

Kitabo struggled to her feet and hoisted him up on to her broad shoulders to give him a better view of the birds. The very next morning as her older children trailed off to the fields, Kitabo wrapped some rotis in a tiffin box and for the first time in his life, sent Jai Prakash to school.

The Harijan Bal Vidyalaya was a six-kilometre walk away but at least it was free. Kitabo insisted that he attend school every day even though there was fierce opposition from Sheoraj, who glowered that the boy's physique was so slight that he should be put to work with the crops to build up some muscle.

Sheoraj had scowled for days when Jai Prakash finished school and then went on to Gorakhpur University, then to

Jawaharlal Nehru University in Delhi where he enrolled for a doctorate. But Kitabo was thrilled and dreamt of the day when her son would write a book.

Jai Prakash worked desperately hard, went to every class and stayed up into the dawn reading everything he possibly could. He completed his Ph.D. on the *Lesser Known Saints of the Bhakti Movement* after eight years; and although it was published by a small publishing house in Lucknow, it hardly sold.

Kitabo would have been shocked at the company that Jai Prakash kept at JNU. Not a single nice girl in a sari, only thin bearded boys with cloth bags. Boys who held up banners and shouted on sweaty evenings.

Change society! Why should fathers pass on legal practices to their sons? Why should corporate houses recruit nephews of retired directors who went to the right schools and spoke with the right accents?

Jai Prakash became friends with Thomas. The bearded man who was working at the computer looked up and smiled, and Kishan, the man in the kurta pajama smiled too and folded his hands in a namaskar.

With Thomas' help, he set up Shiksha Andolan which was aimed at tackling some of the horrible inequalities of education in India. They managed to get a small kitty of funds from an international philanthropist and started work.

Shiksha Andolan translated a few English language books into Hindi, reprinted them as cheaply as possible with help they got from a small publishing house called Peoples' Progress and sent about ten copies to university libraries that nestled amongst stones and shrubs, far away from colleges where people like Umadevi got their degrees.

But after a few years, the international funders of the Andolan lost interest. A small book translating venture was not seen to provide immediate and high-profile relief to large enough numbers. They switched their attention to floods and war widows and the Andolan folded up.

One day while drinking tea in the Teen Murti House canteen, he met a senior academic, also a historian. They struck up a conversation, then another long talk a few days later, followed by a meal.

His friend was impressed by the Andolan and inquired constantly about it. His friend went away but wrote to him regularly, asking for more information. Jai Prakash wrote back saying they had been forced to shut it down. He received a reply to his letter within a week. His friend informed him that the Wingate Fund in London was looking to finance new research ideas.

Jai Prakash sent in an application, hesitatingly, fearfully to the Wingate Fund. They gave him a scholarship to finish his book on Jhalkari Bai, the legendary warrior who was said to be an even greater heroine than the Rani of Jhansi.

The scholarship took him to Oxford wearing, would you believe it, Sambhai, yellow bell bottoms. While he was living in a small room in Summertown and sometimes cycling to Queen Elizabeth House library he had met Christine. She was working in a shelter for the homeless and sometimes came to the QEH to look for books for her course in Development Economics.

She said she had never met anyone as magnetic as Jai Prakash. And Jai Prakash had never met someone as enthusiastic as Christine. She had posters of Mother Teresa all over her room and a little penfriend in Bangladesh who was only ten years old.

Sam looked at Christine still sitting at Jai Prakash's feet and thought that she didn't look much older than ten herself.

Christine's father was a rich lawyer who lived in California and didn't really care what she did. He just tried not to let her feel the absence of a mother (who had committed suicide) by ensuring that her bank account was always healthy. Sam looked at Christine again, and thought how far people sometimes had to travel in search of love.

Christine and Jai Prakash built up their own little world in Oxford. Christine took the world so much to heart that she often became depressed just listening to the news. Jai Prakash had introduced her to Shankhapushpi to which she had unfortunately become slightly addicted.

He had finished his book and come back to India forever now. Christine had come with him. They had revived the Andolan and a few others had got involved. His mother, Kitabo, still lived a few kilometres away from this house. Kitabo, his illiterate mother who had understood his first poem.

Sam's breathing had become heavy and he sat very still. Jai Prakash sighed a there-you-have-it sigh.

The table buzzed with activity. The bearded man switched off the computer and stretched. The yin and yang woman stuffed a fat volume into a brown envelope, sealed it, licked on a stamp, pushed it to a corner and stood up.

"Jai Prakash, I'll start for Delhi now," said Yin and Yang. "See you in a few days."

Jai Prakash stood up. "Theek hai, Premila. Milenge."

The bearded man whispered something to the other man. He nodded and began to write on a notepad.

"Christine has an education from very good college, Yale University," said Jai Prakash, sitting down and stroking Christine's hair, "and she went for holidays to, what is the name of that place, what did you tell me?"

"The Hamptons," said Christine, looking truculently at Sam. He smiled smoothly back.

"See, she's a pucca Boston Brahmin. Nahin?" Jai Prakash's eyes stayed on Sam.

Jai Prakash bent towards Sam. Behind his glasses and floppy hair, his eyes glittered. When he spoke, his voice was low and dogged.

"Come outside, Sambhai. Come. Let's walk towards the field."

As they walked out, an atmosphere of silent anticipation settled in the room. The two men stared openly. Christine looked after them with saucer eyes as they walked out over the dirt tracks and stones, out towards the fields where the shadows were lengthening and the birds clamouring in the trees. Jai Prakash said: "In my life, Sambhai, I have found many true friends. They have helped me. And one of them has helped me most of all."

"Who?"

"I'll tell you someday, Sambhai. One day, I will tell you....But now let me show you Badayun town, then I will cook for you, make you sleep on charpoy, make you smell the woodsmoke and also cowdung and give you...how you say...whole Indian experience." He smiled again and his eyes twinkled.

They walked along the mud path under the trees, talking and smoking, as children ran in front of them and cyclists wobbled to clusters of huts far in the fields. As they got to the end of the path, Sam opened his arms and Jai Prakash walked into them. The sun set on their brief embrace.

The same night, Dhruv stretched out in Zahra's handloom cushion and hanging-plant home.

Next to him, Zahra's hair reached down past her bare shoulders. Her breasts quivered towards the ceiling. A dark down waved on her long wide-hipped pale body. They had made dexterous love all evening and achieved some premium orgasms.

Dhruv hadn't paid much attention to Zahra when he had first met her in Oxford. She had just been Madhavi's prettier friend who seemed to laugh all the time and wear floating clothes. But now after years of cataloguing women into Beddable Bimbos, Bitchy Dykes and Useful Mummys, her luxurious laugh was a salve on his snarling rejection complex.

She seemed relieved to be divorced from her businessman husband. When they became lovers, she had told him that she wasn't in this for commitment. But she had offered to redecorate his house and treated him with flirtatious disdain. She was so beautiful that Dhruv felt ten feet tall just walking by her side.

She looked like a star from the Black and White movies saying her lines next to a moonlit rose bush, with a light shining behind her head. She reminded him of women he had seen while travelling to boarding school in Rajasthan hefting brass pots on their shoulders and rounding up buffaloes. Women from village fairs singing husky songs with facial hair glowing in the sunset.

When he made love to her, he felt as if the relationship between Hindus and Muslims was in fact an intensely sexual memory of love and wickedness. The love of enemies was peculiarly strong. Overcoming historical barriers was an aphrodisiac, speaking the same language across bloody headlines made the knees tremble. She seemed to feel the same way. The sex between them was the best they had ever had in their lives.

He tiptoed romantically around her when she read the namaz, crowded her with Rajasthani trinkets, harnessing handicrafts to his courtship. On his birthday she had a beer and biryani party for him and invited everyone who might be important for his potential job.

Afterwards, he had pushed her against a wall, placed his hands on either side of her face and asked how he should thank her. She had pouted prettily and he had pushed her soft flat belly into his hips.

"Dhruv..."

"Hmmm." His eyes were closed.

"Guess what. I met Madhavi in CP."

"Zahra," Dhruv opened his eyes and held up his hand, "please don't talk to me about her. Please, okay."

"You didn't tell me you had met her also."

"Oh, come on," he snapped. "She came to the Foundation. How could I not meet her? Jesus!"

He didn't tell Zahra that he had watched from the window as Madhavi had walked down Lodi Road after reading Zahra's review. He had found himself looking at her thin jawline. He had lifted his eyes to her face and stepped back, startled. Her face was red and small, her fine eyes bewildered. He had been mortified. He had forgotten how young she always looked.

He had kicked himself for pinning up the review on the bulletin board the previous day, for such a naked display of rivalry. He had torn it down after she left and thrown it away.

Madhavi always made him do the wrong things, made him feel as if he was thrashing around mindlessly lending support to the wrong causes, that his traumas were boring and worthless. Being with Zahra was more restful.

"Why're you getting upset, Dhruv?"

He sat up, his hair ruffled.

"I'm not upset, yaar. Please, Zahra, please."

Zahra stroked his arm soothingly and flattened down his hair. "I should've asked her to come over. She's been in Delhi for a week. Shall I call her for dinner?"

He cupped her breasts in his hands and pictured Madhavi again.

"Forget her, Zahra," he said emphatically. "Just forget her. She's just jealous of you. Jealous."

He pulled her face up towards his and kissed her smoothly and deeply. Her lips smelt the same as her pubic hair: bittersweet.

She turned her face away.

"No, I'm serious. We should call her. Dhruv, why don't you want to see her? I thought you and she..."

"Look, just shut the fuck up, Zahra," Dhruv exploded suddenly. "Just stop going on and on." Zahra looked even more beautiful when she was injured. Dhruv couldn't bear the hurt in her beautiful eyes, like a doll pushed face down on the floor. He cupped her face in his hands in contrition and kissed her palms.

"Pamela must have told her that she's decided to appoint you," said Zahra in a small voice. "She should. She should sock it to her."

He stretched. "She'll know in time. God, baby, you're lovely looking."

He grabbed her shoulders and flung her back against the pillows. Then he threw himself over her and pressed his body down on hers so hard that she wheezed. She pushed his chest back with her hands and kicked him off the low divan onto the soft pile carpet. Then rolled over onto him and bit his finger. He screamed and pushed her. They dissolved into laughter.

In their graduate days, while Dhruv and Madhavi were slogging in the library, Zahra had not been allowed to complete her doctorate. She had been enticed back to Hyderabad by her parents and married off to a businessman she had never seen. Her future husband shuttled between London and Hong Kong but had a bungalow in undulating Banjara Hills and his own swimming pool.

Zahra would be happy, her parents had said. The businessman even played cricket. But she had divorced him in less than a year, declaring that shopping, being seen at society marriages and travelling abroad was not what she wanted out of life. She dug out her unfinished doctorate from her trunk and fled back to Oxford. She had worked with manic dedication, finished her thesis and come back to Delhi as lecturer.

Madhavi had written to her after her divorce, she remembered, instructing her to walk alone, and be strong. But Zahra had come to believe, sneakily believe, that beautiful women worked to their own rules and didn't need to sing *I Will Survive* in the bathroom. Not when the world was full of lovely men like Dhruv.

"Do you think she may stymie your chances?"

"She, stymie me? Arre chchad yaar, Zahra. *No* chance."

He climbed back onto the bed and pulled her on top of him. "No chance. I've done too much for the place. Too much. Could Pamela have got Ikram Gilchrist? Could she have got Lady Lichfield?"

He was good, he knew that. He had felt the excitement of an idea like a thump in the solar plexus, the gathering joy of seeing all the bits of evidence fall like pieces of sculpture into a whole. The sensual thrill of words coursed through his inner thighs and upper arms. The tangible, evident truth was not important in itself. It was an indication of the future, the first signs of change. The crackling power to lie about reality had kept him tied to journalism for so long.

Madhavi wouldn't understand. She was as intolerant as ever. Prudish like all academics. What could she know of the sordid seduction of news? She would gloat at his grovelling letter. She would look quiet and pure and hate him for getting his hands dirty.

Madhavi and her little baby wandering about with packets of sweets and chocolates in the pram, looking lost. She had looked similarly lost when she had come to see him off at Heathrow on his way back to India, almost twenty years ago. She had looked lost because of the way he had changed in England. All his time had been taken up with himself and his fretting about language and identity. By the end, he had had no time for her at all. He had been too busy learning Hindi.

Why had he written her the letter? Had he just been trying to impress her? Impress her enough to give up the race gracefully? No, she would never do that. She was far too resolute. No, he had written the letter because it was somehow terribly important that she didn't misjudge him. That she remained convinced that he wasn't driven only by ambition, that he was still good and honest.

Zahra rested her head against his chest. He rubbed his chin along her hair. Then slid his hands under her and pinched her bottom. She cried out but he grasped her shoulders and laid her down. She shook his chin.

"Dhruv, what're you thinking now?"

"Nothing." His eyes were unfocused.

"I feel bad about writing the review. You shouldn't have pinned it up. I mean, her book wasn't *bad*."

"Forget it," he said his face in her hair. "Just forget it. Forget it. Forget it." He brought a fist to her nose and held it playfully poised.

Zahra's former husband had treated her with stern honour and consigned her to clothes and jewellery. Dhruv always playfully thumped and punched her about and wrestled her to the floor. She loved that.

She curled against him, smelt his body around her, then pushed him aside and got out of bed. She dragged on her dressing gown and asked if he wanted some tea.

He nodded. He didn't tell Zahra that he had in fact seen Madhavi yesterday. Last evening he had wandered down to the Habitat Centre just as she was rolling Mira out. He had asked what she planned to do in Delhi until the seminar. She had said, politely and coldly, that she was going to see a play over the weekend. *Hamlet* in the Shri Ram Centre basement.

"Zahra?" he called after her as she skipped towards the kitchen.

"Kya?" she called back.

"Want to see *Hamlet* in the Shri Ram basement?"

He heard her put on the kettle.

"Okay," she shouted back. "But I'm going for a demonstration in the afternoon. Against the kitab chors. You should also come."

He lay back on the bed. God, it was good to be away from his dingy little *Republic* office with the cartoons of grinning politicians all over the walls. Mooli-farting voices on the phone every night asking why he hadn't covered the prime minister's speech on the front page. His looks and size required a better frame. The Mahatma Gandhi Foundation.

In Delhi with its lopsided fountains and colonial architecture, the flowering trees and fortified residences, the hectic villages and swarming roads, there were people who took a zigzagging route to the rest of India. They sometimes went from State to Religion to Market to Compassion, as Dhruv had done. Or the other way around. To what? What indeed.

Dhruv had searched and searched, but he felt as distant from India as he had always been, perhaps because perversely, he wanted to feel distant. To belong, would be in some ways to admit defeat, to sink in with the rest of the starving hustling horde. It would deny him the hand-wringing prestige of the observer.

He became a journalist almost immediately after he returned from Oxford, while he was still flushed with hormones about the Motherland. His father had suggested he join his older brother in the family business but he chose instead to join the Congress-inclined *Leader* where he distinguished himself by zealous investigative newsbreaks. Sale of secret papers by intelligence agencies and paedophilic orgies at the home of a state chief minister.

Like most of his generation, the assassination of Indira Gandhi and the subsequent riots grabbed him by the jugular and catapulted him into an insecure alertness. He became momentarily euphoric over Rajiv Gandhi and a young and reasonable future.

But he was soon disappointed. Rajiv remained trapped with the cocktail drinkers. He didn't seem gritty enough to Dhruv who continued to look for a single truth, the engine room truth, under the mess of his country.

He had been impressed for a while with the 'social justice' movement for the lower castes. But since it was a movement led by the Left he had fallen out with it pretty fast. He hated India's socialist state and indignantly demanded why it should prevent him from importing a Saab Turbo if he wished.

At this time he had met Rukmini who worked in one of the city's newly built five star hotels and who always phoned to say how much she enjoyed his writing. One day, riding the crest of his own byline, he offered to marry her.

While still in his early thirties, he had been sought out by a liquor baron and asked to create a daily newspaper. He had named it *The Republic* and thrown himself into editing. Sleeves rolled up, young, sleepless and totally unpredictable.

During the religious riots between Hindus and Muslims in the Eighties, he had been contemptuous of the Left's version of events. He had maintained that the social justice group had completely underestimated the potential of religion. There was nothing wrong in being a passionate advocate of the *majority* religion and *majority* culture. This is a country in which the majority are Hindus, damn it, he announced to his friends. Does America try to hide the fact that it's a Christian country? Does Britain? Is the Queen not the head of the Church? So what's wrong in being Hindu?

The Hindu republic was imperative because it was a long overdue escape from westernisation. After all, Resist-the-West-at-all-costs had been his refrain since he had been a student at Oxford.

Rajiv Gandhi was torn to pieces by a woman with a bomb in her chest. Dhruv had mourned his death but felt elated at the liberalisation of the economy that followed. At last, he sighed, there go the socialist files and cobwebs. *Fuck the socialist state!*

Then the Ram Janmabhoomi movement led by Hindu activists had become cacophonous. Their demand to destroy a mosque and build a temple in its place began to electrify. Already, a Toyota designed to look like a mythological chariot had wheeled through India, gathering millions of Hindus into its mechanical innards. It had been a hectic time and *The Republic* seized the mood.

At that time, a tall woman in a sari who said her name was Suguna Shastri had visited him in office and said she wanted to contribute to *The Republic*. Dhruv had been taken aback at the sight of her. She had reminded him so powerfully of Madhavi that he couldn't bear to look at her for long. He had pushed her out of his office and his vision, saying earnestness had for too long been a drag on the nation. He had things to do and hidden meanings to uncover. He had no time for his past.

One December afternoon another great metamorphosis had taken place in his life. Hindu fanatics tore down the Babri mosque, vowing to erect a temple in its place.

Dhruv felt his Oxford-born Hinduism crumble. Once again, his ideas about himself and his country had been revealed as false. He had felt betrayed. He couldn't believe that a movement which he had supported for so long as being an example of true patriotism would in fact destroy a defenceless little monument. He had been horrified that a shrieking Frankenstein's monster had taken over Hinduism's playful gods and its merry festivals. It was a fall, for him, from well-read living.

He had obviously got his patriotism wrong. He abandoned it in favour of a drunken pluralism. He began to see Suguna as often as he could, drank heavily and wrote long essays on the synthesis of cultures in the Gangetic delta. But he hadn't been very convinced and his arguments had petered out.

But curiously enough with the collapse of his ideas, he began to grow better looking. The more confused and insecure he felt, the more handsome he became. His face acquired a ravaged leanness and his eyes became intense and powerful.

By the closing years of the twentieth century, he had come to regard The Market as his only north star. His hangovers had got so bad that he joined a gym and had watched with some pride as his alcoholic fat had turned to hairy teak.

Blair bounded to power in Britain. Amartya Sen won the Nobel prize and convinced Dhruv in an interview that the market wasn't anathema to social responsibilities. He decided that the new potent politics of the Centre was his thing. Besides, to be viscerally opposed to the West was to risk becoming the Taliban. Dhruv, now past forty and more handsome than he'd ever been, veered towards a sozzled middle path.

But he felt curiously bereft. There was no anticipation in his life with the 'third way' or 'middle path' or call it what you will. Not the dancing optimism when thunder had growled on the margins of the full moon and The People were being born. Nor the breathless tears that had hurt his eyes when he had come back to a country constructed by dreams. Nothing.

A few weeks before his forty-third birthday, Rukmini left him for a film-maker. Dhruv felt tired. He felt he was being drawn into the orbits of venal politicians. That he was nothing more but a pedlar of gossip and a participant in other people's destinies.

When he woke up one morning thinking how nice it would be if he could just have a quick drink before the day began, he knew it was time to take a break from his own narrative.

So he gave Rukmini the divorce she had been demanding, resigned from his job and asked Pamela if he could work at the Foundation, first as her additional director, then apply in due course to become director.

And here with Zahra, he felt he could somehow make up for his mistaken passions of so many years. Zahra was Dhruv's ravishing atonement.

He turned on his side and scrutinised her dressing table. He found it useful to judge women from their dressing tables.

Madhavi's had been littered with pens with reference cards stuck in the mirror. Rukmini's had been dusted with gold dust, lockets and earrings. Zahra's was decorated with Biotique lotions, herbal lip salves and a bunch of roses in a glass. And a packet of playing cards. He snatched it up.

He loved building card houses and was extremely good at them. He could see a farmhouse or even a mansion taking shape. This one would be particularly intricate, Zahra would be impressed. He began to build.

First a main house, then an annexe, a third storey, even a garage. Two garages. It could even be a permanent structure. He needn't pull it down after it was finished. Perhaps he could break off a bit of cardboard and attach it around the house like a wall.

He had recently organised an evening on India's nuclear tests. It had been extremely successful, attended by Indian and foreign businessmen, media executives, foreign correspondents from *The Guardian* and *The Independent*, diplomats, a visiting Indian peer from Westminster and even a couple of fashion models.

Pamela had been shocked by the audience. She had congratulated him afterwards and said she was fully confident of him. As students, Madhavi had idolised Pamela, but Dhruv had always been impatient with her old-fashioned ways.

But she was impressed with him, he felt sure about that. Good heavens, Dhruv, Pamela had-mouthed when he had been to see her to ask if he could join the Foundation as her deputy, what have you done to yourself? You look like a film star.

This was going to be his month. The Ikram Gilchrist lecture would be the ballast of his ascent into director. With Ikram under his belt, not to mention the seminar where he would impress Lady Lichfield into presenting an endowment to the Foundation, his takeover of one of the biggest private foundations in India would be innocently automatic.

Pamela would make the announcement and fade into oblivion. And Madhavi would take her pampers and feeding bottles back to New York and her husband.

Years ago, they had cycled out to darkening Port Meadow in Oxford when they should have been in the library.
"Dhruv," Madhavi had asked, "after you finish, then?"
He had climbed off his bike and pushed ahead of her.
"I'm really not thinking that far."
"Will you go back?" she had asked.
"I don't know. I'm just looking at options right now. There's stuff I need to work out. I need to think about things."
"Shall I also come back with you to Delhi?" she had asked. Directly and simply, like a marriage proposal.
He had laughed irritatedly. "Why the hell d'you want to come back with me, yaar? I've got my own life. You've got your own life. Don't be a frigging Miranda House behnji. Get with it. Do your own thing. I can't handle anything else right now."
It had been cold. The grass had stuck clammy blades into his socks. They had walked into the smoke from their cigarettes to feel its warmth. She had brushed her unruly hair back from her forehead. She had looked devastated.
She was so bloody didactic about things and curled up in a shell of some kind which he couldn't be bothered with. He was restless. He had tried to shrug off her intense attention on him. She had been badly hurt by his inward gaze. But he was too exasperated to comfort her. He realised that now.

9

Uma rushed out of the house to get an autorickshaw to her rehearsal. She saw Hari Ram milling about in the distance and crossed the road quickly to avoid him.

The auto bumped along towards the Shri Ram Centre basement. Suddenly, she saw Sam and Jai Prakash walking on the pavement. They were walking close together, Sam bending his head, listening to the much smaller Jai Prakash, long brown ponytail and black thatch bent towards each other on the street. My Friend and I. Native retainer and collector sahib. Local expert and expat journalist in a tropical flesh pot. Rural guerrilla and Christian missionary in a forested dictatorship.

They had their arms around each other and were laughing about something.

"Sam!" shrieked Uma, from the auto. "Hey, Sam! Are you back? Are you back?"

But they continued to walk on as if they hadn't heard, deep in conversation.

"Sam!" shouted Uma again, prodding the auto driver to hurry up. "Helloo! Wait for me! When did you come back?"

But they still didn't hear and began to walk faster as if they were trying to avoid her. They seemed further and further away.

"Sam, wait, I'm coming!"

They walked on, deaf to her shouts.

"Sam!" yelled Uma hysterically, jumping on the seat, and pushing the driver again. "Jai Prakash, wait! What's the matter?"

The sun beat down. The street seemed blurry and out of focus. The trees were dark smudges on a white hot canvas. The buildings rose through the light like black monoliths.

"Sam! Wait, SAAAM!"

But as the auto rounded a corner, they had disappeared.

"Madam," giggled the auto driver, "kya hai?"

"Woh aadmi mera dost hai," she said incredulously. "I know them."

"Udhar koi nahin hai, madam."

She wasn't able to concentrate at the rehearsal later and Aditya had to stop more than once because Uma had forgotten her exits and entrances. As punishment, after the rehearsal Aditya handed her a list of former members of the Shakespeare Society of St Stephen's College, whom she would have to call and inform about his play.

Sitting mutinously at home, she felt furious at Jai Prakash. This was supposed to be her make or break holiday with Sam. Instead this mysterious UP bhaiya had kidnapped him and taken him away from her.

Jaspreet rang to tell her about the book theft from her house and from Kamini's landlady's. Uma said her summer had been ruined too, by Jai Prakash. Oh him, said Jaspreet, he runs a correspondence course. He's not a bad guy.

Uma put the telephone down and stared at it for a few moments. In all the time Sam had been away, he hadn't even called once. Why? She wandered miserably into the kitchen. Misri was frying fish. Soon Anusuya would come lurching in from her bedroom to supervise the seasoning and to scatter dhania leaves all over the rice and dal. The walls of the kitchen were spattered with oil and a film of masala and dust was sitting on the vegetables. The kitchen door to the vegetable patch outside was open and a cool breeze was playing outside. Inside, it was steamy, even the walls ran with sweat. Misri worked fast, coating the fish pieces in haldi, chili and salt and laying them out in a bubbling shining lagoon of hot oil.

Chores, Uma recalled, perching on Misri's stool, had been an area of conflict with Sam. Her lack of experience with opening wine bottles or stacking the dish washer had exasperated him and he had once asked her if there was anything at all that she could do properly.

Of course, in a competition to scrape a tawa with Vim and steel wool she would have beaten him hollow. She had seen even Anusuya scour the kitchen drain with Phenyl, then get the nali man to probe the dark clumps of oil and rat hair out of sewers with his stick and pour in gandak ka tejaab into the hole so that the nali didn't get clogged up again with grease and the sludgy combination of masala and oil.

Jai Prakash was wrong about what he had said to Sam about a revolution. How could he have made such a foolish remark? To be privileged in India was a highly relative term.

Every district collector had to learn to get on with the sarpanches and tehsildars, every Delhi politician would have to befriend the local MLA, every factory owner would have to drink chai with the unions and most Delhi memsahibs would have to, at some time or another, stare down a nali.

She had once sat through a lecture by a celebrated author, who had condemned the audience as 'oppressive' and 'rich'. But surely, she had thought, this celebrity should have known that they had all struggled into the auditorium on swerving autorickshaws and when they went went home in the evening, their houses would be sitting in a carbon monoxide cloud.

They would bumble in the sulphurous darkness of a power cut, tap in vain at a dead phone line and console themselves with the knowledge that at least they were the oppressor class. But Jai Prakash wouldn't understand. Nor would Sam.

Sam who had dark hair on his chest and broad bony shoulders.

She watched Misri skilfully ladle out the pieces of firm fried fish. Plump fair Misri with her smooth round face. I'm a bit up in the air at the moment, said Uma silently, pretending Misri was a colleague in an air-conditioned office. Floating, you know. Floating in a rootless, context-less space, trying to nail down a romance with an Englishman without reneging on 1947 and everything I was brought up to hold sacred. Citizenship, dignity, being myself.

And now with the intrusion of this other rural man I feel I've lost my edge. He'll drift away from me and my body will be of no help, because of course, as you know, he's immune to it.

He will never crush me against him and kiss me madly and furiously strip off my clothes. All he'll do is ask for reading lists on the caste system.

Just then Misri turned.

"What are you looking at?" she demanded. "You're just like your mother. *Chole jao, jao*! Who it is who has cursed me that I have to work in this household and see every kind of sin take place, I don't know. Go!"

Uma sighed and wandered out. Perhaps she should get over the ghastly chore of telephoning the list of strangers about the play. She walked to the telephone, glanced at Aditya's list lying next to it and felt her heart bump at the first name. Dhruv Mathur! The handsome journalist.

Uma and Dhruv had met about three years ago at The Shakespeare Society production of *King Lear*. At the party after the play, she had found herself standing in the same corner as him and being drawn into his easy, charming conversation. He had even given her his card, invited her for tea at the Machan and asked if she would like to consider a career in journalism. Uma had found herself gazing, instead, at his lovely jawbone. But he had avuncularly patted her knuckles and deftly turned the conversation back to the press.

They were both alumni of St Stephen's College, an institution established by English clerics to mould people who were already convinced that they were India's best. They shared an insidious skill in bilingual puns. A comfortable memory of mince cutlets eaten with knives and forks. And the conviction that when it came to Shakespeare's poetry, none could speak it better than they.

But underneath the tentative puns rested the fearful recognition of a diminishing world. Most young Stephanians no longer even lived in India. They had fled to the West, hurt that the country they were educated to rule was no longer theirs. Their cosy labyrinth of superb connections had crumbled like a ruined anthill.

"Hello," Dhruv's voice was quick and questioning.

"Hi, Dhruv, it's Uma. Uma Bhattacharyya. Remember me?"

"Uma! Of course I remember...so you're back!"

They chatted brightly. Whom-did-you-meet-what-did-you-do-where-did-you-travel. Amazing-being-back-it's-like-I-never-left-nothing-changes. Uma told him about the play. So you've come back and started on a play immediately, laughed Dhruv. Now I know that you're in it, I'm definitely coming! So, will all the old gang be there?

"Not many," said Uma, "but I've got a friend here, visiting. This English guy. Sam."

"Ah ha!" said Dhruv, "you're back with your regulation gora. Good, yaar. Get him along. I'll check if he's good enough for you."

There was a pause.

"Actually he's not here right now. He's in Badayun."

"Where?"

"Badayun."

"Jesus. How'd he get there?"

"He went with this other guy called Jai Prakash," said Uma plaintively, "from JNU. He's running some education thing and he gets people to..."

"Oh yah, yah," said Dhruv vaguely. "I think I know the guy. Jai Prakash from JNU. He's called me once or twice at the Foundation for his education programme. Some Andolan or something like that..."

"Yes!" Uma cried eagerly, "he's the same one who's got some correspondence course happening, na? He's producing tutorials for the deprived."

"Yah, I know," Dhruv laughed again, "and the last thing the deprived need are tutes, right?"

"And there's an American woman who's, like, his serious slave."

"Really? I didn't know that. Scary."

"Yah," said Uma sombrely.

"Anyway," Uma heard the affectionate smile in Dhruv's voice, "forget all these weirdos and tell me your news. Chal..."

He changed the subject back to Uma's future plans. He had been impressed with her agitated intelligence when he had first met her at *King Lear* and was pleased to hear from her again after so long.

Although there was bright sunlight outside, Pamela's living room was lit by a small lamp with a tassled lampshade. A set of lithographs of old Calcutta, Chittpore Road and the Hoogly had been taken down from the wall and were propped up against the Jamini Roy which was still standing on the floor, waiting to be dusted.

There were fresh flowers in a vase. The photographs that had once been propped up against the book shelves had been piled on the dining table in the kitchen, next to the cutlery heap.

The photographs — some framed — were haphazardly stacked. Pamela's family house in Lansdowne Road. Pamela in Presidency College, where she had attended the rallies of the undivided communist party. Pamela at a trade union meeting, fist raised against a lockout.

Pamela and Sailen in Darjeeling, decades before the Mall became littered with secessionist posters of Gorkhaland, when the high snow peaks of the Kanchenjunga mountains still shone in a civilised chota peg at the Planter's Club.

The genteel socialists of India and their self-proclaimed duty to guide superstitious masses out of tradition into a scientific way of life. Nowadays they would call it wrong. Paternalistic, westernised. But in those days they felt it was the only way. The early planners of the economy like P.C. Mahalanobis believed it. Sailen believed it. Sailen believed that it was his duty to spread the light among soporific masses. This was 'the Bengali renaissance'. Intellectual agony of sorts from the nineteenth century. Did it really happen? Or were the Bengalis simply ahead in the race to become English?

She looked out into the garden. She would have liked to surround the hibiscus with lawn and leaf, but instead broken cans and bits of paper lay in the brown grass. She would ask Benedicta to sweep the garden. But leave the hibiscus. Leave the hibiscus for the next occupant.

She sat upright in her armchair, the bowl of porridge at her elbow. On a generous October day, a bowl of porridge with cold milk could make up, at least temporarily, for the loss of the Kanchenjunga mountains. On a cold night a snuggly blanket could even compensate for the absence of Antara, who had died a few years ago. But she must be content wherever she was. Antara was always content.

Perhaps this was old age. When even death seems tolerable if there's good food to go with it. The young would call it corruption. They wouldn't understand that growing old meant living only with the fleeting.

She read through a sheaf of papers on her lap, slowly and carefully, as if checking for mistakes. She reached into a Saree Centre plastic bag that rested near her armchair.

As she read, she blinked and frowned and her jaw dropped, then sneered up again sarcastically. She put the books and papers down on the table with the hurricane lamp and reached for her bowl of porridge. Benedicta clicked in with a napkin.

"My husband," she said gesturing with a spoon, "only bought cakes from Nahoum's bakery in Calcutta where they still sell guava cheese and plum puddings. Nahoum's plum puddings, of course, are world famous. They stay well over long distances."

Benedicta wiped Pamela's mouth with a napkin and helped her set the bowl down.

"Bread pudding, madam? I make for you, na. "

Pamela laughed. "I'm just an old buddhi, Benedicta. Too old for sweets."

I'm as old as that church in Bandel outside Calcutta, beautiful old church dating from 1599. Now, they've encased it in white marble and made it shine and put in that garish stained glass from somewhere. It's been declared a basilica, I believe.

And the Kuchaman fort in Rajasthan. They've painted over the seventeenth century frescoes and made swimming pools, I hear in the old baolis. How could they do it to these old buildings? Tarting up old women for profit. This country is in a hurry to forget us all. Forget that we ever existed. Throw out our ideology by all means. But why throw out our tastes and our manners?

The daguerreotypes of Presidency College gifted to her by her father. They would have to be wrapped in newspaper. Presidency College, dedicated to the pursuit of Reason in Bengal. They were both students there, she and her husband, Sailen, when they met. Her father had been a fierce upholder of modernisation, a critic of Indian backwardness. He was shocked at her own communist sympathies.

But she and Sailen — the boy from Brahmo Boys School who had been impressed by her ability to dance the Charleston — weren't fully communist. They were only civilised spectators. They weren't members of the undivided communist party. Simply on the fringes. Generally pragatisheel, was the word. Progressive.

Progressive and extremely English, nostalgic now for the British Labour Party when it was led by Michael Foot.

It's easy to blame my generation now. To blame them all for erecting a false system. But what else were we supposed to do? There was no other way to make sense of the massive swarm of suffering all around us.

Other ways were not rational. Other ways were not so theoretically satisfying. What took us forward? It was the delusion, the stubborn delusion that we too were relevant. That we too mattered in this country where the vast number are untouched by the things we grew up with. It couldn't be that we didn't matter at all.

"Take me with you, na," called Benedicta from the kitchen, rolling chapattis for Pamela's lunch. "I don't got anybody."

A mountain cottage with a rosebush and a view of the hills. That retirement spot for old ladies where she, Pamela, would die. They make a fuss about things these days. *My* freedom, *my* rights, *my* life. If you keep quiet, everything sorts itself out.

Perhaps they don't really want freedom these days. All they want is the fuss.

Antara, Pamela's sister, the dog lover, spurned all her suitors to live alone with her dogs. The only romance in Antara's life was Georgette Heyer and she liked to keep it that way. She never missed not being married, as far back as, let's see now, the Forties. She was a dear, old Antara. Never made a fuss, and no one made a fuss about her. Antara disliked *nekami* above all.

They make a fuss nowadays about growing old too. They don't realise that we're constantly replenished, like birds or fish. After I've gone, there'll be other potty Sens grumbling here. There'll be other Benedictas taking care of elderly ladies. Yet people foolishly believe that they face extinction, not realising that death only completes us, death makes up the whole.

"Come if you want," invited Pamela.

"Come?" Benedicta asked.

"Yes," Pamela felt for her spectacles, "if you want to spend your life with an old woman like me then come with me to the mountains. It's very beautiful."

I'm unfit to live in this city anymore. I wobble angrily on my cane, impatient with the burdens of maturity. I dislike the automatic respect for age in this country. I hate my own old age and don't care if it is ignoble. I shall be what I always was, a 'hoyden' as my father used to say.

"Benedicta, will you check on the hibiscus plant in the evening?"

"Hibiscus, hibiscus, hibiscus, madam!" Benedicta laughed. "All the time you say hibiscus."

Uma lay sleeplessly in bed that night thinking about her life and uncovering incidents of ever deepening gloom.

She tried to imagine what Sam would do if confronted with the sight of her as a moustachioed seven-year-old, playing guli-danda with the outhouse children in the mossy rural palace in 24 Parganas, which had been assigned to Shantanu as district collector. Or in a ganji and knickers eating *luchi* with jam. Sam might never be able to stomach the immense range of her miseries.

When she was thirteen, yes, that old, she had wet her pants in school. The school doctor had told Anusuya that Uma may have been suffering from trauma. What trauma, Anusuya had expostulated. She has nothing to worry about. I'm the one with the dead parents and the uncaring husband. *She* has nothing to worry about. *I'm* the one. Not *her*. Not the sticklike child with the moustache and staring eyes who thinks she's Bertie Wooster.

She heard a rustling sound outside her window. Oh no, thought Uma with a sinking heart. Could it be Anusuya again with her fractured nocturnal trauma? She padded to the window and looked out through the twisted creepers climbing up next to the railings. It was Hari Ram.

"What are you doing?" she accused, staring straight into his fierce eyes.

"Shhhh, chup karo!" he hissed. "Don't wake everybody up. There are some wires tangled up here. Problem hai."

"What are you doing with wires so late at night? Why don't you go home?"

Hari Ram brought his face closer to hers through the railing.

"There's a shop in parathawali gali in Old Delhi that gives scholarships for America," he grated. "They say they'll give my son a scholarship. He has a scholarship business on the side. That paratha shop owner. Paratha bhi bechta hai, scholarship bhi deta hai."

Uma sighed. "It's not a scholarship business, Hari Ram. They're probably taking cheap labour to some industrial country. They'll probably take your son to Canada and send him down a mine. Or to Germany and make him work on an oil rig. Or make him live in a submarine all his life."

"Why?" asked Hari Ram puzzled. "Why will they do all that to him? Why, tell me why quickly."

Because his father is the most insane telephone man in the world, that's why muttered Uma under her breath.

"Don't trust anyone unless you've shown me all the papers, theek hai? Okay, bye bye," she said after a pause.

"My son also needs to get married," fumed Hari Ram. "You can't be the only one getting married. Although," his voice became suspicious, "your jamai babu looks like a terrorist."

"What's getting married got to do with getting a scholarship?" asked Uma, curiously.

"First scholarship, then marriage," pointed out Hari Ram, astounded that Uma hadn't figured out this simple truth. "No scholarship, no marriage. Why not?" he exploded suddenly. "You got a scholarship. You got one. Then?"

There was some more rustling and scraping. Then a long sigh.

"There!" hissed Hari Ram. "Now it's okay. Ho gaya."

Uma went back to bed and tried to sleep. She heard the scrunch of a footfall and the soft sliding sound as if someone was sneaking along the wall. Then a quiet click click sound. Hari Ram again, she thought, turning on her side. God knows what he does with those telephone lines. Sleeps and eats with them perhaps.

She dreamt that Hari Ram was floating underground, swimming through telephone lines as a deep sea diver swims through weeds. She imagined him circling the city, the deity of the telephone, underground and perpetually awake. She dreamt that he was looming over the city like Godzilla with a pair of monster cleavers shredding every scholarship application form ever filled in by the sahibs' children.

The kitab chor struck the home of Secretary, Petroleum that night. Secretary, Petroleum lived in the bungalow next door to Shantanu and Anusuya divided by a long thick hedge.

Jaspreet's father and Kamini's landlady had already filed complaints with the police. Jaspreet's father — the minister of state — had even been sanctioned more Black Cats to guard his house. Books, the Cats had hooted, a thief of books? Bade aadmi ki badi baat.

The SHOs were still being impatient. Believe me, sirji, no self-respecting Delhi criminal would waste his time on books. This is a city where 'criminal tribes' defecate in drawing rooms after they've done their dread deeds as a signature of their presence. They strangle their victims with live wire. They *definitely* don't read books. Kya baat kar rahe hai, sahib.

Perhaps some college kids were playing a prank. Perhaps they had all just been mislaid or perhaps the servants had taken them away to be dusted. Perhaps they had recently shifted house and the books had got lost in the moving.

That night after Secretary, Petroleum had finished his puja and retired for the night and his wife sat at her computer sending e-mail to their son in Brandeis, the gang came.

There was a commotion the next morning. Secretary, Petroleum's white Ambassador raced out of the driveway. Mrs Secretary Petroleum could be heard questioning the guards in staccato indignation. All twelve volumes of the *Asiatick Researches* or transactions of the celebrated Asiatic Society founded in 1784 by the famous orientalist William Jones, among others, and published in London in 1806, which had belonged to Secretary, Petroleum's grandfather, were gone.

10

Sam came back from his trip with Jai Prakash, tanned and preoccupied. Uma felt the blood rush into her face and her mouth split open in a huge smile at the sight of such a bronzed David Copperfield. He dropped his bag, hugged Uma and charged off to the Sacred Heart cathedral, calling over his shoulder that he must go to church and would tell her everything when he got back.

His questions went on late into the night. Uma told him, grudgingly, everything she knew about the Dalit struggle for education. The Panthers of the Sixties, students who had used literature for violent protests. The growing demand for education for people buried for centuries under unseen caste prejudices. The few caged tokens in high places, the gruesome attacks on most.

She gave Sam the names of books he might read. She was conscious of the fact that every right-thinking person should admire Jai Prakash. But instead, the more she heard about him from Sam, she felt an irrational animosity. Sam was *hers*, damn it, *she* was his India, she was his interpreter. Not this Salt of The Earth from the boonies who claimed to be more authentic than she was and had forced her David Copperfield to lapse from English literature into the cow belt.

Sam seemed to be in a daze. Over the next few days he washed and ironed his clothes himself much to Misri's stupefaction. He helped Anusuya dust her family photos and even offered to sweep the garden. He seemed much less formal, almost playful. He pushed Uma around and touched her more than he normally did. The electrical charge in her body had dulled into an ache in her joints and she tore away from him for fear of the inevitable disappointment.

He wore his dressing gown at the breakfast table, unaware of Uma's surreptitious gaze on his tall spareness. She had become obsessed with his body and by how sexy he was.

She heard him talk to Jai Prakash on the telephone and invite him to London. He even gave Jai Prakash Felicity's telephone number and told him to ring her if he ever went to England.

He seemed to drink more than usual. She saw him help himself to two or three straight gins the evening that Jai Prakash and Christine were to come over. Shantanu had insisted that they invite him for dinner. After all, he had taken Sam on a trip and it was only fair that Sam had him over to the house.

They walked into the garden grey and smoky in the murky winter night as they waited for them to arrive. Sam's hair flew out behind him, ship deck hair, streaming under a flag mast. He put an arm around Uma's shoulders. She broke free and walked ahead of him.

"Don't run away from me," he said. His voice sounded thicker and deeper than when he had first arrived in India, it sounded gravelly. Probably the pollution, thought Uma.

"Sam," began Uma reasonably, "It really doesn't take a lot to convince you. That story about his father being a wrestler and mother sending him to school. I mean, please! Don't fall for it. I mean, he's hardly..."

"Shhhh," said Sam holding a finger to his lips. "Don't say anything."

"But how do you know the whole thing is true? You're just falling for it. You just like him because he speaks with that awful accent and lives in a mud hut."

"He doesn't live in a mud hut," Sam laughed out loud, "and his accent is not unlike yours." He ducked as she cuffed him.

"Getting Christine hooked on medicine isn't very nice."

Sam bent towards his lighter. "I'd like to help him a little, that's all." He inhaled and blew. "He doesn't seem to have had too many breaks."

But he hates me, she thought irrationally. He has to hate me. He's programmed Christine to abuse me. He's brainwashed her about me. And because of *your* attraction for him. Because you somehow *like* the fact that he hates me. You're attracted to him. Attraction which is somehow a repudiation of me, don't you see that?

My battle is just as valuable as his. I'm fighting to forge myself. I'm trying to build a homestead on a cultural wasteland. I'm just as important as he is. But now he's made me and everything I'm trying to do look foolish and unimportant because he says that he's more oppressed than I am. So where does that leave me? Just an ugly Indian woman with the age-old colonial problem. Doesn't sound good. Doesn't sound good at all.

She walked a little ahead of him and tore off a few twigs sticking out from the hedges. He came up next to her and reached for her hand. His hand was sweaty and hard. She felt his breath on her shoulders and swayed against his chest. He put his hand on her waist and pushed his hips against hers. She felt him become tense and still. He positioned her against a tree, kissed her lightly on the chin.

"Uma…"

He drew back almost immediately. Her heart which had liquefied and gushed onto her tongue flowed back into her oesophagus.

"I know you'll like him," he murmured.

She felt the excitement in his body and saw the faraway look in his eyes. My God, she thought. He's fallen in love with Jai Prakash.

They arrived exactly on time. Jai Prakash's hair flopped over his eyes. Uma noticed that he carried a mobile phone which he placed on the table in front of him as nonchalantly as one might dump hand baggage into the airport X-ray. Christine wore black and grey clothes. They demolished a couple of bottles of beer while Misri clattered about, particularly loudly in the dining room to convey her disapproval. I don't like to cook for people like *him*, she whispered to Anusuya. Have a care for my caste and family background, please. Think about me also sometimes. Everybody in my family has skin the colour of milk! Milk! Tomorrow you'll ask me to cook cow, I know it. Anusuya smiled vaguely and disappeared into her room.

But Shantanu, Uma noticed, exchanged a warm handshake with Jai Prakash and even clapped him on the shoulders. Shantanu said he had met him before through his office assistant, Mr Aggarwal, who was also Jai Prakash's neighbour.

Of course, Santanu-*da*, of course I know you, Jai Prakash smiled.

"Umadevi," Jai Prakash turned to Uma, "at last we can talk." His gaze was watchful but Uma could see how impressive his quiet suddenness was. He would laugh suddenly. Then suddenly become introspective and distracted.

"I'm sorry about Christine, Umadevi. Believe me, she's young, she has a simple view of things. But I sincerely hope...she did not...how you say it...impose on you...."

Impose, thought Uma. She gives me some medicine that almost paralysed me for life, abuses me for leading the wrong sort of life, but there's no imposing. Don't even think about it.

"Just curious," grinned Christine, "about India's princesses."

"Princesses?" Uma asked after a pause, "but the only precious objects in this palace are the silverfish in that book shelf..."

She stopped as she felt the pressure of Sam's hand on her knee.

"Come come," interrupted Jai Prakash, "let us talk about better things. Forgive us, Umadevi. You see, we are not Ox-phord intellectuals. I don't know good English. I am only a deshpremi. Tell me, do you have any thoughts about your desh, about your homeland? Any thoughts?"

"All the time," drawled Sam.

Jai Prakash and Christine laughed. They told Uma about Badayun. They invited Uma to visit Jai Prakash and his family in Sahaswan. Just to see, Jai Prakash teased, what a real village looks like. Sam said Uma had seen lots of villages but only in Europe. Jai Prakash laughed his uproarious bellowing laugh. If he laughs any harder, thought Uma resentfully, he might have a heart attack.

As they were leaving Jai Prakash performed an elaborate namaskar to Uma so that his hair bounced jauntily. He gestured towards the white Ambassador standing boxily under a tree and inquired with false politeness if madam Uma had ever travelled by public bus in Delhi.

Sam said his memsahib was not as spoilt as they thought she was. He could vouch for the fact that in Oxford she had washed up at least twice in the last two years. Uma glared at him. Sam ducked behind Jai Prakash and they giggled again.

On the evening before her play, he put his hand on her arm and asked her to forgive him but he couldn't come to the performance. He had promised to take Jai Prakash to meet one of the priests at St Columba's.

"Sam!" she wailed. "But why does he want to meet the priest in a school? Why?"

He linked his arms around her shoulders and touched his forehead to hers.

"Forgive me. Father Malcom's leaving. Tomorrow's the only day he has."

But I don't want you to go with Jai Prakash, she thought furiously. I want *you* at *my* play.

On the afternoon of Uma's play, the small demonstration against the kitab chor gang attended by Zahra, Aditya, Kamini's landlady Mrs Visvam, Jaspreet's father and Shantanu's neighbour, Secretary, Petroleum went off quite peacefully. Carefully drawn placards were held up and displayed:

> NAB KITAB CHOR GANG!
> LIBERATE CITY FROM BOOK THIEVES
> POLICE FAILURE, CITY'S WOE!

They marched along India Gate, past the boat club and presented a petition to the President's office. The police, standing by, maintained a respectful distance. This was not an ordinary crowd.

Jaspreet's father, the minister of state, addressed the gathering. This uncanny and coincidental theft of our rare and treasured books over the last few months has taken us all by surprise. It is truly an unheard-of thing. It is absurd and quite mind-boggling. These antique books are as precious as gold or cash. Some of them are irreplacable and we may never be able to get them again. Honestly, these thieves seem to know what to take. These are our books, our property, they belong and have belonged in our families for generations. They are books collected by our fathers and grandfathers. By generations of enthusiasts. Generations of educated visionaries who bequeathed to us their own wide horizons. Generations of collectors who wanted us to have what they had. They can't just be taken away by these gangsters and scoundrels.

Secretary, Petrolueum made a speech too. Perhaps if we could approach these people and ask them what they want. We should think about pooling our resources and offering them a grant to get the basic books that they need. Useful basic stuff on management, career advancement, science and technology and other basic books that can help them. But why must they take our good books?

Why must they take the *Rubaiyat of Omar Khayaam* or Philip Mason's *The Men Who Ruled India* or old editions of *Sanjibani* — the Brahmo reformist journal of the nineteenth century which had raised its voice against child marriage and other horrors of tradional society? Why these books? Why the *Shah Namah* by Firdausi in the famous James Atkinson translation of 1832, (the book that was called the Iliad of the East) or a rare copy of Dadabhai Naoroji's *Poverty and Un-British Rule in England?* They should be given simple inexpensive texts that would help them in life and let them get on. They needed manuals. They needed good instructive digests.

And what about my dance books, pleaded Mrs Visvam. If they want to learn dance, let them join a school. There are so many nowadays at reasonable rates. Cheap dance schools are a dime a dozen. All over the place.

The crowd clapped gently and nodded in grave agreement and dispersed for cups of elaichi tea that had been provided by Mrs Visvam.

The Shri Ram Centre basement auditorium was scattered with a sparse crowd. Among them, a drama aficionado with bright grey hair and a Naga shawl. Two Channel V veejays, a graphic designer, Madhavi in a green and red churidar kurta and Deekay in a shirt signed *Windhoek*.

Anusuya and Shantanu were under strict instructions from Uma not to come in case Anusuya ruined things by walking on stage and dusting the sets during the performance.

Madhavi glanced towards the door as they settled Mira between them and saw Zahra and Dhruv enter.

"What's up?" asked Deekay, feeling her stiffen next to him.

"Just some people I know."

Madhavi gave Mira a Bounty and turned her head slightly. Zahra and Dhruv were looking towards her. Zahra waved and signalled that they would meet afterwards.

The lights dimmed. The cast filed onto stage. Hamlet and Laertes in jeans. Ophelia in salwar-kameez, Gertrude played by a man and the king, played by a woman. Rosencrantz and Guildenstern were both women, short-haired with beads around their ankles. Aditya walked among them positioning them in different postures as they stood like statues against the black backdrop.

"Hello, everybody," he addressed the audience. "Thanks for coming and sorry we're late."

The audience murmured approvingly.

"We wanted to make this different. You know, just have fun, fool around with it, throw it up in the air, let it fall down, push it to you and let you throw it back at us. Masti!"

The audience clapped and the play began.

Hamlet and Gertrude kissed stylistically. Hamlet and Horatio slid under imaginary fences tracking the ghost who had still not appeared. Ophelia wandered through and belted out a Hindi film song. Rosencrantz and Guildenstern goose-stepped on stage and off.

Then there was a beating of a drum and a high-pitched chanting. It grew louder and louder, until at last, Uma, in a cloud of incense, walked onto the stage. She was dressed in a red sari, a mask in one hand and bangles on another. A wig had been crafted to look like a tapering bun at the top of her head. On her forehead, was a huge red bindi decorated with sandalwood.

The audience shifted admiringly.

"Pagan but feminine colours," hissed the graphic designer.

Uma sat cross-legged at the far corner of the stage. She jerked her head from side to side and displayed her palm to the audience, in a blessing. Then she burbled in a low monotone.

"God, what the shit is Uma doing, man," growled Deekay.

Uma rumbled through the ghost's speech with a few 'oms' thrown in at intervals. She ended with an elaborate namaste and slowly blessed the audience again.

"Bizarre, but exploratory," sneezed the drama aficionado.

"Fab," diagnosed the veejay. "Radical."

Madhavi buried her head in Mira's back. She turned to look at Dhruv and Zahra and found Dhruv looking straight at her. She turned away quickly.

The 'players' appeared, dressed as mental hospital attendants, carrying a stretcher. The play within the play was presented as therapy for Gertrude and the king, who were strapped onto the stretchers and carried away at the end of the sequence. A long interaction followed between Hamlet and the ghost. Uma delivered her speech in the same chanting style.

"An Anglo Saxon fable becomes universal," murmured the drama aficionado.

"Good tune," defended the veejay.

The final scene commenced. Aditya walked on stage, followed by members of the crew. They circled around Uma and sprinkled haldi powder over her head. Uma flashed into a series of kung fu movements, directing the director and the crew to move imaginary bits of furniture, let down curtains, wash the floors and help the actors with their outfits. Then without warning, she suddenly ran into the wings.

As Hamlet lay dying and Horatio made the final speech, Uma swung through the stage on a rope, scattering bits of glitter and confetti on their heads.

At the end of the final scene, incense sticks were brought in and lit around Uma as she froze in the pose of a deity. The houselights came on. Aditya bounded into the crowd. The audience collapsed around him in argumentative relief.

Uma stood alone on stage peering around. Her hair was still full of haldi. As she looked this way and that, sprays of powder fell to the floor and lay there in patches next to the burnt-out incense sticks. One of her bangles tinkled to the floor and broke.

Silently she stood in a sari with haldi powder in her hair, Hamlet's father's ghost in Shakespeare's play, thinking about Sam and wishing he was there.

He had occurred in so many recorded histories. His literature and history stretched back through centuries. Other people had done the work for him, written books about him, built his great universities and looked after his languages. She just hung in an odd new morning, without any help from her past.

She had made herself ridiculous in this play. But was it only beyond the ridiculous that there was the hope of an escape from the dominance of Sam?

Madhavi and Deekay got to their feet. Deekay hoisted Mira on his shoulders. Dhruv and Zahra clapped enthusiastically. Then Zahra signalled to Madhavi. *Come.* Dhruv's hand was on Zahra's waist, her hair waved near his neck. He stroked her back and cupped her shoulders, but his eyes stayed fixed on Madhavi. She felt scruffy and chaotic confronting their sleek sexuality.

"And who is this?" Dhruv asked Madhavi loudly, frowning at Deekay.

Deekay looked young and untidy too in his *Windhoek* T-shirt with a baby on his shoulders.

"Oh, hi. Dinesh Krishna," said Deekay, extending his hand.

"At the university?" asked Dhruv shaking it.

"Sort of. Working on my doctorate."

"The great Madhavi Iyer on a date with a student?" Dhruv cackled. "Snatching from nurseries again? Hunting in the paediatric ward?"

Zahra, caged in Dhruv's grasp, leant forward from the waist and tickled Mira under the chin. Madhavi gave Dhruv a look of mature superiority.

"Did you like it?" he shot at her.

"Like it?" Madhavi's voice rose. "It was apalling. The ghost was gross, to say the least." Dhruv and Zahra converged fluidly into another embrace. She whipped behind him and grasped him from the back, as a pillion rider grips her biker. Deekay bounced Mira threateningly on his shoulders.

"I thought, in fact," ventured Zahra, "that it was trying something new."

"Rubbish!" said Madhavi, giving her a stern look. "There's a thin line that separates dishonesty from creativity and in this case the line, to my mind, was crossed. Particularly in the character of the ghost."

"I thought there was tremendous imagination in it," said Dhruv. "Innovation's a good thing. Throws up new questions."

Here's the undoubted parting of ways between us, thought Madhavi. You've thrown in your lot with your muscles and your Body and your fancy clothes. You've accepted the eager endorsements of anything that is anti thought. The hip-talking, off-with-the-old-on-with-the-new swagger and the rowdy, hey-it's-hot-hey-it's-big attitude that governs all our lives.

If it's famous it's okay. If it's shocking, it's even better. If it's not serious, it's the best. The more foolish and idiotic it is, the more creative. I know about it. I live in America. But I'm resisting this disease. Still clinging to hope that there will come a time when the calm and quiet will return. When virtues like good sense, courage, patience and anonymity will not be considered boring.

She looked at Dhruv standing opposite her with Zahra in his arms and remembered one of his parties in his room in Oxford. Amidst the drink and noise, she had kept on trying to talk to him, pull him back from the arclights, trying to tell him, somehow, how sometimes in the cold of her nights, she missed her mother.

But Dhruv had been excited by all sorts of ambitions and pushed her hand away. Please Madhavi, stop being boring. He wanted to travel, he had new ideas about his life and his place in the world. He was discovering so much about himself. An educated Indian. A D.Phil. from England in a country of peasants. An excess of words in a language too few understood. A colonial education that hadn't taught him to love his people but to cringe away from them. Come on, didn't she want to think about all this and meet new people? Why did she always want to stick with him? He just couldn't understand her. If he tried to be nice, she was rude. If he tried to leave her alone, she was rude. She was always rude!

She had called him a shallow attention-seeker. He had rubbed his eyes, shaken his head and said he simply didn't understand why she always found fault with him. Why the hell did she always make such hurtful derogatory remarks?

She couldn't have told him why.

So disdainful. I knew it, he smirked. She fancies herself as a lone clay lamp flickering in the neon. The last outpost of dreary good sense. So happy about yourself. You, the repository of everything that is good and true. You use us to show how different you are.

We're all thoughtless and shallow. You're a person of depth and substance. Cotton. Lamplight.

"People with brown skin," she said firmly, "don't have to be outlandish circus clowns just because they want to reinterpret themselves. We can be normal, you know."

Deekay pushed his hair back from his eyes to get a clearer frame of her. She was fearless and fantastic.

"Ah, but who's definition of normal, madam?" smirked Dhruv. "Does 'normal' also mean being 'westernised'? We must create our own normalcy."

Madhavi brushed a trembling hand across her forehead. "Capering about in this foolish fashion isn't normal."

Her hands shook as she dragged Mira off Deekay's shoulders. Dhruv looked as if he would like to wring her neck. He turned on his heel and walked out of the auditorium. Zahra tugged at Mira's cheeks and followed him.

Madhavi stood very still. Mira twisted on her lap and held out her arms towards Deekay, bewildered with her mother's moods.

The sets were lit by a sharp yellow light, under the white domed ceiling. Shards of glass rose up from the sides of the wall.

She knew he would be waiting for her when she got back to the Habitat Centre and told Deekay that she preferred to take a taxi back alone.

Sure enough when she got to her room, Dhruv was walking outside, looking angry and windblown, saying he wanted to talk to her. He sat on the sofa in tense silence, paying no attention to Mira and waiting impatiently for Madhavi to stop feeding her.

He told her how much he loved Zahra. The simple fact of being together was a repudiation of ugliness. It was a retreat to a room on whose walls Mughal miniatures were arranged next to Tanjore paintings.

To exhibitions of Islamic art and Ashokan inscriptions. That was the world he had chosen for himself and Zahra. The world where she would be safe. The world where he was her protector. He would slay any dragon who dictated that he could not fall in love with this beautiful precious woman.

Madhavi felt as if he was beating her raw nerve endings with a hammer. Was he accusing her of being a dragon? Why was he trying to impress her by his love for Zahra? So he was faithful to Zahra. She would have expected nothing less from him.

She had never been happier in her marriage. Peter was a kind husband and made her feel perfectly at home. Dhruv said whatever had happened between them was part of the past, it could never resurface again because he was far too committed to Zahra.

What did he mean, she asked angrily. What could he mean? How dare he say anything about the past? She didn't care for him. She never had.

And now here they were pitted against each other in this race for a job. It was very important for him. It was very important for her. He didn't think the Foundation should be a sacrosanct millstone. Someone had to get out there and sell it.

She said packaging everything into a screenplay was dishonest and cheap. Jesus, said Dhruv, throwing up his hands, what's wrong in popularity? Popularity, she snapped. Popularity at any cost, even if it means whipping up stupid good-looking lies which promote illiteracy and do no good to kids. Sure, what does it matter as long as it makes you popular, as long as your ratings grow?

He said he would appreciate it very much if she wasn't rude in public, particularly in front of Zahra. She said she wouldn't dream of upsetting Zahra. Zahra had been *her* friend before his. Zahra was *hers*.

Did Zahra know that he had written her a letter? That he had come to see her here alone? That he was here now?

He turned away. He said he was sorry if he upset her but she had been so aggressive that he wasn't able to help himself. She had always been aggressive with him. Ever since he could remember.

Anyway he must go now because Zahra was waiting. She asked if Zahra knew that he had taken her to the play only because he had known that she, Madhavi, was going to be there?

She said she had read his letter. His phrases seemed not to have progressed from his college days. He glared at her and left. She touched her cheeks and found they were burning.

She could only bear his company if she was able to pierce his buoyancy with ridicule and spear him with cold insight.

They had always been mortally wounded by each other. Nastiness had been their only admission of weakness.

Uma refused Aditya's invitation to go out with the cast and took an auto home feeling nauseous. Panic sat in her stomach like a sleeping dog. The play had not eased her into a new comfort. She hadn't found any lost treasure. In trying to be an Oriental ghost in a Shakespeare play, she had ended up becoming a joke.

The cultural tangle was becoming a giant pain in the backside.

The light was still on in Sam's room. She pushed open the door and went inside. Sam was sitting up in bed writing something. As she came in he hurriedly pushed the papers under his pillow.

"Hey," he said, "how did it go?"

She flopped down on the chair opposite him.

"I wish you'd been there."

"No. Forgive me. Do you mind? Jai was very anxious for me to go with him to St Columba's."

"I hope the meeting was useful for him," she said bitterly.

'Jai'? He now called him 'Jai'? 'Jai' she thought fiercely. Constantly crying off plans to be with Jai Prakash. Laughing when Jai Prakash called her Uma*devi* and making fun about the fact that she couldn't speak any language other than English. 'Jai' this and 'Jai' that.

He couldn't see how she had been torturing herself with the king's ghost. He didn't feel sorry for *her*. He couldn't care less that she had made a fool of herself. Jai Prakash had a monopoly on his sympathy.

"Just as well I was home, actually," Sam smiled suddenly. "Your friend Mrs Khurana called."

"Mrs Khurana?"

The last thing she needed was Mrs Khurana. The poor soul was probably calling from a public booth. Perhaps her husband was dying and she didn't have enough money for the hospital. Perhaps she needed a loan or wanted Uma to ask Shantanu to put in a word for her somewhere.

"Yes, her secretary called, that is. From the Aladdin."

"*Her* secretary?"

"Yes, she wants to hire you."

"*Hire* me?"

Mira was crawling towards a phantom cat and Madhavi was sitting at her laptop, trying to prepare discussion points on Dhruv's paper, when the baggage handler knocked on her door and delivered a letter.

She turned it over in surprise. That's funny. A letter? In the evening? Peter's handwriting. But she had been speaking to him regularly on the phone and he had even sent her e-mail last night saying that the leak in the floor had been repaired. Perhaps it was an urgent document.

My Darling, the letter began. He loved her and Mira deeply and always would. But Madhavi had stopped communicating with him for so long. After the baby was born, she had locked herself into a world in which he hadn't been able to enter. She had not stopped to even look at the beauty of the countryside during their driving holidays. She had shown no interest in the house they were thinking of buying in the country.

She had changed. Almost stopped speaking to him. She didn't seem to delight in their time together at all. And her strange desire to take a job in India. She had walked out with no satisfactory explanation. He simply did not understand her. Hadn't understood her for a long time.

He had become lonely. Did she recall meeting Tina Mathews, from China Studies? Tina and he had decided to move in together. Of course, he would give Madhavi all the financial support she needed and she could keep Mira. He wouldn't dream of tearing the little one away from her mother. He was mortified about this letter, he just could not have faced her.

He would continue to love her father, those holidays in Bangalore, he would treasure those times always. He would pick her up at the airport when she came back to New York and they could discuss things. But his mind was made up and *could* she please forgive him, please *would* she forgive him.

He was wretched, he couldn't believe this of himself but he couldn't lie to her, she had been such a good wife, so true. Something about her that was so untouched.

But she must surely admit to herself that perhaps she didn't really love him anymore. And he did have a right to his own happiness. Hugs to beloved little Mira-mine.

She tossed the letter away involuntarily and fell to her knees towards Mira on the carpet. Two letters so far, she thought with insane clarity. One from Dhruv last weekend, now one from Peter. Will there be more? Will there be one from Mira too, cutting off their relationship?

She rushed into the bathroom and looked around aimlessly not knowing whether to pee or brush her teeth. Would Colgate renew her somehow? Would it show the way in a teeth-snapping, advertisement smiling sort of way? She felt faintly sick but was too paralysed to drink water or do anything about the nausea. Then Mira cried out and she rushed out again, wrenched her up and joined her chin with the baby's round jaw.

"Mama-lulu!" Mira twisted out of her lap and fell back on the floor. She threw her colouring pens into the air and launched herself at her mother. Madhavi pitched onto the carpet and pretended to die, clutching her stomach in pain. Mira gurgled and slapped her mother on the face. She gathered up a ball of spit in her mouth and prepared a projectile.

She poured a box of non-toxic coloured rings on Mira's head and dangled a chocolate in front of her nose. Mira rolled onto her back and became a puppy entangled in knitting wool.

There was that one balmy evening when she had wandered with Peter through an open-air concert in Lincoln Plaza watching eager couples pirouette to a soaring orchestra. "When was the last time you people *danced* together huh?" the MC had screamed. All these boom economy riches and yet the island isolation in that billboard bright street.

The partners, there for each other, woman needs a man, man needs a woman. Times Square with the pantheon of mythic advertising: America is a victim of its own myths she wanted to scream at Peter. You cannot walk down Broadway without the entertainment industry nipping at your ankles, inviting you to pay for immortality. You can't sit in a sextime, night-time bar without hearing the plaintive cry from every darkened booth, "Who'll love me, who'll love me?" And you, Peter are a victim of my myth. Me, your amazing wife.

Peter had put his arm around her and asked if she would like a drink. But she had felt listless and sunk willingly into deep disenchantment. Yes, the phrase was deep and the phrase was disenchanted.

Peter used to be curious about how neatly and gracefully she was able to fold away her legs when she sat on a chair. He had paid her the nicest compliment she had ever received. "Your bosom," he had smiled at her gently, "is the loveliest thing I've ever seen." She had been entranced at how pure he had made her breasts sound.

She felt an irrational rush of goodwill towards him.

What media occurrence can guide me now in my future actions? What are the options that the paperbacks and movies provide? What does a woman who has received a letter saying her husband wants to leave her, do?

Should I plunge into despair and drink myself silly, wake up in the morning in another man's, in this case, Deekay's arms? Or pack my bags and take the next plane back, and fall weeping at his feet, pleading for my child's future? Or spend the evening in dim loneliness, listening to sad songs while a panoply of images cross my mind about our life together. Or perhaps walk in the park and let the wind ruffle my child's hair? No, none of the above.

Mira played with her rings. "Mama!" she suggested. "Nomanee, nomanee."

No, tomato*kutty*, money wasn't a problem. Mama was an empowered woman, with an education and a job. And Daddy would be generous, she was sure about that. In many ways, Daddy was the best guy in the world. Perhaps he had known all along that her decision to apply for a job in India with or without him was a milestone. A milestone which had zipped by without her noticing the markings on it.

I've painted myself into a corner with my memories and my baby. I rattle around all over the world by myself with my baby. I watch Sunday afternoon families while I sit with my baby on my lap, filling her space with food and toys, but no people. I go to book launches, drinks parties and lectures. But I never go to births and deaths. When was the last time I went to a funeral, for God's sake?

It's my fault, of course. Everything inevitably is. I pushed Peter away. I made him a victim of my post-natal patriotism. Poor guy. He must have been pretty bewildered by my hangups, how I would pounce on him if he ever pronounced my name wrong or couldn't remember which state I was from. And if he missed even a single nuance of Indian politics, I would pour White Male Guilt all over his ice cream.

She had met Peter in Oxford at a dinner given by the Black Jays, a group of South Asian women. Peter had come with his then Sri Lankan girlfriend but spent the evening chatting with Madhavi. After the dinner he had sent her a note saying how impressive she seemed to him, he couldn't believe that she was from India. She hadn't responded to the note at that time. She was too busy being awful to Dhruv.

After she completed her doctorate, she had looked for work in India for months, but after being assigned to a room which was to be shared by three other new lecturers, without a computer or a salary to buy one, she had flown sheepishly to America, and bumped into Peter again at the house of a common friend. He was teaching East Asian studies at Columbia and helped her get the job she now had.

She sometimes — only sometimes — admitted to herself that perhaps she had married him in the first flush of the realisation that home was a professional precipice.

Peter had treated her like a delicate symbol of his committed liberal politics. He took her to Democrat rallies and proudly introduced her around. His friends were delighted to meet her and she was so grateful for his protectiveness that she dismissed the hidden conditionalities attached to his aid. There was nothing wrong with a little pampering, she told herself, even though it made her feel like the Elephant Man.

She couldn't blame Peter. How could she when he admitted so disarmingly that for someone born and brought up in India, she was 'amazing'.

Bangalore had receded into a holiday destination. What could he — foreign policy analyst and China expert — have possibly done in India anyway? The last time they had been to Bangalore he had been scathing about the power and water cuts. No wine, no money, no public transport, no fun. He was sorry to say that this was not what he wanted out of life.

She gathered Mira up and laid her on the bed, swiftly changing her pampers and pushing on a pair of shoes.

She needed to go out. She had to get out and walk among people. Her mind was like rapids on the Ganga, white water mind, an ice-brook raging over whirlpools and sharp stones.

She would ring Peter in the evening. He would be abject but steely. She would rush to fill the distance. Yes, she too had been conscious of a certain winding down. Yes, she had lived more and more within herself these last few months. Recoiled at sex. Forgotten that he didn't eat red meat.

She picked up Mira's bag, swung it on her shoulder, heaved up the fold-up pram, and placed Mira on her hip. Come on, gypsy child. Come with your nomad mama.

She decided to see if Deekay was home. Whoever laid down that life happens in straight lines, from point a to point b to point c was wrong. Life happens in circles, or triangles or squares, not straight lines. Progress need never be a straight line. I can go backwards and still have improved.

She ran along towards the taxi stand. Deekay's lights were on, faint music filtered from his flat. She jumped up the stairs two at a time with Mira jumping on her shoulder.

He was working on his computer. She sat tremblingly on his bed while Mira played with his computer and said she had come over because she had just read about the leukaemia afflicted girl who was not being allowed to sit for examinations in a Calcutta school.

They discussed the issue until Mira fell asleep and Madhavi said she should be heading back, she had a phone call to make. But instead of Peter, she rang her father in Bangalore.

"Hello, Appa."

Her father sitting on the balcony in the tea planter's chair that he had splurged on after his retirement. He would have eaten his frugal meal by now and finished watching the Doordarshan news. He didn't trust the new cable channels and still read the Reader's Digest. When he went to bed later, his rubber sandals with the single band across the toes would flip across the neatly wiped cement floors.

When she went home, he would put on his Frank Sinatra and Harry Belafonte records and light a Tortoise mosquito coil so that she wasn't bothered by the mosquitoes. They would laugh about the routinely unsuccessful *arangetram* preparations of the Swaminathan's daughter next door. Anjaiah would bring in plates of curd rice. Her father would offer to order a vegetarian pizza from the newly opened Domino's if she wanted. "No, thanks Appa," she would say, "haven't had *thayir sadam* for a while."

"Ah, Madhavi. How are you, *kanna?* I just can't wait to see you."

"Okay, Appa. How are you?"

"Carrying on as usual. Everything all right with you, my dear?"

"Everything all right, Appa. How's Anjaiah?"

"Anjaiah?"

"Yes."

"Are you ringing me up to ask about that fellow?" Her father chuckled.

"Yes."

"He's," her father sighed, "giving me a lot of trouble. A lot of trouble. His drinking habit is pronounced. He has no sense of time, and on top of everything, he is not taking care of the car. Has a bit of blood pressure also, I think. Today, he took the car *just* when he knew I needed it. He..."

She cradled the telephone next to her ear, listening to his quiet voice. Anjaiah wouldn't be too exercised over her divorce. In his hometown, he would say, it happens all the time. Men leave women, women leave men. Rangamma had three sons but did that stop Murugesan from leaving her for a girl old enough to be his niece? Anjaiah would just go back to his tea and dismiss her sorrows as easily as his lifetime of slavery. Poor Anjaiah, with the thin arms and stooped shoulders, sitting alone in his outhouse with his philosophies and his beedis.

After she had put Mira to bed, she sobbed as loudly as possible about Anjaiah.

Mrs Khurana not only owned the Aladdin but lived in a new double-storeyed house in Delhi's Vasant Vihar where diplomats' Dobermanns patrolled hushed walkways. Mrs Khurana's Cowley Road stall had only been a small business on the side. Mrs Khurana was rich.

Mrs Khurana, the sad affectionate immigrant, needed Uma's sympathy as badly as Indian women needed fertility pills.

Mrs Khurana beamed broadly and hugged Uma tightly and informed her that she had just received an invitation to a gala reception at the Mahatma Gandhi Foundation that was to be held two weeks from now after the name of the new director had been announced. Mrs Khurana had promised to make a small donation to the Foundation, as a duty to her homeland.

But now, could Uma please help her aunty? She had hired a young girl for her sales promotion for the Diwali season but the girl had backed out at the last moment. Mrs Khurana said that they had planned a special show for the festival season, now that Diwali was almost round the corner and could Uma please step in? Uma nodded absently. Mrs Khurana called all the department supervisors around her to announce that Uma would be the new shop assistant at the Aladdin. Arre guddi, it is zyour shop. The future belongs to zyou zyoung people.

This was Mrs Khurana's plan. Uma was to wear different types of Indian fancy dress and stage a few dance performances. Could she do that? One day she could emerge out of a clay jar like Aladdin's genie. At another time she could be a Rajasthani folk dancer, hopping among plastic sand dunes. Then a turbaned Scherehzade reclining on a Persian rug. Or a North-eastern basket weaver. *The Aladdin Diwali Show!* Just for this season, that's all. Mrs Khurana skipped with entrepreneurial adrenalin. Please guddi. Please. You'll help me na? Gazing at her kind tear-marked face, Uma simply couldn't refuse.

The Aladdin was well-equipped with costumes. Rows of outfits —dancers from Rajasthan, Baul singers from Bengal, a Kashmiri flower seller, a Delhi nawab, a South Indian prince, a priest, complete with sacred thread and wooden sandals — hung expectantly in a little anteroom at the back of the shop.

Every day Uma could choose what she wanted to be. In the store room she would find cardboard oceans, tinsel palms and foil paper stars which could be dressed in the window according to Uma's needs.

As if these pleasures were not enough, Mrs Khurana would bring photos of Gurleen to show her. Oh, what fun we will have, guddi.

She strapped her dupatta to her waist and hugged Uma repeatedly. Uma thanked her and walked quickly out of the shop wondering what her grandfather, the late S.N. Bhattacharyya, star of the Oxford Union would say.

What would he say if he saw her frozen on one leg in a shop window? What would he say to Mrs Khurana who, with her v's that sounded like w's and her s's that sounded like y's and her nylon salwar kameezes and her rexine shoes, was far kinder and far richer than the late S.N. Bhattacharyya could have hoped to be.

Uma began her job at the Aladdin. She struggled out of a giant amphora clad in shimmering veils, silk pajamas and a turban, while the shopping crowd gasped admiringly. This girl is from a wery good family, Mrs Khurana told the transfixed visitors. A *student* from Oxford Zhuniversity, no less.

She surveyed Uma's thinness, maternally pronounced that she must eat paratha and achar in the mornings and brought her tiffin boxes of food every day. She even offered her a permanent position as a professional buyer for the Aladdin after the fancy dress show contract was over.

She could work as part of Aladdin's managerial staff, decide on new products, and be based in Delhi. It would be of such help to Mrs Khurana. It was so difficult to find young people of taste and education these days. Think about it, beta.

But Uma was too distracted to think about jobs. She simply breathed reflexively at pictures of the heroin-thin Gurleen and bought gifts for her parents and Sam with the money she earned, saying to them that she had friends in high places nowadays.

Sam looked more alluring than ever. There was a faint beard on his cheeks and since he wore T-shirts all the time his body perpetually dominated her vision. His face was growing more ardent by the day. His eyes didn't flit anymore, but moved, under their forests of eyelash, deliberately from one object to another.

Misri had told her that while Uma was working at her job the Englishbabu spent all his time with that black man from UP. So black, shuddered Misri, the same colour as dadababu's shoes. Misri was an impoverished Brahmin from a village outside

Calcutta. I may be poor she told Uma proudly but my skin is as pale as a queen's.

One evening she asked him again about Jai Prakash's work.

"I've told you," Sam looked surprised, "he runs a tutorial programme. It's called Shiksha Andolan. He sends reading material to people. He calls them Study Packs. Anyone can subscribe. He's a little unsure about his plans, though. All over the place. He needs to sort out a number of things before he begins."

"Begins?" asked Uma after a pause, "begins what?"

"His...school."

"But he's using you!" she wailed. "You've taken him to St Columba's. You've given him Felicity's number. That's more than enough. You needn't do more."

"Oh, what the hell, " he shrugged. "I'm going to earn a lot of money soon. Helping rich people get richer. Helping rich people buy more things. Helping rich people help other rich people."

Oh no. Sam had cast Jai Prakash in the role of the saviour. Uma tore at the dry skin on lip and felt along a craggy ridge.

"Sam, for God's sake!" she almost screamed. "You've been completely brainwashed by that fraud. Believe me, there are lots of people like him here. Lots. Godmen, fakes of different kinds, all beneficiaries of Poverty Incorporated. I can't believe you've fallen for this."

Sam laughed. "Well, maybe I'm using him too, Uma. Maybe he's," Sam narrowed his eyes, "useful for me too. For mah dogma, man! Me and mah dogma."

He rocked backwards with an imaginary electric guitar and fell to his knees in an impromptu rock concert.

"He does need a bank account and a spread-sheet, though," he said, getting up.

"For what?"

Sam's eyes dropped over his aquamarine pools. "For his work. He needs to make it more systematic."

"He's just an ambitious careerist," she snapped.

"Like me. I too am an ambitious careerist."

Sam's smile, when he was happy, could be magical. It lit up his face and transformed him from a grave Mohican to a good-looking playboy. She suddenly wished she could stage a drinks party on a freshly mowed lawn in which he could skip between circular tables holding a tennis racquet.

He said he must go in search of draft beer. If he ever lived in India, he said, he would have to arrange a wholesale supply of booze. The lack of bars in Delhi was becoming a trauma for him. He seemed to be in a very good mood.

She was about to turn off the light and go back to her room when the telephone rang. It was Jai Prakash.

"Ah, Umadevi" said Jai Prakash. "*Aap theek hai?*"

"Haan," she said guardedly.

Jai Prakash chatted for a few minutes, asking her to accompany Sam to his house sometime, saying he hadn't seen her as much as he would like to. "Sambhai pampers you too much," he said.

"But I have my own work," said Uma defiantly. "My own job."

"He will miss you," he said suddenly, "if you don't join him."

"Join him?"

"Join him in his work. He's very scared, Umadevi. Too scared."

"Who?"

"Sambhai. Of you. The word is...how you say...terrified. He's terrified of you. And I keep on telling him that he should not be terrified of you. Why should *he* be scared of *you*?"

"Terrified of *me*?"

"I also was surprised too. But...ah...how you say...the word was...'intimidated' and 'terrified'...that is what Sambhai told me."

She couldn't believe him. Incredible that Jai Prakash actually expected her to believe him. Had Sam, six foot two and omniscient, actually confessed to being intimidated by *her*?

The thought seemed to her so ludicrous that by the time she got to her bedroom she had convinced herself that Jai Prakash was simply cracking a slimy joke, which he would no doubt, laugh about with Sam later.

But for the first time, as she lay in bed that night, she let her fantasies become uninhibitedly carnal. Sam and her and miles of dissolute beach. And nearby, Jai Prakash being slowly devoured by a rare breed of shark.

11

Jai Prakash and Christine drove to Bharatpur bird sanctuary in his red Maruti.

Zahra and Dhruv went to Nimrana Fort in Rajasthan, but were too turned on to admire the restoration of the medieval fort with the stony walls and the rough steps, and spent forty-eight hours in bed.

October wound on beautifully and the first crackers began to burst with the imminence of Diwali. The afternoons were warm and deliciously alcoholic. The evenings were balmy and hectic with dinner parties and gambling. The Delhi Gymkhana card rooms were packed. Card parties stretched into festive early mornings. Friends and Contacts exchanged baskets of fruit and boxes of pistachios, cashewnuts and almonds, cut-glass vases and even carpets. Nothing like the festival of lights to establish new alliances, jettison the outworn and start a new company. Maybe.

Lodi Garden was *en fete*: the tombs glowed happily in the sun and the grass grinned. Even Lajpat Nagar looked dirtily radiant.

Madhavi and Deekay played with Mira and went out to restaurants where Madhavi only ate dosas because she said for some reason she had developed an aversion to anything resembling a hamburger. In Madhavi's voice, the plaits with the ribbon at each end were coming loose. Deekay had realised that something wasn't quite right when she had come to his flat that night, pale and trembling. Even he, Deekay had deduced, wouldn't be as moved to a personal crisis about the girl with leukaemia as she seemed to have been. No, it wasn't the cancerous girl in the newspaper. It must be something else.

He had rung the next day and asked if she was all right. She said she wasn't. Since then Deekay cooked for her, played with Mira, let her ramble on about her life with Peter and said admiringly that she gave him hope for his ancestors. But she seemed restless, kept twisting with Mira's flaxen hair and whispered to him disjointedly about her marriage and childhood.

When he went to see her one afternoon at the Habitat Centre, he found that her eyes were red and she was still in her T-shirt and track pants. Mira's face was smeared with porridge and chocolate. Her pampers hadn't been changed and she smelt of potty. Madhavi had been up all night typing out ideas for a future book. But this morning they all seemed idiotic and she had deleted them. So, she said laughing breathlessly, she had nothing to show for her night's labours.

Deekay put his arm around her and suggested she send an e-mail to Columbia asking for a sabbatical. She seemed mentally exhausted.

She did. They wrote back saying they could discuss it further if she could suggest a replacement for her position because there had been a great deal of interest in her course. She replied that she would try to think of some names.

She had begun to dread the seminar next week and the announcement of the name of the director of the Gandhi Foundation, that would follow.

She was losing hope about the job. Dhruv was clearly the director designate. Pamela had left most of the organisation of events in his hands. It had been his job even before she arrived. She should have known that she didn't really have a chance.

She had seen Pamela walking in Nizamuddin, swinging her cane, holding the heavens at bay with madness. Madhavi had studied her for signals, wondered if the grimaces between her wrinkles were nasty or kind.

"Pamela*di,*" Madhavi had drawn her pram alongside her. "Hello ma'am. *Kemon acchen?*"

Pamela's hair was pulled neatly at the back as if brushed down by someone else. She leaned heavily on her cane and peered for an autorickshaw.

Pamela dressing up to see *The Importance of Being Earnest* in London, reading out passages from *Gora* and *Ghare Baire* during supervisions. Her music collection, S.D. Burman and Edith Piaf.

The 'correct' accent: when Pamela most disliked someone, she would call him 'bounder' or 'knave'.

"Pamela*di*, my husband is leaving me," said Madhavi addressing her bent back. "He's met someone else."

There was no answer from Pamela. She continued to peer at the dizzying road where tractors, bicycles, trolleys, horse-drawn carts and buses were trying to cut a path through her stomach.

"I've been packing all day," burbled Pamela, "I've had no time to think."

There was no break in the wall of insanity. She hadn't opened any doors. Pamela coughed. Her jaw slid sideways, her eyes blinked several times, her mouth became slack then her lower lip curled cruelly towards her nostrils. But just as Madhavi was about to turn away, Pamela said:

"The same thing, as you know, happened to me. Not exactly the same thing. He died. And I was left alone."

Madhavi stopped short. Pamela's presence was like a puddle of water on a plastic sheet, as unpredictable as an amoeba. The liquid amnesia in her eyes was daunting but was it real?

An auto screeched to a halt next to her. A cyclist shaved past. Pamela walked shakily towards the auto.

"It's not a tragedy," she said firmly, "Untimely death and incapacitation are life's only tragedies. This was only," she climbed in with the driver's helping hand on her upper arm, "an inconvenient necessity." She squinted out at Madhavi through her heavy eyes. "As you get older, you know, you separate things out. Put things in their proper place. Tidy up."

Felicity telephoned to say that Sam's official appointment letter had arrived from McKinsey's. He was firmly in. Apparently they had been so impressed with him that they had agreed to place him in London even though there was a more urgent need in San Francisco.

Now, he said to Uma, sounding strangely unmoved, a shockingly wealthy job awaited him after he went home, awaited him in a fancy apartment and a fancier car.

Uma whooped with loudly concealed disappointment. His future was bright but more perpendicular to hers than ever. Of course he would join McKinsey's. He would join McKinsey's and come to India once a year for his favourite interesting holiday. With Jai Prakash.

That evening a huge bouquet and box of chocolates arrived from Jaspreet and a bottle of champagne from Kamini all of which Sam dumped in a taxi and took over to Lajpat Nagar with a note saying, '*For Jai and Christine. Love, Sam.*'

Shantanu and Anusuya looked pleased too. To celebrate, said Shantanu, let's go out for lunch on Sunday.

They went to Pickwick's at Claridges. To the memorabilia of nineteenth century England. Colonial lamps hung above smoky pork chop sizzlers like phantom emblems conjured up above a druid's cauldron.

Anusuya wore a pale chiffon sari with a powdery purple bindi, her shining pageboy hair dancing around her cheekbones. Her heavily blackened eyes flicked disdainfully around. Her head revolved loosely on her neck, as if secured only by a slender tissue which could snap at any moment. Her black enamel cigarette holder dangled between her fingers and she blew smoke into Shantanu's face at regular intervals.

Shantanu perched thoughtfully next to her, carefully holding a glass of beer. Several comparitive administrative problems between India and England crowded into his head. Bars, as existed in England, of course would have to be policed in India, and then there was the question of licensing.

He had already pointed out triumphantly to Sam that even England had not dispensed with the Official Secrets Act.

Across the glasses and plates of food, sat Uma and Sam.

"Well, here we all are," said Uma.

Her accent had been a gymnast for the last two years, walking high above the heads of Sam and her parents, taking care not to fall either on one or the other side. Every word if not adequately supple could do untold physical damage.

"Interesting," said Shantanu, cutting a potato into two halves and waving one half at Sam, "how rivers are cleaned in your country. The last time I was there I noticed how the river, you know, the one with the punts going about, was being dredged."

Sam smiled and was about to say something when Anusuya interrupted.

"River?" she cried. "You think those were rivers? They were not rivers. They were nalas. Drains, small sewers. In our country," she said inhaling hard and addressing her gin, "this is where you see rivers. Real rivers."

"Hasn't the Ganges always been rather dirty, though?" smiled Sam.

There was a pause.

"It used to be," said Shantanu. "But it's being cleaned. Some people are trying. It's dirty because of the ghats. The burning of the flesh. From the bodies. Hindu custom."

"Our family has suffered at the hands of the British," introduced Anusuya loudly, "no family has suffered the way ours has. My father and grandfather were beaten by lathis by them." Tears glistened in her eyes and she blinked rapidly, her eyeliner smudging her lower eyelids.

Uma looked urgently at Sam.

"Jai Prakash tells me," Sam sipped his beer, "that a caste apartheid — he used that word — exists in India."

There was another long pause.

"In some ways, yes," said Shantanu.

When Jai Prakash and Christine had come to dinner, Anusuya had said Jai Prakash was obviously a very good man because being an Untouchable and so low caste, he still managed to smile, wear decent clothes and talk politely. Uma remembered Anusuya's mother Kamala, the jitterbug queen of the Calcutta Club, whisper *'scheduled* caste' into her husband's ear when being introduced to a particular politician.

"But it was *not*," said Anusuya, rolling her eyes, "as if the British ruled over *anything*. Who were the British? Just a small number of puny people. They were only there because we let them be there, that's all. And the minute we got tired of them, we threw them out. Quit! Quit India. That's what we said." Her pallu fell down from her shoulders.

"The empire had nothing to do with me," said Sam uncharacteristically loudly, "My family was never upper class enough to participate in it. Could I have another beer?"

"Please don't talk so rudely, please," whispered Uma while Sam was trying to attract the attention of the waiters.

"Why?" cried Anusuya in Bengali. "Did you hear how he said he hates me because I'm black?"

Shantanu ate in silence.

"Ma," pleaded Uma, "he never said that."

Two glasses of beer for Sam and a gin and tonic arrived for

Anusuya. Sam drank beer like busy office goers in Connaught Place hurriedly downed quick swigs of raw coconut water.

"All the British were involved in the empire," intoned Anusuya. "They're trying to cover it up now in their films and books. They still don't know how we all suffered. They don't know about the Bengal Famine."

"Castes," Shantanu said to Sam, fluttering his fingers on the wooden table, "have been an unfortunate part of Hinduism."

"I have no doubt that Hinduism is very spiritual, but it doesn't seem very rigorous," said Sam.

Shantanu smiled conspiratorially to himself. Anusuya's eyes misted over again.

"My father," she declaimed, "used to cry when our national anthem was played. He used to stand up and cry. He was a member of the Congress until he died. One day he was beaten by a British policeman. He was only a child then. After that beating my father joined the Congress."

Uma drank some water. "Shall we go for a film this evening?"

"Hinduism," said Shantanu indulgently, "is the opposite of, say, a religion of the book. Complete opposite. It relies, you see, on personal evolution."

"But that seems to me," Sam lit a cigarette and inhaled deeply, "its main flaw, if you don't mind me saying so. It refuses to accept that the human being, in himself or herself, is simply not good enough. That's probably why there's hardly any Hindu political theory."

"Why? What is the reason, in your opinion?" Shantanu stared suspiciously at a herb and separated it out carefully from his food.

"Well, from what I've read of Ambedkar and Gandhi, Hinduism has suffered because of its castes. It has suffered because knowledge was monopolised by the priest. Knowledge was used to maintain old privileges and not to create progress," said Sam.

Anusuya's head rotated on its single tissue. It fell to one side, then jerked up again, only to roll back to the other side.

She replaced her cigarette in its holder, using only the tips of her long painted nails. Sam lit it at once. Anusuya threw her pallu over her shoulder and ran a trembling hand across her forehead so that her bindi became a jagged pink stain.

"Do you want Uma to convert?" she asked suddenly.

"Ma," said Uma urgently, "please!"

"That's up to her," Sam's eyes were bright.

"I wonder," said Shantanu talking to an absent Cabinet committee, "if you have ever taken the time to peruse the *Panchatantra* stories. There are some English translations, I believe. Excellent political and moral fables."

"Will you," asked Anusuya, reaching for her drink, "put pressure on her after the marriage?"

Uma glanced at her mother's handbag. A medium-sized leather bag, worn down to its last layers, patches of white poking out through the black cracking skin. The zips were rusty and the flaps frayed. Only the central clasp gleamed bravely.

"We're not getting married, Ma," soothed Uma. "There's no question of us getting married."

"Why not?" demanded Anusuya turning on Sam, "why is there no question of you getting married? Do you not want to marry a black person, is that it?"

"I didn't say it," said Sam looking down at the table. "Uma did."

"You have a different religion!" Anusuya shouted, her teeth drawn across her face. "It's not the way we live. You can't understand the way we live. You live in a different way! Look at the amount you drink all day."

Now, that's rich, thought Uma. Drinking is surely the one area where there is complete understanding between cultures in this particular case.

"I just said I'd like to know a little more about Hinduism." Sam's eyes flashed, "That's all."

Anusuya's hair swung out angrily towards him.

"Then why don't you go back to your Book?" she shouted. "Go back to your church. Go back to all your angels and devils and blood. All that foolish stuff. It's all stupid. Don't dominate my daughter. I won't allow it. I know what it's like and I won't let it happen to her. I won't let you dominate her!"

Sam looked up slowly from his glass. Uma saw a red stain leap up from his chest towards his temples. His eyes were arctic green caves.

"You're just very spoilt!" he cried, his voice shaking. "Why don't you have the sense to see what's going on in your country? You're fucking disconnected, you lot! You're just piss-artists, leading a fucking privileged life."

There was a catastrophic silence. The plates of food on the table looked apocalyptic. The fish and chips were smothered by a mayonnaise ice age and rained on by a primal hailstorm of boiled peas.

Uma felt Sam breathe heavily next to her. Shantanu continued to eat, curiously unconcerned. Anusuya's food was untouched but she had drunk three gin and tonics. Uma was sure she would take her Valium this evening.

Anusuya gathered up her bag and pallu, which had become entangled in an intricate knot and rose like a flock of geese rising up from a lake.

The pallu and bag had become a single menacing entity. As she threw the pallu viciously over her shoulder, her bag rushed up behind her and knocked the back of her head.

"I'm not staying here," she announced. "I'm going."

Uma sighed and looked helplessly at her mother. She only looked as if she was having lunch at Pickwick's. In fact, she was marching with Gandhi's satyagrahis, marching to the sea to defy the colonial salt tax and whip up indigenously produced salt.

Poor Sam. How could he possibly know that Anusuya had invested him with the same authority as Irwin the Viceroy and was reacting to him with only natural rebelliousness.

Sam's face was scarlet. He buried it in his hands.

"I'm sorry. That was unforgivable. I'm sorry. Please forgive me."

But Anusuya was already meandering out of the restaurant holding her cigarette aloft, tightly bound in her bag and pallu.

Uma turned to Sam. "Don't worry. She's bananas."

"She's always been unstable," explained Shantanu. "Come, let's just carry on."

Sam remained standing, looking at his hands. Shantanu and Uma looked at each other, then back at Sam. He was still flushed. He pursed his lips. His eyes were sad forgotten lagoons enclosed by eyelash forests.

"I can't believe I said that. Please forgive me."

He ran out, leaving Uma to sit with her father who smiled slyly and said that it would appear that her English boyfriend had met his match in her mother.

Sam ran up next to Anusuya as she sailed down the stained marble Claridges lobby.

"Anusuya, please don't be angry," he said breathlessly. "I'm very sorry. I'm very sorry if I upset you. Here, let me help you."

He bent to pick up Anusuya's bag which had fallen to the ground. Her hair was askew. Her bindi was crumbling and pink powder sprinkled the bridge of her fine nose.

Anusuya frowned at him. She tried to pass him but he blocked her passage.

"Please let me take you home."

"NO!" she screamed.

Sam ran his hands through his hair.

"I won't be able to live with myself if you didn't forgive me.

I've never met anyone like you before. But you haven't given me a chance. Ever since I arrived you…"

"What?" she demanded.

"You've treated me like a piece of shit. I don't understand why."

Sam walked around her. She staggered a little, turning her eyes away from him. Her eyeliner had spread all over her eyelids. Sam got a taxi at the hotel entrance and pushed himself in after her. By the time they got to Lodi Estate she said if he was really sorry why didn't he go down to the INA Market and buy them some fish for the evening meal. Sam was relieved to be given this task and sped off.

Sam loved the INA market, although he didn't dare to tell Uma in case she accused him of being a slave to exotic India. The ground ran with acidic rivulets of blue-green liquid and rough muddy stones dirtied the bottom of his jeans. Urchins flew at him offering road maps, pens and ganja but Sam knew the ropes by now. Not everything I do has to be 'West' eating up 'East', for God's sake, Uma, he muttered to himself, shaking off the little boys. Give me a fucking break.

Indian markets seemed so well digested by time. The wares they dispensed were like well-gurgitated food, churned over centuries to their present form, containing much more than simply plant and animal extracts but also disparate pieces of human civilisation. They proved so casually that mighty empires were encrusted by grime at the edges; that the thrones on which kings sat were not any less grand because they were smutty and frayed; that rituals of purity were lined with shit; that rare herbs were stuffed into dirty fingernails. Like the human body where organs beat in healthy perfection through the blood and the mucus. Like Anusuya in whom beauty festered under layers of powder and oil. Whoever said that perfection had to be clean? The need to be neat must place a limit on the human genius, thought Sam wildly.

By the time he rushed back to the house with the fish Anusuya was changing her clothes in her bedroom. Sam stood weakly in the kitchen exchanging remorseful sign language with the cynical Misri who snatched away the fish, smelt it, wrinkled her nose and slammed it under the tap. As she washed and shook the fish dry, she gestured in the direction of Anusuya's bedroom and loosened the nut in her head. Sam relaxed a little.

After an hour Shantanu and Uma arrived and Shantanu insisted it was time for some chai. As they drank in silence in the living room, he informed Uma and Sam that his single expectation from Anusuya was that when she died she'd make it quick and convenient. If for example she had walked under a bus outside the hotel there would have been terrible complications with death certificates and passports. The hotel management would have to be informed. God knows how many documents would have been required.

Anusuya wandered through presently in a printed kaftan, smelling faintly of attar and gin, on her way to the kitchen. She examined the fish, pronounced that it wasn't of bad quality at all and began to cook, shouting over the sizzles to Misri that she would never get used to an English son-in-law. Uma peeped in to see if Anusuya was all right. Her mother whispered to her that on the way back from the hotel, Sam had called her 'wonderful' and 'unbelievable'.

Sam came into the kitchen. He leant against the kitchen door and looked out at the small row of cauliflowers set among the clothes lines in the vegetable gardens, and said that if Anusuya didn't forgive him, his feeble Western stomach would revolt and he would be ruined by a severe dose of food poisoning. That made her laugh her sly and kittenish laugh. She tucked her face into her chest, looked up with amoral eyes and giggled the way schoolgirls do when another girl drops food down her uniform. She laughed with ghoulish delight at the thought of Sam's Delhi belly. Sam watched her laugh at his impending destruction and thought that she looked like Kali herself.

Misri smothered fish pieces in haldi and chili, rolled her eyes and muttered under her breath that she didn't know why she worked in this degraded house where they invited shudras for dinner and drank alcohol all the time. Anusuya seemed excited. Her eyes were bright and she cooked furiously, pushing at Misri and opening bottles of masalas and chutneys at the same time.

At last the fish of peace was cooked and left to simmer. They sat in the living room together, trying not to listen to Misri's imprecations about the household and how sinful it was. Shantanu buried himself in an old issue of *The Independent* magazine, Anusuya painted her nails, Sam chain-smoked and Uma said that the legendary Ikram Gilchrist was delivering a lecture at the new Mahatma Gandhi Foundation tomorrow evening. Anusuya immediately said she would like to go.

"Ikram Gilchrist?" inquired Shantanu looking up from *The Independent* magazine. "What do you know about him? Better that you spend the day watching video."

"I'll take you, Anusuya," said Sam quickly. "I'll take you to the lecture if you want."

"But Uma's mother," said Shantanu, grimacing towards Sam, "won't enjoy the lecture. She can't read books or take lectures in the right spirit."

"I've read all Ikram Gilchrist's books," said Anusuya loudly.

They watched television in silence. Then Sam rose, saying he needed to take a shower and phone Jai Prakash. She drove me to an edge that I didn't think I was anywhere near, he said to Jai Prakash, running his hands through his hair. I lost it completely. Be calm, Sambhai, advised Jai Prakash. And don't drink too much.

They ate Anusuya's delicious fish stew for dinner cooked with badi, brinjals, palwal and young bananas. They ate in relief and studied amnesia. Only Anusuya said charmingly that she felt much closer to Sam now that they had had a good fight. Gusts of smell escaped from her hair.

From this point onwards, Anusuya's every wish became Sam's command. He would have broken off the dome of the Rashtrapati Bhavan if she wanted. Or agreed to buy her fish every day from INA market. He felt as if he could turn a somersault of relief in her forgiveness, as if he was pulling down the burning rags of an anger that had begun in Badayun, with a cool Excalibur. Through it all, Anusuya was unfailingly elegant.

As she placed her holder gingerly in her mouth, he lit her cigarette and looked at her as Neil Armstrong might have gazed on Planet Earth from the moon, with wonder and a strong sense of discovery of her power over him.

"You look very beautiful this evening," he whispered to her.

In his bedroom that night after the meal, Sam put his arm around Uma's shoulders and leaned his head against hers.

"*My* mother's my problem too."

"Oh, really?" She was uncertain about this conversation.

"She's an ex-hippie, you see. A Third Worldist. The Seventies' notion of Western groupies of the Third World. I've never agreed with people like my mother who apologise indiscriminately. Apologise all the time. Apologise for being guilty. Apologise for being Western. Apologise for things that happened without my vote or consent. My mother's favourite phrase is, musn't be *Western,* darling. But I've always argued that I *am.* I *am* Western."

Uma hadn't thought of it like this before.

"Of course you are," she said in surprise, "you should be."

"Yes, but my mother says I shouldn't be. You see, for my mother being Western is the same as being almost evil. But I've always argued that I should be free to say what I like and don't like. I've always felt that's more honest."

"I agree," said Uma.

He squeezed her closer to him and sighed. "Oh God. Ewe-ma, Ewe-ma, Ewe-ma," he whispered.

She felt her cheek against his chin. The familiar unbearable electricity started in her knees and abdomen. Could she just turn and leap on him, just grab him anywhere she could? No, he might shrink away in defeated alienation.

"You must hate me for what I said."

She sat still in his embrace. His breath still smelled of beer from the afternoon. He had never called her 'Ewe-ma' before. He pulled her even closer and pushed her head down onto his shoulders. Her conversation with Jai Prakash crowded into her mind. Here she was in the bosom of her parents while he was all alone, trying to make sense of it all.

"She was being horribly rude to you, Sam. I know how provocative she can be."

"D'you despise me, Ewe-ma? Sometimes," he laughed helplessly, "I feel that you loathe me."

She was too surprised to speak.

"Loathe you?" she asked at last.

"You feed me so much crap. I can tell. I'm not an idiot."

But would he be able to take the real her? Would he be able to absorb her into his experiences? Would he understand that when Shantanu read the *Times Literary Supplement*, it was a bulwark against all sorts of unknowns. That if Anusuya decided to embrace Absolute Values, she would have to kill or maim others on the street.

Uma shifted away.

"It's complicated, Sam."

"Why, Uma? Why is it complicated?"

Uma felt along her lower lip. There was an unknown valley in it.

"Because..."
a) You're white and I'm brown and I treasure your language
b) Your ancestors created my family
c) It would be easy for us to think bad things about each other
she didn't say.

He held her by the shoulders and looked down into her eyes. "It isn't complicated," he said.

"It isn't for Jai," he said again after a pause. "Jai's on top of it."

Uma leaned around to kiss him on the cheek. As she did so, he pushed his hand inside her hair and twisted his fingers around her scalp, as she had seen film stars like Michael Douglas do when trying to convey destructive passion. She felt his hand on the small of her back and around her waist. She felt him edge towards her buttocks but he pulled away immediately.

OH NO! she yelled in silent horrified disappointment. He kissed her forehead. She got up and ran out.

Could it be that he was just as scared as she was? Could Jai Prakash have been right?

She walked back to her room feeling strangely excited. She rang Jaspreet.

My mother, of all people has pushed us face to face and made it all raw. It's almost as if we're much closer, somehow. But still no kiss. No kiss on the lips. And I wish he wouldn't keep mentioning the word 'Jai'.

But Uma, protested Jaspreet, this is a little unfair on you.

Sam sat up with his diary, writing eloquently about Uma's beautiful face and limbs and the sweet smell of her body and her long athletic legs and her unaware little girl sexiness.

My beliefs and my reason for living in a particular way, he wrote, and the choices that I've made in order that we build something that would endure, help us face what will be a difficult life together.

But without love, without commitment to love, or an admission of love, can there be a future? Or should I simply leap into the unknown without knowing what her feelings are except for the worries about losing herself to me and everything I'm supposed to represent. I had thought that we both knew what culture was and how to deal with it but we don't appear to. This is agony.

And Anusuya, Sam wrote, was even crazier than Felicity. A brightly coloured Bird of Paradise with her bottles of medicines and booze. A woman strangely free of any artifice. A woman made of earth.

The famous writer Ikram Gilchrist flew into Delhi from Mumbai to deliver the inaugural lecture at the Mahatma Gandhi Foundation. A few tourists at the Taj Mahal hotel craned their necks curiously as Ikram's black Mercedes pulled up outside the hotel. His face looked familiar.

Ikram walked through into the hotel lobby, frowning. He had the lengthy grandeur and the white sharp-boned face of his Parsi mother and the piercing navy blue eyes of his Anglo-Indian father. He tapped impatiently on the reception desk with a long blue-veined hand.

"Now, my little behnji locked in a Rajouri Garden hovel with Rohtang Pass fantasies of hill rolling Bollywood," he said, "do me the kindness of freeing yourself from long socks and oily plait memories and send me to my haveli. Later, after I've walked again in the city where I once wept and spat, we might talk about your Sachdeva Travels tourism in Simla."

"Yes, Mr Gilchrist," smiled the receptionist. She was young and dark with long foxy eyes. Her hands were balled into fists on the counter. They looked, he mused, like hooves. A jackal-girl. A juvenile she-devil.

"I hope you'll enjoy your stay here, Mr Gilchrist," she said.
"Thank you," replied Ikram.
"We are all fans of yours," she said insincerely, tapping on her computer. "Although you don't write books about…" she bared long yellow teeth, "people like me who live in hovels."

"Please," he held up his hands, "Don't say that. I know it's not true. Let me burrow back to my homes in Lonavala in the Western Ghats, and on the Isle Of Wight. The former, a Hindu forest, where the river runs even in summer, past the villas of witty scions. The latter overrun in short spells by sailing girls and sailing lads at weeks of Cowes, but basically, a pensioner's retreat of elderly observant affluence. In such deathly ease, I have grown unaccustomed to the mercury of celebrity. Please don't abuse me. Leave me the space to crawl away to my room and pout into the mirror of my writer's block. I pleased you all once. But I can't anymore. Let me saunter," he hunched and turned away, "Quasimodo in dullness, inappropriate, nowadays, for viewing."

"How well he talks, na," whispered a diamond-studded lady. "Even though he's no more what he used to be."

The receptionist smiled. Her smile was wicked and her eyes flashed. Does she fly around on her broom at night, Ikram wondered.

"Your room's ready, sir," she said, "please go with…the boy."

The bellboy scurried up the stairs with Ikram's three identical black bags. Ikram plodded heavily after him.

In his room, he peered at the curtains.

"Silk," he deduced. "Silk, that great myth of the Occident," he sighed at the bellboy. "Blinded horses fighting through medieval blizzards taking this fabric to the Victorians, steeds on the Taklamakan desert, ferrying their dreadful merchandise to uncaring royalty. Silk, skirting the descendants of the Golden Horde, circling the Great Gamers, the steeds pressing ever forward. Samjhe?"

"Ji sir," agreed the youth.

Ikram paid the bellboy and gazed down towards Shah Jahan Road.

Ikram's first book, *The Death of Zarine Naoroji* written about his mother's life in the days when Napean Sea Road in Bombay (before it became Mumbai) and the Congress party were still fashionable, had become a sensation all over the world. So had his second book, *Park Street*, set in Calcutta during the days of dancing in Trinca's and listening to Pam Craine croon at a bar called Mag's, about the Anglo-Indian ladies of Calcutta in their tiny printed dresses and plump legs stretched out in rickshaws travelling to New Market for their bread and cakes. Since then he had won several literary prizes, created two successful screenplays, one about Mohammad Ali Jinnah's last days, the other about a feudal dynasty in Rajasthan, written a couple of defining essays on world politics and had received a Padma Bhushan.

Clinking glasses on chiffon-clad evenings overlooking the Arabian Sea or sipping a dry Martini at eleven o'clock at the Bombay Gymkhana bar, or eating Chicken Tetrazzini at Sky Room in Calcutta wearing paisley silk shirts and suspenders, he had once been charming and brilliant and always made sure he remembered everybody's names and faces. He had rushed between India and England several times a year, a pivot of the Indo-Anglian chatter.

But for the last ten years, inspiration had deserted Ikram. He seemed unable to tear himself away from base camp, now becoming crowded with more energetic climbers. His twenty-year marriage had begun to falter as he examined every physical and emotional experience for novelty.

He lived in fierce seclusion in the hills near Bombay most of the time and his little house on the Isle Of Wight when it became too hot in the Ghats. He had travelled on the Silk Route, visited the West Bank, jostled in the evening arti at Kashi Vishwanath temple in Varanasi, read about the legend of Roopmati and Baz Bahadur on a trip to Mandu, studied Inuyet carvings, lain on a beach in the Algarve, smoked incessantly on an Alaskan cruise, tried to create a Japanese rock garden in his home in Lonavala, but with no success.

He had even thrown away his computer, blaming technology for separating the primeval self from creativity. He preferred to write long hand anyway. He tried to write an article on the dictatorship of technology but instead found himself plaintively describing how all imagination was being knocked out of him by the computer and the microwave. He wrote a complaint about the rise of religious fundamentalism, but it was indistinguishable from a routine editorial. He had come to the cynical conclusion that the world was full of unhappy people trying to make each other meaninglessly happy only because they wanted more and more money. His deepening misery had not spurred his genius.

Instead, his critics had begun to snigger. The great Ikram Gilchrist, they had said, had finally lost it.

He tried his hand at a sci-fi thriller called *Rahu, the Last Spaceship* but it bombed. He wrote a proposal on a television serial called *Kalashnikov Kali*, based on the growing number of female terrorists in the world but it was rejected by Channel Four as too 'patriarchal' and 'mainstream' in its viewpoint.

As he stood looking down on the Delhi streetlights, he was a white-haired wizard with a sharp chin. He wore a long black achkan, closed at the neck, embroidered with gold thread along the sleeves. Under it he wore a white churidar and mojris with spotless white socks. Around his neck hung a thin iron chain with the characteristic skinny dancing figures of Bastar.

Educated in the same private schools as Uma, Dhruv, Madhavi and even Shantanu and Anusuya, Ikram, at sixty had been quite shocked to receive the letter from Dhruv inviting him to deliver a lecture at none other than the acclaimed Gandhi Foundation.

He had, at the time, been thinking about how he might dignify his retirement. With amused maturity or perhaps portly relaxation? He had even contemplated starting Buddhist chants to provide him the peace of mind which he needed, to face the fact that no one wanted to listen to him anymore. Dhruv's letter had taken him back to the old days.

He unpacked his suticase and arranged the books he had brought with him from Lonavla, above the television.

They came when he was sleeping and took away his *Hobson Jobson* and two volumes of his *Hindu Manners and Customs* by the French traveller the Abbe J.A. Dubois printed at the Clarendon Press in 1897.

Ikram rang the police in the morning. They barked that there was nothing they could do and could he please understand that the communist party was protesting about the fate of under-trial children in Tihar jail, a group from Calcutta were staging a demonstration against another planned wedding at the Victoria Memorial monument, and they simply didn't have time for rich people's whims about books.

12

As the day of the seminar and the announcement drew near, Madhavi felt her heart push into overdrive every now and then and began to find it difficult to sleep. There was no way of knowing who would win. Pamela was giving nothing away.

She brushed her hair while she waited for Deekay to pick her up for the Ikram Gilchrist lecture, looked at the amount of hair that had come off on the brush and decided she only had a few good years left.

She decided to wear a sari and leave her hair loose instead of bunching it up at the top of her head.

She studied her reflection. No, not the sari and long hair. She looked black and mad. She pulled out a pair of brown pants from her suitcase and matched it with a white sleeveless shirt. Better. She painted a line on her forehead, but rubbed it off. Mira snorted and fell back on the bed in disgust.

She tried on her high heeled closed shoes but rejected them as too formal. The kolhapuris were casual but undergraduate. She rifled through her suitcase, feeling panic-stricken at her own ugliness. The lines around her eyes and the droop of her mouth made her look thick and plodding.

Mira uttered a sharp 'toffee' bark.

Stupid, awful hideous child. Shut up *shut up*. She picked her up, threw her back on the bed, pushed her on her side and shoved a milk bottle in her mouth. Mira looked up at her through petrified eyes and pushed the bottle away.

Madhavi ignored her and went back to scrutinising her shoes. She opted for the last remaining pair of sandals, but they were shiningly black and looked too eager. They would also make her look taller and she had always been self-conscious about her height. Dhruv used to pull her shoulders back and tell her not to hunch.

She had been speaking to Peter on the telephone almost every day. He was being loving but distant. He cared for her and Mira deeply and always would. They had memories of such good times. Those summers in Bangalore: 'Beautiful.' 'Important'.

Peter loved building immortal remembrances and legend from trivia and nonsense, she thought unkindly. What holidays in Bangalore? It had only been two years ago and she had been sick and pregnant.

But for Peter they were Memories with a capital M, the stuff of grand emotion. She felt angry at him for being sentimental, bitchily told the mirror that Peter was so immature that for him a drive to the chemist was suffused with historical photo-ops.

There was a knock at the door and Deekay came in. Mira cried out at the sight of him and held out fat arms. He swung her into the air and rubbed his head on her stomach. She laughed approvingly. Don't trust mother! her eyes shouted. Mother's a traitor! She flung her arms around his neck and pressed her little rear admiral face next to his beard. I'm mad about you, darling, he told her. Madhavi gathered up Mira's bags and lifted the fold-up pram from the bed in quick preoccupied movements.

"Let's get out," she said.

"I've never actually heard Ikram Gilchrist speak before, eh, is he still as famous as he used to be?" he asked.

"There was a time," she shrugged, stashing a bottle of milk into her bag, "when he was everybody's hero. But I think he's a bit past it now."

They walked downstairs. Mira, safe on Deekay's shoulder, flung a scowl at her mother. Stretching across Lodi Road, outside the Gandhi Foundation, a waving banner announced, '*Ikram Gilchrist inaugural lecture!*'

Dhruv was standing at the entrance in a dark suit, waiting to welcome Ikram. Zahra stood next to him, stunning in a green sari with flowers in her hair. Behind them, the lecture room was packed and television crews spilled onto the pavement.

"Quite a crowd," said Deekay in surprise.

"Oh that's just Dhruv's doing," Madhavi grated back. "Nothing to do with Ikram."

She felt plain and dirty. She wished she had worn a sari, instead of this tatty white blouse. Whatever she wore, Zahra always made her feel badly turned out. Zahra's fingernails were fresh and cool, she kept little tissues and mints in a small black purse and she always smelt of an after-dinner liqueur. Madhavi's untidy haversack contained crumpled papers, rubbery toffees, crumbling bits of tampons and pens that didn't work.

"I called you after the play but your answering machine came on," said Madhavi accusingly to Zahra.

Mira spread her hands behind her, she was Supergirl on Deekay's shoulder. Zahra ran a hand along the globular cheek.

"Choti bachchi baby," crooned Zahra. She would much rather talk to Mira than Madhavi. "Do you know how naughty your ammi was when she was tiny?"

Mira shook her head as if she didn't want to know and beamed toothlessly. She became a hang-glider, her arms stretched back. Then she opened her eyes and asked what do you think of that. Deekay leant his head on her stomach and carried her over to the back rows.

"Little, little baby," babbled Zahra. "Come. Come to me."

"Your bearded friend seems to be in a hurry to get a seat. Never heard the famous author speak before?" drawled Dhruv.

"I was hoping we could spend some time, Zahroo," said Madhavi, ignoring him.

"Baby, baby, hello baby."

"You must be nervous," Dhruv tossed his head, "about Pamela's decision."

He slid his hands around Zahra's waist and down towards her bottom, but his eyes stayed on Madhavi's face. Zahra arched towards him, her breasts brushing his tie. He pushed his hips against hers. She lifted her arms slightly to give him a better grip.

You're using her, she thought jealously, using her to assure you of your exceptionality. Using her to make a statement about yourself. She's your victim, not your lover. I'm banal, the same as you. She gives you your multicultural halo.

"I don't think it's going to be me," she snapped, moving away.

The long room with the white polished floors was packed with people. Rabindranath Tagore's portrait looked marginalised on the wall. A podium had appeared below it.

A television crew filmed the poster of Ikram pasted outside the centre. Journalists huddled together. Academics brushed unwashed hair from library-stained eyes. Silk-clad socialites with bouffant hair, careless intellectuals, women in Sonia Gandhi chic — handloom silk sari and string of pearls — fashion designers with crew cuts and queues of students. The ubiquitous machine gun flashed between the guests as they were put through elaborate security checks just in case any one of them specialised in assassinating authors.

Pamela sat in the middle of the front row in a grey silk sari with a thin gold border, a scarf tied around her head, holding her cane like a drawn sword.

Uma, still wearing her Aladdin costume sat a few rows in front of Deekay thinking about Sam's lips that hovered only a few inches above her head. She watched his chest rise and fall, the dark hair near his neck. She glanced up at his eyes, the aquamarine seas were calm as he looked straight ahead towards the podium.

This was their festival time. Sam's body seemed constantly by her side. The air was scented and every day could bring something new. She hadn't torn at her lip for the last twenty-four hours and the edges of skin had sunk into soft pink sponge. She sat between Anusuya and Sam, looking forward to every minute.

Five minutes after the appointed time, Ikram's Merecedes drew up. The tourists and students gathered outside began to whisper and rush to their seats. Inside, the audience fell silent. Tourists stood up and craned their necks. Academics applauded civilly. Madhavi settled Mira on her lap.

Ikram stepped smilingly out of the car and put a paternal arm around Dhruv who was beaming at the door. He walked down the aisle, with Dhruv in tow, but stopped when he spotted Anusuya. He bowed. Anusuya smiled back uncertainly.

"May I introduce, the one and only Ikram Gilchrist!" shouted Dhruv, looking around the audience. "He needs no..."

Ikram dashed a silencing hand on Dhruv's shoulder and ran up to the podium. He stared at Anusuya's gleaming mop and huge bindi in the middle of the audience for a few seconds then began his lecture.

"Ladies and gentlemen," he smiled, "I crawl, cur-like, from continent to continent, furious for genuine joy. I am squeezed in McDonald markets where suggestive popular tunes imply that one shouldn't worry but remain happy. My name, for what it's worth is being trampled on by the bloodhounds of the young. But I still submit to you The Savage Child."

The audience clapped. The tourists whispered. Anusuya reached into her embroidered pouch for her cigarettes, having failed to see the No Smoking sign.

"When the earth cracked, a child emerged," he cried.

A hush fell over the audience.

"The child," he continued, "lay on the moonscape, writhing in agony at its birth. The fallopian tubes of imperialism clawed at its breath and the blood of past conquest gushed from its eyes."

Ikram closed his eyes and shivered as if a chill wind had just blown through the room. Deekay straightened up in his chair. Mira sucked her thumb.

"It had two heads you see," complained Ikram, "One stared deep into its own belly where the bile of injustice and poverty churned. The other looked outwards where the icy pines stood cold and arrogant against a grey sky. The two-headed child began to grow, to feed on the thorns that were scattered near its mouth by the pines when they shook with an ostentatious zephyr."

"Surreal," supported Dhruv from the back.

Sam pinched Uma's hand.

"Very naked," said Zahra, leaning her head against Dhruv's shoulder.

"But wait!" cried Ikram suddenly. The audience froze. "The child has found a plaything. What does it hold between its stump-like hands, to feed itself, because no force in that yawning landscape of the imagination will come to its aid?"

"Shhhh," said Dhruv, to a group of whispering students. "Ikram doesn't like people talking at his lectures."

"It has found a vacant uterus," shrugged Ikram in wonderment, "In this uterus of the epochs was it born, and it is this uterus upon which it will feed. It will feed upon its own shelter to grow...to find...to seek...the sun."

Suddenly there was the sound of loud coughing and a blowing of the nose. Then a loud sneeze, another bout of noisy honks and a phlegmy clearing of the throat. Then a loud spit-gurgling hawk. Ikram stopped.

"Er...which member of this gathering is impatient with the life of a bloodied child?" he inquired politely.

The audience looked at each other.

"Let me participate with you, whoever you are," Ikram's gaze swung along the rows.

A bespectacled man raised a hand from the back rows.

"I am sorry, sir. I am sorry," said Jai Prakash.

Sam clutched Uma's palm and shifted in his seat, turning to look at Jai Prakash.

"Oh God," Ikram put a hand out as if trying to staunch a flow of blood, "what a voice. The voice of the shepherd god, blue-skinned Krishna, in his milk republic of seedy politics. Where are you from, sir?"

"I am from Uttar Pradesh, sir. Please forgive me," said Jai Prakash. "But I also studied in Ox-phord."

"The state of noble dissent now ruined by stultifying poverty. Still chained to the commas of imperialist discourse, it reminds me of the miserable prurience of the Indian state spawned by the dvija in 1947," Ikram said to himself.

"I am from Sahaswan in Uttar Pradesh, sir," said Jai Prakash again.

Ikram slammed a hand on his white mane. "Has the Capitol been breached? Have the cowherds streamed into the citadel leaving dung in the footsteps of the sages? When Oxford becomes Ox-phord," he mimicked, "does one assume that the *demos* is finally upon us in all its demonic size?"

The crowd began to shift and look at each other. Uma felt Sam blush and become tense. Dhruv and Zahra giggled.

"Sit down, sit down please," said Ikram. "Ox-phord. Ox-phord. I ask you! Nehru's abode in the plains has diseased beyond belief. Tractors and carts cross the civil lines into debased plebeian dictatorship."

The audience turned to look at Jai Prakash. Ikram made mock-supplicatory movements.

"Vaat arre vyou doing, saar," he mimicked. "I'm gnaat underyisstanding, saar," he mocked. "The language, friends, of the sad swarm that has ruined speech as we know it. Paan-English. Chai-English. Vai you are interrupting my shitting, saar? Wort for are vou gnat giving me munnie, saar? Vai you are not signing on my bum, saar?" Ikram shuddered.

"Excuse me, Mr Gilchrist," Madhavi's voice was tightly plaited and she was on her feet.

"Yes?" Ikram whirled.

"Spoken English often need not impede learning or erudition, Mr Gilchrist. And I'm sure the gentleman here didn't mean to interrupt. I don't think he deserves such vilification."

"You're right, of course," Ikram smiled. "Of course, you're right. I have no right to vilify. Curse me for it. But," he leaned forward on the podium, "I believe, madam that sometimes some of us shouldn't *be* right. Some of us should be wrong do you understand? We have the duty to be wrong. To be wrong is as important, as it is to be right. Do you understand what I mean? Let me argue on the side of what is wrong, while others like yourself necessarily, uprightly and quite correctly, uphold what is right."

The audience began to talk. The bouffant settled her hair and sari.

"You see, Madam, refinement and aristocracy are bad words nowadays," Ikram cried out over the murmuring. "They have been dumped in a dustbin overflowing with junk food wrappers. We must all bow to the dung people as they sweep away our hard-earned country. But! Let there at least be the great But!"

Madhavi frowned into Ikram's eyes across the rows of heads.

"I just don't think you should judge the gentleman so harshly, Mr Gilchrist. There's no need to be hurtful and so personal."

"Good God, Madam," said Ikram boxing his own temples, "must I be molested by the idiot swarm in the few hours that I am among you?"

The audience began to talk louder. Ikram made an open-armed gesture towards the heavens as if to say, part the clouds, ye gods and let a shaft of sunlight descend. There were a few disinterested murmurs. Ikram's gaze turned back to Anusuya. The embroidered cloth pouch hanging from her wrist fell to the ground.

"Not a very compassionate line of argument," said Madhavi, sitting down. Ikram waved in her direction.

"Ah, my interlocutor retreats," he smiled, "in the face of my aged spleen. Right," he continued, "Apologies for that little foray, ladies and gentlemen. Back now to the Savage Child."

Madhavi shrugged at Deekay. Jai Prakash turned to look at Madhavi from the back of the room.

"It, the child, that is, has gnawed. It has slavered over the tissues which once sheltered it. It has eaten up the fluids of past legends and the skin of holy scriptures. Now it rises, speaking in a series of tongues, advancing, retreating, growing, towards the moon, which it must remove from its universe in order to find the sun. Will the child die, child?" he asked suddenly looking straight at Uma. "Tell me."

"No, sir, it won't," she shot back.

"Correct," smiled Ikram serenely, "the child won't die. But wait..." he held up a thin arm and pretended to hear, "what is this?"

"What?" murmured the stricken crowd.

"Mahisasura," introduced Ikram.

"Who?" whispered Sam.

"A demon, sort of a folk symbol of evil," said Uma.

"Mahisasura crushes the giant child's skull," said Ikram performing what looked like a slow Taichi sequence. "The child, falls to the bad earth. Far away the cold arrogant pines chortle.

"Mahisasura is strong. He detaches one of his ribs and slices the child in half, it lies severed in two unequal parts, writhing, bloodied. Far away the pines turn their heads away, twirled in a rich cloud."

Ikram laughed cynically. He circled his hands above his head like a windmill. Then he lifted his head and looked at the crowd. "Who is this child's mother? Will no one call it their own? Who is its father? Yet!"

He leaned forward and looked at Anusuya again. She bent and scrabbled hurriedly for her little embroidered pouch with small cross-stitch flowers and shadow-work leaves, which had fallen to the ground.

"The sun dithers. A small rebellious ray will not let the child down. It pulls the bloodied bits of baby back from the crevice. The child survives on such a cold wasteland, lit by a small sun. The small weak ray is still there. But for how long?"

The audience was silent for a few minutes then broke into whispering, shuffling disgust. A few 'awful's' and 'bekar's' and 'waste of time's' rose from the students. Tourists got up and left and chucked a few scraps of paper along the aisles. Academics sniggered. The bouffant tittered.

Benedicta, who had accompanied Pamela shook her head from side to side in melancholic disapproval.

Ikram stood next to the podium, in his carefully chosen clothes, appealing to them to understand the sensitivity of his soul but they just turned their backs on him and left. His head began to droop downwards. Failure hung around him.

It was the failure that attaches itself to shabby old waiters with bravely starched coats and declining political parties with fierce, tattered manifestos. In his achkan and his carefully combed mane, his clean hands, his polished shoes, his Shakespearean accent and his records of Sibelius, Ikram was, in India, pathetically solitary.

He would sit in his carefully designed home, reading books that tied him to Western metropolises, elaborately trying to recreate a cafe in his drawing room that would have to be policed by security guards. He would employ a string of bent skinny cooks to toss him a European style green salad which he would eat pretending he was in Florence. And when the electricity went off, his achkan would drip with sweat and his starched shirt inside would have to be sent back to the dhobi to be redone again in the angrezi style.

And all around him a new India would hurtle and disco, and stake its burning claim to new freedoms.

And Madhavi looking at Dhruv felt a familiar fleshy sympathy for him. Which part of his Civil Lines heart, touched by gentle breezes across lawn leaves, still worshipped at Ikram's dusty pedestal? She had an image of him, handsome and sharp-suited but with his ankles chained to a wobbly post.

The crowd pushed out of the auditorium and conspired in small groups. Dhruv walked rapidly to Ikram as he stepped sadly away from the podium and started to thank him.

"Dhruv, dear," Ikram reached for Dhruv's hand, "Don't thank me. Me, the stubbly dog. But!" he said with determined cheerfulness, "tell me, who is that turbaned Calcuttan?"

"That's Uma Bhattacharyya," said Dhruv.

"Young lady," Ikram looked towards Uma, "Come here."

"Sir, if I could only tell you, sir, how much I admire you and er…sir…how much…er," stammered Uma, thinking how closely he resembled Saruman the evil wizard in the Lord of the Rings.

"A Bengali convent princess," ascertained Ikram.

"Yes sir, Bengali, sir, sir…how did you…know er…"

"I know everything," pointed out Ikram miserably. "That's my trouble. Unknowing eludes me. I yearn not to know. That's why I'm no good anymore."

He peered searchingly in Anusuya's direction. She was still sitting in her chair, motionless, apparently uncertain whether the lecture was over or not or which part of it to believe.

"And tell me, who is she that sits beside you?"

"My mother, sir," stammered Uma, motioning Anusuya to join them.

Anusuya rose from her seat and advanced towards them looking like a decorated cruise ship. The embroidered pouch flapped on her wrist like an old standard. Her face had been perfect in youth and Ikram saw it.

"The red scar across the forehead of the peninsula, searing through historical memory like a blood-soaked marker of violent epochs," breathed Ikram. "Madam, what are you but a pretty tragedy?"

Anusuya folded her hands in a namaskar. Her pallu was wound around her chest, its extremities bouncing under her chin.

"Beautiful," sighed Ikram. "A collapse of Bengal, her clothing in shreds, sinking slowly into the putrid bay of ideological compromise."

"Yes," said Anusuya confusedly, "we are Bengali."

"Bengal," Ikram uttered a sharp hiss of laughter, "from where the tributaries of sperm and the deltas of ovum, belch forth passport-seeking skinny legions that beat at the doors of an entirely European Union offering recipes for mutton korma."

"No, no," smiled Anusuya brightly. "Mutton korma is not a Bengali dish."

Ikram gave her a long look. The crowd boiled on the peripheries of their circle, craning to hear what the famous author was saying. Sam stood apart from them, talking quietly to Jai Pakash, with a hand on his shoulder.

"The slushy shops of Calcutta," mused Ikram bringing Anusuya's palm to his lips, "and the fly infested fish women ruining Rabindranath's songs with the thin voices of the inbred."

"Thank you for coming, Mr Gilchrist," said Dhruv bustling up and pumping Ikram's hand.

"No, no, Dhruv, dear. Don't thank me. I should thank you," said Ikram bending away from Anusuya, and turning a gimlet eye on Dhruv. "Bye Dhruv, my Mathur patrician. Bye, beautiful madam. I must go before I disgrace myself any further."

Ikram waved blindly at the scornful, hawking, hate-filled crowd and walked to his car, his head still bowed.

A Hyundai Santro whizzed by on the road. Under the front seat: *The Great Moghuls* by Bamber Gascoigne and the *Annales and Antiquities of Rajasthan* by James Tod and *History of India* in three volumes by H. Beveridge published in London in 1865.

Pamela rose slowly from her seat and reached for her cane. Madhavi, who had been explaining the Ikram phenomenon to Deekay, pushed through the crowd with Mira on her hip and touched Pamela's shoulder.

"He seems," she whispered to her, "finished."

Pamela brought out a lozenge from the depths of her sari and popped it in Mira's mouth. Mira demanded another.

"Find something else for your child," she croaked, fumbling in her blouse for another sweet. "Educate her. By the way," She raised her cane, "I'm glad you spoke up."

"You also would have, ma'am," said Madhavi.

Pamela waved her cane again and began to walk towards the exit.

"Bah!" she snorted. "All rubbish! I must ring Zerbanoo and tell her that her son is at sixes and sevens. I've never known Ikram to be so bitter."

Dhruv and Zahra came up behind them.

"Chatting up Pamela*di* again, Madhavi," sniffed Dhruv, "complaining about everybody again?"

Madhavi looked towards Pamela for support but the old woman was walking away, waving to no one in particular. As she walked unsteadily out, an unobtrusive figure came quietly up to her and unobtrusively helped her out of the depleted room.

"Why d'you keep putting everything down?" Zahra's voice rose.

Madhavi felt a hot irrational stain on her cheek.

"I've been putting things down?" she shouted, inappropriately, "I've been putting things down? What about you, Zahra? What have you been doing? Why this unnecessary crusade on Dhruv's behalf? What's in it for you?"

Zahra turned away.

Madhavi braced herself to look at Dhruv and the air between them became still. Flesh is incorrigibly neutral. Driven by dishonest chemicals. Fantasies crowded into her mind. Perilous rock face arguments, skipping teasingly away in a crowded flea market. Old friends. What has friendship got to do with any of this sudden hostile game? She snapped her gaze away. He marched out.

She looked down at Mira. She had been holding her so tightly that there were red welts on the baby's bare thighs.

Uma, Sam and Anusuya walked across to the India International Centre bar. Imagine the famous author actually talking to them, and kissing Anusuya's hand? And how did he know about them? Did you see how he looked at Anusuya? How strange that my poor little mother should attract the attention of the great Ikram.

There was a new spring in Anusuya's step. Sam had said she was beautiful and now, so had Ikram Gilchrist. She was suddenly at a New Year's Eve dance. In that large crowd, Ikram Gilchrist had noticed only her. He had looked only at her several times. Sam tried to hold her by the elbow to escort her across the road, but she shook him off and stalked ahead, with her nose in the air.

"The Sens," she flung over her shoulder at them, "have always been friendly with famous authors. My grandfather even went to a party once with Pearl. S. Buck."

Uma shoved her hands into her pockets. "Poor Ikram. He's had it."

"How so?" Sam asked.

"Because he's realised how irrelevant he is. That's why he attacked Jai Prakash. See, the British should never have let us happen. People like me, my parents, Dhruv, Ikram, old Sen, the director, we're the irrelevant Indians. The irrelevant Indians from Oxford.

"Jai Prakash. Mrs Khurana. They're not irrelevant. But my parents are doomed. And me and my friends will travel in small immigrant packs. Like Venu. Like Shravani-Rani. Wriggle into other peoples' histories. Talk in other peoples' voices. Dye our hair blonde and live other peoples' lives in other peoples' bodies in other peoples' countries. That's what'll happen to us."

There was a silence. Sam reached for her hand.

"But that's far too harsh, sweetheart," he said at last. "There's so much for you to do here. If I were in your place, hey, I wouldn't have a minute to spare."

He pulled her towards him but she pushed him away. On this stretch of the road, he couldn't help her.

13

At last the day of the first Gandhi Foundation seminar arrived: the big seminar and the big announcement. Madhavi felt tense and overwrought and Dhruv's pulses raced. Ikram was to attend the seminar too but he apologised to Pamela, saying he was not feeling well and left for Mumbai. Nevertheless, all the other participants gathered punctually.

As befitted a new Foundation, the L-shaped seminar room on the upper floor looking out into a line of gently playing trees had dispensed with the routine semicircular table with microphones. Instead it was decorated like a drawing room, suspended between a library and the Cottage Industries Emporium in New Delhi.

In the far right of the room roses and lilies shot out of a brass amphora. On the left corner two Khajuraho-style brass figurines writhed plumply. On lamp-lit armchairs, the participants chatted. Among them, eminence was a routine gasp.

As soon as Dhruv and Madhavi arrived, Pamela announced that someone called Jai Prakash was also to participate. Inspite of their nervousness, dry throats and thumping nerves, they were shocked.

Jai Prakash? The man with the vernacular accent and the awkward clothes, the target of Ikram's wrath and their sympathy? He was, apparently, known to Pamela. Pamela had put his name down on the seminar list at the last minute and decided that there was to be a third speaker. After Dhruv had finished reading his paper, and Madhavi had responded, Jai Prakash, Pamela declared, would also read a presentation.

But who is this Jai Prakash and why should he suddenly read a paper, Dhruv exploded. He had seemed like an uneducated fellow at the Gilchrist lecture. Oh yes, he had talked to him on the phone a few times. He had been harassing him for funds for his education programme. He had often telephoned asking Dhruv to arrange for some reportage on something or other. But why should he suddenly be included here? He has something interesting to say, Pamela had insisted. Madhavi was puzzled too. She didn't understand why Pamela had all of a sudden introduced this third soldier into what she assumed would be a battle between Dhruv and herself. They settled down in their chairs, shrugging and glowering, curious about Jai Prakash, angry with Pamela.

They looked closely at him when he walked in with Christine. Dhruv dismissively thinking about Uma's description of him and Madhavi with faint sympathy, thinking about Ikram's pathetically brazen snobbery.

Jai Prakash inclined his head towards Madhavi. Namaste, madam, he mouthed. Pamela, sitting in the armchair closest to the food table, waved him in and asked him to introduce himself. He said he was a 'humble teacher from Badayun'.

He was dressed in his usual neat trousers and white shirt. As he smiled and shook hands, his hair flopped over his glasses.

After her disagreements with Dhruv and Madhavi, Pamela refused to exchange pleasantries with anybody and sat in a shrouded world, eating greedily and trying to ignore everything around her.

On her right sat Zahra in a flowing white salwar kameez, keeping unobtrusively quiet. Zahra didn't say much at seminars — except laugh supportively at others' jokes — and was often designated note-taker whose job was to transcribe the proceedings and send copies to interested journals.

Dhruv sat next to Zahra. He was a seminar veteran who knew all the tricks. Keep the tone measured. Make a joke after a serious comment to win over hearts. Figure out who the main rivals were and vanquish them by summing up their views more pithily than they could.

He had reason to be proud. The lecture may have finished Ikram but it had been a media success. The audience reaction had only added to its exclusive appeal. *Gilchrist loses Muse,* the *Times Of India* had reported. *Famous author Ikram Gilchrist was humiliated today,* Star News television had gloated. Dhruv had filed a despatch for *The Republic.* 'Excitement at the new Mahatma Gandhi Foundation,' had been his last line. The seminar was just a formality now. Gandhi was already his.

He had made innovative love to Zahra last night. First slow and effortless, a bite here, a nip there, sudden squeeze of the pressure points. Her breasts had quivered towards the ceiling like upright kulfis and driven him to greater strength and passion, followed by a moaning sigh of mutual performance.

She had run her hands along his shoulders and tight stomach and said he looked like Roger Moore. She had bent backwards to let him write his name on her abdomen with his tongue.

On Dhruv's right sat Arunava Sinha, a pudgy historian from Delhi University.

Between Arunava and Madhavi sat Ian Stephenson from Cambridge, thin and pink with a North England accent and a goatee beard. Ian spoke fluent Hindi and was on his way to Bihar for a year to study political corruption.

Madhavi sat next to Ian, diagonally across from Dhruv, wearing a silk sari, her hair piled on top of her head and her haversack askew.

She had slapped Mira to sleep last evening, sat bolt upright in bed savagely marking and scoring out portions of Dhruv's paper. She had written furious notes and drawn silly faces along the margins. Perhaps you are unused to our ways, she mimicked, hasn't your friend heard a famous writer speak?

Everything that he had said to her at the Gilchrist lecture seemed unbearably insulting. She had written him a hurried long letter clogged with ironical hatred but torn it up. She had rung him on his cellphone at night but disconnected when Zahra answered. She had rung Peter too and disconnected when Tina answered. Why had Dhruv written her that letter about his problems with journalism? Did he think she cared? She *didn't*.

For the seminar, she had ironed and tied her sari in between milk and potty interludes, rubbed off brown tentacles from-God-knows-where that appeared suddenly on her pallu and called Deekay half a dozen times to screamingly ask him if he intended to keep his promise of picking up Mira for the morning.

She had bathed the child in water that was so hot that she had cried out. I'm *sick* of facilitating your life, she had told her, looking at the baby with hard eyes. She shook her so hard when towelling her dry that the little curls darted out from her head as if blown by a strong breeze.

Ghastly baby mewling all over my equanimity. I want to spend time on my intellectual *evolution,* and on my *clothes* but no, *you* come charging in everywhere. Mira had shrunk away from her, horrified.

When Deekay arrived, she had clung to him and averted her face from her raging monster-mother.

Next to Madhavi sat the baby-faced Zai Cheever (Jaideep Chibber in another life), film-maker and short-story writer from Mumbai. Zai's film *Narasimha at Home* about a middle-class patriarch who holds an honourable office but secretly sodomises his son and dresses in drag was skilfully filmed and had been shown at the Cannes Film Festival.

Zai couldn't take his eyes off Zahra. I don't care a hang about where anybody comes from, he mouthed to her, as long as they excite me. Zahra giggled.

Next to him sat Kumudini Rai, actress and dancer who had just finished collaborating in a production of the *Mahabharat* with a troupe from LAMDA. Kumudini had long straight hair, blue shadows above her eyes and a bindi the size of almost her entire face. There was a whiff of sandalwood as she leaned across and extended a tight hand movement towards Madhavi.

At the far end of the circle in a straight-backed chair, was Lady Lichfield, with a face like a well-bred spaniel. Lady Lichfield had completed a doctorate on Indian textiles and had hinted to Dhruv that she might be willing to endow a fellowship on the study of Indian fabric.

A little detached from the group, on Pamela's left, respectfully behind Pamela's chair, Jai Prakash and Christine sat on hand-painted Gujarati stools.

"We better begin," grumbled Pamela stuffing a pastry into her mouth. "The presenter is Dr Dhruv Mathur and discussant is Dr Madhavi Iyer, followed by a supplement from Dr Jai Prakash. Start, please, start."

Dhruv sat up.

"Good to see you all," he smiled.

There was a faint whisper from the back of the room. Dhruv nodded.

"Oh yes, before I begin, I'd like to welcome you all to biscuits. Fish fingers for those of you who are inclined towards fish. A cheese dip with fresh greens and some excellent samosas. And also some fresh Coorg coffee."

"Sorry, sir, coffee nahin hai, sir. Only tea," came an unobtrusive voice from the far corner of the room, a white-coated attendant, frayed guardian of restless educated palates.

"Alas," Dhruv turned his eyes heavenwards, "no fresh coffee. So with or without coffee let us proceed now to Indian politics and the myth of popular government."

He began his diatribe. India wasn't a democracy. It had never been. The vote was a tax, the MP was a local king.

"Bhoof!" coughed Pamela.

Zai suppressed a quick yawn.

Zahra winked at Zai who pretended to be knifed in the breast and die. Zahra's adoration of Dhruv never came in the way of serial flirtations with men. Simply an act of philanthropy, she often thought, nothing serious.

Pamela crumbled pieces of biscuit on the table top and began to arrange the crumbs in single file on her lap, for their entry into her mouth.

Kumudini placed her chin on her palm and shut her eyes at the glacier of gooky biscuit and tea which had formed in Pamela's mouth and slowly advanced down her chin.

Zai rolled his eyes and mouthed, "This is a bore" to Zahra. She frowned back.

There was a silence around Jai Prakash and Christine, their faces turned from one seminarist to another in curious interest.

Ian began to ask Arunava anxious questions under his breath.

Jai Prakash bowed his head, tugged Christine's trousers surreptitiously and looked at her from under his lowered brow.

The drinks glittered under the lamps.

Zahra squeezed a twist of lemon into her tea.

Arunava guiltily helped himself to a huge glass of tomato juice slicked some dip onto a cracker and slid it sideways into his cheek.

India's politics dominated the room.

Madhavi sat up straighter like a warrior readying for combat and arranged her sari on her shoulder.

"The small ones," Pamela said loudly.

Dhruv stopped in mid-feudalism.

"Excuse me?"

"I want to eat the small buns," said Pamela simply.

"Immediately ma'am, immediately ma'am," cried Arunava, gesturing towards the attendant, "When I think," he said turning to Ian, "about Dr Sen's contribution to the field. Immense, absolutely immense."

Dhruv continued.

Pamela chewed slowly.

"The manner in which the landed class traditionally colonised the voters' bodies continues today," continued Dhruv.

"You know," drawled Zai to Kumudini next to him, "the more I hear all this stuff, the more I think that it's all ultimately about the body. You know, flesh, tissue, tongues. Body. Body. Body. All about the B-O-D-Y." He moistened his lips and turned his gaze to Zahra.

"Body," he mouthed to her.

She placed a pale finger against her lips.

Madhavi took a sip of tea and coughed.

"It's nice here, isn't it?" she asked Ian loudly. For some reason Ian Stephenson reminded Madhavi of Peter. She found herself hating the way his mouth turned downwards when he smiled. When he asked if he could help her to some tea she refused rudely.

"Oh, definitely," said Ian.

Arunava drank a huge gulp of juice and goggled approvingly at Dhruv. He hadn't heard a word of what he was saying, but he was far too hungry to care.

"And thus we can safely say that the Congress Party was not really committed to representation but conquest," proclaimed Dhruv.

Pamela drowned large pieces of cucumber in a creamy dip. Holding the cucumber upright, her tongue snaked out and swept off swathes of dip from the vegetable.

"Who's a lesbian?" she asked, looking around.

A whiplash of silent laughter shook Zai. He rose up from his chest and fell back concave against his armchair.

Zahra held a white hand over her mouth.

Lady Lichfield looked thoroughly bewildered.

Kumudini knitted her brows.

"Er…sorry? No, I don't think sexual orientation in particular was mentioned…" clarified Dhruv, looking up from the government.

"Oh," subsided Pamela. "Can somebody please show me the black biscuits with the white cream on top? What is it, is it yogurt?"

Zai's chest curved up again. He sank into his chair and his cheeks bulged.

Lady Lichfield searched urgently for her feet.

"Please gentleman, please gentleman," cried Arunava appealing to the attendant, "please help Pamela*di*. The legend of our times, her authoritative study," he said again turning to Ian, "on Gandhi was a classic. Classic."

Pamela thumped the table with an arthritic hand.

"Where are the black biscuits with the white cream?" she cried.

"Just coming, ma'am, just coming," Arunava called, "Please take, ma'am, please take."

Ian looked at Madhavi. "Fascinating."

Madhavi wagged her finger at him. "*Fascinating?*"

Ian nodded.

"Modernity was duly monopolised into Brahmanical society," droned Dhruv.

"No," said Madhavi.

"You think not?" asked Ian solicitously.

"You see, I don't think India is fascinating," said Madhavi, "On the other hand, I think England is fascinating. I found it strange and magical. Everybody I met there was an alcoholic or an eccentric or both. I found America fascinating too. Fascination, yes. You used that word. Fascination's a useful tool, isn't it? It distances but so nicely. My husband, that is, my former husband, also found me fascinating. If I had my way I would ban the word 'fascinating'."

"Ah," said Ian, looking hunted.

Dhruv finished his paper and sat down.

Kumudini and Zai applauded.

Pamela gestured towards Madhavi without looking at her.

"Discussant, please begin. Then we'll have comments from everyone."

Madhavi felt cruel. As cruel as a cocaine addict and driven by an animus against the world. When she began to talk she found herself sounding ill-tempered and hectoring. The plaits in her voice were tight and there was no ribbon at each end.

"Mr Mathur's noble attempts," she announced, "at fighting the forces of political corruption are themselves corrupt."

Zai looked hurriedly towards Zahra.

Lady Lichfield popped a liquorice stick into her mouth.

"If Mr Mathur is so worried, why has he saved his reformist zeal for this seminar. He has preserved his revolution for a dining room. He has saved his flagellation for a very friendly audience. He is a hotel lobby revolutionary!"

Zai rolled his eyes.

Lady Lichfield looked towards the door.

Zahra stopped taking notes and stared angrily at Madhavi.

Arunava started to eat fast, fearing the worst.

"His presentation is a distressing example of how certain words have become the currency of power, to the detriment of the very groups they seek to uplift. 'Empowering the people' and 'democracy'! Just words! Words! Everybody has the words. Everybody talks the talk. And because of this, the words have scarcely any meaning anymore. They are used by the upwardly mobile. They are used by job seekers. They are used by those who think nothing of kicking an ideological brother in the shins just to be able to take their conscience to international forums.

"And they are used by media carpetbaggers, who are dishonest about their own lives.

"They are the words of the commercial conscience. Words that have spawned a chain of conferences stretching from Berlin to Botswana. Will any good come of such an industry? Some will argue that it will. My own opinion is that it will create tribes of seminar vikings, who will rape the world for their own plunder."

"Dr Mathur," she almost screamed, "is a rapist. He's nothing but a hurtful uncaring rapist! He just doesn't care about what he does to his subject, he just wants what he can get from it! He doesn't care about anything beyond himself. He just doesn't care!"

A silence grew in the room like a tree grows in an animation film. Tears flowed down Madhavi's face. Pamela listened with her head to one side.

"Ma'am, this is really intolerable rudeness," Dhruv half stood out of his chair. His eyebrows were joined on his forehead. "Really, this is a totally unforgivable tone. A completely wrong tone for our Foundation!"

"Whose Foundation, Dhruv?" Madhavi's voice shook. "Whose Foundation? It's not yours! Not yet."

"Shut up, Madhavi," he snapped, his eyes dark circles of fury, "stop making an ass of yourself in public!"

She glared back. "I'm an ass? Let's take a referendum around this room and figure out who's the biggest ass!"

"Look," he yelled "there's a world out there. Dog eat dog. I choose not to spout dreamy stuff about being Deep. I choose to engage. You're just an egoist. You're an egomaniac!"

"Me? I'm an egomaniac. Look who's talking!" she shouted, tears streaming fast now, rushing towards her chin.

"Yes," he shouted back. "You are! Your ego is much bigger than mine. It always was and it always will be. Morality's your thing. Being above it all is your thing. You won't stoop so low as me. You just want to be aesthetic all the time, leaving others to look ugly. You're not fucking human."

The wounds that former lovers bring to seminars! The hatreds that they feel when they confront their adored adversary across the faceless discussion tables, the desire to be closer, to forget everything, to throw yourself over the papers and the seriousness and seek comfort, any comfort, for all life's tribulations. The rejection of the past, the missed opportunities, all those times they could have dispensed with hard wit and cold puns and stepped dumbly and placidly into flowering happiness. They could have but they didn't. It would have been so easy. Yet the terrible realisation that that comfort will never come, that this, this cold seminar room is where their paths now lie.

Pamela continued to eat. Bits of food fell to the floor.

Arunava picked up the morsels and heaped them carefully on a napkin.

Kumudini made a calming wrist gesture. "Please, this is senseless. Senseless negativity," she said.

Zai made a knife slicing through neck action at Zahra.

Lady Lichfield moved her chair and made little abstracted gestures.

Jai Prakash looked intently at Madhavi, but she was staring, wildly and intently, at Dhruv.

Ian looked out of the window, wishing he was back in Cambridge.

Zai wondered if they would come to blows.

The flower arrangement in the corner of the room swayed and one of the roses drifted to the floor. The discussion teetered on the brink of terror. Fissures of pain began to crack open near the armchairs.

Nobody wants me, Madhavi thought desperately. Peter doesn't want me and Dhruv doesn't want me. How idiotic of me to think that Dhruv would have any feelings left for me. Why should anyone want a haggard woman with an eager manner and a huge vocabulary, not to mention a baby?

The tears stopped suddenly at the thought of Mira and she sat up.

Lady Lichfield who had been looking across at her anxiously gave her a small relieved smile.

Then Jai Prakash stepped into the traumatic centre, gathered up the terrible vibes into his palms and said he would tell them all a nice story.

"Pamela*di* and friends," began Jai Prakash, standing up and looking around the room "Let me tell you all a funny thing? Let me tell you all a nice funny story. Nothing intellectual. Just a story. But first, how should I thank you for letting me be here amongst you?"

Madhavi felt as if her cheeks had been singed. A mad train spun around inside her, round and round, heedlessly.

"You are all famous intellectual from good families. You are doing me a big favour. A big favour."

Jai Prakash smiled. A freshly shaved energy dashed out from him. "I have no idea for what reason Pamela*di* brought me among all you big intellectuals. Really, I have hardly any idea. But I will tell you about something nice. That is what I will do."

He waved his paper around like a magician shows off a newly extracted pigeon from his hat.

"Do tell us your story," Lady Lichfield's head darted forward.

"You are all," said Jai Prakash glancing around, "you are all high people. Perhaps you will not know much about the ordinary people. About ordinary people and small lives. I will tell about this interesting story about ordinary people. This is the subject of the seminar paper that I have chosen to tell you."

A sigh went around the room. Jai Prakash shifted the burden of their discomfiture onto his shoulders and began his story. This is the story, he said, of the Nat Devi of Sahaswan.

In western UP, near his birthplace in Sahaswan there flourishes the ashram of the Nat Devi. This cult began at the time of the great spiritual churning known as the Bhakti movement of the fifteenth and sixteenth centuries.

India, as you know, said Jai Prakash, is full of little shrines and temples. Small agricultural deities, deities of the harvest, deities of manufacture, all sorts. This is a different kind of deity. She is the devi of dance and drama.

You see, the interesting thing about this ashram is that it is made up only of women. You have to be a woman to know about it. You have to be a woman to do the puja and you have to be a woman to learn the mantras.

Because Nat is a pantomime goddess. She wears many disguises. In every festival her face changes. Sometimes she's a man or a demon or a tiger, sometimes a queen. Anything.

Legend has it that she had been a woman performer in the area, a minstrel of some kind who wandered through villages and took sick and unhappy women away with her to a secret place to heal their illnesses through song and dance. Then brought them back, healthy but devoted to the Nat.

The movement is ancient and secretive. Through Mughal dynasties and colonial rule, the cult had continued untouched by state power, its message handed down through generations of daughters.

The nuns who keep the order alive live in a self-sufficient community and are supported by lay members. Members are ordinary wives, mothers, mothers-in-law, nieces and daughters who make secret donations to the Nat.

But they are sworn to secrecy. If an outsider approaches, he will never guess that they're not just plain housewives because they are adept at dialogue. By day they live within traditional rules, but by night, they pray to the goddess of the double life.

"What sort of double life?" asked Madhavi, sweaty and drunk on Peter and Dhruv.

"They act, madam. At home their heads are bowed. In the ashram, they spread their legs."

"Spread...er...legs?" interrogated Zai.

"They cast off their conventional roles and become themselves," Jai Prakash clarified.

He continued with his story.

The practices and rituals of the Nat were unknown. Suffice it to say that when dark-skinned and ugly daughters go missing, when abnormal and crippled girls go missing, they are taken in and sheltered by the Nat. When women want to give up family duties then too they are taken in by the Nat. The Nat looks after all those poor village women who do not want to be poor village women. A sad woman, a woman who has nobody, she need not fear. Because she is sheltered and loved by the Nat.

Dhruv stood up suddenly and faced Jai Prakash who was also standing.

For one tense second, burning brown eyes stared into bright black ones across a choppy gulf of historical wrongs. Dhruv had fought for himself and his dilemmas, for his generation. Jai Prakash had fought the world, for himself. Dhruv was much taller and bigger than Jai Prakash, but Jai Prakash looked as if he could fight him to death. Then Dhruv flounced over to the window and stared outside.

Yeah. Yeah. Just another bizarre local icon. Every journalist worth his notepad had his fund of these. An ashram financed by the local drug don, a prostitution racket maybe. What the hell was this bugger trying to pull?

Kumudini fluttered her eyelids. "Can it be real?"

Zahra stopped writing. "Not new, though, is it?" She looked fearfully at Dhruv.

Zai surveyed Jai Prakash through narrowed eyes.

"These communities of nuns, how do they find new recruits?" asked Madhavi.

"Can absolutely *anybody* join?" asked Lady Lichfield.

Jai Prakash smiled and continued with the story.

Ian's face had become avid. "And what do they do in the ashram?"

"Quite interesting, I must say, a sort of private health care," said Lady Lichfield.

"The address and location of this ashram are all in my article. Unfortunately," said Jai Prakash, blinking at them, "I am sworn to secrecy and cannot share it with you. But I will give you some more interesting facts."

Today the Nat Devi ashram was growing in number. All sorts of women were seeking refuge there. And the only goddess they worshipped, was the goddess of make believe. The goddess of pretence.

"So, you see, doctorsaab," said Jai Prakash looking across the room at Dhruv, "politicians can come and go. But people look after themselves. For these women all the things that you talked about — government, elections, state, nothing matters. Only their secret goddess matters."

Madhavi felt her limbs becoming stiff after sitting still for so long.

"How do we know any of this is true?" she asked in a hoarse voice. "If it's all so secret, how do you know about it? What's your proof?"

Jai Prakash laughed in a way that made the water in the glasses tremble.

"Ah, madam Madhavi. Always suspicious. Always angry. Always...how you say...critical...of doctorsaab. But," he held up his paper, "it's all in here."

"Can I see the paper?"

"Of course, madam, of course. In fact, one of the things that Pamela*di* always says to me is, show it to Madhavi, show it to Madhavi. Let Madhavi see it. And it is to *you*," his spectacles turned towards her, "that I will show it."

Madhavi turned to look at Pamela. Did she know this Jai Prakash? How? She had never mentioned him before. Where had Pamela met this seminar gatecrasher with a story on a secret cult? The old woman was still eating, her head bent low. The seminar broke into hushed whispers.

They crowded around Jai Prakash. Ian began to fire artillery rounds of questions. Zahra and Zai nudged each other.

"What a lovely story," said Lady Lichfield. "Gives me so much hope."

"Triumphant autonomy. Power of a kind that is unbelievable," said Zahra.

Zai clapped his hands. "Believable, teasingly believable."

Dhruv remained standing by the window, alone. Even Zahra had forgotten him.

Pamela began to drink tea, holding the cup in an unsteady hand. Madhavi broke away from the group around Jai Prakash and bent towards Pamela. Was it possible that Jai Prakash was just having everybody on by this tale? Was this just a joke on the protected and gullible?

Madhavi brushed some crumbs from Pamela's shoulder. Pamela hadn't taken this seminar seriously until Jai Prakash had started to speak. "What do you think?"

Pamela lifted her grey head towards Jai Prakash. "I have decided to believe him." A blue mist came over her eyes and she gripped her cane. "For my own sake."

"Go and meet these secret women," Pamela continued, looking at Madhavi straight in the eye. "Go and meet people who don't know about seminars and fame and all the other things you say you despise. Go and study them."

Shades of the old Pamela. With her mile-long reading lists, her hopelessly unfair expectations, her shoulder at failure.

"You didn't seem to care about Dhruv's paper. You didn't seem to care." Madhavi's voice trembled.

"I occupy two worlds now. This one and," Pamela's head jerked heavenwards, "that one."

Tears sprang into Madhavi's eyes. Pamela was dying. And she knew it. Perhaps that's why there was an impatience with niceties. That's why she had changed. The premonition of death must bring rudeness.

Madhavi looked towards Jai Prakash at the centre of the group. A seed of an idea popped into her brain. It sank into the mud and bubbled under the surface. Small shoots sprouted and pushed out of the earth. She began to understand why Pamela had refused to recognise her. Why Pamela had journeyed to a place beyond seminars to an irritable angry one-sidedness. Why Pamela didn't want to hear any debate anymore and had pretended to be senile this afternoon.

Pamela had decided on the truth. Pamela had abandoned her own world. Pamela, once the gentlest of arguers had sunk thankfully into an aged unapologetic intolerance. In the final push to the finishing line, Pamela had broken free.

She understood at last what Pamela had been trying to tell her all this time. Pamela couldn't help her anymore. She didn't want to. Pamela had finished doing her duty by Dhruv and her.

She had steered Madhavi to the edge of the cliff and shown her how to spread her wings. She had seen to it that Dhruv grew stronger and learnt to trust himself. There were other claimants now on Pamela's love.

Madhavi saw what Dhruv was unable to, so when the final announcement was made she was well prepared.

She glanced at him. He was standing quietly by the window and staring straight at her. His hair was tousled like a schoolboy's and his eyes were watery, as if had just finished a bout of secret tears.

A blue light in a hotel room, sheets and silence, curtains blowing in a clammy breeze. Dhruv, hairy, naked and young, jumping on the pillows. His long wild hair and his thin body and never-ending talk about himself and everything he planned to do with his life. She shook her head to block it out. He turned his face away.

"*He*," Pamela's eyes were on Jai Prakash, "*he* is our greatest resource. He is," she quoted, "our parent and original. He can undo the damage of the past. The rest doesn't matter."

She creaked to her feet, and dusted out the crumbs from her lap. A spasm jolted through her face again and her mouth fell open. She slapped her cheek with an angry hand and walked purposefully out of the seminar room with Madhavi frowning after her, Dhruv in tears by the window and Jai Prakash at the centre of a jealous, gasping crowd.

Madhavi took an auto to Deekay's flat to collect Mira. Deekay sat at his computer, typing slowly. On the same table next to the computer sat Mira with a set of reference cards arranged on her fat thighs.

She pulled Mira to her lap, fell back on Deekay's bed, let the child rush into her stomach and breasts and realised that all this time she had appointed Pamela as her mother. Mothers who raise hopes in their own omnipotence and then, irritatingly, die.

Pamela put up her announcement on the bulletin board. "The board of trustees of the Mahatma Gandhi Foundation has appointed Dr Jai Prakash as its new director.

Dr Jai Prakash has impressed us by his commitment to the written word. And to exploring the limits of what is readily apparent.

After almost fifty years in the service of History, I am convinced that it is in the search for the invisible and in the hidden that the liberal arts can find new strength.

Signed, Pamela Sen, Director (retired)."

The night of the seminar, while the city slept and the pavement tradesman tossed and turned under the tamarind trees, small groups of people tiptoed stealthily through the darkness.

They stole along the walls and down long corridors, inside hotel rooms and up wrought iron staircases. In Jaspreet father's house and in Mrs Visvam's beautiful home, in Secretary, Petroleum's bungalow, in the Presidential library and in the bare spaces of Dhruv's flat.

And they returned the books.

Jaspreet gave back her father's books, which had been taken by Deekay and Kishan. Kamini gave back Mrs Visvam's. Christine gave back Aditya's. Thomas gave back Dhruv's. The hotel receptionist posted Ikram's back to him in Bombay. And Shantanu gave back what he had taken from Secretary, Petroleum's bungalow and from the Rashtrapati Bhavan library.

Stealing from the President's library had been quite an operation. Shantanu, as Secretary, Education, had access to it but had had to seek numerous clearances, including one from the President himself. He had planned it well. The census records of the British government were not available anywhere else in the city but Shantanu had been obsessed and determined. He had printed dust covers which he wrapped around flat wooden boxes and placed in the shelf, so that they looked like the books that he was taking out.

He had taken two volumes out everyday over a period of a month and a half. Shantanu's camouflage had worked so well that the missing books weren't discovered for a month. And by the time that happened, the books were safely in Badayun. And nobody dared to ask such a senior officer in the government why he wore a long overcoat even in summer and what he was carrying in his pockets. Besides, he had a special letter from the President exempting him from security clearances.

The others, Thomas, Premila, Christine and Leslie and Dawn (the brown-haired English couple at the Lajpat Nagar flat) deposited all the books at the front doors of the other houses they had taken them from.

"Why are you giving them back?" croaked Jaspreet's father.

"We never stole them, daddy," smiled Jaspreet. "It was just the press that gave us that horrible name because everybody ran around filing complaints. We had just borrowed them."

"*You're* a member of the kitab chor gang?" whispered Anusuya as Shantanu climbed into bed.

"Yes."

"Why?"

"That's the wrong name for us. There was no chori involved at all. It was a borrowing programme. A lending library."

"Why? What?"

"I wanted to help him," said Shantanu dabbing mustard oil in his nostrils to stop himself from snoring. "That's all."

"And the others?"

"Young people who are not what they seem to be. I was pleasantly surprised. Not everyone is like you, you know. Things," he pulled his blanket upto his chin, "are not always what they seem. And some people," he smiled at Anusuya, "have perfected the best camouflage. Nobody knows what they do, but others thinks they do."

He turned on his side and began to snore.

When Sam had visited Jai Prakash in Badayun he had been unable to sleep at night. Dogs had barked in the alley and the snores of the neighbours filled the air. Sam had lain curled up sleeplessly on his charpoy under the blankets. Late at night, Jai Prakash had come to sit by his charpoy, held his hand and taken him into his tiny library, next to the kitchen, a room which Sam had noticed was always kept locked with a giant padlock.

Distemper peeled off the walls of the room, lit by a single naked bulb overhead. Iron book racks stood coldly against the peeling walls, a couple of cockroaches scuttled away under a crack. Sam peered. The complete *Encyclopaedia Brittanica*, the M*emoirs of Zehir-ed-din Muhammad Baber,* written by himself in Jaghatai Turk in the famous Leyden and Erskine translation of 1826. The complete works of Mahatma Gandhi. There were contemporary books as well. Kennedy's speeches. The Third Way. WTO. Civil Rights. Welfare economics. Affects of the global market. Politics of the media. The Environment. Failures of the women's movement. And plays. Anouilh and Chekhov, Becket and Brecht.

In the centre of the room was a wooden table with a steel chair behind it, for reading and taking notes.

When Sam met Jai Prakash and Deekay in Chandni Chowk (where he had in fact learned that Deekay's surname was 'Shah'), they had told him that they had embarked on an education programme that was different from anything he knew.

They wanted to create a bank of teachers. Gather together a group of people who could be teachers for a new school.

Committed educators for Untouchables. Teachers Sambhai must have had. Teachers Umadevi must have had. But teachers that I, Jai Prakash, never had.

But their work was attracting too much attention in the press and if Sam was prepared to join them he would have to keep it a secret. One emotion motivated them, they said: love. Love of the books that had been written by the great travellers and historians of India. If Sam had it, he could join. If he didn't, he should stay out.

"The kitab chor?" Sam had blinked in Badayun.

Jai Prakash had sat him down on a mura and brought him a cup of tea to wake him up. Then he had sat down at his feet, a small figure with a thatch of hair and big glasses that almost obscured his face.

"No, Sambhai. Not chori. Not stealing. Simply borrowing. Borrowing what we would never get normally. And in any case if people are hoarding and keeping others deprived, then stealing is all right, nahin? I mean, look at, how...you say...that...person in your English history, that Robin..."

"Robin Hood."

"Yes, Sambhai, I am the Robin Hood of...how you say...knowledge. You see, Sambhai, you do not know what is thirst...how you say...thirst for...for knowledge. You don't know what it is to be denied knowledge. You take it so much for granted that you are bored with it. You don't know why it is my obsession. Generations in your family have grown up with books. Generations have seen books.

"But this is *my* library. My borrowed how you say...legacy. Me an Untouchable-scavenger with my library of precious books in a small Uttar Pradesh town. Me with my black skin and my bad acccent, here with my borrowed education. My illiterate ancestors will be proud of me, nahin?

"My illiterate grandfather who had to go all the way to Panama Canal to eat his food, grandmother, great grandfather, great grandmother. Don't you think they will be proud of me, Sambhai? You know, sometimes I come here at night and sit and look around me. And I pretend that my grandparents left me these books. That my grandparents, like your grandparents, left me the knowledge of how to read and how to write."

"What about libraries, the internet, second-hand bookshops?" Sam had asked.

Jai Prakash had looked puzzled. Looked down at his hands. Then looked up at Sam with glittering fierce eyes.

"No, Sambhai. This is my andolan. My revolution. My passion. Of possessing these books. Touching them. Bringing them to this part of India, where my ancestors dug the ground with bare hands and cleaned other people's shit. They are my grandparents' wish."

"Will you give them back?"

"I told you. I am sharing them with my friends. We are sharing the wealth contained in them, wealth that to me is far more valuable than cash or precious stones. For some time. After we have finished, we will give them back."

"But why?"

"You do not know so much Sambhai," Jai Prakash sighed. "There's so much you don't know. Someone like you can't understand what it is to be born to parents who never saw a book, let alone touch it. You do not know what it is like to be born into a family which has been illiterate for generations. For generations, Sambhai, understand? Umadevi's grandfather went to Ox-phord. Your parents went to Ox-phord. But my grandfather carried shit on his head. Other peoples' shit.

"We had to cut off our thumbs if we learnt archery because our caste was too low. We were executed if we sang God's praise because our caste was too low. We could not learn Sanskrit because our caste was too low. We were prevented, banned for centuries from reading and writing because our caste was too low."

The naked bulb shone in his glasses masking his eyes. As he leaned forward, Sam saw there was froth in the corner of his lips.

"But I've heard that there's affirmative action now, reservations?" Sam asked. "In schools and colleges? Is education still not available?"

He laughed. "But what if, Sambhai, what if I don't want to be what the affirmative action laws want me to be? The government in its wisdom has decided, oh these are Untouchables make them study in some government schools and then make them clerks in the government.But what if I don't want to be a government clerk, Sambhai? What if I don't want to go from being a slave in society to a slave in the government? What if I want food for my brain, not only for my stomach? What about that, Sambhai? What if I want to be a poet? Or a composer or an author or an architect? What if I want to be Rabindranath Tagore or Dostoevky? What if I want to be Kalidasa or Panini? What if I want to be Milton or Tolstoy? Such things I can't be, Sambhai. I can't be such things."

"But why," cried Sam, his face red, "why can't you be what you want to be?"

"Because," Jai Prakash explained, "knowledge is still not free in India. Knowledge is an...how you say...how Christine says ...instrument of...er, domination. Knowledge is...politics. Only priests know the prayer mantra. Only the kshatriyas are supposed to know about the art of warfare. Only traders are supposed to know about trade. And Untouchables are supposed to know...nothing.

"Of course, it is changing. There are a few who escape, Sambhai. But they are like the American negroes. Once they get ahead, they forget about those left behind in the ghettos. About those who did not manage to escape."

Sam placed his head in his hands and looked around the room. A dark cabin of a room with insects running along the green walls, and a naked bulb. Rare books looking out into the fields and the railway tracks beyond.

Jai Prakash picked out a photograph from the shelves. A thin man with small eyes and a thin moustache. A Tamil bank clerk or a Bengali school teacher.

"Who's this?"

"It doesn't matter who he is, Sambhai. It matters not. The fact is that there are hundreds like him, thousands like him. They are my friends, members of my library and my andolan. They don't live in villages. They are not victims of famines. They are not the India to whom the World Bank is giving the aid.

"But they too are hungry. Not for food. Not for water. They have food although they are not rich. They have degrees, worthless bits of paper but their knowledge is very limited. They are hungry, Sambhai, for thought. They don't only want to be what the...how you say it, Affirmative Action laws want them to be.

"They don't want *their* education, Sambhai. They want *your* education."

Sam shoved his hands deep in his pockets and peered along the shelves, a cigarette burning in his mouth. He was flushed. A deep red stain had crept up from inside his T-shirt towards his face. His eyes were misty, blurred with lashes.

Jai Prakash walked to the book shelves like a father to his brood. He pushed his hair away and Sam saw his eyes. He saw that he was daring him to laugh at him, his chest was thrust forward pugnaciously challenging any power in the world that would deny the truth of his words.

He offered him his cigarettes and Jai Prakash helped himself. He smoked with his hands in a fist with the cigarette poking out between his fingers and he inhaled slowly and sensually.

He said he wanted to start a public school for Untouchables. A public school like Sam attended, but only for Untouchables. Giving what he called Quality Education. A school for the best. For the *best* among the *worst*.

"What will you take classes in, Sambhai? In Western culture?" he laughed and stuck out his belly in a mock paunch. "You will teach my illiterate father. And my illiterate mother will teach you how to make rotis. Theek hai na? And I will make you paapri chaat to eat."

Sam didn't laugh. "Let's get serious," he said stubbing out his cigarette and lighting another one. "I'd like to do more than that. I'd like to help you."

Jai Prakash's eyes glimmered through the combination of spectacles and hair. His eyes were guilelessly bright.

"You should."

The idea of 'borrowing' rare and old books had been Jai Prakash's dream. It was a dream that Christine had been determined to fulfil for him. She had met Jaspreet, Kamini and Deekay through her gym, met them while she was jogging in Lodi Garden, met at parties where they were supposed to enjoy themselves but had ended up staring emptily into the bright darkness of manicured lawns. When Christine had told them her plans, they had been similarly determined. Why? What was it that had frought them together? Because they had gazed at the jams and gin and pickles and cakes on their tables and felt sick with fat and sugar. Because they had woken up every morning and felt a yawning empty cave open up in their stomachs and had not known what to do to stop themselves being sucked into it. Because they had been hot and anxious and brooding and they had gossiped and shopped and had sex and wept but none of it was good enough. Because they had not wanted to act in plays or in a fancy dress show. Uma, poor Umadevi, she needs help, Sambhai."

"Why did they help me, Sambhai? I don't know. But when I met Shantanu sahib through Mr Aggarwal my neighbour, I was astonished by his attitude also. He said he had a sorrow in his life that he wanted to make up for. That he had done a wrong thing to someone and wanted to make up for it. He said he knew what lack of education does to people."

The idea had been to create a library, a rotating library and take and return books without anyone knowing. But they hadn't counted on the vulnerability of the educated citizens of Delhi who had immediately begun to file complaints to the police and the press had given them that terrible name 'kitab chor' which had made them all very angry and which had made Jaspreet and Christine cry.

"And I must say, Sambhai," Jai Prakash grinned wickedly, "when I see the panic on the faces of the...how you say...big people of Delhi...I feel...I am sorry to say...quite good inside."

They kept the books here in Badayun because this was where the work of reading the books and taking notes was done.

"In Delhi," smiled Jai Prakash, "there are so many distractions. Besides, we have our computer system very well set up here. By Jaspreet's friend, Mr Mathew Kutty V.C."

A few days later back in Delhi, sitting with Shantanu over a drink in the evening, Sam said Jai Prakash reminded him of the rugby players in his school who wandered nakedly in the dorm, amiable louts with strength in their thighs, but dishevelled and scatter-brained. A man with so many raging plans inside that he simply couldn't see how he could accomplish them and did some foolish things sometimes with his gang of restless young people.

Jai Prakash seemed, Sam said to Shantanu, too satisfied in a private war of words with Uma, easily content with proving himself to Christine. He seemed too happy with short term triumphs. He didn't realise that it wasn't enough to prove a point to Uma. That he needed to move beyond rhetoric.

Shantanu said Sam was obviously impressed by him and wanted to provoke him to higher successes. Sam seemed excited by Jai Prakash's life. He smiled mysteriously and revealed to Shantanu a plan that made the older man almost fall out of his chair.

"Tell me," Sam had asked in Badayun, "these potential teachers that you want to train for the school, how many of them are there?"

"Twenty," said Jai Prakash, "There are about twenty volunteers who are ready to help us. They receive Study Packs from us regularly. We prepare these Study Packs so that we can have teachers with a difference. With a *difference*. Teachers who have disagreed with the great impressions of the Asiatic Society of William Jones or felt the thrill of reading Babur's memoirs.

"Stay in India, Sambhai. Stay on in India. There you will see how much work you can do."

They talked into the dawn.

There should be, suggested Sam, a trust to administer the project and Jai Prakash should decide on the trustees. And what about opening a bank account? Where was the money — basically drawn from private donations by members of the Andolan —

being deposited so far? In Premila's account, said Jai Prakash. Sam shook his head. That won't do at all, he said. Open an account in the name of the Shiksha Andolan, deposit the money and set up a trust. And stop the young kitab chors before they got out of hand. Instead, write to rich Indians abroad appealing for donations. Set about acquiring property.

When Christine woke up and went into the kitchen to make them tea and asked what they had been talking about all night, Jai Prakash smiled that listening to Sambhai, he had understood at last how these sahibs had built the mountain roads in India, put down the railway tracks and codified a population whose languages they had to learn from scratch.

14

The day after the battle at the Gandhi Foundation, Sam drove Anusuya to the India International Centre. As they ate lunch sitting out looking at the fountains, surprisingly conversation did not falter. The kitab chor secret lay buried in them both.

In her blue and green Bengal cotton sari, flat chappals and small embroidered pouch dangling from her wrist, there was an undefinable delicacy about Anusuya. She ate in tiny quantities, waiting patiently for Sam to settle down to his food before she began to eat and used her knife and fork with her elbows tucked deep into her stomach.

She asked Sam if the *Cutty Sark* in London was still in use and looked puzzled when he said it wasn't. But why not, she demanded, such a big ship shouldn't be allowed to just lie there.

She said she hadn't liked the Chinese food in Chinatown in London, saying she couldn't eat noodles without coriander. The last time, Anusuya swore, she had found pubic hair in the Beijing duck.

She said that if Uma tried to wear tongue studs or tattoos, she would beat her until she was black and blue. Sam said hitting children could become a punishable offence in England, to which Anusuya replied that if mothers couldn't hit their own children then who could they hit?

As she sat opposite Sam smiling through her vast eyes, smoking with her fingers in a tight fan with her melting shoulders and tiny face, he thought she looked like an icon lit by candle light.

He asked about her religious beliefs. She said in her puja shelf at home there was a carved Ganesh, an illustration of Zarathustra and a photograph of the Bom Jesus church in Goa. Sam discovered that she treated God like a close and troublesome companion and became indignant and reproachful every time He was mentioned.

She confessed to Sam that she was worried to death about Uma. Had Uma forgotten her mother? Had she grown away from her while she was at Oxford?

No, Anusuya, said Sam. He could recognise love when he saw it. And he had seen it in little Uma. Uma's feelings for anyone else would never compare to her love of you. Anusuya smiled proudly, saying she was happy that Uma had turned out the way she had, except for the fact that Anusuya didn't really understand what Uma was saying most of the time.

By the time Sam and Anusuya came back that afternoon, mellow from civilised sunshine, they were exchanging secret looks and conspiratorial glances around Uma, as parents do when they're hiding a delicious secret from a child.

That evening Sam asked Uma about Anusuya's life. She told him, fearfully, edgily, still a little worried. But after she had finished her story, he just lay back in his bed, threw his head back against the pillows and said even if he went back to England he would have to come back to India at least twice a year.

Uma knew the Anusuya story well. Anusuya had been married off at the age of eighteen, just before she was to join college. But Uma was born soon after her marriage and she had missed out on university altogether. Her mother-in-law, the accomplished Umadevi with a first class in English Literature, dismissed her as nothing but a pretty face and insisted that she start her day by fixing meals for Shantanu.

As her husband grew more successful, Anusuya's curries became spicily resentful, but Umadevi said her food was so good that she must go on cooking. Sam said Umadevi had probably been jealous of Anusuya's beauty from the start.

Anusuya and Shantanu were married by the diktat of his dead great-uncle. This ghostly ancestor had conveyed his instructions to his parents by means of a planchette. A frenetically swaying 'medium' had goggled into their faces, possessed, he insisted, of the uncle's spirit.

He had scribbled madly on several sheets of foolscap and said that the spirit had decided to uproot the coconut trees and kill all male servants in the house if this young civil servant was not immediately married off to a certain fair short girl with a large fortune.

The 'medium' had rushed through the house dressed in the red robes of a tantric and finally managed to rid himself of the opinionated spirit in the servant's toilet. After several smart swipes of the trishul and payment of the marriage fee, he had transmitted the spirit into the next dimension.

Anusuya's mildly reformist parents were appalled at such superstition, but since Anusuya was already eighteen and Shantanu was a promising young officer in the civil service, had married her off with a discreet dowry.

In those days, her beauty was her contribution to every gathering. Shantanu confessed to being pleased by her shy and unexpected smile which he likened to various Hindi film heroines. When the lights went off at a government inauguration once, the minister had turned to Shantanu and said, "You are the only man lucky enough not to need electricity. Your wife lights up the room."

After Uma was born, Anusuya hummed and curled in her bed like a luxuriating caterpillar next to her naked baby. She hadn't known then that it was not birth but death that would be her constant companion for the next decade.

Within a couple of years, one by one an astonishingly large number of family members, including her father, died. Her grandmother, three uncles, a cousin and an aunt and her son, the last trapped alive in a burning car, made the transition from being gossip partners on the telephone to ancestors speaking through a planchette.

The remaining family scattered. Her brother and cousins emigrated and her mother's kidneys began to falter. Gatherings of the clan became a thinly attended register of absence. Then her father died too. Her father's death made Anusuya hate him for not giving her adequate warning. She threw a tantrum and said she would never speak to him through the planchette.

By the time she was thirty, Anusuya had become a death expert. She developed a capricious relationship with death. She knew all the shraddha mantras by heart. She grieved and felt lost when famous people died. She wept at train accidents and floods reported in the newspapers and read books on the astral body. By the time her mother died Anusuya was running on a deserted road that streaked towards an absurd sunrise.

At exactly the same time Shantanu began ascending the bureaucratic ladder. They acquired a social universe that demanded that Anusuya express intelligent views on newspaper op-eds. But her heart was full of rajnigandha and incense. And mantras about the fourteen male ancestors who had lived and died before her father.

At the presidential At Home when the conversation was thick with federalism, Anusuya volunteered a few comments on the indignity of death and how her father had been bleeding from the ears even after his spirit had left his body.

Shantanu had dug her sharply in the ribs and told her to take a reasonable stand on how Karnataka and Tamil Nadu might share their water resources.

Valium and gin came to her rescue. Gin made her interested in fundamental rights in this life and banished her timid obsession with the after-life. Valium made her articulate about the judiciary. She also found it easier to sleep.

Soon, the treasured pussycat of Shantanu's boyhood marriage mutated into a painted addict. He escaped into service to other innocents.

Sam asked Uma why she hadn't told him this story earlier. She said she had been too scared. As she got up to go he held her hand and asked her to stay for a while longer. But she refused in a quick reflex because she thought he was only asking out of pity.

After she had gone to her room for a bath, Sam sat in his room and sketched Uma's face in his diary and tried to imagine the house she may have lived in as a child. Then he wrote that he couldn't bear it anymore and even alcohol and cigarettes weren't helping his self-control and he'd have to do something before he lapsed from virtue completely. Best to make a clean breast, he told himself, no pun intended.

By dinner time, Anusuya was refreshed by a long nap. She billowed about under the glare of Shantanu's dissatisfaction. She had changed into loose pants and shirt and informed Shantanu that she would like to talk to him. He took a second look at her face. Anusuya had taken off all her make-up and scrubbed her face until it glowed pink and smooth. Even the dark kohl was gone. Her short hair shone around her ears.

She said casually that Sam's mother Felicity had invited her to England for a holiday. She had been speaking to Felicity on the phone and she had invited them to stay with her. Sam had mentioned that Felicity might drive up to take her to see plays and drive her around in the moors and in Jane Austen countryside near Chawton. She would see the places where Elizabeth Bennett and Emma had lived, could he imagine that?

"*Jane Austen* countryside?" Shantanu became genuinely concerned. "But what do you know about all those things?"

"I know a lot. Why don't you also come?" Anusuya smiled.

"Where?"

"To England" she giggled. "You thief."

And for the first time in her entire life Uma saw her parents smile at each other, smile as they had in the photograph of their wedding during the *shubhadrishti* when the sheet is lifted and the bride sees her bridegroom for the first time.

"Wow, Ma," Uma said.

Anusuya looked years younger, like a tiny Venus de Milo.

"What wow?"

"You look lovely."

"Same. Same."

"No. You've washed your face."

"Trying something."

Later, as Shantanu sat reading his *Guardian Weekly*, and Sam smoked in the garden, Uma noticed that there was a suppressed hilarity in her father's manner, as if he was hiding a private joke. He listened with interest to Anusuya's description of her day with Sam. After a while he said he had to go out to congratulate a friend who had just got an excellent new job.

15

On the morning that Uma finally lost her virginity, Shantanu and Anusuya left for a two-day trip to Jaipur to attend a wedding. The wedding season was upon them and phoo-phoo bands boomed through the city. 'Electricity theft' areas were being cut off for a few hours at a time: illegal megawatts were being consumed by the fairy lights on houses and the floodlights in the colony maidans and shamianas.

As Uma was preparing to leave for the Aladdin, Misri shouted into her room to say there was a call for her.

"Uma?" It was Dhruv.

"Oh hi Dhruv," said Uma cheerily. Her voice was beginning to swing upwards these days.

"How are things?"

"Good. Good generally, Dhruv."

There was a silence. He coughed like a TB patient.

"Uma," his voice sounded thick and slow and there were long pauses between the words. "I need a small favour."

"Sure, Dhruv, anything."

"You asked me about a guy called Jai Prakash, do you remember?"

"Jai Prakash! Don't I know him."

"Can you help me?" Dhruv's voice began to rise. Uma said of course she would, wondering what the matter was. Dhruv said he wanted a research paper that belonged to Jai Prakash. But there had been a misunderstanding and Jai Prakash would never give him the paper if he asked for it. Could Uma ask Jai Prakash for the article, to read, just as a matter of interest. Then pass it on to him? He wanted to have a quick look, that's all. Then he would give it back. He would be most grateful.

"An all woman cult?" she asked curiously.

"Yah, something like that."

"Probably bullshit."

"Maybe. Just want to find out what this guy's trying to do."

She jigged to one side and jigged back.

"I'll ask him for it. He loves Sam. He'll give it to me."

"I won't forget this, Uma. I'll never forget it."

"No problem, Dhruv."

"I won't forget your kindness towards me."

"Hey, Dhruv, relax, yaar. No problem."

"No, I mean it. I won't forget."

"That's quite okay, Dhruv, believe me, not to worry."

"You've really helped me, you know. Really."

"It's okay. Seriously. By the way…"

But he had disconnected. She put the telephone down, puzzled. He had sounded most peculiar.

What could possibly have happened between Dhruv and Jai Prakash? She couldn't imagine Dhruv being depressed. And that too because of Jai Prakash, of all people. Jai Prakash, the North Indian wrestler's son. The blight in many lives. Uma yanked grimly at the bamboo mat she was supposed to be weaving as she sat in the Aladdin window display.

Her costume was particularly resplendent today. She was a Naga woman once again demonstrating the art of weaving a bamboo mat. She wore a short red skirt, red blouse and canvas sandals. Two yellow scarves were wound around her back and front in a cross and then tucked into her skirt. Around her waist she wore a bejewelled dagger secured by a brown leather belt. A large bright red feather was fastened to her scalp. Her spectacles added distinctiveness. She looked like a tribal fogey.

Her live act as different Indian characters was drawing an interested audience at the Aladdin. Every day shopping ladies would stop by. Uma staged small dances, enacted scenes of harvest time, washed clothes by the river or cooked on small wood fires. Today, as she sat at the window, demonstrating the art of mat weaving, shoppers grinned and bought. She knitted her brows in concentration and licked an imaginary string.

"Oh my God," screamed a lady diplomat, "it's so interesting!"

"Red is there. Green is there. And blue is there," said a kitty party lady wearing purple lipstick.

Mrs Khurana bustled up.

"As you know, this dress is from the Nagaland, madam," said Mrs Khurana, waving her jiggling arms. "Nagaland. This young girl, she is dressed today as a Nagaland woman who is making," she gesticulated grandly, "mat."

Uma wove with gusto, clenching her teeth and shoulders. She looked out of the window. A cadaverous caprisoned horse struggled by bent under the weight of a mammoth bridegroom wearing a garland of currency notes.

Just then Jai Prakash and Christine walked past the Aladdin. She peered to see if Sam was with them.

"Arre beta, arre, where are zyou going?' called Mrs Khurana as Uma flung the imaginary mat to one side and stood up.

"I've just seen some old friends, aunty!" said Uma. "I must meet them. I'll just be back."

"Finished?" said the lady diplomat. "Has she finished making the mat?"

"This is trouble with India," said the kitty party lady, "no pride in the verk."

"But beta, will zyou go out on street in Nagaland costume?"

"Oh that's quite all right, aunty, not to worry," she called back. "Yeh to India hai."

She dashed out of the Aladdin. A Maruti honked and a couple of cyclists stared as she walked past, her feather sailing above her head and the sword bouncing at her side.

She followed Jai Prakash and Christine down around the far corner of Khan Market, past Bizarre and Fashion Flash. Christine turned her head suddenly and Uma had to lunge into the Masihi Sahitya Sanstha, straight into the arms of the lay preacher who worked there.

"What-a!" exclaimed the Malayali lay preacher.

She saw them turn into Bengal Sweet Home and hopped after them.

"Hello," she said, looming up. The waiter stared in extravagant incomprehension and the paapri chaat man dashed extra chili powder on his chaat.

"Umadevi!" said Jai Prakash in surprise, "What are you wearing? Going to a fancy dress party?"

Christine looked up at Uma. Uma had noticed that every time Christine looked at her, a shadow of dashed hopes passed over her features.

"Join us, Umadevi. Have coffee," said Jai Prakash. "Why are you dressed in those clothes?"

"Oh part of my employment structure, Jai Prakash bhai," sang Uma in a tuneless falsetto, "part of the employment structure. It entails wearing the clothes of the motherland and convincing foreign diplomats to feast their eyes and empty their wallets on the pleasures of the Orient."

"The dress of an Indian capitalist farmer," Christine grinned, taking a quick sip from her hipflask and pushing it under her blouse. "The sword is designed," she waved her hands, "to demonstrate a brutal disregard for the human rights of defenceless tenants," she finished with a flourish. Jai Prakash laughed and thumped the table.

Oh shut up, you revolutionary bimbo stroke freelance guerrilla, thought Uma nastily. I need to know about this piece of paper which has pushed my friend Dhruv to some sort of personal disaster. Tell your information don to hand over his vernacular ravings about folksy spirituality. Support my Stephanian-in-arms.

It seemed unjust and unfair to her that Dhruv should invite Jai Prakash for a seminar and Jai Prakash should refuse to share his paper with him. Everybody had to donate things to Jai Prakash but Jai Prakash wouldn't give anybody anything. He was the permanent recipient, the king of a guilty kingdom.

"So what are you all doing here?" she asked, sitting down on the black rexine seats.

"We are waiting for madam Madhavi," said Jai Prakash. "Do you know her?"

Uma's dagger pushed up her stomach. It's sharp jewels poked through to her skin.

"No."

They chatted about Sam. Jai Prakash said Sam and he had become like brothers. Christine asked if Uma had heard of the recent announcement at the Gandhi Foundation on the new director. Uma said no, but hadn't Dhruv already been appointed? Jai Prakash changed the subject hurriedly.

The feather in Uma's headband dipped and rose as she drank her coffee.

"I did hear about your seminar paper," said Uma after a pause.

Christine raised her eyebrows.

"Paper?" she asked.

"You know, the one you presented at the seminar. Sounds terrific."

Jai Prakash and Christine glanced at each other. His hair flopped over his spectacles.

"Umadevi, thank you."

"Can I have a look at it?"

"It's kind of confidential?" Christine's tone was even.

"Oh come on, Jai Prakash! Can I see it? I was very excited about it."

There was a silence around the table. God, how she disliked this man. His easy conquest of Sam, the devotion of Christine, the sneering way he called her "Umadevi" as if she was a feckless good-for-nothing.

She felt judged by him, put on the defensive, a focus of his condescension. She knew that Sam sneaked off most nights to see him to help with God knew what. Sam was far more excited about him than he was about her. He hadn't come to see her play because of him, he talked about him constantly. She kicked the table.

"The paper contains, know what I mean, like, details?" said Christine. "He just does not want them to be made, like public? The people, the movement he has described relies on sort of complete — um — confidentiality for its success?"

"Umadevi," asked Jai Prakash, "who told you about it?"

"Oh I just heard," she said airily. "Everybody's talking about it. I just wanted to read it for curiosity's sake. Do you have it here?"

"Yes, as a matter of fact he does, but I think you should respect the fact that Jai doesn't sort of particularly want to show it to, like, around?"

"But Jai Prakash and I are old friends," exclaimed Uma. "We are manumitted from the ideas race, we are forging a living on the streets. I'm sure he won't mind if I have a quick dekko."

"Umadevi," a smile played near Jai Prakash's lips, "you are a very clever Ox-phord intellectual. Why do you want to read my small work in poor English. What is it about this humble goddess of naach-gaana that all you Ox-phord intellectuals are after her?"

Spare me the social comment, pal, Uma gnashed her teeth. I'm an old hand at this. I know this routine. Who's more deprived here, anyway? You've got your own language. You've got the blonde groupie. What have I got? A bizarre mother. A boyfriend who won't sleep with me and adores *you*. The cultural vacuum.

"Arre, bhaiya, kya baat kar rahe ho," she said. "All I actually want is just your article. I'll read it and give it back in a few minutes. You see," she said reasonably "it gets very boring in the shop. There's nothing to, you know, *read*."

"All right, Umadevi," said Jai Prakash, silencing Christine with a gesture. "A quick look, but that's all, theek hai?"

Uma grabbed the paper so eagerly that she bumped the table with her knees. It lurched to one side. The coffee cups bounced and one of them spilled to the floor.

She read the title out aloud. *The Nat Devi Ashrams of UP* it said. It was closely typed. There were intricate maps marked with red dots.

"I'll just take it and read it at the shop, all right? It's so boring at the shop. Deadly."

She jumped to her feet, her feather bobbing up and down and walked quickly out of the restaurant, tucking the sheafs of paper into her belt.

Christine and Jai Prakash stood up in unison.

"No, no, Umadevi, wait, give me that paper, you can't just take it like that. Wait, I can't give it to you. Please, read it here." cried Jai Prakash.

But Uma pranced away. Jai Prakash hurried after her with fast strides. Uma ran back past Fashion Flash, Masihi Sahitya Sanstha and Bizarre, rounded the corner and sped past Binny's textiles, pushing shoppers out of the way.

A Honda City honked furiously, but Uma ran uncaringly past Alfina towards Sugar and Spice.

"Come on, hey, what do you think you're doing?" cried Christine, laughing and gasping at the same time as she trotted after Jai Prakash. "You can't walk away with it like that?"

"Umadevi!" Jai Prakash called. "Don't be silly. There's nothing in it for you. Please give me that article, come on, give it back!" They broke into a run behind Uma, slid around the streaming shoppers, circled prams and dodged shuffling senior citizens.

I'm a runner of the information trade. Give me the virgin forest and I'll give you the TV script. Give me the freaks, I'll supply the screenplay, give me a secret goddess, I'll give you my education. Give me the secret of India Out There, because if you don't, I'll snatch it away and steal it and make it mine.

She looked back. Jai Prakash was breaking free of Christine and gaining on her. She put on more speed. Just as she was nearing Saluja Dairy, to cross the road to the Aladdin, she collided head first with Hari Ram.

He gazed at her with a bright intensity that she hadn't seen before. She felt a chill of fear settle on her moist legs like daubs of new paint on rotting wood, but shook it off. It was only Hari Ram, for God's sake. She had known him for years.

"Uma sir, I was coming to meet you. The paratha shop was not a fraud," he chattered rapidly into her ear. "If it hadn't been for you my son would have been in America, by now. The paratha man would have sent my son. But you unnecessarily gave me the impression that it was illegal. But it was not."

He dodged this way and that refusing to let her run on.

"Could you move out of my way?" demanded Uma. "Move!"

She looked around. Jai Prakash would be here in seconds.

"Come on, please let me pass," she said breathlessly.

"Bio-datas: given," Hari Ram counted on his fingers. "Birth certificates: given. Ration card: given. Still more is being asked.

And it's basically due to you. You said I should show you the documents but when I went to your house you had gone for some natak."

"Oh come on, behnchod, let me through!" cried Uma desperately.

Hari Ram started back.

"You gave me a gaali? Uma sir, why did you give me a gaali?" He shook his head as if he couldn't believe his ears.

"Haven't I seen you grow up, Uma sir?" Hari Ram's voice soared in a quivering arc. "Didn't I come limping at four o' clock in the morning when your father told me about the fault in his restricted access line? What not have I done for you, Uma sir? What not have I, Hari Ram, Hari Ram, the telephone loafer, done for you? No respect? Nothing at all?"

Before she knew it, a sharp push landed on her shoulders, another at the side of her stomach. She stumbled and fell outside Saluja Dairy. She felt a sharp pain shoot up her arms and back. She felt her elbows scrape against concrete. The papers flew into the air, the Naga skirt spread around her stomach like a pool of blood.

"I don't like gaalis," he screamed. "Not from them. Where will they go without me? Where will they go? When I'm the one that looks after them." His eyes popped out of his head. He had stormed the bastille.

Jai Prakash and Christine ran up. Jai Prakash had been talking into his mobile telephone as he ran. He had called Sam. He pushed Hari Ram away strongly so that he almost collapsed onto a passing car and bent towards Uma in a fluid movement. Christine knelt beside her.

"Hey, are you crazy or what?" asked Christine.

She reeled out some tissue from her pocket and dabbed at Uma's face.

Jai Prakash propped her up against the wall and inspected her with a doctor's precision.

He whipped out a handkerchief, packed it with tissue and tied it around Uma's elbow. Then picked up the loose sheafs of Nat Devi and stashed them safely away under his powder blue jumper.

"What," said Christine "the hell possessed you to run off with Jai's article? Are you crazy? You can't just *do* that, you know?"

She pulled out her hip flask and offered it to Uma. Uma drank thankfully and stood shakily against the egg racks of Saluja Dairy.

"Jesus," she moaned, "that Hari Ram's a maniac. He's been harassing me ever since I came back. How awful to be targeted by the marginals in this foul fashion."

A crowd began to gather. Christine turned towards them and pointed to Hari Ram.

"Dekho, dekho," she cried. "He pushed this woman. Did everybody see? I hope everybody saw."

"Did he know Who he was hitting?" murmured Jai Prakash, pushing his hair out of his eyes and trying to keep a straight face.

"But she gave me gaali," urged Hari Ram, craving for understanding. "I, who spend days with lines in my mouth and my feet in a nala, she used a bad word. And I didn't hit her, I just pushed her. Like I would push my own son."

A policeman strolled up slyly. "Theek hai, theek hai."

"Aiye havildar sahib, padhaariye," Jai Prakash grinned at the cop.

The lay preacher came panting out of the Masihi Sahitya Sanstha, fat and outraged.

"Bad-a. Very bad-a. Fussht of yoll, this poure adivasi was-a running-a," he shouted, "The poure adivasi was running-a vith some papers-a, when he pushed-a into the telephone man-a. Then the bad-a man jussht-a kicking and jussht-a shoving. That poure audivasi jussht-a falling-a. The tribal-a could-a been bad-a hurt. Bad-a."

Uma blinked. U. Bhattacharyya, BA,(Oxon), a *tribal*?

"Come on, let's get outa here? Let's scram," said Christine.

Mrs Saluja from Saluja Dairy swelled by Uma's side. "Bada bravely face kiya isne. Bravely face kiya!"

"Uma sir," reasoned Hari Ram, "gives scholarships to people. She gets them and she gives them. And myself, I fix the telephone."

"Chal, tu aaja," said the policeman to Hari Ram.

"Bad-a," asserted the lay preacher.

"Stupid idiot, that telephone fool," inserted the girl from Raja Ram chemist.

"Hey, who's been hit?" asked a familiar voice. "Kaun mara?"

Sam pushed through the crowd. His hair was loose and blowing back and his eyes looked like the sea tossed by a whipping wind. The crowd began to whisper at the sight of this enraged angrez. He had rushed to Khan Market as soon as Jai Prakash had called.

"What happened to you, Uma? What's up?" Sam looked questioningly from Christine to Jai Prakash. "Who hit this woman?"

The crowd shuffled and pointed.

"Brother, the tribesman-a was jushsht running-a. That telephone man-a jushsht come-a and jushsht hit-a," shouted the lay preacher determinedly.

"Stupid idiot that telephone fool," said the girl from Raja Ram chemist.

Sam shoved past the policeman and grabbed Hari Ram's throat. He was unexpectedly strong. He lifted Hari Ram a little off the air and threw him against the low wall of eggs and bread piled against Saluja Dairy. He was a bespectacled avenging angel. Hari Ram struggled free of him and wept noisily.

"Sahib," he addressed the crowd, "I was the one who gave them the modem. I was the one who lost a finger when there was a short circuit. Uma sir," he wailed, huge tears running down his cheeks. "My son. What about my son? What will happen to my son?" he sobbed theatrically. "And his mother's found a girl, also," he added. "For him to marry now. That's the other problem."

"Why did you hit Uma?" yelled Sam rather inappropriately, advancing like a defiant boxer. "Are you a mard that raises a hand on a girl?"

"Chalo chalo, sahib," leered the cop. He signalled to Sam to keep calm and squeezed Hari Ram's cheeks. "Kya?"

Hari Ram burst into another round of sobbing.

"Bravely the Naga has faced it. Just faced it," said Mrs Saluja.

The cop was about to haul Hari Ram away when Jai Prakash slipped him a note. Instantly, his grip on Hari Ram's neck loosened. Hari Ram broke free and vanished. So did the cop.

Sam touched Uma's arm. "Are you hurt? Let me look at you." He rubbed her hands and stroked her hair. "Are you okay, darling? Sure you're okay?"

Uma hadn't stopped looking at him since he appeared on the scene. My God, what had she made him do? He was so thin and hopelessly out-muscled even by the ravaged Hari Ram but he was so brave. He was trying to live up to the burdens she had placed on him.

Here in her own country, he was trying to be her Heathcliff and Captain Blood and Sargeant Troy who had to defend her against telephone warriors.

"That-a adivasi not seen the citty, poure fellow," said the lay preacher. "From rural-a background-a."

The crowd began to move off. Christine and Jai Prakash clustered around Uma.

"Did he abuse you, Uma?" asked Sam gently, "Did that creep abuse you, my love?"

Uma couldn't have spoken if she had been gifted an island. She was not only his darling but also his love.

"He pushed her?" said Christine. "It was good that you happened by? Come to think of it," she smiled, "Uma does look a bit like a tribesman?"

"I like my women tribal," Sam mock-growled.

Uma smiled sheepishly at Jai Prakash and said she was sorry for such a stupid scene.

Jai Prakash clasped Uma's hand, wriggled his eyebrows in a mock pantomime and said she must never play games with the Nat Devi. Sam let his arm rest on Uma's shoulders. Christine scurried away, produced some ice from somewhere and held it against Uma's grazed elbows. Then she extracted some cotton from her bag and wiped away the dirt from Uma's forehead. Her touch was soft and considerate.

Sam squeezed Uma's arm and said he would take her home.

As they walked back from Khan Market to Lodi Estate, Sam delivered a short ringing speech against the failure of Third World governments to create social safety nets and control lumpen rage. As he helped Uma cross the road, he raged against the fact that crime for crime's sake had replaced crimes of poverty or passion. He mourned the fact that governments failed to push the message of hope at the grassroots and despair and violence boiled under the surface.

He waved the clucking Misri away, made Uma a plate of pasta with Maggi Hot and Chili Sauce and insisted she take the day off and be spoiled by him. As she changed out of the Aladdin costume, he even rang Dhruv to try and tell him what he had put Uma through but there was no answer on Dhruv's mobile.

Uma ate in silence while Sam steadily drank beer, occasionally stroked her arms and asked if she would consider marrying him because his greatest pleasure would be to protect her all his life.

He said he had been in love with her since he first saw her. But yes, as he had confessed to Jai Prakash, he had been far too afraid to tell her. She was so theoretical, so prickly about her heritage, so suspicious. Most of all, she professed not to believe in love. He had been terribly hurt when she had said that love was just a commodity. He hadn't known how they could talk about a future without love. If she didn't believe in love, surely she would laugh at him. But now he simply had to tell her how he felt because it would be wrong not to. It would be wrong because it would be a lie. He had followed her to India because he couldn't live without her.

She said she loved him too but couldn't bear to use the word and would probably never be able to say it again. Please could he understand and not force her to say it again. She was disabled. There were certain words she couldn't use easily.

He understood her disability. Understood her crippling need to save herself. If he hadn't come to India and hadn't seen her life he mightn't have. But now that he had, he did.

"But I have to be at home for a while," she said shocked by her own clear direction. "I can't live anywhere else at this moment."

"Why not?"

"I've just begun to get used to things here. It's liberating, in a way, to think that I'm not standing in a queue for a US green card. I've realised that I've got to fight all my life. Fight for the suitable accent."

He told her to stop being clever. She didn't need to be clever anymore, not with him. He said he didn't care where he lived because God lived inside him wherever he was. But he couldn't see himself living in India forever. Perhaps they could compromise. Live life, from now on, five years at a time.

Uma sat up suddenly. "But Sam, what about McKinsey's?"

"What about it?"

He took her to his room. Roderick Strange and Tolstoy were still arranged on his bedside table. In addition, Uma noticed *Aquinas* by Antony Kenny. *The End of the Affair* by Graham Greene.

He was generously masterful. For someone who hadn't had any practice he was surprisingly expert. His body was long, sinewy and covered with soft dark hair. When he took his spectacles off his eyes seemed bigger and more like the sea than ever. He was gentle with her bruises and her lack of experience. She tried to bend her thin dark legs under her but he stretched them out and kissed them. She shut her eyes and pretended it wasn't happening. He had seemed overwhelming in her imagination. In reality he was younger and thinner.

Jaspreet came pounding into the house on the way home after a jog in Lodi Garden, looked into the guest room, accurately muttered, "oh, fuck," and left as fast as she could.

And so Uma lost her hymen. It was more reassuring and far less important than she thought it would be. Maybe because it had happened so often in her imaginings. And maybe because by the time it happened, her anxieties had galloped along to another stable. The pain between her thighs seemed as normal as the ache in the legs after sitting in the same place for too long.

She could not have imagined that it would be Hari Ram of all people who would finally push Sam and her over the edge of politeness. Although Jai Prakash would probably say that this was only the Nat Devi working her magic.

Madhavi rushed into Bengal Sweet Home, with a hastily dressed Mira, a little late for her appointment with Jai Prakash. He was sitting alone at a table and offered Mira a sweet which she quickly grabbed.

"Congratulations," Madhavi said, as he ordered a coffee for her and Mira sucked her sweet. "You beat us all to it."

Jai Prakash waved his hands impatiently. Madhavi set Mira down on the floor.

"You Ox-phord intellectuals are leaders of society. People like me, we follow where you lead." His eyes sparkled with combat.

"That's funny coming from someone who's just been appointed director," she replied.

"You're right," he grinned. "I was, as they say in America, only kidding."

She laughed. His eyes softened. For a woman who had just had a baby she was remarkably thin. Tall and thin in white shirt and beige jeans.

She reminded him of someone. Someone he had just seen but couldn't place. No, wait, he *could* place her. He knew.

"Do you know Uma Bhattacharyya?" he asked suddenly.

Madhavi looked up. "No, sorry. I don't."

Jai Prakash leaned back and pushed his hair out of his eyes. "You," he waved his hands, "remind me of her."

Madhavi raised her eyebrows.

"I'm sorry, I don't understand."

"You are like a grown-up version of Uma," Jai Prakash snapped his fingers and laughed, "You're the same person. The same woman. When Umadevi grows up, she will become you. Tall and thin with...how you say...rough hair. Both of you are deshbhakts, both of you have," he tapped his temples, "a lot of things happening up there. Both of you are torturing us men."

"Torturing?"

"Only a few differences," he shrugged, "otherwise same. For you," he grinned naughtily, "Sahaswan must be very very far away. Yes, you and Uma, Uma and you: Nat Devi ki kamaal!"

His gaze became watchful, keenly judgmental.

"I know Sahaswan, Jai Prakash," she said calmly. "I've been there several times during my own research. I've travelled there on election campaigns too. I studied the United Provinces during colonial rule."

"Oh that's good then. Because there's been no change since then."

They both laughed. The atmosphere between them shifted. Give us social change for another decade, she thought, and we'll be sitting in the same classroom.

She liked his floppy hair and rough hands and honest hang-ups. She knew more about him than he gave her credit for. Knew about the daily wage mothers who ran back from fields with breasts engorged with milk because the landowner would allow them only half an hour to feed their screaming infants who they couldn't see until nightfall. Knew about fathers who never knew intimacy because they spent all their time away from their families, tearing out food from their limbs. She knew, underneath her own disappointment, that Pamela had run with those sprinting chasing mothers.

She felt waves rise up from her belly. Waves of passion and anxiety. She had a brief fantasy of burning the houses of parliament. Another of cheering on a new messiah. She felt her heart thump in the familiar way that it had always, all too briefly. She pushed the waves down. No. No. Jai Prakash was all right. He was here. He had won. She musn't burden him with her patronage and her naive hopes and her search for love.

He offered her a book project. Based on research into the Nat Devi cult, she could write on the local gods of UP. It would be the first major book financed by the Gandhi Foundation. She could spend a year or two with the women and write about them. They wouldn't open up easily. She would have to spend time with them, get to know them, convince them that she was on their side.

"But," she guided Mira with her foot, "why me?"

"Simply because," he looked down at his tea, "it's your field."

He told her how much he had appreciated her defence of him with Ikram. Pamela always spoke so glowingly about her, she was very proud of her, prouder of her than anyone else.

He invited her to his house. She was impressed with the Andolan and the plans to start a school. He said her books were bloodless and over rational. Didn't she feel enough? She was far too young to be so stodgy. The Nat Devi would set her right.

She agreed to meet him the next day to work out the final details. Now she must go down to the travel agency and book her ticket. Where to, he asked. Bangalore, she said. Not the US? No, not back to the US. I'm never going back to the US. I'm staying on in India.

As she tied and tucked Mira, she wondered if Peter had been put off by her realisation of most things. By her ordered universe. Had Peter disliked her for not being tactile enough, by choosing not to live in the world of showy feeling? Perhaps Dhruv was right. Her attempts at seriousness and maturity made her inhuman.

She didn't mean to be superior. She had been brought up not to be an exhibitionist. Only when there was no language, like with Mira, was she able to admit to the basics. As soon as there were words, Madhavi found herself ordering them into analysis, leaving feelings knocking at a closed door. Serious thought was not about feelings. She had always hated being praised for womanly virtues like 'instinct' or 'descriptive ability' and fought the urge to say, "I feel...", fearing such a phrase would lead her to be perceived as frivolous and too much of a woman. She had taken care to argue reasonably and advance serious, factual views.

Jai Prakash would probably disagree. Things were so because you felt they were. That's the Indian way of thinking, he would say.

Just as he felt, incredibly, that she and someone called Uma were the same people and would lead the same life. What a ridiculous idea. Well, whoever this Uma is I hope she's not leaving India to get married and worrying about herself the way I did. If she is, then she *will* probably grow up to be like me. Just as I will probably grow up to be like Pamela!

16

Uma slipped on a white dhoti and vest handed to her by Mrs Khurana. This was her last day at the Aladdin. A week had trundled by and her life had changed so quickly and easily that she wondered why she had not been more clairvoyant.

Things had been hectic since the belated rupture of her virginal tissue. Organising the wedding ceremony — first the wedding in church then Hindu rites — visas for Felicity and Michael to come to India for the wedding, plans for gifts. Jaspreet, Kamini, Deekay and Aditya in and out of the house.

Uma's body felt cleansed and well worked out. She found herself questioning why human society had evolved garments that hid their beautiful bodies. When she went to buy her contraceptive pills — an issue on which Sam said he had changed his mind since coming to India and disagreed with the present Pope — she couldn't help a triumphant handshake with the girl at Raja Ram chemist.

She felt a thrill of closeness every time she looked at him. He had cut his hair to a crew cut saying he didn't want to get married looking like a hippie. He looked stunning. She wished she could place him on a manicured pillared lawn where he would drink pink gin with powerful powdered parents. She wished she was more aesthetic but he didn't seem to mind.

Mrs Khurana handed her an oar. She sidled into a wooden catamaran and embarked on a strong battle with the waves of an imaginary Arabian sea represented by blue cardboard whirls. She rowed with straining drama, gibbering under her breath. Today was Kerala boatman day.

"A fisherman!" screamed the lady diplomat. "From Kerala."

"It's a hard life, oh yes, very very hard, " observed the kitty party lady.

Uma smiled a tight labouring smile. Mrs Khurana looked up proudly from her receipt books.

"She is my bachchi. She is from zyou know, the zhuniversity in England."

Uma bared her teeth in a show of Herculean rowing prowess and headed out into the open sea. She was about to begin an arch towards a killer wave when she saw Anusuya and Shantanu wander by. They signalled at her to come out.

"Beta, where are zyou going?" shouted Mrs Khurana. "Wait!"

"Just one minute, aunty, I'll just be back," whispered Uma, climbing out from the boat.

"Beta, again that telephone fellow will beat zyou," wailed Mrs Khurana, "don't go."

Uma ran out to her parents standing across the road and smiling at her. Anusuya's hair was freshly washed and hung wetly around her face. She wore lemon yellow pants and a short white kurta. Her tear drop beauty glowed against Shantanu's shabby coat.

"*Khukumoni*," said Anusuya, after a pause, "We came to buy some things. For your wedding."

"Yes."

"He loves you a lot," Shantanu confirmed.

"Yes."

"Will you live all your life in Delhi or not?" demanded Anusuya.

"I'll have to work it out with Sam, Ma. I don't think it'll be *all* my life. No."

"Oh," said Anusuya.

Her parents bowed their heads. As they walked back, they walked close together and their shoulders drooped a little. For the first time in years, she saw Anusuya slip her palm into Shantanu's hand. And saw Shantanu extend three stiffly embarrassed fingers and brush Anusuya's cheek.

No, she screamed after them quietly, you're *not* to feel that you're losing me. You'll be off and away soon. Off for an English holiday. It'll all be for the better. You'll have a different life because of Sam. Throw away your medicines. Throw away your gin. Show Felicity your transliterations of Tagore's poetry. Show Michael your sketches from Abol Tabol. Feed Sam your *daab chingri*. Dust out your old tanpura and play.

One day she would surely leave with Sam. Leave the cultural dilemmas, sit in a moderate park, thinking back to raucous Sunday afternoons. Anusuya's triangular shadow would grieve in the garden, peering for her jewellery in a steel cupboard, brooding in shabby artifact-filled drawers. Cockroaches would stare out from behind book shelves bending under the weight of world encyclopaedias. The torn lace curtains in her bedroom would flap dryly and giant family photographs would be filmed by dust.

She gazed into a vision of her parents' future. At Uma's marriage, Anusuya would recover her young heiress self. She would return to being the sweet socialite she had once been. She would go to ikebana exhibitions and cocktail parties, decorated with her embroidered pouch on her wrist.

Shantanu would put all his money together and buy himself more books. In his library, he would hang a photograph of *INS Vikrant,* and his vests. Every year after the monsoon, the dusty government house would be whitewashed and Anusuya's empty bottles and broken photographs would be dumped on a truck and thrown into the Yamuna.

Her face would become classily free of make-up, her hair would shine in a neat large bun at the nape of her neck and the gracious movements of the Tea Planter's Wife would return to her demeanour. The neighbourhood Rays would tell everybody that Anusuya's English son-in-law had introduced her to a new life.

Her parents would thus live on until the end of their days, never certain why the fates had decreed that they should occupy the same house, exchanging the odd word every fortnight and wait for Uma and Sam, by then perhaps far away somewhere.

And when they finally froze into statistics in the Indian census records, their understanding of themselves and where they had belonged wouldn't have progressed beyond a trunk full of new and old clothes under their bed.

"Uma, beta, zyou look so sad," said Mrs Khurana as Uma came back into the store.

"No, no aunty," said Uma tremulously.

"What is it, beta? Poor motherless girl!" Mrs Khurana's eyes filled with tears. "Zyou know zyou can tell your aunty anything. Anything. When my Gurleen is sad, who is there for hurr, beta, who is there for hurr?"

Uma looked at Mrs Khurana. A soft mound of a woman with her pudding face and her jiggling arms. Caramel custard and paratha with jelly. Bursting in after school, the after-school mother time when all the spaces that you hadn't seen had been filled with love. Lunch love, room tidying love. See-what-I've-cooked-for-you-love.

Mrs Khurana and her opening arms, come beta, come *puttar* come, see I'll make sarson saag for you, only for you. See how much I will cook for you, bachche See what what I will make. Come guddi. Come guddi.

Uma clutched Mrs Khurana, and buried her head on her shoulder and began to cry. Mrs Khurana wrapped her arms around her and cradled her head.

"What happened, mere bachoo?" she shrieked. "Kya hua? Who has hurt you again? Tell me and I will myself beat them."

Uma clung to her soft bosom. Mrs Khurana rocked from side to side.

"What will my parents do without me, aunty?" wept Uma.

Mrs Khurana rocked and sighed. "A mother's life is full of sorrow, beti."

Uma asked if Mrs Khurana remembered offering her a permanent job at the Aladdin. Mrs Khurana nodded vigorously, wiped her eyes and said she would arrange everything.

And so Uma got a job as a buyer with the Aladdin. The job would keep her based in India — at least for as long as she and Sam decided to remain there — and bring her a nice salary.

The salary was not too high of course because when it came to money, mother or no mother, Mrs Khurana never let business interfere with maternity. But one look at Mrs Khurana's toffee face convinced Uma that there could be no more secure launching pad into her unknown future with Sam. She felt curiously comforted to be linked with Mrs Khurana.

Sam had already written to McKinsey's refusing his job. He hadn't told them that he was going to stay in India to start a school, simply that he had decided to continue with his studies.

He had told Uma the complete kitab chor story now. Told her that since he arrived in India, he had been meeting Jai Prakash and Deekay but had been sworn to secrecy because of the way the whole thing had been blown up by the press.

The fund-raising for the school had got off to a good start. With Jai Prakash now director of the Gandhi Foundation, it had been decided that the Foundation would sponsor the establishment of the school. They had even decided on a name: The Pamela Sen Secondary School. Jai Prakash had hoped to persuade Pamela to become principal, but she was determined to grow old and had refused.

Jai Prakash and Sam would work together. The kitab chor gang now re-christened the School Committee would become members of the school board.

Felicity's wedding gift to Sam had been a stake in her now booming company. He no longer had to worry about a personal income.

"Perhaps you'll become a well-known educationist," predicted Uma, "in the tradition of the Jesuits. You'll dash about in a Range Rover. Trek through sun and sand." Sam laughed saying he didn't think it was going to be so glamorous. Simply a lot of hard work.

Uma watched him make a list of things to do. Jai Prakash was probably the reason why Sam had made the decision to live in India. He didn't love her less but Jai Prakash had shown him a way which she could never have. He would respect Jai Prakash, but play the fool with her. He would admire Jai Prakash but he would love her. She would be his 'Ewe-ma' and his memsahib, but Jai Prakash would be his serious responsibility.

If Jai Prakash hadn't come along perhaps Sam may have remained what he had always been: tipsy, hating his parents, reading all the time. Jai Prakash was more important to Sam than she could ever be.

He looked up and waved his hands in a wide arc:

"Why don't you join me? Like Jaspreet and Deekay. It's more worthwhile, surely, than acting in plays and working in a shop."

"But what's the point," she said after a pause. "We're going to pack up and leave in a few years, anyway, right? So what's the point?"

"We're not leaving immediately," laughed Sam. "There's time."

It's not a question of time. Don't you see that I've made a choice. Don't you see that I've thrown aside my brave ragged mother who is also my country and chosen you. Chosen a life with you and not her, fled from a past I can't find. I'm hanging on to your coat-tails now, pleading for escape. I've chosen to go away. Chosen to leave the gin, the dusty portraits, the telephone lineman and the language question. I'm going. I'm saying goodbye. So there's no point in getting involved, you see, no point in service. No point in trying to like the people I've been educated not to.

Only Mrs Khurana gives me hope. Reminds me of mothers and what they could be.

As Uma padded after Sam, sneaking her hot hand into his and timidly glancing back at her cast-off self, she knew that if she had Sam, she could not have herself to herself. But that was the trade-off. That was why she was what she was and Jai Prakash was what he was.

She couldn't have told Sam, though. He believed that her dislike of Jai Prakash made her unfit to live in India anyway.

Madhavi and Deekay walked back to the Habitat Centre.

The sky rested among the layered branches of a sheesham tree, the leaves spreading from its trunk like a cancan from a girl's waist. My cancan under my stiff pink dress with white socks and pink bows in my hair.

She had met Zahra a couple of days ago. She had been wandering in the Foundation reading room, rifling through recently arrived magazines when she had heard a familiar voice.

"Madhavi,"

"Hi Zahroo," Madhavi had extended her hand. But Zahra had remained standing where she was.

"I hear you're leaving," said Zahra.

"Zahroo," Madhavi danced up to her with Mira bouncing on her hip and threw her arms around Zahra's neck. After some hesitation, Zahra returned the embrace.

"Let's stay in touch. Please. I don't want to lose you."

"Of course you won't lose me, darling," Zahra laughed. "How silly you are!"

Zahra opened her arms to Mira. *Please please* come to me. Oh *please* let me hold you. She dragged Mira away from her mother's lap, ran over with her to the window to point out a bird and buried her face in Mira's hair.

As old friends get older, Madhavi thought, they can only express their love for each other through their children. Because old friends dislike each other too much to hug and kiss.

"We all get so caught up in our lives. It gets difficult," Zahra said looking back at Madhavi over the baby's head.

She jigged Mira on her lap, kissed her hair and cheeks and continued to look out of the window.

Madhavi had rung Dhruv on his mobile phone a few times but there had been no response.

She put Mira to bed and started to make coffee for Deekay and herself. But he said he'd prefer a drink.

"So, Deeks," she said opening a bottle of whisky, "I want to be with Gandhi but Gandhi doesn't want me."

Deekay laughed. He looks nice when he laughs, she thought. The way his shoulders shake and he throws back his head. A man's laugh at a woman's joke is normally surprised and a little patronising. But Deekay's was a happy tribute.

"Forget it, Madhavi. You're too good for the place."

She kicked off her shoes. Deekay lay back on the sofa.

"Fucking behind the times. This was your job. It was meant for you. You're the only thing," he looked down at his drink, "that makes sense to me."

Oh no, young man. You don't understand. I can't be your pure alternative. I have flowery bedsheets at home and I buy my child Barbie Dolls. I take holidays in India. We took a decision not to live here because my husband was scared Mira would catch the plague. Of course I would never admit to being bourgeois, oh no, never. You'll never catch me doing that. But I am weary of being cast as 'the radical alternative' just because of the way I look.

"Deeks, I'm not what you think I am."

He smiled. "I know what you are, Madhavi. I've been thinking of changing my job. Maybe I could. Maybe," he bit his lip, "we could talk about it."

I'm just nasty and old. I wallow in memories all the time. I can't offer you anything. You need a brave young fighter who will take on the world with you shoulder to shoulder.

"You've been an angel with Mira, Deeks. I'm really touched. I want you to know."

"She's my darling."

"It won't work with us, Deeks."

"But why?" his eyes were wide above his beard and his shoulders looked bony and responsible.

"Because I have nothing to offer you."

"But we could work it out, Madhavi. The baby and us. Maybe you could come to Mumbai with me. Just as soon as I finish my doctorate. My folks'll love you, man. They're cool about the age difference and all that."

He sketched an animated life for them. They could travel to different parts of India, there was so much work to be done, so many exciting things happening all over the country.

"I can't do it, Deeks. If I did it I would only be using you," she said.

"But people do use each other, it's fine to use each other."

She should never have confused him with Dhruv. How could she have been so cynical? Deekay loves a baby he doesn't know.

A baby he feeds and puts to sleep as if it were his own. A baby who can do nothing for him, return no favours except fat little pats on his beard. She couldn't imagine Dhruv being good with babies.

He kissed her gently on the temples and said since it was her last night before she left for Bangalore, he would sleep over on the sofa.

She asked him to sleep as long as he liked in the morning because her flight wasn't until the late afternoon and she was all packed already. Mira was fast asleep. She would remain, foetus like, in bed for the next six hours. Mira never woke up at night. Her steadfast snooze through the noisiest of nights was one of her many kindnesses to her mother. Madhavi rubbed some cream on her cheeks.

She put her into the bed and stroked her hair and smoothed down the quilt. She propped her rag doll next to her and turned the lamp towards the wall. She bent to check if she was asleep. A pulse leaped in the fat folds running around her neck. She bent into the roundness.

Talcum powder and toffee smells rushed into her nose and softness crowded into her lips. She rubbed some cream onto the pendulous cheeks. The little face was far away, eyelids resting together, as lightly as breath.

She fell to her knees beside the bed and felt tears on her chin. Eager, comforting Mira. Optimistic, soothing Deekay. They were both hopeful for Madhavi, they trusted her, thought she was exemplary and important. Yet these weeks in Delhi had thrown her upon herself in a way she could not have guessed.

Her marriage was over, she had decided never to go back to America, but to go back to her father. To fling herself at his rubber chappals and expect him to give her his world because she had failed to create one for herself. The house with the dirty railings and the rusty swing would be witness to the prime of her life, to her child, to her future.

Oh God, Amma, Amma, where are you. I'm embarrassed to burden Appa with my failures. Embarrassed that Mira's the landscape on which I've built my hut. If you were here, Amma, I wouldn't have been so embarrassed.

She needed to go out. To bright lights, to a cup of coffee and an expensive successful pastry. A five star hotel coffee where she would watch the hard bright world spin by, comfortingly dismissive of the small dowdy changes of direction in her own life. She needed to go to a world of airline crews and blase socialites. People who travelled, divorced, ate and moved on easily without feeling any of the stomachy palpitations that she was experiencing.

Sleep now, little one, sleep for a while.

She pulled on a sweater, looked at Deekay snoring gently on the sofa and for the first time since Mira was born went out at night leaving her behind.

Dhruv lay in bed, fighting off waves of drunkenness. Zahra was asleep by his side. Since the announcement, he had been sleeping into the afternoons and drinking into the nights. Zahra had given up on him. This evening she had snapped that unless he got a hold on himself she would go to Mumbai to stay with her married sister.

She had refused to go out with him, saying she wanted to be alone. He had wandered down to the Delhi Gymkhana bar anyway and found that she was there with Zai. He had smiled inebriatedly but they had been embarrassed and Zai had left. Zahra had stared at him balefully and pushed his shoulders so hard that he almost fell over.

"Why did your friend leave, yaar?" He laughed shrilly. "Call him back."

"Just calm down," she brought her face close to his and grated. "It's just another job."

"Just another job." He had nodded. "Who cares?"

Later, he had slumped in Zahra's dark living room. Back to bloody *Republic* and those voices. Back to a long endless life. Without the job. Without *her*. He knew she was leaving tomorrow. Let her go. Let her leave him in peace.

He decided to help himself to another drink before going to sleep. By the time he had staggered up to Zahra's bedroom he hadn't been able to see the stairs.

His body ran with sweat. A bristle had already started to crawl on his cheeks. He was in a steel grey skyliner, a deadly fire starting in its wings as it fell towards the globe.

He stared at the wall. Madhavi's right. My achievements are a huge gathering snowball of nought.

Musafir hoon yaaron, na ghar hai, na thikana. When in doubt, Hindi film songs, those markers of different phases in life. How many Indian men had grown to manhood to the tenor of Kishore Kumar?

Tomorrow, work would begin. The obsessive import of work. Ideas all absorbing, deathly important, the painful process of writing. He would have to finish his book, urging the Congress to give way to newer plebeian leaders and cast aside the feudalism of the earlier years.

He felt infuriated at himself. How could he have dreamt up such an argument? He would go back to *The Republic* and whip his staff into writing stories supporting the rich. He would turn his back on The People and begin a foundation to help the cause of the polo players and heedless hedonists who may not have brains but at least had the right accents. He would engage cobblers, sweepers, parking attendants, small farmers, barbers and mechanics in political debate and beat them down by repeated allusions to Western classical music. He would challenge Jai Prakash to a gin drinking competition and defeat him.

Gin with angostura bitters. Gin and lime. Gin with Indian tonic water dashed with quinine to keep the memsahibs protected from malaria. Gin with soda. Straight or on the rocks. Or with bitter lemon. Gin at the Gymkhana. Gin on the verandah. Gin at the club with cocktails at six o' clock. Gin was liquid colonialism.

Dhruv sighed. How could he not have known? How could he not have known that he was an inhabitant of a riverine island which would disappear if there was a strong enough flood? The thin wavering line of some of the most educated people in the world, clinging to the edge of a sea of the world's poorest.

Nausea began to knock at the door of his brain. It became a tight ball inside his stomach and grew into a spreading liquid which engulfed his arms and legs. The centre of the nausea was like a galactic black hole pulling his senses into its magnetic depths. He decided to go out.

He raced shoulder first towards the mirror, mistaking it for the door. Zahra's roses crashed to the floor. He ricocheted off the wall and teetered out of the room, down the steps, scrabbling for the car keys he knew she always left on the side board and out of the front door. He squeezed himself into Zahra's white Maruti and felt blindly for the ignition.

He revved past Andrewsgunj, down Ring Road and up towards the Hyatt. Booze. More booze. He veered this way and that, drunkenly joyful that there was no traffic so late at night.

Pyramids of vomit began to rise from the walls of his intestines again. He must find a toilet. He dumped the Maruti with the parking attendant at the Hyatt where a brilliantly white lobby shone with flowers and mirrors. Cabin crews were on their way in and out.

He burst through the doors, zigzagged into the lobby and bumped into the central flower arrangement. He staggered backwards where a bottle of champagne in a bucket stood on a table between two antique chairs. He bumped against the table and the champagne bucket tipped over and fell off. The ceiling came bending towards him. He heard faint sounds of a bell and the sound of running footsteps. The staircase down to the coffee shop reared up and became the tail of a dragon, lashing crazily into a cloudy Arcadia.

He lurched backwards. A yellow stream came gushing out of his mouth in a steady arc and landed on the carpet. He fell back.

The gathered company at the Hyatt stared in giggling horror. Chee, chee. Ulti kar raha hai. He's being *sick*. Arre, jaldi aao, bhai. Please hurry up.

One of the guests, overpowered by the smell of stale drink collapsed on the sofa. Dhruv lay under the glittering lights, still handsome but sprayed with vomit.

Nat Devi of Sahaswan appeared before his eyes. She waited for him in the green beyond. She floated with Aquarius as it emerged above the fields. She flashed like a glow-worm on cricket-calling nights as he stumbled through dark mud, falling face down on soft leaves. She smiled at him in the bark of a banyan. Or in a crowded tenement, in a chanting crowd, he saw her again, the deity of drama. She was mocking him, she was a tease. She would never be his. India would never be his.

Madhavi walked in for a coffee and stopped in surprise.

Dhruv was standing, or rather swaying in front of the receptionist. A crowd huddled opposite him, whispering.

"No, no," Madhavi heard the receptionist say coldly, "champagne bottle, price is fifteen hundred."

"Pleash pleash, it'sh not like you think...Sir, please maaph kar dijiye, dekhiye..." stammered Dhruv, his eyes bloodshot and his hands trembling. "It'sh, I don't have any murrie, er money..."

Madhavi stepped forward.

"Dhruv?"

He turned slowly as she came up to him and for one awful moment, his lips trembled and his eyes filled with tears. He extended his hand towards her, she grasped it firmly and faced the receptionist.

"Is there a problem here?" she asked.

The receptionist turned and looked down his nose. "Are you known to him, ma'am?"

Madhavi held his hand firmly in hers and squared her shoulders.

"Yes. I'm known to him. I'm Dr Madhavi Iyer, from Columbia University. This is my husband."

That night at the Hyatt she hugged and kissed him, unmindful that his mouth was stained with puke, comforted him as one comforts a child, paid the receptionist as much as he wanted, took him into the Ladies and washed his face and hands, then led him downstairs to the coffee shop and gave him cups of hot sweet tea. She pushed his hair out of his eyes and smoothed it down.

Dhruv sobered up a little.

She noticed the wrinkles under his eyes and the hollows in his cheeks and forgave him for leaving her twenty years ago.

He looked at her sitting opposite him, tall and upright with her fine intelligent eyes and unkempt hair and realised that she would always be his queen.

"What will you do?" she asked.

His face was pale and his eyes were dead.

"No clue. No clue."

"What about Columbia? Teach Indian history there?"

"Like you?"

"I've resigned. They need a replacement desperately. And I can recommend you. They'll take you like a shot."

He laughed drunkenly. "I don't need handouts from you."

"You need handouts from someone. I'm going back to Bangalore."

"To what?"
"To nothing. To Nat Devi of Sahaswan."
"Maybe it's just shit," Dhruv nodded scornfully.
"Maybe. If it is, I'll get a job at St Joseph's or Mount Carmel." She drank her tea. "I'll grow old in the city of my birth. My matter-of-fact voice will be sometimes heard in newspapers and I'll become more tolerant with age. But still," she wagged her finger at him, "retain my fetishes. Never teach my child roller blading and never allow her to watch Action Channel."

Let me crawl away somewhere in my little Third World hole with my little baby. Put my head down and live out my life in a narrow municipality. And know that when I die I will be remembered for a few good lectures at Columbia and that article in the Modern Asian Studies, if that."

He rubbed his eyes. "You've got it all mapped out. Nobody fits in to your life. Only you fit in."

She let him touch her hands across the table.

"Go to America, Dhruv," she whispered urgently, "You'll revel in America. Accountability. The market. Free competition. All the things you thrive on."

"Touché, madam. I'm the brainless market freak. You're the deep thinker."

"You'll be appreciated. You'll become even better looking."

"So you think I'm good looking?"

"Of course you are."

"Of course you are," he mimicked, drank thirstily and wiped his mouth. "Pamela said I should've been a film star. Shit yaar," he sighed and leaned across the table, "let's get married."

"Stop being an ass." Her heart leapt towards her neck. "Go to America. It's made for people like you. People who want to forget their history and forge ahead. You'll be happy. Seriously."

He bent his head into his hands.

"Shit Shit Shit Shit. You fucked it up for me."

"It has nothing to do with you or with me," she replied quietly. "It's Pamela and her view of herself. She wants to go down ranged on the side of the fighters."

"Fighter?" he almost wept, "That creep's a fighter? That Jai whatever guy?" Dhruv put on his Imperial accent. "Just because he's an Untouchable, I say." He groaned. "Jesus Christ, man."

She drove him back to his own flat in Zahra's Maruti. He asked her to come in and she agreed because she couldn't bear to be parted from him so quickly after so long.

She sat on his bed, looking like a little girl with her long legs dangling down from his high mattress. He showered and brushed his teeth.

"Thanks for your help, by the way," he said, emerging from the bathroom, wrapped only in a towel. His hair was wet and dripped down his bare back.

"No problem. You were pretty wasted." She kept her eyes firmly on his books.

"I'm still wasted," he said, walking out towards the fridge in the kitchen and taking out a bottle of beer. "Want?"

"No."

He drank again and burped. "Sorry."

"No worries."

"My show's off the road. I'm a back number."

"That's not very nice."

"You're not very nice. You're a bitch."

They knew each other too well for romance. They were far too close to bother with the formalities of foreplay and the tedious exercise of trying to make compliments sound original.

At the same time in their lives, they had watched *Sahib Bibi aur Ghulam* on election night TV when they used to show films between the results.

They had danced to Abba and Boney M at school socials and eaten their first hot chocolate fudge at Nirula's, when there was no McDonald's or Wimpy's. They had listened to Engelbert Humperdinck and Neil Diamond on *In The Groove* radio shows when there was no MTV.

They had smoked and lain on the grass at Mood Indigo at IIT Powai, won dumb charades competitions in college, marched with 'Chipko' demonstrators, trying to save the tree and posed on a rattletrap Yezdi trying to look like Ryan O' Neal and Ali McGraw in *Love Story*. They had played their Leonard Cohen tapes on scratchy cassette players (CD's? Unheard of in those days) and read *The Little World Of Don Camillo* in bed. Now their world was over.

They had set off on the narrow highways of their metropolitan youth, lit by street lamps that were puny but had still cast their light on a new generation of sharing. She felt as if they were spooky turn-of-the-century people who had lost entire tranches of their past. Gained only sadnesses that they must adultly laugh off.

He said she was too good for him. He couldn't deal with her purity, her strict rules and morals. She made him feel small. They were bad for each other. They had always been.

She rolled with him on his rumpled bed reliving moments that were dead, whichever way you looked at them.

Her hair spun out under her neck. She felt his arms squelch into her sweat. She dozed, suspended between sleep and awakening on his shoulder. She felt intoxicated and warm.

Car headlights moved across his wall like the sun in fast forward across the sky. She looked at their legs together on the sheet, ghostly in the light of the flickering streetlights — tree stumps lying across a rainy highway. His profile — Ozymandias in the desert — a broken face in the bits and pieces of her memories.

The past is gone, fully and completely gone. To try and recapture it is only greed. Other Dhruvs would stomp angrily down

Oxford streets arguing about India. Other Madhavis would cycle, wearing odd clothes, speaking in a changeable accent. And other Pamelas would stare into the vacant night and set off towards unconsciousness. God, Dhruv, how betrayed we all are. Betrayed by our fat stupid sense of importance. We're children of another time, of a peaceful and iniquitous time, of an unliberalised, unfair and grammatical time.

The constant absence in my life, he murmured. I live with a constant absence of something. You. You're the absence in my life.

No, she had answered sleepily. It's not me. That's just mushy rubbish. Zahra's more real to you than me. You love Zahra and she loves you. I was closer to Peter than I ever was to you. Between us there is only angry obsession and the certainty of competition.

She shut her eyes and slid closer to him. Placed her ear next to his rib cage as she used to and listened to his voice as she used to. Hi, dumb man. Hello, public school jock. Here's my rasam mouth and my kadhai black skin. Here's my coriander brown elbow and my Chandrika soap hair. Here's me with my busy and happy life without a soul to remember me.

Here's me, on my way home.

Her road was glancing ahead through a swinging door.

And in another room, on a forgotten bed, Mira woke up. Whimpers at first then sobs and then full-blooded wailings. Long cries seeped through the closed door, as the child searched for her mother with her body. She squirmed over the sheets and clawed at the pillow. She was a little Sphinx who crouched, lifted her head and began to shriek.

On the sofa, Deekay leapt to his feet. He rushed into the bedroom and stood looking at the abandoned bed. He wrenched Mira up and walked up and down, his beard on her head.

Come on baby, come on, baby, mama's just coming. Mama's just coming. Where the hell is mama? The faster he walked and jumped, the louder she yelled. Her screams pierced the window and ran up the trees outside the window.

Deekay thumped and bounced her frantically but she arched backwards and screamed even louder.

He tried to put her in the pram but she held her arms up and bellowed. He hopped to the kitchen and pushed around for a bottle, but couldn't find one. He poured some milk out into a saucer and held it to her lips expecting her to suck like a kitten. She threw her foot against the saucer, milk tumbled over his shirt.

"Mamamamam!" Mira yelled.

"Arre, yaar, chal, chal, there you go, darling, there you go, mama's coming. Eh, come on...just take it easy."

Darkness began to turn grey behind the trees.

Deekay ranged through the room like a panther on the hunt.

Mira choked on her cries. Deekay became crazed with the noise.

His eyes fell on Dhruv's invitation card for the Ikram Gilchrist lecture stuck in Madhavi's mirror. A telephone number scrawled in black ink.

Dhruv's mobile rang. Madhavi picked it up and peered at the number display. The Habitat Centre.

"Yes?"

"Madhavi, Mira..." Deekay hissed under the child's cries.

She ran through the night. Ran barefoot, naked except for her kurta, to a taxi stand. The taxi rattled too slowly towards her orphan.

Which other woman in history had abandoned her child? She could only think of Sita. Sita, the ideal of Indian womanhood, was, in fact, a bad mother. She had egoistically chosen self-sacrifice over her sons. She had sunk into the earth and left them to their father. Bye bye, kids, she had said. Mama's leaving you.

She looked to the side. Another woman sat beside her in the cab. A terrifying woman, wreathed in silks and wearing masks. A performing clown of a woman who changed her face like the trees change leaves. A bad naughty woman who lived a secret life. The woman smiled at her as she sprinted away out of the window into the trees.

She burst into the room. Mira's desperation coursed down her cheeks and onto Deekay's shirt.

She grabbed Mira and stuffed her into her chest. She felt Deekay's gaze like the Spanish Inquisition on her face, blinding her momentarily by its sharp focused rage.

I told you I was no good. A pure upholder of the conscience? Forget it. I abandoned my baby and ran off to sleep with a man who doesn't love me. That's what I am. I'm as impure as that. This is your awakening.

She collapsed on the floor with Mira and pressed her into her ribs. She had stopped breast-feeding two months ago, but dragged out a breast and pushed it into the baby's mouth. The child's eyes fluttered open and her body went limp. She sucked in remembrance and appetite. Deekay towered above her.

"She woke up a long time back," he said in a voice she didn't recognise.

He flung out of the room, leaving her to sit on the floor.

The maniac in her stomach flung her head back and yelled and stomped. Yes, I abandoned you, flung you to one side, propelled forward by the fluids in my groin. My craven need for flesh, me with my ugly fat waist, my hanging breasts and pig eyes. You're the reason for my life, but I threw you aside. What are you, you silly little baby compared to the potent powers of my former lover?

Tears came like avalanches.

Benedicta had done a very good job. Pamela's books and papers were neatly ordered and put away into boxes. Her bed had been made. Her saris, trousers, some Argyll wool sweaters and a wrap from Harrod's was packed in her suitcase. She couldn't bear to be parted from her Wedgewood tea set. Yet she'd left it behind.

She was to hire a car to her mountain cottage. Her lithographs had been wiped and arranged on the walls. Her Jamini Roy original had also been cleaned and straightened. Her blue porcelain crockery pieces and single hurricane lamp were arranged on the floor. She was not going to take them away with her. No, they were her offerings to the next occupant of the house. She had bequeathed him everything. Everything except her books.

Her cane stood at her side as she sat in her kitchen. Her kitchen too had been polished and cleaned and put back as conveniently as possible. Ready for the next occupant.

She pottered to the living room and looked around. Huge boxes stood by the bed. She had given him everything. Sofa, bed, dining room and chairs. She had even given him her antique chest and stained glass table.

She bent towards the floor and noticed how dirty it was. It would need a scrub, the windows would have to be opened and the light allowed to flood in. She went outside.

Her garden was dark, dry twigs curled up against the front wall. She bent down on painful knees and began to pull at the soil. She dug with twisted fingers, making little rabbit holes here and there.

A broken pot stood in a corner. Pamela kicked it with all her might so it broke into small pieces. She bent again and powdered the small pieces with her fist and let them lie there in a heap. Her magnolia tree had withered and died and around it weeds had sprung up noisily. She pulled at them ferociously, but her nails were weak and she couldn't get a grip.

She checked her hibiscus plant. Yes, the soil around it was damp, Benedicta had watered it. Amidst the ruins of her garden, the hibiscus was healthy

She stroked the hibiscus. Grow now. Grow. Be a friend to him. Grow with him.

She tore at the dirt. A broken cup with a picture of her college, a crushed empty box of agarbattis, a kolhapuri slipper, torn and dirty.

She squinted at the watch on her wrist, climbed painfully to her feet and tottered to the kitchen. She was covered in mud and dust. She came back with a broom and bag and began to sweep the dirt into a pile. She piled the mud, slipper, dead leaves and scraps into a small hill. Then bent and scooped it into the garbage bag.

Clean. The house must be clean for the next occupant. She must bow out cleanly, leave him her legacy but take away her debris.

Pamela had been captivated by the desire in Jai Prakash's eyes when she had met him at the Teen Murti House canteen. She was the one who had sent him to Oxford, spoken to the Wingate Foundation for a grant for him and become an interested consultant in the Shiksha Andolan.

Told him about the great books of the world and in whose houses she had seen them.

When she first met him, his ideas tumbled over each other, ungrammatically and clumsily. She watched as he slowly began to stand away from himself and acquire a sense of humour.

But she worried sometimes that perhaps she valued him more as a category than as an individual. She hadn't bothered to really get to know him, so impressed had she been by his existence. It struck her that she didn't even know his surname. She only knew him as 'Jai Prakash'.

She walked out to say goodbye to Humayun's tomb. Like you, my neighbourhood opium-addicted emperor, my 'son' is greater than I could ever hope to be.

17

Pamela sat in the back seat of the car that was carrying her to her cottage. She nodded into her dusty shirt, smelling a little of fertilisers and dead leaves. A couple of handbags collapsed near her feet. *Mono mor hongsho bolakar pakhay, jai ure.* My mind sits on the wing of a swan. This world has outgrown me. This world has become fast and beautiful and ugly History teachers like me must quietly die.

She inhaled and coughed until her face turned vermilion. Benedicta, next to her, snorted.

"Pahar mein not smoking, madam?"

"I'll be fine, Benedicta. Wait until you see the cottage." Pamela pulled her trembling jutting chin sternly in check. Wait till you see the red roof and the rose bush and the blue hills below the aged chill peaks. Peaks that are bloodied by sunset and sanctified by prayer.

Benedicta sniffed. "I don't got anybody but you, memsahib."

Pamela's jaw dropped and snapped upwards. Her lower dentures smartly caught her lower lip just as it began to insinuate itself away from her face. She bit down on her cheroot.

"Here," Pamela pushed a translation of Tagore's *Gora* towards the mountainous woman with the thick lips and barrel bosom. "For you."

"No read, madam."

"Just keep it. It's about...well...a group of young people. And all their problems about a country Tagore sometimes called *Bharatvarsha.*"

Sailen would have liked Benedicta. He liked bosomy women who could cook well.

"Lord not making people like you anymore, my dear," said Benedicta softly.

When they had come to say goodbye Jai Prakash had bent in a pranam. So had Christine. Pamela had watched the straight hair fall untidily over his big glasses. And noted how Christine still stayed a little behind him. As she shuffled into her car, she had looked over her shoulder to see if they were still there, waving. But they had gone. They were in a hurry to do something, of course. At their age she had been busy all the time. They were going to name their school after her, they'd said.

Good heavens. I never thought I was grand enough.

Sailen would have been proud of her for her decision. So would Nehru, perhaps. Proud that she had chosen the rational way. The nation-building way.

My footfalls have no business in this world anymore. I am ready to leave it.

The pines danced past. She switched on the old Walkman which she had bought over a decade ago. Ah, Handel. Water Music.

Madhavi sat in the plane on her way home to Bangalore. Mira boiled in a downpour of sweets created by air-hostesses recently enslaved by the pink cheeks. She reached out and inserted a finger into Madhavi's mouth. Mother had been good today, good as gold. She hadn't screamed even once. Mira was pleased. If mother continued to be good she might consider co-operating in the next round of potty training.

Madhavi read through Jai Prakash's paper.

Perhaps this strange cult does in fact exist, an invisible deity for men, an integral part of a woman's life. The goddess of make-believe. Replete with possible concepts and potential seminar papers. An icon outside mainstream Hinduism, a nascent feminisation of devotion, an expression of subaltern autonomy, pretence as practice, masquerade as domestic duty. Important light on the nature of contemporary Hinduism. Oral histories of the cult would give evidence of early politicisation of women, albeit in a segregated sphere. Would Jai Prakash be able to understand all that?

Nat Devi of Sahaswan waited for her. Mischievous woman of the many disguises, naughty goddess of lies. She would track her with her notepad and her tape recorder, smash open her shroud with her empirical skills.

Deekay hadn't said goodbye. He had obviously been too deeply shocked. She had disillusioned him about scholarly women. But he would come around. She was sure he would. You never believe people when they tell you that adulthood is a collection of unspoken failures. You have to discover them yourself. Just as you have to discover that as you get older the things you laugh at are, in fact, your life's anchors. Like baniyans. And Kwality's Choc-bar.

He had left a little doll for Mira at the Habitat Centre with a card saying, *love, Deekay*. She had decided to interpret it as a peace offering and left her e-mail address at the Habitat Centre reception.

Dhruv had waved her off at the airport.

"Sorry the baby woke up," was all that he had said.

Her father would be waiting at Bangalore airport an hour in advance, with Anjaiah. They would pile into the black Ambassador with windows which had to be pulled up by hand.

Mira catapulted onto the seat from the table and extracted Madhavi's hand mirror from her bag, preparing to hurl it at the air-hostess.

"No, *kanna*," cried Madhavi, pulling the mirror away and pushing a pen into the chubby fist. Mira doubled up and drew a pattern on her bare legs.

Madhavi saw a face flash in the mirror. Pamela's face, old, angry and alone. She peered closer. No, wait not angry. Not angry at all. She had misjudged the picture. No, there were lines of fun twisted around her mouth. Her eyes were merry, twinkling with abstruse jokes when she thought nobody was looking. Her brow was smooth and calm not furrowed as she had expected it to be.

She dragged Mira onto her stomach and leaned back on the seat. She patted the soft bottom and peered to see if the eyelids were closing. Thank God she was too small to remember that night. Mira would never know.

She was her attractive mama, her wise mama. Her mama with the clear voice and sheltering arms who wandered about with a maniac hidden in her stomach.

Uma and Sam rattled towards Badayun. He wanted to show her Jai Prakash's house, take her to meet Kitabo, Jai Prakash's mother. Take her to the site where they might build the school. She looked at Sam's sleeping face.

All he seemed to want to talk about was the school, *his* school and its immense possibilities. He hadn't mentioned McKinsey's even once and didn't seem too interested in Uma's job with the Aladdin either.

She tried to picture him in the Jesus and Mary church in Delhi, near St Columba's school. After that, drifting into Gole Market, eating rabri. Sam and herself in Bengali wedding dress,

Sam on Janpath, looking like St Augustine in beads and kolhapuris. How would he react when he saw Uma reflected in the light of an inverter during a power cut? In her mother's family home in Calcutta he might feel imprisoned by the mosquito net, balk at the bartan vendor's invasion of his Inner Quiet.

She would explain everything to him. She was this city, the city was her. The city existed in her explanation of it. As she explained, she too would understand. From the clandestine hillocks of Lodi Garden to the dark fumblings under a sulphur lamp on the Delhi Ridge. Is the kiss Western? Do Indians *kiss*, she had asked the captain of the chess team and son of Secretary, Petroleum, or do they *lick*? Her hunch was that they didn't kiss, at least not in the Clark Gable and Vivien Leigh way.

She would tell him about that night when Anusuya had become muddy in the garden. About other nights when the lawn had been damp and chocolatey, and Anusuya had sat on the grass crumbling the soil between her fingers and flipping through pages of her family album.

She would have to tell him about it. She would tell him that most of her life she had struggled to prove that love need not satisfy any rules. That even burra memsahibs play with mud in a Very Important Garden. That pillars of the state wear torn vests and stumble on kutcha roads outside their delusory office rooms.

Sam stirred and put an arm around her shoulders. His aftershave smelt reassuringly banal.

She would never know if he admired Jai Prakash more than her. Whether he thought Jai Prakash was more real than she was. Or whether he had decided to stay on in India because of Jai Prakash or because of her. She would never know if he loved her, or if, in fact, he loved Jai Prakash. But it didn't matter because she didn't *really* know either. Didn't know whether it was him, or whether he was her revenge on the British empire.

That evening there was a grand reception at the Mahatma Gandhi Foundation. Jai Prakash made some delighted announcements.

Zai Cheever, Kumudini Rai and Zahra were all given fellowhips. Zai would work on projections of the Hindu karta in popular cinema. Kumudini Rai would create a ballet combining jazz dance and the Kamasutra. Zahra would compare images of the historical Enemy in the media in India and Pakistan.

And Madhavi's work on the Nat Devi cult was to be the first book commissioned by the MGF.

Jai Prakash held his arms back. His body twitched with excitement. His mobile phone twinkled in his trouser pocket. His smile was as roguish as ever and he shook his head from time to time in a resigned joke. That he, grandson of a scavenger-labourer on the Panama Canal was now Lorenzo the Magnificient, grand renaissance patron seemed to confirm that this world was indeed maya.

The audience clapped politely after every announcement. Zai puckered his lips at Zahra and reached for her hand. She was a fresh white lily in a white salwar kameez.

"By the way," he whispered, "are you coming to his house-warming party later tonight?"

She grinned. "All very arty-farty in there now."

"Completely," said Zai, widening his eyes. "Sen's house, is…" he made twirling movments with his hands, "all re-done. Christine did it. They moved in just this afternoon. Lots of zany stuff everywhere. Oh man. Amazing."

"But I hear Pamela*di* left some stuff behind?" asked Zahra.

"Sen left behind her hurricane lamp and her Bong paintings, can you imagine?" laughed Zai. "Christine wanted to junk them, but Jai Prakash won't hear of it. Honestly, he treats her stuff as if it was sacred. He says if anything happens to Sen's things, he'll be struck by lightning…" Zai rolled his eyes.

"And I hear they've moved in with silk sofas? God, yaar. Talk about, *you know*."

"They're getting a tent from the Aladdin," Zai conspired raising his eyebrows, "for the party. I'm serious. From Mrs Khurana, the owner. She's lent him a Rajasthani tent. Wild, na?"

"And you know what?" Zahra shook with a suppressed giggle, "she" she nodded towards Christine, "wants me to go shopping with her. For clothes. For *him*. For JP. C wants to buy clothes for JP. Allen Solly shirts." She shook her head. "Poor Pamela*di*."

"Why?" inquired Zai. "She should be happy, yaar. This guy," he jerked his head towards Jai Prakash "is going to do great things. And she'll get all the credit."

Jai Prakash said something funny. The crowd threw up their hands in the air.

"By the way," said Zai, after a pause. "Where's your...er... your...er...? Kahan hai?"

Zahra shrugged. "He must be here somewhere," she said airily.

Zai grabbed her hand and they plunged into the crowd of the teacups, glasses and printed silks.

Jaspreet, Deekay, Kamini and Shantanu, officials of the Foundation, dancers, writers, poets, members of the history department from the university, and even Shantanu's minister with the cellphone ear, streamed around to greet Jai Prakash. All good wishes to the new director and the Foundation! Lady Lichfield, bearing flowers and words of congratulation came with a cheque and a list of names and addresses of funding agencies. The former Indian high commissioner to London galloped about glistening with slippery new networks.

Mr and Mrs Khurana came too, richly dressed with promises of support. They were accompanied by the bank manager of the National Westminister Bank in England who had flown down to organise the grant that the Khuranas were about to make to the

Foundation. The Khuranas' Cowley Road stall had been sold. They now owned a flat in Mayfair in London that was on rent to a Pakistani industrialist and had bid for shop space in Heathrow airport. "Airports, guddi," Mrs Khurana had whispered to Uma. "The business traveller has no time to shop in the city. Only in airport he has time. Airport is big shopping area now."

Jai Prakash's eyes were bright. His glasses had changed, he now wore spectacles similar to Sam's and his hair was as long as Sam's had once been, but slicked away from his face so that it no longer masked his eyes. The powder blue shiny jumper had disappeared. He wore a tweed jacket and polished shoes. But Christine, by his side, still wore her black and grey clothes and her nose ring glittered firmly.

Lady Lichfield tittered and wafted. The high commissioner swelled proprietorially at Jai Prakash's side. Sarojini Pande, wife of the vice-president and doctorate in late Mughal painting, magnificient in a turquoise sari exclaimed at the pencil sketches of Lucknow on the wall.

Rabindranath Tagore looked admiringly down from the wall. A white glow emanated from the freshly painted walls. The atmosphere settled around Jai Prakash like clouds of piety. He was the prize exhibit in an art gallery, the sanctum sanctorum in a new temple.

Coffee and tea were passed around. Plates of vadas and samosas were offered. The new director's obsession, breathed the guests, was a school. Apparently, in addition to his academic work, he was determined to start an activist education programme. The foundation would sponsor a school, created along completely new ideas.

Arunava and Adrian raised a toast. Zai giggled with Zahra and blew a kiss at Jai Prakash.

Jai Prakash made some other announcements. The Shiksha Andolan and the School Commitee was to become the

Foundation's main philanthropic project and shift its base from Lajpat Nagar to Lodi Road.

And now, said Jai Prakash spreading his hands as if asking God to raise him up to heaven, the best announcement of all. The announcement that gave him such pride that he felt as if he was walking a few feet above the ground.

Here it was: Sam O'Toole, brother and friend, was to be the organiser of the Pamela Sen Secondary School. Sam had given up his job at none other than McKinsey's Consultants to remain in India. Can you imagine? At a time when most people are running after such big jobs, Sam had actually given McKinsey's up.

The school would be established either on the outskirts of Delhi or in Uttar Pradesh. Sam had taken full responsibility. Our old friend and supporter Shantanu Bhattacharyya would be a tower of strength.

The audience clapped and looked around for Sam. Sarojini Pande smiled approvingly at the ceiling. The former high commissioner looked as if he was about to burst. Zai and Zahra nudged each other.

Jai Prakash clapped his hands and said he would like to show them around. As they trooped after him, through the heads and bodies, Jai Prakash suddenly noticed Dhruv, leaning against the mantelpiece, looking thin and red-eyed. He detached himself from the crowd and trod lightly to him.

"Doctorsaab, doctorsaab," Jai Prakash clasped his hands, "we have been so busy shifting that we haven't had time to invite you here before. Sorry. I am sorry."

"Shifting?"

"Yes," said Jai Prakash happily. "We have just moved into the director's house. Into Pamela*di*'s house, didn't you know? She has left, you see."

"Congratulations."

Jai Prakash shook Dhruv's hands again. "Thank you for coming here, doctorsaab. You know what this means to me. I know what is in your heart. But you are great. Let's be friends. I would like to be a friend. Believe me. I don't want you to be suspicious of me. Tell me, what are your plans?"

Dhruv extricated his hands from Jai Prakash's grip.

"I'm going to apply for Madhavi's job in Columbia University."

"Achcha," Jai Prakash inclined his head. "That I know. I know you and madam Madhavi are old friends. I also know that I'm not a part of your friends' group. But," he spread his hands again, "if you ever need any help..."

Dhruv inclined his head.

"The school, doctorsaab," whispered Jai Prakash, "it is my dream come true. Like me or don't like me but at least come and see what work we have done. Then you will know. Forget about me. Forget about me and my..." his eyes sparkled, "social complex. Just see the work. That's all I ask of you."

And try as hard as he could Dhruv couldn't disbelieve him. He could recognise a time when he saw it. After years on the trail of events, he had come to understand when a particular moment throbbed with an unstated future. When a particular time became telescoped and dense with energy.

As he looked into Jai Prakash's intent eyes, he felt his own features become slack and over-used. His mouth felt anti-climactically dry and the lights in the room made him shiver. He felt as if he had just been discharged from hospital, as if the smell of medicines hung on his clothes. Jai Prakash's hands were warm and ruddy. He looked, to Dhruv, like he'd just come in after a game of golf.

"I don't have time now. I'll come later, guruji. Achcha phir." Dhruv folded his hands and looked away.

Jai Prakash was about to say something when a crowd of other guests arrived. Foreign correspondents, a school principal, bureaucrats. He bounded away to welcome them. Guests spilled into the little back garden, around the greenhouse, glowing with laughing twilight.

Dhruv stood at the Foundation window and looked down the road as if expecting to see Madhavi come wheeling past with her pram.

He had dropped in to see her early this morning as she was preparing to leave. After the amount of alcohol that he had consumed the night before, his head had felt as if it was a seismic zone waiting for the first tectonic rumbles. She had been packing. There was a faint darkness around her eyes.

"Stupid of me to..."

She had looked gravely up from her suitcase. "I'm as much to blame as you."

She had lifted her baby up and nuzzled her face in the little stomach. She had kissed the baby once, twice, then again.

"You know my little Mira, na? My little Mira, my doodoo little Mira."

"Hi Mira," he had said.

She put the baby down on the bed and gave her a rag doll to play with. Then continued with her last minute packing, screwing the caps on toiletries and pushing in bits and pieces of toys. The child had rolled on her back and kicked her legs. Her face had seemed swollen.

"You didn't tell me about your divorce."

"How did you know?"

"From Pamela. I dropped in on her on my way here."

"Oh really. Why?"

"To kill her."

She had laughed. She said she admired Jai Prakash because he was a warrior of a kind that she and Dhruv would never be. But she found his constant send-up of English-speaking silliness and crusade against gentility irritating. They had a mutually assessing relationship and it was good to keep it that way.

She told him about the night. The baby had woken up and she had lost a friend. Deekay who had been so good and so kind, now hated her for wantonly abandoning her baby. Deekay hated her. She hated herself.

"So," Dhruv had tried to change the subject. "You're off."

"Yes."

"Cancel your trip and spend the rest of your life with me."

She had picked up her baby and pressed her face next to the infant's.

"And what about this little person? Her father doesn't want her. Shall I check her into an orphanage? Dump her in an institution for motherless children? Give her to the Nat Devi ashram? Throw her away for ever? Shall I just forget her as I did last night, knowing she has no one to complain to?" She had squeezed the baby and her eyes had begun to fill.

He had jumped to his feet and held her shoulders. "Okay, okay, just take it easy."

He had lifted them both — the baby and her — off their feet, and set her down on the sofa. Then staggered back against the door as his breath rushed out of his mouth. The baby had sniggered nastily.

He had driven her to the airport only a couple of hours ago.

If only she would suddenly, miraculously appear. He had begun to feel that he existed with all his being in her understanding of him. He felt as if the damp subterfuges of his past dried and crackled when put out in the sunlight of her honesty.

He would tell her that when he saw her. If ever he saw her.

Somebody patted him on the shoulder. It was Zai, asking him to join them at the party later tonight at Jai Prakash and

Christine's new home. Come on Dhruv we'll all be there. We've organised some champagne. Come on, forget what happened, yaar. It's party time.

He said he had another engagement, said a formal goodbye to Jai Prakash and walked out of the Foundation.

Dhruv needn't have been so depressed, though. Because when he was dispirited and love-lorn he looked more handsome than ever and several heads turned to look at him as he passed. From the garden door, Zahra watched him leave and wondered if there was enough food for him in her fridge at home.

Later that night the party was in full swing. He drove past the Nizamuddin flat, opposite Humayun's tomb. In the front garden, the soil had been dug up in preparation for a new lawn. Bits of china, old tins and a torn chappal were shovelled and heaped on a lumpy churning of earth ready to be dumped somewhere to make way for a new green.

The curtains were drawn back and the room inside was crowded with people. He could see Zahra's white salwar kameez in the middle of an admiring circle. On the walls hung a very original painting. In place of Pamela's lithographs, Dhruv noticed big Andy Warhol posters. A globular white lamp shade in the same place where Pamela's hurricane lamp once sat.

Laughter rose from the ornamental tent pitched in the back garden. Someone had even started a barbecue and smoke gushed upwards into the sky.

He lingered outside the house for a few moments then walked back to his car. As he walked past the garden, somewhere crumpled in the dirt, Dhruv saw the dead limbs of a hibiscus plant.